"Take us in, Hotdog!" t
his head mike. "I got to

The pilot complied w
both Brody and Snakem
tained machine-gun bursts at Viet Cong squads running through the jungle below.

Suddenly, there was a massive explosion.

"Fucking animal; twenty claymores feels like," Gabe, the chopper pilot, clicked in. "Hold on to your balls, ladies!"

The blast nearly knocked *Pegasus* from the sky, but Gabe somehow managed to keep her level and flying.

Brody was leaning halfway out the hatch, held aboard only by the thin monkeystrap lifelines attached to the bar along the hatch. His M-60 started heating up fast as he fired five- and ten-round bursts back along the target tree line.

The red tracers seemed to glow a bit more as dusk took hold of the land, throwing jagged shadows through the tree line as they ripped through the stick figures racing for cover below.

"Yeah!" Fletcher yelled, throwing a fist in the air. "D'ya see that, Whoremonger? Smoked me at least five for the body count that time, dude!"

"Way to go, Snakeman," Brody answered, throwing him the thumbs up victory salute.

"Your turn comin' up, bro'! Got to spread that voodoo around."

Includes a complete GLOSSARY of military jargon.

Also by Jack Hawkins in Sphere Books:

JACK HAWKINS

Chopper 6
Suicide Mission

SPHERE BOOKS LIMITED

For "Saigon Commando" Jonathan Cain, who
volunteered for The Nam despite a draft number of
363. All he ever wanted was to be a good door
gunner, but Uncle Sammy gave him an MP's foot
beat on Tu Do Street instead. And for Lu Le Khanh,
who tricked him out of Vietnam before it was too
late. I am convinced they will someday return to the
Pearl of the Orient. Together.

A SPHERE Book

First published in Great Britain by Sphere Books Ltd 1990

Copyright © 1987 by Butterfield Press, Inc.

Printed and bound in Great Britain by
Cox & Wyman Ltd, Reading

ISBN 0 7474 0479 8

Sphere Books Ltd
A Division of
Macdonald & Co (Publishers) Ltd
Orbit House
1 New Fetter Lane
London EC4A 1AR
A member of Maxwell Macmillan Pergamon Publishing Corporation

AUTHOR'S NOTE

In the fall of 1966, the U.S. Army began field-testing its controversial "search-and-destroy" tactics for the first time. Dubbed Operation Attleboro, its purpose was to penetrate northwestern Tay Ninh Province along the Cambodian border—specifically, Dong Minh Chau: the longtime enemy sanctuary located 25 to 30 miles northwest of the capital, Saigon.

American and South Vietnamese military commanders believed that large groups of both Viet Cong and NVA soldiers were hiding in dense jungle west of the Michelin Rubber Plantation there, and, on September 14, the 196th Light Infantry Brigade was assigned the task of routing out the communists.

The 196th—or Americal Division, as it was more commonly called—was assisted by elements of the 1st Infantry Division, the 173rd Airborne Brigade, the 3rd Brigade of the 4th Infantry Division, and the 11th Armored Cavalry Regiment.

Though Doc Delgado, Gage Ruckter, Reece Jones, "Snakeman" Fletcher, and Brody The Whoremonger may remind readers, and First Team vets, of soldiers they knew in The Nam, they are fictional characters. Other than well-known public and historical figures, any resemblance these characters may bear to actual persons, living or killed in action, is purely coincidental.

Echo Company's gunships had been using the Special Forces camp at Dau Tieng now and then for recreation and resupply ever since 7th Cavalry returned to War Zone C from unscheduled duty in the Mekong Delta. The hops through Dau Tieng were far from official—the Airmobile troopers were supposed to be part of a larger contingent battling Cong to the north, in the longtime VC stronghold of Binh Dinh Province. But with Colonel Neil "Nazi" Buchanan in charge, things did not always go as planned.

Jack Hawkins
Little Saigon (Garden Grove)
California
30 April 1987

CHAPTER 1

Dau Tieng Special Forces Camp

Sgt. Treat Brody's world had turned an ugly shade of crimson.

What had always been a routine and reliable olive drab was now red—there was blood everywhere in the gunships's inner belly. Splinters of bone clung to his hair and eyebrows. The air was filled with the stench of it.

"MEDIC!" Brody had never cried the word so loudly before. His arms were full—a trooper nearly twice his size but missing one foot was propped semi-conscious against him. Brody's fingers were busy trying to keep a severed femoral artery plugged.

Pegasus was still 30, now 20, feet above the perimeter wire, cruising in over tent tops and guard towers, but corpsmen were already running to the helipad, chasing after the smoking Huey.

When Gabriel pranged her across the rippled tarmac, three medics rushed up over the landing skids, crowding the hatch.

"My God!" one of them—a newby fresh from back-to-back tours in Guam—recoiled when he saw the mutilated bodies piled up against the port doorgunner. The corpsmen on either side ignored his shocked reaction and set to work relieving Brody of his charge.

"What the hell happened?" one of them asked, as sev-

1

eral more casualty-laden choppers dropped from the skies onto the Green Beret camp.

"Somebody misjudged Charlie's strength coupla klicks to the whiskey," Brody muttered, pointing westward. He made no immediate effort to leave his post, to abandon the hatch gun.

"Obviously."

"An F.O.B.?" The medic from Guam had quickly collected his wits again, referring to a fly-over-border mission.

"Beats me." Brody finally stood. He moved over toward the doorgunner who was leaning out the opposite hatch. "We just responded to their Brass Monkey—I don't even know what the exact cords were. We were part of a gaggle limpin' in from contact along the Dong Minh Chau . . . weren't even supposed to get involved in no one else's troubles. I think your customers are from the 196th. . . ."

"Yep, looks like an Americal patch to me," one of the other corpsmen decided.

"You okay, Snakeman?" Brody rested a hand on his best buddy's shoulder.

Spec-4 Elliott "Snakeman" Fletcher wore a death head's grin when he turned and looked up to face Brody. "It's gonna rain, Whoremonger," he drawled. "I can taste it on the sticky fuckin' air: monsoon's rollin' in. That's a good sign. . . ."

"It is?" Brody's disbelieving expression was a mixture of relief and irritation.

"You can bank on it."

"I mean, you're sure you didn't catch any flak back there?" Treat asked deliberately.

"No sweat, pal. Eight and skate. Gimme another mission, brotha'!"

"Eight and skate, you *wish*." Brody removed Fletcher's

frozen fists from the M-60 and gestured toward a waiting jeep below.

The medic from Guam was shaking his head, too, as they carried the wounded soldier away. "Talk about *gung-ho* . . ."

"More like we been working double gross-outs, if my time card's half-assed accurate." Brody's gaze dropped to the jeep. "Let's borrow that fucker and boogie on over to the mess tent for some—" he began, but Snakeman interrupted him.

"Hey, don't they have a club here?"

"I don't know, but I'll find out, brother."

He climbed down out of *Pegasus*—so named because a bright mural of a winged horse was painted across its snout—and headed for a maze of tent tops and sunken bunkers.

"Stay within earshot!" the gunship's pilot called through a shattered web of Plexiglas.

"No sweat, Gabe!" Snakeman replied with a thumbs-up gesture.

Brody glanced back at the pilot, who was still inside the helicopter's cockpit. Beside him, his copilot sat motionless at his position, head back, arms rigid, a puddle of blood and gristle in his lap. His Adam's apple was missing. A single VC machine-gun round had slammed up through the craft's floorboards and struck him in the throat as they were lifting off from the extraction point only minutes before.

He was one of the new men. Peter pilots, or copilots, almost always were. Neither Brody nor Snakeman had ever taken the time to get to know him. Now they were glad they hadn't. Gabe assumed the task of assisting medics with the body bag.

Brody glanced over at the other ships flaring into the narrow helipad. Rotor tips almost touching, they pranged across the rough tarmac with screaming sounds as bent-over corpsmen braved the downblast to hustle the casualties out of blood-stained hatches.

They didn't need Whoremonger's help, that was for sure. Medics seemed plentiful today. Only one W.I.A. had been aboard *Pegasus*—the one-footed man—and he'd already been spirited away. Everyone else was dead. Everyone except him and Snakeman. And Gabe The Gunslinger, of course.

Brody gazed beyond the camp's perimeter wire. Hills covered with dense elephant grass and razor-sharp reeds rose above the sagging coils of concertina. And past the hills, smoke. Thick, black columns of it rose to the northwest.

He knew it was opposite the direction they had just left, but the smoke brought it all back to Treat Brody, made him relive, over and over, the bewildering events of the last hour. . . .

They had been headed for the Dau Tieng Special Forces camp on a routine mailbag ash-'n-trash relay flight when the call for help came in: Some grunts in an Americal unit had been ambushed on the western edge of the Ben Cui Rubber Plantation after walking into a claymore boobytrap. Most of the nine-man squad received serious wounds from the first blast. The radioman confirmed that at least three had already been killed, and managed to give out his coordinates before the radio went dead.

When *Pegasus* and eight other gunships arrived on-station, the bodies of the dead GIs were immediately visible around the edge of a clearing. More than a third of the squad was now dead, but one M-16 rifle muzzle kept sending short bursts into the surrounding jungle.

Peg's pilot, Cliff Gabriel, concentrated on the shadowy

forms darting about the western tree line—black pajama-clad shapes zigzagging closer to the clearing, bearing the unmistakable silhouettes of AK-47 assault rifles, bayonets fixed.

"Take us in, hot dog!" Brody could still hear Snakeman Fletcher's taunting chant as if it had only just been yelled. "Take us in . . . so I can *get me some*!"

Snakeman was already dropping sustained machine-gun bursts down at the Viet Cong with his hatch-60, but instead of descending, Gabriel abruptly banked to the left. Fletcher, who was manning the right-side MG, sent a burst of red tracers up into the lazy cumulus clouds drifting castle-like above the battlefield.

"So sorry, Snakeman!" The Gunslinger clicked in with his best Fu Manchu accent. But there was no need for further explanation. Fletcher and Brody both felt the gut-wrenching sensations as roaring choppers swooped past on either side of *Pegasus*. There were just too many birds in too little sky!

Gabriel opted to allow one of the other Hueys first pick at an LZ, but the bird flaring in alongside *Pegasus* also pulled up without warning—another armed force was moving toward the clearing from the east. They too appeared to be clad in black, but closer examination by crewmen in the third ship verified that only the faces were black. They wore tiger-striped fatigues, and the uniforms blended in well with the surrounding terrain. That was why they had not been spotted earlier.

"With greasepaint on their pusses, over. . ." Brody monitored the metallic crackle of ship-to-ship radio conversation.

"An Americal element?"

"Appears so, Gunslinger."

"That'd be my guess, too, Python-Lead."

"Rodg," Gabriel responded without emotion. "Eat clouds while I make another pass. Will advise, how copy?"

"Complying..." came the acknowledgments, one after the other.

So they were Americans after all. *Pegasus* was circling back after a tight turn along the jungle's edge while the other ships ascended so as to avoid possible collision.

"Eyeball everything that moves, ladies," Gabriel told them over the intercom. "I wanna check out who's the white hats and who's the Indians 'fore we commence to droppin' shit into the fan."

"Rodg," Fletcher replied dryly. He already had a new ammo belt fed into his hog.

"You got it, Gabe-baby," Treat Brody leaned into his monkeystrap as they raced back down toward the clearing. "Permission to bust caps on Charlie if—"

"It's up to you guys," the peter pilot riding on Gabriel's left anticipated his request. "Just make sure your ricks don't force one of our own birds down 'n dirty." "Ricks" was short for ricochets, which didn't even apply, as far as Fletcher was concerned. The copilot was really referring to missed shots or clean thru-and-thru's. He wanted the two gunnies to keep the entire sight picture—including the background—in mind. It was an unnecessary warning. Snakeman Fletcher and The Whoremonger were not pogues fresh off some newby convoy from Anh Khe.

The terrain was unusual. A patchy network of overgrown clearings on the edge of dense jungle extended as far as the eye could see. Low, distant mountains rose up on the east and stretched along the horizon into the sunset, but they were of little consequence as far as immediate developments were concerned.

The "animal" exploded as *Pegasus* swooped low over the clearing's center. An animal was a cluster of 12 to 20 claymores—deadly anti-personnel mines—jury-rigged to

6

detonate simultaneously. The blast nearly knocked *Peg* from the sky. It definitely did its job on the ground.

The phantom force in blackface and tiger-stripes was a separate contingent of Americal troopers rushing to the assistance of their besieged brothers. They, too, had monitored the Brass Monkey distress call, and managed to cover the two klicks separating both squads in less than 30 minutes, despite the dense foliage surrounding the interlocking series of clearings. And Charlie had been waiting for them.

The eight reinforcements were killed instantly. The ninth man was alive, his leg severed just above the ankle. The concussion left trickles of blood below the noses and ears of *Peg*'s crew. Somehow, Gabriel managed to keep his craft in the air.

Brody was already leaning halfway out the hatch, held aboard only by a thin but durable canvas-and-fiberglass lifeline the doorgunners called monkeystraps. The straps were connected to his web belt like suspenders. The other ends were brass hasps that clipped to a metal bar running above the hatch.

Brody's M-60 was also suspended by a similar device, allowing him to lean into it with few restrictions, firing below and behind the gunship at odd angles. Even as *Pegasus* was roaring out of the billowing explosion within the clearing, Whoremonger fired five- and ten-round bursts back at the target tree line.

In contrast, Fletcher's hatch gun was mounted on a metal support, which permitted a more limited sight picture. His versatility was half that of Treat's, his range of targets far less.

Ascending above the treetops and banking to the right, *Pegasus* swung around for a new pass as the other gunships remained in a broader holding pattern outside the kill zone. Brody's M-60 went silent—his hatch was facing the gold sky and setting sun now—and Fletcher resumed firing out his side of the craft.

The red tracers seemed to glow a bit more as dusk took hold of the land, throwing jagged shadows through the tree line. Glancing across the cabin and past Snakeman's station, Brody watched the powerful rounds rip into stick figures racing for cover.

"Yeah!" Fletcher yelled, throwing a fist out as Gabriel banked sharp to the left and began climbing for another diving pass. "D'ya see *that*, Whoremonger?" His chin rested on a shoulder as he gauged Brody's reaction. "Smoked me at least five for the body count on that last run! D'ya see it, dude?"

"I saw it, Snakeman." Brody's eyes seemed to light up with a spark of excitement.

"Your turn comin' up. . . ." Fletcher warned, but they continued climbing when *Peg* should have started her dive, and the radio net became a din of garbled chatter.

Both doorgunners frowned with disappointment: Gabriel was giving the other ships a shot at the enemy. "Don' wanna press my luck, ladies. . . ." he clicked in the mild apology.

"Yeah," Brody muttered. "Gotta give the other boys a chance at Charlie."

"Gotta spread the voodoo around some." Snakeman nodded.

Climbing a thousand feet above Void Vicious, they watched as two, then three, then four gunships swooped in and unloaded on the suspected VC positions with mini-gun fire. Puffs of alternating black and silver smoke erupted behind the craft as rocketpods emptied their ordnance beyond the clearing—just in case a larger force lay in wait.

By the time it was *Peg*'s turn again, Gabriel saw fit to air the okay: "Python-Lead's gonna visit on this pass," he

8

advised. "Two, set down on my port. . . . Three, prepare to go to bat as soon as we lift off with casualties. . . ."

"Rodg, Lead."

"The rest of you remain airmobile 'til we air a sitrep, how copy?"

Circling the cluster of clearings just under the thousand-foot safety ceiling, the remaining pilots acknowledged in order of their numerical call signs.

Two Cobras—sleek, heavily armed gunships containing a pilot, gunner, and no room for passengers—suddenly appeared among some palm groves. Keeping well out of the way, they darted about the hostile tree line, laying down a screening cover fire while *Pegasus* began her final descent.

"Nice to see you could make it, Sharkskinner," Gabriel mumbled into the ship-to-ship frequency.

"Sorry 'bout that, Gabe . . ." Warlokk's transmission carried the crack in his voice. "But we were a good twenty klicks out. . . ."

"At Tay Ninh's most notorious steam-and-cream, no doubt," an anonymous comedian broke in.

Several acknowledging responses followed on the radio, then there was a tense silence as the deadly business of combat resumed.

Whether it was gut instinct, bad vibes, or just a whim, Gabriel did not use the adjoining clearings to land all the other helicopters. Had the ships been loaded with cavalry-men—that would have been a different matter. But they were all empty, save for the pilots and doorgunners—all involved in routine ash-'n-trash paperwork or equipment relays when Americal's Brass Monkey call for help went out.

Thus, landing all eight ships nearby would serve no useful purpose. There were no charged-up, hard-core

9

troopers eager to leap from the hatches and engage the enemy—just empty slicks.

The wounded soldiers were all in one clearing. Gabe would talk the ships in two at a time, and he would lead by example until they had extracted the last casualty.

"Bamboo in the grass!" Snakeman was yelling suddenly. He had spotted something the others had missed. But it was too late.

A thick bamboo stake, 12 feet high, punched up through *Peg*'s floorboards—nearly impaling Brody against the helicopter's roof. The spearlike tip left a gash in the cloth cover of his flak jacket.

A second stake struck the tail boom and shattered. Its top half cartwheeled into the rotor blade. Bamboo splinters showered over both Hueys. Debris was sucked into the engine cowling and, though Gabriel managed to set *Pegasus* down, black smoke soon began billowing from her turbine.

A few shots bounced about, some entering the cabin, as Snakeman sprayed the tree line, 20 feet away, with machine-gun fire.

Crouching in his hatch, Brody searched frantically for something to shoot at, but he saw no muzzle flashes, spotted no Vietnamese slipping through the bamboo—only bodies. American bodies. Everywhere. They were motionless beneath the swirling blanket of gunsmoke.

"Don' look good, don' look good," the peter pilot was saying as Brody un-assed and jumped down out of the hatch. "Don' look good, Gabe, I'm tellin' ya.... I got a feelin' about this one."

Brody listened for cries amidst all the discharges. Voices, shouts—anything. The second chopper was setting down—its pilot managed to avoid similar stakes set at a deceptive angle on the other side of the clearing—and all

10

he could hear was the violent flapping of the rotors as the pilots nervously waited for the ascend signal.

Brody didn't envy them—the pilots were sitting ducks, even with their chickenplate armor. But he didn't have that easy a job either. He could find no signs of life, so he grabbed the nearest wrist and began dragging the dead man toward *Pegasus*, 10 feet away.

Fletcher was soon by his side. They were no longer taking hostile fire from the tree line, but both soldiers were experiencing an ominous feeling about this place—it was as if they sensed hordes of Viet Cong rushing toward them through the void. Void Vicious was that shimmering sea of treetops on the edge of every battlefield Brody had ever fought in. It was the strange stretch of rain forest racing by below the gunship skids that seemed to call to every trooper in The Nam. The trees became more than just "alive" during a firefight fly-over; they seemed to fly into a frenzy, swaying to a silent song of war-zone magic, trying to mesmerize you, bewitch you, so that the gnarled branches could reach up without warning and snatch a ship out from under even the most experienced chopperjock.

Some said that the trees didn't move at all, that it was an optical illusion—at most, a shifting in the layers of triple canopy as the helicopter dropped or ascended to various altitudes during the mission. It was definitely not downblast from the rotors. Whatever, Void Vicious was jungle hell.

"I'm gettin' bookoo bad vibes about this one, Treat!" Fletcher was yelling above the clamor of nearby rotorblades. "Sump'n tells me it's gonna be a rat-fuck at best. . . ."

Brody read Fletcher's lips and nodded. A "rat-fuck" was the GIs bastardization of "Romeo-Foxtrot," which in turn was radio phonetic for a failed mission—one that had been doomed from the start.

11

They rushed back and forth, dragging, lifting, carrying, dropping, dragging again two, four, a half-dozen bodies before they finally found the man with one foot. He was beneath the bodies of his friends, in shock, suffering a severe loss of blood.

It was obvious he had not expected to be rescued. He hadn't bothered trying to stop the blood. He just clamped his lips together, sealing in the pain, and dropped back beneath the unmoving corpses, playing dead. Better to bleed to death than die from a VC bayonet thrust in the belly.

The wounded man was the last American they carried over to *Pegasus*. "That's it!" Gabriel called back as he watched Warlokk pass back and forth in front of his nose cannon, saturating the tree line with mini-gun fire. "We're overloaded as it is. . . ."

"Oughta leave some o' them bodies behind 'til after this LZ is secured," the peter pilot muttered. "We can always come back for 'em. They ain't goin' anywhere. . . ."

Gabriel did not answer, but concentrated on his instrument panel. He didn't think Charlie had any fight left in him, but there were VC survivors out there. Of that he was convinced. And The Gunslinger knew what Charlie did to the bodies his sworn enemy left behind. He didn't want to return and find them strung up on the bamboo poles, their lips sewn together with fishing wire, their genitals hacked away and "missing."

"You up back there?" he called over one shoulder.

"We're up!" Snakeman replied after Brody slid backwards through the hatch on his haunches, dragging the wounded soldier after him. Wrists under the GI's arms and locked against his chest, Brody pulled him free of the earth even as *Peg*'s tail began to lift.

"Take her away, Gunslinger!" Fletcher urged while guiding the unconscious man's legs into the cabin.

12

Without further ceremony, *Pegasus* jerked upward. Tail boom swinging to the left, her landing skids barely cleared the treetops.

The engine seemed to sputter and cough, and for a moment Brody and Fletcher locked eyes, fearing the worst. Gabriel's laughter did little to reassure them. "Come on, you feisty bitch!" The warrant officer's feet were rising and dropping as his hands remained committed to a successful ascent.

Something was purged, or seemed to catch in the whirling shaft and swash-plate assembly overhead. There was a series of forward jerks, and then the familiar purr they all were used to returned.

After he finished wrapping the wounded GI's leg and applying a tourniquet, Snakeman clasped an ammo support beam rising along the port wall. "Come on, *Peg*, ol' girl," he said, flattening his lips against a smooth plank of fiberglass. "Hang together . . . just this one last time, honey . . . just this one last time. . . ."

"You're gonna be okay, buddy," Brody was whispering to the man in his arms. "We'll have you in front of some ace medics *rikky-tik*!"

A splitting *crack*! echoed through the cabin, and *Pegasus* seemed to shudder. A whistle filled their ears, and out of the corner of one eye Brody saw the glowing green tracer punch up through the gunship's roof after exiting the top of the peter pilot's skull. A random farewell shot from Charlie, it had come up through the floorboards as they rose to that false plane of security above the landing zone.

Snakeman was saying something, but Brody could not hear him: The air was a din of shrieking turbines and rotorblades pulling pitch as the Cobras darted about, dumping more rockets into the jungle only 50 yards away.

Brody watched Gabriel give the copilot but a brief glance before returning all his concentration to the controls

13

and the mission at hand: getting the lone survivor and his crew back to Dau Tieng.

Out the opposite hatch, Brody watched Phantom fighter-bombers swoop down through the darkening shades of purple twilight to unload their ordnance. For a brief moment, the skies turned golden again as balls of floating napalm wafted up through the crackling treetops, but then *Pegasus* was abruptly climbing the spiral staircase of clouds and he focused on stemming the wounded man's flow of blood.

A grainy, haphazard daydream later, they were flaring into the Special Forces camp, medics were everywhere, and he was safe again. They were all safe. He was drunk on adrenaline, it seemed, for his legs wouldn't work at first—and if another Brass Monkey danced on the radio waves he'd be the first to volunteer his services—but, for the time being, he could relax in the comfort and deceptive security of the base camp.

Treat Brody realized that he was walking alongside Elliott Fletcher and that they were approaching what served as the outpost's informal club, but he could still see and hear and feel battle all around him. The flashbacks were drawing themselves out, only to collapse in on each other each time his eyes blinked—an odd sensation, to be sure.

The flashbacks were just beginning to re-run when Snakeman's words turned on the lights and Brody's mental images vanished.

"This ain't like 'em," Fletcher stared at the padlock on the NCO club's hootch doors. "This ain't like no god-damned Green Berets *at all*!"

"Maybe they're out on a patrol or ville P.R. job or some such shit." Brody scratched at a series of mosquito bites on

14

his gunhand. He glanced back at the welts and saw blood caked in the folds of his jungle fatigues' sleeve. Quickly, he averted his eyes.

"They would have taken their medics along, doofus."

"Right."

"You boys need a *drink*?"

Both doorgunners froze on hearing the husky voice. The images in Brody's head formed a grizzly bear that could talk. Finally, he and Fletcher both turned around.

"Uh, yeah..." Snakeman stared at the stocky red-headed master sergeant, a good foot taller than either cavalryman, standing a fist's throw away. "A bottle o' *ba-muoi-ba* to wash down the dust would feel real fine right 'bout now, Sarge."

Brody did not immediately say anything. Not many sights impressed The Whoremonger. An orgy at the Crown Hotel in Bangkok back in '65 had come close, and there *was* that stripper on Patpong Road who could "smoke" cigars using only the lips of her pussy. But he was in awe of the gorilla standing before them now, his green beret cocked on the edge of his close-cropped crown.

"Brody," The Whoremonger said finally, "Sgt. T. Brody, and Spec-4 Fletcher, Sarge. Seventh of the First, at your service..."

The big NCO's appraising scowl split into a toothy grin. "Glad to meet ya, T-Bone. M'name's Frisk," he extended a hand to Elliott first. "But you can call me—"

"You mean, like..." Fletcher was about to describe a police body search, when Frisk grabbed his wrist, whirled him around, and threw him against the creaking plywood.

"Up against the wall!" Frisk bellowed a laugh so loud it gave Brody an instant headache. "And you can call me 'Pat *down*!'" He grabbed Snakeman's buttocks and propelled him *through* the locked front door.

CHAPTER 2

Dau Tieng SF Camp

As pieces of wood still fluttered to the ground, Brody cautiously peered into the dark club after Sgt. Frisk followed Fletcher through the shattered doorframe. He could barely see Elliott rising to one knee from behind several crates of PX liquor.

"I hereby declare this club *open!*" he heard Frisk's voice rise dramatically. In the background, the last of the choppers were swooping down into the camp.

Frisk flipped a switch, and a small light bulb in the center of the ramshackle hut began burning dimly. "Homey," Treat said sarcastically.

"Welcome to the hell hole." Frisk's right arm made a sweeping gesture as he backed up to give Brody a better view of the place and the doorgunner shook his head, grinning. "You got a problem, bucky?" Frisk asked him.

"Naw . . . no," Brody replied, shaking his head. "No, I was just . . . we used to hang out at a . . . our bunker up in the Ia Drang . . . we used to call *it* the hell hole, too. . . ."

"Shit, man," Frisk ambled over behind the makeshift bar and rummaged through some coolers until he came up with three beers, "*every*body calls their bunker the 'hell hole.' This is The Nam, for crissake!"

"Yeah," Fletcher muttered, rejoining the two. He began

17

brushing his trousers off before accepting the Vietnamese brew.

A huge shadow suddenly filled the doorway, and the two cavalrymen tensed. Brody's M-16 hung from its shoulder sling against his hip, horizontal with the ground. Instinctively, he rested his gunhand on the pistolgrip.

"What the fuck, over?" came words from the shadow. The voice sounded like an older man's. Fifty-five, perhaps sixty, Brody decided.

"Come on in, Top," Frisk was busy assaulting a huge block of ice with a rusty screwdriver.

"Openin' the bar early, you fat faggot?" snapped the voice, and a soldier with a set of first sergeant's stripes on his tightly rolled fatigue sleeves sauntered into the club. He nodded to the strangers, but Brody and Fletcher were exchanging apprehensive glances. Snakeman was still upset about his bottom being manhandled.

They turned to look at the six-foot-nine monster in the green beret. Snakeman began shaking his head in the negative. He gave Brody a familiar look. No way he wanted to tangle with this dude.

"What happened to the friggin' door?" the first sergeant asked.

"Goofy over there," Frisk motioned toward Fletcher, "tripped and stumbled head first into—"

"Cut the shit, Frisk," Top interrupted him with a knowing grin. "I saw you grab the young girl's tight little butt! You gotta quit gettin' so excited every time fresh meat arrives in camp. . . ."

A noticeable shiver ran down Snakeman's spine. He downed an entire bottle of beer in one long, desperate swallow. Frisk and Top paused the obligatory few seconds, then both NCOs broke out in laughter. Frisk walked over, handed Fletcher another beer, then punched him hard on the bicep.

18

Elliott hadn't been struck so hard since his last promotion, when it was semi-traditional to "affix" chevrons or Spec-4 patches with a good-natured all-or-nothing punch. "You didn't really think I was of the limp-wristed persuasion, did ya, fella?" Frisk slurred his speech as he walked over to the other side of the room and sat down on a bar stool. He waved at Snakeman with an exaggerated swish and blew him a kiss.

"Well, fuck me till it hurts," Brody muttered under his breath to Elliott.

"Wrong choice of words, Whoremonger." Fletcher shook his head again.

Top laughed again. "Don't let Frisk bother you," he joked, reaching for a beer himself now. "Not much pussy around these parts, and—"

"My balls are a-draggin'," the stocky sergeant admitted. "*Anything*"— he batted his eyebrows at Snakeman—"is beginning to look good."

Top sensed it was time to change the subject. "Appears you gunship jockeys took some shit out yonder." He glanced through the open doorway to the choppers cluttering his helipad.

"We don't take no shit off nobody," Fletcher corrected him.

"It was a Brass Monkey," Brody explained. "Americal unit ate an animal."

"Ahh." Top's brow furrowed in deep thought as he tried to picture the battle scene.

The first sergeant studied the two cavalrymen closely, gauging their physical features and attempting to size them up by their stance and their manner.

The buck sergeant—"BRODY," his nametag read—appeared to be in his early twenties at most, Top reckoned. Standing an inch under 6 feet, Brody boasted a lean, hardened frame and probably weighed in at about 175. Unruly

19

blond hair, but at least he kept the sides short and up off the ears, the first sergeant noted, nodding ever so slightly to himself. The mustache could use a trim, though. He wore two rings, and neither was a wedding band. The one on his right hand seemed to be from some high school back in The World. The one on his marriage finger was recognizable even from this distance: an Army Airborne ring. Over the C.I.B.—combat infantryman's badge—on his left breast were subdued parachutist's and aircrew wings patches.

The other soldier was tall and lanky. Top detected a bit of a southern twang in his voice. He wore no fatigue blouse under his flak jacket—only a torn and ragged o.d. green T-shirt.

"What the hell you got slitherin' around in yor' helmet, son?" Top asked, folding his arms across his chest skeptically.

Fletcher's helmet, its chinstrap riding a web-belt keeper, hung upside down against his hip. Something—or several things—with scales, was moving about inside it.

Brody answered for the trooper. "Snakes, Top," he said. "That's why we call him Snakeman."

"They're my good-luck charms," Fletcher spoke up. "And they—"

"So long as they ain't goddamned poisonous." Frisk moved toward Elliott who backed away, holding out a cautioning hand.

"You got that look on your face, Sarge!" his eyes warned the NCO to keep back as well.

"What look, youngblood?" Frisk grinned from ear to ear.

"That *fucked-up* look I've seen before on another Green Beret's face . . . that *goofy* look that says you're in a bitin'-off-snake-heads mood."

20

Frisk replied with a hearty laugh. "You is blessed with telepathic powers, *amigo*!"

"One of 'em's a two-step krait viper!" Brody interjected, as Frisk seemed about to lunge.

"Yeah!" Fletcher affirmed. "A righteously poisonous two-step! And he *hates* gung-ho Green Berets, Sarge!"

"My favorite!" The NCO called their bluff, but froze when Fletcher grabbed a waving tail and pulled out a small, 2-foot long reptile with multicolored circles on its scales, beginning behind the snout.

"Then you can *have* him!" Snakeman tossed the harmless serpent at the sergeant.

Frisk caught it with both hands, started to rip it in half, then abruptly changed his mind. Instead, he kissed the creature on its nose and tossed it at Top.

"You *son-of-a-bitch*!" the senior NCO did a frantic dance as he raised his hands in front of his face. The snake landed directly on them. Its coils wrapped around both thumbs, eliciting a nervous chuckle from Brody.

"Top just *haaaaates* little snakies," Frisk advised them with another wink.

The first sergeant flew out of the club, calling for men outside to remove the reptile before it bit him. "I'm gonna *kill* you, Frisk!" they listened to his distant threat while the offender brought forth another round of beers.

"It won't bite 'im." Fletcher was frowning. He wasn't truly affectionate toward his reptilian pets, but he did worry for hours afterward whenever he lost one of the creatures on a jungle patrol or out the gunship hatch. Being among strangers could be even worse—especially since this *was* a Green Beret camp! Snakes didn't stand much of a chance at an SF outpost.

"It *wasn't* really a two-step, was it?" Frisk asked after downing his *ba-muoi-ba* in one gulp and reaching for still another.

"Naw." Brody nudged Elliott as the three of them listened to the sound of an approaching helicopter's rotor-blades beating at the sticky, humid air. "Ol' Fletch's truly a snake charmer, but *nobody's* that good!"

"He's gonna be pissed worse than a water buffalo with a punji stake up its ding-dong," Frisk sighed, referring to the first sergeant. "Hopefully I'll be soused beyond feelin' any pain before he makes his way back here, hey-*hey*!"

"Top'll get over it." Fletcher spoke as if he had already known the man for a tour or two.

They drank in silence for a moment, listening to the Huey set down on the helipad a hundred yards away. Turbine idling, its rotors continued to flap at a slower pitch. "He ain't shuttin' down," Brody's ears perked slightly as they listened to a single set of boots approaching the club.

"And he ain't takin' off," Fletcher noted.

Frisk glanced at his watch. "Mailman," he decided.

"This time o' the evening?" Fletcher could see that some of the brighter stars were already coming out. In another few minutes, it would be pitch-black out there. And it would be Charlie Hour.

"Sometimes HQ sends out a carrier pigeon with worthless intel after the 1700-hour Hanoi Hannah broadcast. Worthless crapola, but you know how the game's played."

A growing shadow filled the doorway, and then a bent-over corporal with a duffel bag over his shoulder entered.

"Greetings and salut*Asians*!" The corporal did not look up but began looking for somewhere to set down his duffel.

"This ain't the orderly room, *amigo*," Frisk rummaged through the beer bottles, searching for his hidden cache. "Ahhh!" He sounded surprised when golden brew from the Kingdom of Thailand showed up. "*Singha!*"

"I know this ain't the orderly room." The mail clerk wiped sweat from his brow after propping the duffel

22

against the makeshift bar counter. "It's the club. I been carryin' mail on this route for eleven brain-fryin' months. In ten lousy days and a wake-up, it'll be *twelve* months, and I'm *outta* here. . . ."

"Almost a single-digit midget," Brody said with mock envy.

"So I oughta know where I'm at, okay?"

"Okay." Frisk did not sound impressed. "So now that you know where you are, go take a hike, you REMF son-ofa—"

The clerk did not appear intimidated by the "rear echelon Motherfucker" label, but he was quick to interrupt the towering Green Beret. "You *are* Sgt. Frisk, are you not?" He unlocked the duffel's top security rings.

Frisk glanced up from his beer for the first time and glared at the clerk suspiciously. "Naw, that ol' fuckwad Frisk got his gonads blown away goin' on two weeks now, kid . . . so why don't you just pack up your little—"

"I happen to *know* you're Sgt. Frisk because I passed Top on the way up from the helipad, and he said you were playin' with yourself inside the club. He described you to a tee: 'big seven-foot-tall ape wearin' a green beret.'"

Swiping the beret off almost comically, Frisk set his beer bottle down with a sharp crack and folded his massive forearms across his chest. "So which one o' my lousy ex-pud pullers sent me a subpoena through Uncle Sammy?" he asked, referring to his five former wives. A slight tic developed at the edge of his left eye.

"No divorce papers." The clerk's shallow laugh filled the room as he removed a box that appeared to take up the top half of the duffel.

"What the hell . . . ?" His curiosity suddenly roused, Frisk moved around from the back of the counter.

"I've been tryin' to deliver this to you for over a month now," the mailclerk said.

23

"I move around a lot," Frisk replied sarcastically.

"Make sure it ain't addressed in green ink," Fletcher advised them. "The Cong are usin' green ink on their letter bombs this month."

"Any return address?" Brody responded to the suggestion of a bomb.

"Nope," the Special Forces sergeant was grinning. "But I'd recognize that Savannah scrawl *anywhere*!" He began tearing the package open.

"You gotta sign my clipboard here, Sarge." The clerk produced a sheaf of papers from inside his shirt.

Frisk ignored the mail clerk's name tag, which read "MALONEY." "Later, peckernose. This here box is from my man Pruett, down in the Delta—as in *Mekong* Delta! He promised to send me his *Playboy* collection as soon as—"

Frisk fell suddenly silent. He appeared extremely perplexed. Beneath the box's top flaps was a bundle of thick plastic. It was tightly sealed.

"Well?" Snakeman asked.

"Sonofabitch . . ." Frisk whispered. "He did it. That damned Pruett finally did it."

"What?" Brody stepped back a couple of paces.

Swallowing loudly, Frisk carefully grasped the knot on top and pulled the bag out.

It was filled with a crimson-streaked liquid and long, black strands that made the doorgunner think of licorice.

As the bag rotated slightly in Frisk's grasp, it quickly became apparent that there was a human head inside.

"Pleased to meet you," Fletcher mumbled matter-of-factly as the four men stared at the bloated face. It had belonged to an Asian male with long black hair. The eyelids were tightly closed and wrinkled, the sunken cheeks a sickly yellow.

Maloney the mail clerk was aghast—to think he had

24

been lugging this hideous parcel around for nearly five weeks! And the way these grunts took the shocking contents in their stride—as if this happened every day!

"Anyone you know?" Brody tried not to laugh, but there was no mistaking the amused lines creasing his cheeks.

Frisk glanced up and stared at each one of them in turn. "As a matter of fact, yes," he finally said after a dramatic pause of several seconds. "Lam Tre Cuc. A VC cell leader down in the Mekong Delta, where I spent a tour prior to Dau Tieng."

"Cuc?" Brody cut it. "I thought that was a girl's name."

"Yeah, we called him Cuc-sucker," Frisk quipped. "Boy was good with a bayonet. Never carried a firearm. Just the bayonet stolen from a sentry at Cho Gao as he slept."

"Did he kill the guard?" Maloney stammered.

"Nope." Frisk chuckled and tilted his head to one side sheepishly.

Brody read a guilty plea in the expression. "The guard was *you*," he said without pronouncing judgment.

"Yep," Frisk admitted. "Pruett was a-tiptoein' through the wait-a-minute vines toward my LP at the same moment Charlie here lifted my Mattel-manufactured blade, boys! Saved my ass, and managed to ding the zip bastard—but also made me the laughingstock of the Delta in the process.

"Charlie here got away with a flesh wound and my bayonet, and I finished out my tour and transferred up here to Dau Tieng with rotten egg on my face."

"I woulda tracked this dink motherfucker's ass down and filled him full o' two tons o' tracer," Snakeman said confidently.

"Oh, I promised myself even more satisfaction than that, sonny-boy." Frisk's face turned dead serious. "Hunted Charlie here for two months straight. Bagged bookoo VC, too, but never this long-haired hippy bastard."

"He was pretty damn slick for a 'long-haired hippy bastard,'" Maloney taunted the Green Beret sergeant.

Frisk directed a granite-melting glare at the mail clerk. "And who the flyin' fuck asked a clerk-'n-jerk-off for his goddamned opinion?"

"*Xin loi*," the clerk replied with the Vietnamese equivalent of "Sorry 'bout-that."

"Anyways,"—Frisk cleared his throat to end the interruption—"the clowns in my unit got together and raised a hundred-buck bounty on Cuc-sucker here"—his smile returned with the memory—"and started wagering which one of us would be the first to bag the bastard—me or Pruett. By the time I transferred up here, the whole scene was pretty much forgotten."

"You thought." Brody laughed.

"Right." Frisk snickered. "I—" He froze in mid-sentence, glancing back at the door.

The pitter-patter of little feet reached all their ears at the same time. Brody and Snakeman dropped into a defensive crouch, low among the shadows.

Treat was first to recognize the panting sound. He allowed the M-16 to drop back against his hip. "Choi-oi, you goofy mutt!"

Fletcher sighed as a blur of fur bounced through the dark doorway. He recognized the wagging stub of a tail and also lowered his weapon.

Brody grabbed the heavy mongrel and lifted him off his feet until he was reclining in the doorgunner's arms. Choi-oi glanced over at Snakeman with chops open, teeth gleaming, and tongue still hanging out. The brown, short-haired mutt was panting hard.

"Get that shit-eatin' grin off your face, dog, or I'll sell your worthless ass to those mama-san con-cunts at the main gate," Fletcher threatened.

Choi-oi seemed to understand, for his ears perked, and

26

he barked at Elliott until Brody began brushing back the fur over his eyebrows reassuringly. "No, no, no," he whispered in the mongrel's right ear. "Fletch was just fuckin' with ya, pal. Nebbah mind."

Then Choi-oi froze. His eyes seemed to lock onto the plastic bag in Frisk's hand, and he began growling. Again, his ears shot forward.

"It's okay," Brody continued brushing the nervous animal's coat. "Not your type o' meat, boy." He pretended to strangle Choi-oi with a playful headlock, and the dog responded by gnawing at The Whoremonger's forearm. Choi-oi let out a couple of sharp yelps, directed at Frisk, then managed to jump free of Brody's grasp and leaped up onto the bar, where he dropped into a prone bird-dog stance—nose pointing at the huge Green Beret, eyes locked on the item dangling from his hand.

"Hey, this is an honorable establishment!" Frisk pointed at the dog with his free hand. "Has Dinky-dau there been dunked for fleas? Get his freeloadin' butt off the counter. I run a respectable—"

"No sweat." Brody lifted another beer from one of the coolers. "He's as clean as The Whoremonger's whanger. And his name's Choi-oi," The Whoremonger added. "Not Dinky-dau."

"Same-same." Frisk frowned.

"Not quite, Sarge, but anyways. . . ."

"So, anyways," Frisk wasn't one to miss his cue. "I guess ol' Pruett smoked young Cuc with that illegal grease gun he always carried around in his ruck for sterile ops, if you know what I mean. . . ."

"We know what you mean." Fletcher grinned in recognition.

"When this war's over," Frisk nodded in time to his thoughts, "the boys in the War Room oughta authorize some Agency spooks armed with similar 'works o' art' to bust a couple caps on the Berkeley campus—where the real commies are."

"Nothin' but nationalists around The Nam anymore," Snakeman agreed.

"You're tellin' me." Frisk dropped the plastic bag on the bar, and Choi-oi almost shot forward to steal it. Instead, he whimpered, struggling against the self-discipline Brody had instilled in him over the months.

"What's *this*?" For the first time, Sgt. Frisk noticed a small envelope taped to the side of the bag.

"A love note from Pruett?" Brody smiled.

Before Frisk could think up a clever retort, his fingers had ripped open the envelope. The top edge of a wrinkled C-note appeared. "One hundred smackers to go with the skulljob," Snakeman laughed.

Frisk did not seem quite as amused. He pulled out the greenback, held it up against the light for a brief inspection, then stuffed it down into a thigh pocket.

There was a short note in the envelope as well, and as he began reading it silently to himself, two additional heads popped in through the doorway. "Is this watering hole open, or what the fuck, over?"

Both Brody and Fletcher glanced back over a shoulder at the same time, but neither cavalryman recognized the two faces. "FNGs," Snakeman muttered loudly enough for the strangers to hear. Fucking New Guys.

"Sure, come on in." Maloney waved the privates into the club. "Sgt. Frisco here was just about to read us one of his love letters." Surprised by the mail clerk's sudden show of bravado, Brody and Fletcher exchanged puzzled glances. "Is it smothered in perfume, Sergeant-sir?"

"It's Frisk, turd-brain, not Frisco, and just who the hell asked *you* for your opinion?" said the Green Beret before returning to the letter.

Brody, meanwhile, was inspecting the two newbies.

Both whites, one appeared to be about nineteen, with close-cropped brown hair and a baby face no different than that of a dozen other troopers in Echo Company except that he had larger-than-normal ears. The other soldier looked ten years older. He had black hair, slightly longer than regulation, and wire-rim glasses. He reminded Treat of Shawn Larson, "The Professor," who had been on the K.I.A. rolls for some time now. Both troopers wore E-2 chevrons—private 2nd class, one step up from the bottom. The vets called these stripes mosquito wings, in honor of the Vietnamese "national bird." But the soldier wearing glasses had obviously been in The Nam some time already: A MACV patch adorned his right shoulder. Probably a troublemaker transferee, Brody decided. Wearing a combat patch and still only a PV2 meant the soldier had been busted down from E-4, or at least from private first class.

"Is there a Sergeant Brody in here?" MACV Patch asked with mild annoyance.

Treat could read the troopers' name tags from across the room: The older one with the combat patch was Jones; the kid with the big ears was Karter.

He started to respond, when Frisk said, "Shut the foo-foo up, girl. I'm 'bout to grace you glory-fucks with a bit o' masterful writing from a bloodbrother down in the Delta."

"We're all ears." Jones's companion actually commanded his ears to wiggle noticeably. Snakeman burst out laughing, but Frisk just stared at the show for a moment, then dropped his gaze to the letter and began reading.

"'Dear Frisky'"—the sergeant glanced back up at them—"Ol' Pruett calls me that when he's in a good or goadin' mood," the Green Beret explained with mild embarrassment. "'Here's Cuc-sucker's skull, as promised. Be sure to mount it in an appropriate fuckin' place, you hear,

29

slimeball? If you're still runnin' the club there in Dau Tieng, mount the damn thing right over the bar.

"'I went through hell to nab the ratfink,'" Frisk continued reading, "'and decided to enclose the hundred-buck bounty as well—you sure need the booze money more than myself, if you're *still* doin' time at Dau Tieng! I heard through Rumor Control some First Cav doggies are hangin' out there these days. Triple bummer, Trenton. . . .'"

He glanced up, but Snakeman beat him to the punch. "That's your first name," he surmised.

"Rodg," Frisk replied with a wanna-make-something-out-of-it spark in his eyes. "'So keep downwind of Charlie, and maybe we can take in a Thailand R&R together someday—Reilly told me Sattahip ain't been the same since we left Camp Samae San's Mars Hill. Still in Singapore, J.P.'"

"So you're a C-note richer," Fletcher reminded the Special Forces NCO. "Gonna buy us all a round o' Singha, or what?"

A worried grimace creased Frisk's face. The Singha was obviously his private stash. Suddenly light bulbs seemed to gleam in his eyes. "Better than that!" He reached down behind the bar. "I'm gonna treat you no-class clowns to some fine—"

"Aw, no," Maloney groaned as the fiddle came into view.

"You can actually play that thing?" Brody seemed genuinely interested.

"Actions speak louder than words." Frisk beamed, bringing the instrument to his shoulder.

With the first drawn-out, out-of-tune note, Choi-oi sat up and began howling, causing Maloney to laugh and Frisk's eyes to bulge with mock fury. But Brody and

Snakeman knew the mutt was not voicing his displeasure with the recital. His ears had tuned in to something else.

"Everybody *down!*" Treat dove behind the counter. An instant later, the first mortars began whistling down onto the compound.

CHAPTER 3

Dau Tieng SF Camp

Gunship rotorblades were music to Brody's ears.

As Dau Tieng's Green Beret commandos swarmed about the outpost, checking on the Strike Force guards and beefing up their defenses, First Cav warrant officers were busy bringing their helicopters up to pitch power before the rain of mortars could devastate the helipad. Their first priority would be to get the birds up into the night air. Their second would be to seek out and destroy the enemy still on the ground—no easy task in the dark.

One Huey, the victim of a direct hit, was already lying on its side and in flames as Brody and Snakeman rushed from the club, Choi-oi at their heels. They raced for *Pegasus*, but the Cong seemed to be after something else: Most of the eighty-two mike-mikes were walking across camp toward the Command Post—a poor tactical decision, for Brody watched the two Cobras ascend with a roaring scream even as he and Fletch were climbing over landing skids and past hatch-60s.

"Oh, *shit!*" Fletcher muttered as a powerful *thump!* reached their ears even above the climbing whine of *Peg*'s turbine.

"They're closer than I thought!" Brody checked his M-60 to ensure the ammo belt was riding smooth, then slammed the bolt home and double checked his lifeline.

"Eighty-two mike-mikes," Snakeman decided as they listened to several more mortars being fired a mere kilometer away in the tree line somewhere beyond small arms range.

"Nope," Brody disagreed. "That's American-made noise, Snake!"

"Eighty-*one* mike-mikes?" Fletcher readied his own machine gun, then glanced back over a shoulder.

"*Captured* eighty-ones." Brody nodded almost solemnly. Gabriel, up in the cockpit with a new peter pilot, chose that moment to pull pitch. *Pegasus*'s tail boom lifted, and the ship shot out over the perimeter fenceline.

Brody felt a tap on his shoulder and whirled around to find the two newbies from the club crouching in the center of the cabin, their rifles at the ready, but tense anxiety in their eyes. "Hold on to your assholes," Brody yelled above the rotor downblast, "and enjoy the ride!"

"You both know how to operate M-60s, right?" Fletcher locked eyes with Jones.

"Of course!" Karter replied.

"Good!" Fletch popped two thick wads of bubble gum into his mouth. "If me or The Whoremonger over there takes a hit, drag our ass outta the way and take over the Hog-60, you got that?"

"Yeah." the baby-faced private wiggled his ears again for Snakeman.

"We got it." Jones nodded also.

Brody glared at Fletcher and his casual suggestion of catastrophe, but Fletcher only shrugged.

"Black hats off the port skid," Gabriel interrupted the verbal exchange with his sighting.

Brody leaned out the hatch, held in only by the monkeystraps attached on one end to the back of his web belt, and on the other to a bar above the hatch, and immediately spotted the five-man squad of VC, silhouetted by Green

34

Beret illumination flares. He couldn't see any mortarplates or tubes, but five zips in the bamboo were enough to warrant unleashing the wild hog. He sent a sustained burst of several dozen bullets down into the tight clearing, but no sooner had he pulled the trigger than more treetops obscured his view as *Pegasus* raced above the triple canopy. "Fuck," he muttered.

"Did you get 'em?" Snakeman yelled, as excited as Brody had ever seen him.

"Yeah, I think I tripped up two or three of the little bastards. . . ." He clicked into the intercom. "Take us back, will ya, Gabe? Take us back directly over that same spot."

"No can do, Whoremonger," came the metallic reply. "Cherry-red smoke comin' up on our whiskey. . . . Neil Nazi's Loach spotted some Victor Charlie up ahead . . . believed to be the mortar team. Stand by for an increase in the pucker factor, ladies, it's gonna be lima-lima all the way over. . . ."

"Lima-lima" was radio phonetic for low-level. They would be racing a foot or two above the treetops from here on in. They were over dense jungle now. Jagged branches shot up through the canopy without warning at several spots. And they were flying blacked-out. Gabe was guiding on the faint light at dusk.

"Buchanan's in the area?" Fletcher clicked in. He didn't sound very enthusiastic.

"Not in a C&C capacity," the copilot replied. "Just goofin' off as usual."

"Sharkskinner advised the colonel's already topside, watchin' our moves from two thou'," Gabriel clicked in.

"Wonnerful, wonnerful." His peter pilot's words were soaked with sarcasm.

"*There they ARE!*" Fletcher was blasting away out the chopper's left hatch.

"Seven, eight, *nine!*" Brody counted pith helmets in the

35

night gloom. A set of Ho Chi Minh sandals reflected in the light of the parachute flare as several of the high-powered bullets catapulted a fleeing guerrilla head over heels.

"Keep it up, Snakeoil!" Gabriel advised with satisfaction. "They're all yours. I can't mini-gun 'em from this angle, how copy?"

"No sweat!" Fletcher yelled as his hundredth or so bullet —a tracer—exploded from the smoking MG muzzle, glowing white-hot all the way down into the narrow clearing. A black tube flipped through the air amid several bodies, and sparks danced off the mortar's baseplate before Snakeman's sight was obscured by a series of high tree lines.

"He got the damn mortar itself!" Turning to the newbies, Brody yelled with glee. "Did you chumps see that? He blasted the friggin' tube with his Hog-60."

"We're only fifty yards up." Elliott's modest reminder was really a low-key boast. "And it *was* an eighty-two, Whoremonger, not an eight-one."

"Eat my shorts, Snakeskin." Brody couldn't stop laughing.

Gabriel did his best to keep the clearing in sight of the doorgunners as he brought *Pegasus* back around for another pass: It seemed the other helicopters were going after the earlier clearing full of sappers, for there appeared to be no other aerial activity in the immediate vicinity.

"We're takin' 'er down, Gabe?" Fletcher's voice was laced with anticipation.

"One more pass," The Gunslinger advised. He swerved from one tree line to another, then abruptly dropped below a long, meandering line of palm fronds as they returned to the mortar team's last-known location.

Eyes glued on the ground, Fletcher advised the newbies to get ready for the real fun. "Prepare to un-ass and *kick* butt!" he told them with an evil leer. Even before the clearing shifted back into his gunsights, Fletcher was firing long, unceasing bursts down into the shifting multihued layers of rain-forest green.

"Us?" Karter locked disbelieving eyes with Jones.

Fletcher glanced around the cabin even as he continued to fire. "You see any other nose-pickin' pogues aboard this ship?" He flashed a bright set of teeth.

"But there's only the *two* of us!" Jones rose from his crouch and was nearly thrown out the hatch when the helicopter tilted onto its side to maneuver through a clump of leaning tamarinds.

"And we don' have any . . . any *training*!" Karter was quick to point out. "I mean . . . we just *got* here, for crissake! You haven't showed us how to do it your way. How the hell do you expect me to—"

"Snakeman's greased every guerrilla within two klicks o' the clearing. All you two girls gotta do is retrieve the mortar tube, take a body count, then beat feet to your sierra-echo, where *Peg*'ll be waitin' to extract ya."

"Who's *Peg*?" Karter yelled back at Brody. His words were all but drowned out by the hatch-60's discharges and the rotors beating hectically overhead.

Brody answered the big-eared trooper first. "*Peg*'s short for *Pegasus*, asshole," he said, pointing at Jones's combat patch.

"Fuck you!" Jones replied angrily.

They were getting nearer the chosen LZ. *Pegasus* was dropping—already her landing skids were only a few feet off the earth. Jones knew there was trouble waiting on the ground. He knew that not *all* the Viet Cong were dead. He knew Sgt. Treat Brody was sending him to his death.

"*What?*" The Whoremonger rose to the challenge. But Fletcher didn't give them a chance to argue.

"We got dinks at three o'clock!" he was swinging the M-60 from side to side as he fired nonstop at shadows darting about in the night tree line.

37

"Fuck!" Brody muttered as he began unsnapping both his monkeystraps and the heavy machine gun. "Don' gimme none o' that 'three o'clock,' Hollywood crap, Snake! Where's the—"

"Right there, and *there*, and THERE!" Fletcher pointed with his MG muzzle as he fired. Most of the Vietnamese were cut down in their tracks.

"Jesus!" Both doorgunners heard the copilot's exclamation as Gabe brought the ship in for a sideways landing. The skids pranged across several protruding tree roots, and then shoulder-high elephant grass was slapping at the hatches.

Finally, *Pegasus* slid to a bumpy halt. "Follow me!" Brody flew through the smoke-filled opening and disappeared into the shimmering sea of sharp reeds beyond Snakeman's glowing machine-gun barrel.

"Don' worry!" Fletcher called out confidently, "I wasted 'em all for ya, Whoremonger—I think!" But he was still firing away.

Jones and Karter again locked eyes. For a moment, the two of them just sat there without moving, frozen in fear. Then Fletcher was yelling at them. "Move it!" he screamed. "That's my best friend down there! You'd best get your asses down there and cover 'im, or you're dead meat." The machine gun in his hands was filling the cabin with smoke, and empty brass piled up around their boots. Already, the helicopter began to rise back off the ground, its tailboom swinging around.

"You clear back there?" Gabriel's worried voice filled the intercom in Fletcher's headset.

"That's a roger!" The angry doorgunner continued firing his mounted M-60 with one hand as he grabbed and threw the two reluctant cavalrymen out the hatch. "We're *ba-moui-ba*-light back here, Mista Gabe. Take her up!"

CHAPTER 4

Jungles Outside Dau Tieng

The punji stake cracked and split apart instead of penetrating the sole of Brody's boot as he jumped from the chopper hatch into deep elephant grass. "I owe you one, Buddhabuddy," he muttered under his breath and glanced up at the brightest star in the dark sky.

A steel plate runs along all army-issue jungle boots, between the rubber sole and inner lining. Though originally designed for just such grassy encounters, it had also been known to stop one of Charlie's favorite booby traps. Treat tripped one of these next, and the blast threw him off balance. He slammed against an earthen bank at the clearing's edge.

"Damn!" Pain tightened his jaws. After breaking the punji stake, he had stepped on a buried bullet trap.

Charlie was good at concealing empty, sawed-off 50-caliber cartridges in the earth. Against the shell's bottom primer plate, a tack or nail was soldered. A push-button pen's spring was placed around the nail, and a live M-16 round gently inserted into the brass, nose up. Then the entire contraption was buried in soft dirt up to the 5.56-caliber bullet's lead nose. The first person stepping on it would force the bullet down onto the nail's tip, setting off the primer. The M-16 round then discharged, sending a bullet up through the victim's foot.

39

"This place is a goddamned buried-bullet mine field," Brody watched *Pegasus* hover overhead briefly, then dart off, blacked out, disappearing through a break in the tree line, silhouetted against the stars. He ran the palm of his hand against the earth and felt several more bullet tips barely protruding above the surface. Simply touching the lead-nosed rounds was not enough to detonate the makeshift anti-personnel mines. A man's full body weight had to be applied, and with sudden, sharp force—otherwise, the M-16 cartridge would shift about and misfire, rendering the boobytrap dangerous but no longer as deadly as intended.

Happy to be receiving no immediate welcoming fire, Brody was nevertheless startled by two bodies that hurtled through the elephant grass without warning, slamming into him just as he was rising to one knee again.

"We heard an explosion!" Karter grabbed Brody's arm.

"Don't move!" Brody warned. "This whole place is a cemetery waitin' to happen!"

"Tripwires?" Jones wiped sooty sweat from his brow and glanced about frantically.

"Not that bad," Brody reassured him by holding up the jury-rigged cartridge.

"Shit." Karter's eyes grew wide. Brody next lifted his boot so they could see the missing chink of rubber tread where the bullet had left its signature. Karter's lower jaw dropped. "Oh man! It must hurt like a—"

"Felt like somebody hit my foot with a sledgehammer." Brody nodded. "From the *bottom*!"

"So what's the plan?" Jones turned his back to them and began searching the twilight for the enemy.

"I wasn't planning on the unexpected obstacles." Brody motioned toward the slight impressions in the dirt where his palm swipe had uncovered the tips of a dozen bullets.

40

"A good grunt always plans for the—" Karter began, but he fell silent when confronted with Brody's icy glare.

Pegasus flew past again, low against the treetops, closing up a counterclockwise circle, with Snakeman still blasting away with his Hog-60. Jones watched red and yellow tracers drop from the hatch and float down into the palm fronds to the southeast.

Brody stared at the temporary trail they had blazed through the elephant grass. "We obviously didn't blow any bullet traps up to this point," he said, "so they must start right here."

"And the doorgunner up there is layin' his line o' fire back in the direction we originally came from," Jones observed.

"I don't see anything of special interest happenin' directly ahead of us," Brody said. "Maybe Snakeman *did* manage to waste all those dinks we saw."

"So we backtrack," Jones said.

"Correctemundo, *amigo*! First thing we do is get out of this clearing. . . ."

"You call *this* a clearing?" Karter was nursing several deep cuts from the shoulder-high, razor-sharp reeds.

Brody ignored his complaint. "And back into the tree line," he exchanged nods with Jones. "What's your first name, by the way?"

"Reece."

Brody contemplated Jones's reply for a moment. Reece Jones. He'd heard the name before, but couldn't quite remember where. "And yours?" He gave Karter an annoyed glance.

"Toby," the kid said. "Toby Karter from New Jersey. At your service."

Brody frowned. He would never be able to remember their first names. They would have to remain Jones and Karter.

"Hey, let's get a move on before Gabe thinks we dropped into a tunnel or somethin' and he gives us up for lost. I don' want my name on no M.I.A. roster. And last thing we need is for Neil Nazi to give the okay for a napalm strike to sanitize the area."

"We never should have dismounted without a radio," Jones protested.

"In Echo Company, we don't do things the way you're supposed to," Brody was not apologizing as they slowly followed his step-by-step zigzag through the reeds.

"So what would your Echo Company cronies do *now*, Sarge?" Karter asked.

Brody froze. He glanced around, making sure there was still no enemy activity in the immediate vicinity, then locked eyes with the private. "*First* off, shut the fuck up."

"Just tell us how you want to work this rat-fuck," Jones cut in. "Brief us, then let's get it over with."

"Fine." Brody's scowl softened somewhat. "First, we sweep the bush toward the sierra-echo. Oughta be comin' across the bodies of those Cong Snakeman wasted. We take a count, retrieve as many weapons as we can carry, booby-trap the rest, then make our way toward the pick-up point —meanwhile keeping an eye on *Pegasus*. We'll guide on her. Our main objective is to retrieve one of the mortars. The Brass got the word from Special Ops about a new Soviet-made mortar south of the DMZ. M. I. wants to get a look at it, though I think Charlie was just usin' an old Soviet 82 to lob shit at us tonight. It's as clean as that."

"Let's fucking do it," Karter brushed past Brody and began blazing his own trail through the tall elephant grass. The cavalry sergeant rushed and caught up with him, jerking the young trooper back into a face-to-face confrontation.

"You ain't been in The Nam long enough to lead the way into or *out* o' the sticks—you got that, *newby*?

I don' wanna lose my ding-dong 'cause you don't know shit!"

Jones rushed past. "Well, *I* fuckin' for sure have been in The Nam long enough," he said before vanishing into the deep reeds.

Gritting his teeth, Brody released Karter, paused, then followed in Reece Jones's bootprints.

The bodies had fallen precisely where he'd estimated they'd be from the air—in an adjoining series of clearings a football field's run from the LZ where *Pegasus* had set down. All ten VC sappers were armed with AK-47 assault rifles, and Chinese stick grenades. "Forget the mortar," Treat Brody advised Jones, who was down on one knee, examining the weapon's heavy plate.

"But I thought it was the main reason we set down in the first place." Jones wondered why he was protesting. The damn thing was *heavy*.

"It's an 82 mike-mike," Brody said. "Soviet, for sure, but we've already captured a shitload of 'em. Like I told ya: No big secret about the eighty-twos. Just carry as many AK's as you're comfortable with."

"Right."

They'd lost sight of *Pegasus*, but there was gunship activity several hundred yards to the southeast—in the general direction where Brody and the newbies were supposed to be extracted—so they headed that way, Treat in the lead this time.

Dense brush rose behind the tree line, so they kept to the edges of an interlocking series of clearings. Here, there were less thorns to contend with, but all three troopers were more exposed. The elephant grass had dropped to waist level in most areas.

Clouds suddenly drifted below the full moon, throwing a blanket of darkness across the land, and Jones cursed under his breath as he stumbled on an exposed root.

Some soldiers like to fight. There are those who'd sell their left testicle for a righteous battle. Of those soldiers that like to fight, only the odd one prefers an after-dark skirmish to one in broad daylight. Treat Brody was one of them.

A flare burst overhead suddenly, and all three soldiers dropped down into squatting positions. They watched the shadows of branches dance in the flickering golden light. As it passed overhead, they could barely make out the white silk parachute. A silver smoke plume, its edges being dispersed by the muggy night breeze, trailed behind it.

In the distance, they could see the reflected silvery-blue halo of *Pegasus* prowling back and forth over the jungle. Spurts of red and yellow tracer shot down from the halo now and then, the dull reports reaching their ears five, ten seconds later. *Peg* was a good thousand yards away.

"The more we hump through this godforsaken stretch o' sticks," Karter complained so softly the others could barely hear him, "the farther away that chopper keeps drifting."

"Shut up," Brody hissed.

"Are they fuckin' with us or what?" Jones asked.

"That's their goddamned job." Treat moved ahead of Jones, taking up the lead again. "To take the fight to Charlie. We get there when we get there."

A point-blank burst of AK rounds 10 feet in front of him temporarily blinded Brody and blackened his face with powder burns, but the dozen or so rounds all sailed harmlessly over his helmet.

Falling back onto his haunches, Brody unloaded on the VC's outline while the imprint was still fresh on his mind.

He fired an entire banana clip. Thirty rounds on full automatic.

The night was filled with a wounded VC's screams.

Also blinded by the drawn-out muzzle flash, Karter dropped to one knee beside Brody as Jones raced past. "Watch your ass, Reece!" he heard himself calling out to the soldier. "There might be more of 'em! We might o' walked right into a goddamned ambush—"

Jones had already sprayed the elephant grass in a 180-degree arc. He was flipping the taped double mag, ejecting the empty clip and inserting its fresh side.

"I just count one!" He struck the magazine's bottom with the palm of his hand to ensure it was locked in place, hit the release lever, and listened to the bolt slam home on a live round. It sounded as though he was checking the dead man over. "And you only managed to ding him once —outta thirty rounds," Jones added. "But I guess you made it count: dead center in the forehead. Wonder what the sucker's last thoughts were before—"

"Keep down the chatter." Brody was back on his feet. "Where there's one, there's more." Wiping his eyes, he moved to Jones's side. "What the hell you think *you're* doing?" Brody noticed Karter for the first time. The kid was stripping the Viet Cong soldier of his web belt and pack.

"Hopin' there *are* more easy kills around," Karter flashed an ear-to-ear grin. "I'm gonna open a war souvenirs mail-order business back in The World when this abortion's over."

"Christ . . ." Brody muttered, wondering why he even wasted wind trying to explain. "Half this shit can't be sent home even if you—" All three Americans dropped prone in the dust as a huge shadow rushed past, low overhead. It was only one of the gunships, racing fast and silent over the treetops.

They didn't have much time to contemplate further. Two short men in black pajamas, brandishing SKS carbines with bayonets fixed, appeared behind them and began jabbering directives in rapid-fire Vietnamese.

Brody recognized "*De sung xuong!*" and "*Dung yen!*" This was Vietnamese for "Drop your weapon," and "Don't move or you die, GI!"

CHAPTER 5

Tay Ninh Province

The tattooed woman jabbed a pin in the back of Gage Ruckter's neck, an inch or so below the base of his skull. Then, using rapid karate chops, she began beating him between the shoulder blades with the edges of her petite but powerful hands.

"Harder, honey." Sgt. Ruckter allowed a chuckle to escape. The chuckle became a sigh, then a moan, as the Vietnamese masseuse went to work on him.

"You're really into pain, aren't ya, Sarge?" A short, dark-haired buck private lying face down on the table beside Ruckter's challenged the big NCO in what sounded like a drunken slur.

"Sex and violence," Ruckter responded as he rolled onto his back and out from under the small towel. "In The Nam that's the name of the game. He caught one of the masseuse's hands and guided it toward his crotch, but she slid free of the stocky American's grasp with little effort and commenced pounding his pectorals.

"Only game in *this* massage parlor," said the short, slender woman with a no-nonsense smirk, "is 'be good boy or yo' gone, *bwana-san!*' "

Frowning, Ruckter rolled back onto his stomach and tried to relax against the harsh rattan table. The masseuse used only one hand now as she rubbed hot lotion onto his lower back. Her free hand was preparing the next needle for insertion along the top slope of his right buttocks. "Only three mo' needle," she announced. "Then, no stress, GI . . . no pain."

Already, dozens of pins dangled from Ruckter's sides and the fleshy joint behind his knees. He looked like a human porcupine. "No pain, no gain, babes."

"What you mean 'gain,' babes?" she imitated him crudely.

"Nebbah mind, woman. Just do yo' thing and let's get it over with."

"What's your name, anyway, honey?" the soldier beside Ruckter asked from beneath several steaming white towels.

"I tell you before—" her smirk broadened into a sly, Korean-style grin, though every drop of blood flowing through this woman's veins was 100 percent pure lowlander Vietnamese—"my name Shirley." She applied more pressure than was necessary while inserting the next pin.

"Shirley?" Ruckter chuckled again. "Surely you *jest*, babes."

"You mean . . . like Shirley Temple?" Ruckter's buddy asked. The name tag on his uniform, which now hung from a hook on the wall, read "FELLOWS."

"That's American," the sergeant interrupted before she could reply. "What's your Vietna*mese* name, babes?"

The masseuse stuck a needle into one of Ruckter's earlobes before saying, "You would not be able to pronounce Viet version, Joe."

"Try me," Ruckter responded dryly. "And it's not Joe," he added. "Call me Gage, okay?"

"Gage?" her palms began kneading the muscles along his shoulders.

"Like twelve-gauge *shotgun*." Fellows sat up. He began removing the towels one by one and piling them up on a nearby stool.

48

The masseuse appeared slightly perplexed. "My English not so good," she finally admitted.

Ruckter glanced over at her. Maybe twenty-eight or twenty-nine, he decided . . . thirty tops. Short and slender, probably all of 5 feet tall and 99 pounds soaking wet. The mandatory long black hair falling to the bottom swell of firm haunches. Mahogany-dark thighs flared from beneath a white miniskirt. The legs were smooth and shapely— muscular, in fact. Probably from squatting instead of sitting on chairs all her life, he decided. And "smooth" wasn't the word for her—nylons had probably never touched this woman's hairless flesh. He doubted they ever would, especially here in the tropics. Proud, jutting breasts pressed against a white T-shirt with "GIMME HEAD TILL I'M DEAD" emblazoned across the front in day-glo pink.

Ruckter chuckled after reading it. Probably a present from some long-forgotten GI. He wondered if she knew what the words really meant.

"So anyways"—Ruckter shifted his head until he was facing Fellows—"what the flying fudge was we talkin' 'bout, partner?"

"Minh Thanh." Fellows sighed, as if it were a beautiful woman's name.

"Ah, yes . . . the battle for Minh Thanh Road," Ruckter promptly ruined the moment. He glanced back over a shoulder at the woman kneading the dips in his backbone. "You shoulda been there, honey-san," he said. "We really kicked Charlie's butt."

"Charlie?" she playfully slapped the back of his head until he lowered it again.

"VC," Fellows translated the GI radio jargon. "Victor Charlie."

A frown of extreme contempt creased her features. Shirley was beginning to look dangerous. "VC Numba

49

Ten." She all but spat the words. "Numba *fucking* Ten. I hate all cocksucking VC. *Sat Cong*!"

Ruckter recognized the Vietnamese for "*kill communists*." "You *do* have a way with jizz words, babes," he laughed. The lines at the edges of Ruckter's eyes seemed to deepen as he drifted back into old memories. "But yeah . . . we truly brought some smoke on Charlie down at the old Minh Thanh."

"It was July 9th. . . ." Fellows began, remembering not the battle itself but the way Ruckter had leaked word of the mission into the local Vietnamese community.

They had done it right through this very massage parlor, in fact—though a different masseuse had been attending them then. She was now in Chi Hoa prison, spirited away from her home in the middle of the night by *canh-sats* so that the local whores wouldn't know what had happened to her. Pretending to be drunk, Ruckter and Fellows had told her all about the battle they had just survived—Srok Dong —and of an upcoming mission: Minh Thanh.

That had been on July 4th. Independence Day. Five days later, they walked into hell, via Minh Thanh Road. . . .

"The Brass sent Arc-Light a few miles to the north, as a diversionary tactic," Fellows continued, though Ruckter was not sure Shirley was picking up on all the words. "The B-52 bombing run was supposed to attract North Vietnamese and VC attention away from Minh Thanh for a few hours on July 9th. . . ."

The information Ruckter and Fellows had leaked included the juicy tidbit that a single cavalry contingent—little more than a company, or less than 100 men—would be passing down Minh Thanh. The Americans were ambushed at precisely the spot anticipated. What Charlie did not know was that, in reality, two cavalry troops were sent to clear the road—and they were reinforced with infantry units.

The Viet Cong sent their 272nd Regiment in, and the

50

U.S. Army responded with attack helicopters and CH-47 Jolly Green Giants—huge twin-rotored Chinooks. "The choppers had only just swooped in and started to pounce," Fellows continued, "when the Brass called 'em off, and radioed in arty instead."

"That's GI talk for artillery," Ruckter told Shirley.

"Cannon." She seemed to know already.

"Right, babes."

"Hell, the C.O. even called in the Air Force when his Loaches told him he had an entire Cong regiment closin' in for the kill!"

"The flyboys flew nearly a hundred air strikes south of the main kill zone," Ruckter explained, tracing a map in thin air with fingers a foot above his face.

"Some twenty-two thou arty shells were called in practically on our own positions"—Fellows's eyes grew wide as he relived the raid—"but Charlie was really dug in. After the first lull in artillery barrages began, the VC rushed the original ambush site and managed to *fini* four APC's and a tank."

"The other tanks managed to blast 'em out o' their Ho Chi Minh sandals, though." Ruckter nodded with satisfaction as flashbacks of the battle flickered in his mind.

"This was back when we just changed over to the M-16 from our trusty old 'fourteens." Fellows's eyes gleamed as if he were reminiscing about a prized automobile.

"But the dust of Minh Thanh Road really jammed the Mattel toys Uncle Sammy issued us. To make matters even worse, Colonel Lazzell caught a round. We fought through the night as best we could, takin' into account the jams and all."

"By high noon the next day, Charlie had melted back into the bamboo, and we retook Minh Thanh Road." Ruckter continued the story as he rolled over onto his stomach again.

51

"Bloody as a bitch in heat, but well worth the effort."
Fellows smacked his lips.

Shirley clapped her hands enthusiastically, then leaned
down and kissed Ruckter on the back of the head. "You
'mericans always won'erful," she said. "Keep Vietnam
free of VC!"

"We nearly lost that one." Ruckter seemed to be ignoring Shirley as he spoke to Fellows. "Yep, choppers made
the difference. We coulda taken the road back that first
day," he added, "if only we'd had those half dozen APCs
from Charlie Troop, like I'd told the captain. Bravo Troop
didn't have enough manpower to pull a counter-ambush
like that. If only we'd o' had a couple dozen more swingin'
dicks from Charlie Troop, all woulda been——"

"You talk just like a goddamned traffic cop, Gage, you
know that?" Fellows asked.

"Ram it in and break it off, shit-for-brains."

"Sounds painful, dick-breath."

Shirley interrupted the exchange of insults. "I no understand difference: Bravo Troop, Charlie Troop . . ." She
tilted her head to one side inquisitively. "You say 'Charlie'
mean same-same VC."

"It would take eight weeks of Boot Camp indoctrination
and brainwashing for me to explain the . . . intricacies of
army commo chatter to you, babes." Ruckter smiled like an
older brother. "So nebbah mind. Don' mean nothin', okay?"

"Okay,", she said, but quickly asked, "You GIs with Air
Cavalry?"

"Yep," Fellows said proudly as he rolled over to face
Ruckter's table again. "We're with 1st Squadron, 4th Cav,
to be precise . . ."

Gage shot him a stern look, and Fellows went silent.
Shirley caught this exchange and laughed. "Don' worry,"
she hastily reassured them. "Me no VC."

"Just a godawful nosy cunt, right?" Glancing back over

a shoulder again, Ruckter locked eyes with her for a moment. Shirley's hands slowed to a gradual halt.

"What is . . . 'cunt'?" she asked innocently.

Fellows erupted into laughter, but Ruckter simply lowered the side of his face back down against the lumpy, satin-covered pillow. "Nebbah mind," he said. "I guess it only applies to American women anyway. . . ."

"Means 'godawfully gorgeous,' honey," Fellows informed Shirley.

"That nice,' her smile returned, and she resumed massaging Ruckter's shoulders.

In the distance, twin Phantom jet fighters were descending toward an American Air Force installation. The roar of their engines reversing as they touched down and approached the runway's end reminded Ruckter of those first days of his return to The Nam—down at Camp Alpha, on Tan Son Nhut air base. The scents of Saigon returned to him briefly, but he found himself unable to hold on to the flashbacks intruding on his memory . . . unable to summon forth the sights and smells, the tastes and emotions of that week in South Vietnam.

All the other recruits had been terrified to venture beyond the security barricades and MP roadblocks—especially with martial law curfew in effect—but not Gage Ruckter. Gage Ruckter had friends in The Nam, and they spirited him past an uncaring and poorly motivated air cop at a dimly lit back gate facing Quang Trung Boulevard, and the night had belonged to them. Tu Do Street would never be the same. . . .

The battles for Ia Drang Valley had just ended. A sense of esprit de corps and brotherhood ws strong in his unit—the 7th Air Cavalry of the First Division—but that shorttimer's uncontrollable desire to be done and damned with

53

The Nam won out, and he left his buddies to return to the safety and false security of The World.

Life stateside had been torture, however. The nightly round of free drinks at his neighborhood bar quickly grew old, and he soon tired of telling war stories to his old high-school pals, whose closest brush with jungle death came from Hemingway novels they bought at the corner bookstore. Life became insipid for Gage Ruckter. Insipid and painfully boring.

It took three months out of the military for Ruckter to realize army airmobile had been the greatest thing ever to happen to him—cruising above the treetops of the Central Highlands and hunting Cong was more fun than anything he had ever done before. After all, what civilian occupation could provide such job satisfaction? He was never prouder than when wearing the First Cav combat patch on his right shoulder.

Ruckter had heard horror stories from other vets about scenes at airports back in The World—the antiwar movement was really beginning to roll, and uniformed soldiers were an easy mark for radical activists. There'd been no shortage of marchers and protesters at Los Angeles International, where he'd caught a connecting flight for Reno—his eventual destination was Topaz Lake, south of Carson City—but they gave Gage Ruckter a wide berth.

A recruiting specialist was exiting the Federal Building in Las Vegas when Ruckter arrived for his reenlistment interview. The Spec-4 had read that combat-hungry look in Gage's eyes. Ruckter still had the Far East tan to go with all the scars, but the specialist goaded him anyway. "Why you wants to re-up, Sarge?" the black enlisted man taunted. "They just gonna send yo' lilywhite ass back to The Nam. You don' wanna turn into no lifer, does ya?"

Lifer.

The word had always struck fear into the hearts of normal, red-blooded American boys marking bold X's across their short-timer's calenders overseas.

But now, after three months as a civilian, Ruckter knew that being a lifer was no big deal. And he knew the lifers' secret: enlist at 18 and retire at thirty-eight—still plenty young enough to begin another career with the federal government or, after a couple of trade-school classes, in the civilian sector.

So Gage Ruckter reenlisted. The contract read six years this time, and he insisted on the First Air Division again. But when he arrived at Camp Alpha, snafu after snafu complicated his life, and the personnel specialist assigned him to a Fourth Cavalry roster instead.

"But I re-enlisted for my old unit," Ruckter protested, "the Seventh Air Cavalry."

"The contract simply reads 'First Air Division,' slick." An adamant Spec-4 had the rulebook on his side. "Be it seventh, fourth, or ten-thousandth Air Cav, they all fall under First Division command, *Sarge*. And Fourth Cav currently has a shortage of grunts—especially grunt *NCOs*."

"Well, if this don't suck the big one . . ."

The reenlistment counselor back in Navada had admitted there was no way the Army would allow him to get more specific with contracts than brigades or divisions. "But there shouldn't be any problem," he insisted as Gage began scribbling his signature across the bottom of the long form. "Not for no double vet like yourself, Sgt. Ruckter."

Ruckter realized later why he had felt as though he'd been dealing with a used-car salesman. But at least he was still an infantryman. And they had allowed him to keep his noncommissioned officer's rank. And this *was* The Nam. And he was making new friends among gunship cavalrymen—not cleaning latrines in Danang, or scrubbing pots and pans in Saigon. Or wearing rent-a-cop uniforms in Las

Vegas and guarding the back door to a casino's vault room. That was *something* to be thankful for.

". . . And we crashed through the disabled tanks, reopening the roadway. . ." Fellows's words returned Ruckter to the present. "It was hell, honey . . . but we beat Charlie back. The choppers helped, of course, but without me and Gage, here, it might have been a VC victory—and *that* would have been hard to take to *my* grave, if ya catch my drift. Now we're gonna help the legs reopen Thunder Road, down outside Sin City and boot Charlie's ass back to—"

"You talk too damn much, kid!" Ruckter lifted a weary arm and elbowed the private.

"I no VC." The masseuse repeated her earlier assurance. "You can talk 'round me, okay? No sweat. I no tell nobody *nothing*."

"Shit," Fellows snickered. "I've heard *that* one before."

"The NVA knew we were gonna sweep the Ia Drang Valley last year a week before we went in because the old bitch who cleaned our hootches was doing *more* than sweeping," Ruckter added.

"She was Cong to the core, honey. And not a word of small talk went over her head."

"Did you catch her?" Shirley asked.

"She now graces the bottom of a maggot-infested mass grave on the outskirts of Bong Song, babes," replied Ruckter. "Got any booze around here, babes?" he turned to face Shirley again.

Shirley opened a small PX fridge beneath his table and produced two bottles of Vietnamese "33" beer. Five minutes later, the slur was back in their words, and Ruckter's needles were all in place. "Yep"—Fellows rolled off his table and dropped into a squat—"I feel great now. Fucking invigorated. Ready to kick ass and take names."

"You're drunk," said Gage.

"And ready for another six-pack," he admitted. "Then we could *definitely* reopen that Cong-infested stretch o' Thunder Road."

"And party with Charlie." Ruckter sat up and slowly swung his legs over the edge of the massage table.

"*Now* you're talkin', Sarge. . . ."

"I think it's time for us to exit the premises, babes." Gage winked down at Shirley after standing up. He swayed slightly on his feet, and she rushed up to steady him. "No sweat." He used the opportunity to kiss her. His lips brushed against the bridge of Shirley's nose, and he drew in her scent before she playfully pushed him away.

At the doorway, Ruckter leaned close to Shirley's ear and whispered, "You didn't hear *nothin'* 'bout no Thunder Road, right babes?"

"Right, Sergeant." She saluted Ruckter as he escorted Fellows outside into the harsh mid-afternoon sun.

"You don't salute sarges," Fellows told her. "Sarges ain't officers, and you only salute officers," he revealed. "Sarges ain't sirs—they work for a living."

"Right-o!" Shirley dropped the salute sharply as the two Americans staggered off down the dust-choked roadway through the middle of town. Ramshackle huts and dilapidated shacks rose up on either side of them. A pack of orphans rushed out to challenge the two GIs for money and bubble gum.

A knowing smile crept across Shirley's features as she watched Ruckter and Fellows freeze cautiously at first— more than a few smiling war waifs had been known to rush up to Americans with grenades in their handshake or C-4 satchels taped beneath tattered Berkeley T-shirts—but the

Americans quickly relaxed and began digging for treats Made in the U.S.A.

She watched Gage Ruckter reach deep into a thigh pocket of his jungle fatigues and pull out a handful of butterscotch kisses—candy he had told her he had received in a CARE package from home only the day before. He threw the small plastic-wrapped candies over his shoulder and high over his head. The children went wild with excitement, filling the street with cries of laughter as they chased and fought over the treats.

Ruckter and Gage continued walking, and Shirley's eyes followed them, watching puffs of pink dust rise from the soles of their jungle boots until they disappeared beyond a bend in the road. Then she turned, walked back into the massage parlor, and called for the next customer.

When they were out of sight and clearly too far from the steam-and-cream to be heard, the two cavalrymen's gait took on a pronounced determination. They fell into a bit of a speed-march, in fact—a sober trot.

"You think she bought it, Sarge?" Beads of perspiration were rolling down across Fellows's forehead, but he was far from out of breath.

"In this crazy country, there's no tellin' for sure," Ruckter could taste monsoon threats on the air. He glanced up at dark storm clouds advancing across the land.

"Well, I suppose we'll know in a couple days. When we beat feet down to Thunder Road."

Sgt. Ruckter did not appear to be sharing Pvt. Fellows's enthusiasm. He sounded slightly out of breath when he said, "I'm getting too old for this."

CHAPTER 6

Near the Dau Tieng Special Forces Camp

Brody wished he had a god to pray to, for he was convinced this was the end of his short but glorious air cavalryman's career. The two Viet Cong soldiers stood directly over them now. One bayonet was snugly against the base of Brody's skull, the other pressing firmly against Jones's. Karter lay unmolested, between the other two Americans, his forearms locked over his terrified face.

Toby Karter was fairly sure these two communists were going to kill them. Brody was as depressed. *If only the VC had "picked" Jones or myself to get a fighting chance at escape*, he thought to himself, and bit into a swollen lower lip. *But not Karter!* Brody was positive the private would make no attempt at resisting or trying to flee. He was lying on top of his rifle—they all were. But only Karter had a chance.

Brody found himself wishing the Cong would make it fast. He hoped they would not mutilate his body beyond what was necessary and expected. He wished they would leave his corpse where Gabe and the others could find it, so the folks back home could give him the required hero's funeral. "Buried in Hollywood before he could truly leave his mark on the world." What an epitaph.

Treat Brody wondered how many VC widows hated his guts and prayed for his slow, torturous death each night

59

before retiring alone to their cold and empty sleeping mats. He wondered how many VC children were told about his deadly deeds by their VC *mama-sans*: "*Sergeant Bro-dee*," they would say. "*Sergeant Bro-dee kackadau papa-san*. We spit in his face and dump garbage on his grave." Yes, Treat Brody had ruined many a marriage. The words *Widow Maker* weren't scrawled across the side of his helmet for nothing.

Despite the unwavering point against the back of his head, Brody managed to roll over without being shot. "*Chao ong*," he greeted them in formal Vietnamese. When one of the guerrillas appeared slightly taken aback, The Whoremonger added, "Yo mama-san's a *du ma*, asshole!" Definitely fighting words. The exclamation point to his statement was an obscene gesture, which brought the rage back into Charlie's eyes *rikky-tik*.

He brought his rifle up, stomped on Brody's chest with his Ho Chi Minh sandals as if to bayonet the American between the eyes, and cut loose with an ear-splitting war cry.

He did not ram the blade home, however. Hearing something in the distance, he hesitated. His war yell faded on the rain-forest breeze—to be replaced almost mystically by a soothing cry . . . a long, drawn-out musical note, to be more precise. The rising song of a string instrument.

Brody's ears perked. A rush of hope swirled through his veins. It was Frisk's fiddle.

A burst of tracers the color of blood sizzled past above The Whoremonger's face. Then the string of red-hot bullets disintegrated the enemy soldier's face. Their impact nearly tore his head away. Brody watched the lifeless torso flop back onto its haunches.

"Hey-*hey*!" He distinctly heard the Green Beret sergeant's confident laugh before the second burst ripped VC Numba Two's belly open.

The Viet Cong private was still standing. Knees slightly bent, he clutched at the gaping hole where his web belt had once been, trying to keep his insides from flopping down into the mud and muck. On the ground in front of him, Brody stared up at the Vietnamese, unmoving, his lower jaw agape—in awe, perhaps, that Charlie could take a half-dozen machine-gun rounds to the midsection and remain standing.

Brody's boot came up slowly. He placed its rubber sole against the Viet Cong's belly wound, and, with a sudden ferocity, kicked the staggering zombie back off his feet.

Frisk lowered his fiddle and motioned for Special Forces troopers and local Arvins waiting in the shadows behind him to fan out and check the area for additional VC. "You sure like to sleep with danger, kid."

Confident the guerrilla was now history, he walked over to Brody and extended a hand. The younger NCO latched on and was jerked to his feet.

"And you believe in waitin' 'til the last possible second to effect a rescue, right?" Treat asked the tiger-striped musician.

"Rescue?" Frisk laughed heartily as his men began filtering back in through the bamboo with negative nods. "Hell, boy, we wasn't out lookin' for you rooks! We was out huntin' for our midnight chow."

"Midnight chow?" Karter looked up for the first time since all the gunplay started. He began brushing twigs and dust out of his hair.

"Sure." Frisk ignored Karter and helped Jones to his feet instead. "Tree gibbons, boy."

"Monkeys?" Reece Jones sounded suddenly irritated.

"That's a raunchy rodg." Two troopers standing behind Frisk spoke in unison. One of them added, "The female's crotch is especially delectable."

Jones wanted to say he thought they were all sick. Instead, he muttered, "Should have expected as much from a clusterfuck o' Green Berets!"

"You're welcome for gettin' your worthless ass saved, boy!" Frisk was laughing again. Lowering his voice, he turned to Brody and asked, "What is he—one o' those liberal, commsymp, campus radicals or something?"

"Or something," Brody picked up his rifle and checked the magazine and safety. He walked over and gently kicked the two Viet Cong guerrillas, but they were already chasing *joss* smoke beyond Buddha.

"Good job, soldier."

Lt. Jacob Vance went from man to man in Dau Tieng's tiny, makeshift club, patting backs. "Final body count just topped twenty." The twenty-three-year-old officer pulled out a huge cigar and fired it up. It was not often he smoked, but tonight was a special occasion. "Twenty zips and not a single friendly got zapped. Not bad for a routine mortar-barrage scramble. Not bad at all."

Sgt. Frisk stared at Vance. The lieutenant was of medium height and weight, but the hawkish nose and black crew cut made him appear bigger than he actually was. "You don't say. . . ." Frisk appeared to be nearly twice Vance's overall size as he blocked the officer's path. The Green Beret's hand was extended, palm up.

Startled by the NCO's sheer bulk for a moment, Vance quickly recovered. His smile returned, and he withdrew another Havana special from his thigh pocket. "Uh, right, Sergeant. Twenty more for Westy."

"We're gonna win this goddamned war." Frisk allowed the lieutenant to light the cigar. Then he puffed a huge cloud of smoke down into Vance's face.

"It's a police action, Sergeant." His smile remained intact. "Not a war."

"What are you, a fuckin' politician?" Frisk's chest expanded importantly.

The entire room fell silent as ten or fifteen cramped cavalrymen and SF advisers waited to see if Vance died a hero, or just died, period. "Me?" The officer's smile did not seem to waver. "No, Sergeant, I'm a lieutenant in the United States Army. Now have *you* got a fuckin' problem with that?"

Brody and Snakeman both sensed it: Their fearless leader was winding up to throw a dirty punch. That was the only way the lieutenant would be able to win: Strike swiftly and deadly—aim for the gonads, or deliver something fancy to a pressure point and hope for the best. "The lieutenant's okay, Frisk." Brody slid to a stop beside the two soldiers. "He's good people."

"That's right, Sarge." Snakeman arrived on the other side of them. "He ain't no pussywillow like *some* ossifers."

"Hhmmph." Frisk did not seem very impressed. "Nam puts me in two kinds o' moods and *only* two kinds o' moods," the stocky Green Beret stated. "The lovemakin' mood, and the castratin' mood. And I sure don' wanna take this sorry-assed West Pointer up to my rack!"

"Speakin' o' romance"—Vance, ignoring Fletcher's whispered warnings to beat a hasty retreat while he and The Whoremonger wrestled Frisk to the ground—"I'm sure in the mood for some classical crap. You SF types need a jukebox, bein' way out here in the boonies and all . . . a jukebox with some classical jazz in it—electric violins, or something."

"Violins?" Frisk's hands were no longer clenched. His features softened as he searched Vance's baby-blues for some sign of sincerity.

"Yeah." The lieutenant abandoned all military bearing. "Some Henry Mancini would fit the mood right now. Have you ever heard—?"

But before Vance could name his favorite string songs, Frisk lowered his fists and rushed back behind the bar, where his ruck was stashed. "Hell, Lou"—the club seemed to brighten with his smile—"why didn't you say so."

As Frisk began playing his fiddle, Maloney the mail clerk returned. "For you and you and you." He dragged his duffel bag over to a table crowded with Special Forces personnel.

"Right smart of you to miss the alert." Someone tossed an empty beer can at the clerk.

"Hey, I'm a lover, not a fighter." Maloney did not seem disturbed, especially since the can missed. "You guys would've probably lost the battle tonight if I came along!"

"He's right," someone in the back of the room called out.

Maloney was digging into the bottom of the duffel bag now. "Missed my ride out, though," he complained, "thanks to you guys."

"My heart bleeds for you, ya no-account REMF bastard!" Another soldier let fly a peeled tangerine.

"Listen up, all you First Cav blues and Arp team gunnies!" A tall black NCO with his head shaved bald made a quick pass through the club. "Nightly shuttle for Binh Dinh now departin'!"

"Brody!" Maloney called out, ignoring everyone. "Is there a Brody in the room?" He held up an envelope bearing a military battle scene across the front in o.d. green. "I seem to recall meeting a Bro—"

"Present!" Treat had contemplated remaining silent, but his curiosity won out. Who would know he was temporarily assigned to Dau Tieng? Not even his parents back in California were aware of his unit's present status. He was getting so bad at writing, in fact, that his mother recently sent him a card that said, "Well, if you won't write..." And on the inside cover, "Draw." Enclosed in the envelope was a crayon and blank piece of paper. In Vietnam, APO postage for American GIs was free. The Asian sun had melted the crayon, of course, but it was the thought that counted. Feeling guilty, he'd sent her a postcard the last time he was down in Saigon. He doubted it had ever made its way all the way back to The World. That was nearly a month ago.

"Don't look like a lady's handwritin', slick," the man who threw the beer can at Maloney taunted him now.

"And it smells more like dirty socks than perfume." Brody ran his nose along the top after breaking the seal. That elicited a rumble of laughs from the back table, and then they left him alone.

"Well, if it ain't from old Gage," he muttered under his breath after scanning the return address. A loud laugh escaped Brody. "Hah! They stuck him with Fourth Cav! *In Tay Ninh Province*, no less!"

"Anyone I know?" Snakeman was beside him now, but before Treat could elaborate, Reece Jones's shadow fell across the short, one page note.

"Gage *Ruckter*?" the newby asked.

Brody's eyes rose from the green-tinted stationery. "That's a rodg," he said. "Know him?"

"Real goofy fuck. We served back stateside together couple years ago. Both got our RVN orders 'bout the same time. I managed to delay mine. He didn't. Didn't want to, he said."

"Gage wasn't all that goofy in my book." Brody's smile was fading. "I pretty much considered him a level-headed guy, actually."

"Everybody's entitled to his own misguided opinion." Jones shrugged and turned away as if to leave.

"Wait a minute!" Brody grabbed a shoulder and whirled the man around. "Me and Gage were *real* close. You don't just go bad-mouthin' a buddy and expect to walk away with that shit-eatin' grin on your face."

"What do you plan to do about it, Sergeant? Punch out an enlisted man?" He ran the palm of his hand across his mouth, dramatically wiping the smile away. With his other hand, he pulled a pamphlet from a back pocket and slid it between Brody's fingers. "*That*'d only get ya five-to-ten at the LBJ stockade."

Behind them, Frisk was already beginning Vance's second request. The fiddle was squalling like a cat in heat.

Treat glanced down at the gray-and-white brochure. The words *Vietnam Veterans Against the War* were emblazoned across the top. He let the leaflet drop onto the floor, which was sticky with spilled beer. "I don't waste my time reading that commsymp crap!" he flared.

"Whatever." Jones turned to leave again.

Once more, Brody stopped him. "Gage Ruckter is a good man," he said. "He volunteered for a second tour over here in The Nam. Why you want to bad-mouth him, Jones."

"Well, that's what we're *all* fightin' for in South Vietnam, ain't it, Sergeant—the right to freedom of speech and one's own opinion?"

"What the hell are you, Jones?" Snakeman interrupted. "A college drop-out from Berkeley or some such shit?"

"University of Colorado at Boulder, if you must know," Jones answered. "Uncle Sammy drafted my young ass in my senior year."

Snakeman laughed. "Hah!" he snorted. "'University of Colorado at Boulder.' Same-same, GI. No difference at all. College towns and college sympathizers crawlin' outta the goddamned woodwork. Couldn't you get a deferment? I suppose you majored in fucking sociology or something."

"Something." Jones was not backing down.

"Knock it off, Snakeman." Brody sounded as if he was ready to go for the throat. "Apologize," he told Jones, who promptly replied with a burst of laughter.

"Apologize for *what*?" Both men were almost yelling at this point.

"Apologize, Jones, or these stripes come off, and it's just you and me . . . man to man."

Jones's eyes bulged. He puffed out his cheeks in mock shock. "I'd kick your ass, mister."

"You'd get one chance to try." Brody's grin came into play. "Then I'd be all over you like flies on a body bag."

Jones was having second thoughts. He glanced around the room. For the most part, the Green Berets were ignoring them. But Brody's Air Cavalry buddies were paying close attention to the argument. Gage Ruckter had many friends in the Dau Tieng NCO Club tonight.

"It's not worth scrapin' flesh over," Jones decided. "I take it back"—jerking his arm free of Brody's grasp, he turned to leave—"even if I *am* in the right."

Brody grabbed Jones's shoulder again and whirled him around a third time. "Just what the hell kinda gripe you got against Gage *anyway*!?" Now Brody's eyes were bulging.

"Ruckter's truly Looney Tunes, Sergeant-sir. He's one of them weird devil worshipers, and if you stick up for him, then you must be a goddamned devil worshiper, too."

CHAPTER 7

Binh Dinh Province

Echo Company did not spend much time at Dau Tieng over
the next few days in November. *Peg*'s crew chief, Zack,
who spent an hour trying to drag Brody's people out of
fiddle-pluckin' Frisk's good-time bar and casino, had them
running search-and-destroy missions up and down the
length of Binh Dinh Province.

Binh Dinh had long been regarded as a Viet Cong sanctuary—and the rumors proved true—so 7th Cavalry of the
First Air Cav Division was kept as busy as any of the
regular infantry units. And that left little time for Brody to
argue politics or anything else with his new doorgunner
trainee Private Reece Jones.

He never got a chance to respond to Gage Ruckter's
letter, either. Jones's accusations had bothered Brody going
on five nights now. Devil worship? Gage? It had to be
bullshit.

"Not that sacrificing naked cherry girls by the light of a
full moon would be all that *dinky-dau*," Treat did not realize he was talking to himself out loud.

"Say again?" Fletcher nudged him.

Brody glanced up from the Saigon phone book.
"What?" he asked, a dazed look in his eyes. Trying to
focus on the blur of treetops racing past outside the gunship's open hatch didn't help matters any.

"I asked what you were mumbling away about," Snakeman shook his head from side to side in mock resignation.

"Fuck, Snake . . . you know? I don't even remember now."

"You been working too many double shifts." Fletcher nodded solemnly.

"We've *all* been working too many shifts," Brody agreed.

Fletcher glanced back at the shimmering rice paddies extending out beneath the midmorning sun as far as the eye could see, but there was no sign of any activity below the landing skids, other than a few farmers guiding plows behind lazy water buffalos. Brody sat on a low stack of metal ammo boxes. Elliott stared at the phone book still lying open in his lap. *"That's* what you were daydreaming about." He pointed at the endless duplication of surnames: Phuc. A very common Vietnamese name, indeed.

"Yeah, I guess I could use a shot o' Vietnamese pussy right about now," The Whoremonger admitted.

Fletcher started to voice a sarcastic reply about the scarcity of same when Reece Jones cut in. "And I could use a little more how-to instruction on this hatch-sixty," he said.

Brody did not look up from his reading material.

"You point it at the dinks running around on the ground and pull the trigger," Fletcher said. "Simple as that. Like pluckin' heads off gophers with a .22 single-shot—'cept you get bookoo more chances at takin' down your target, slick."

"But what about lead time?" Jones sounded serious. "What about rates of fire and maximum effective range? What about the tracers? Can somebody tell me about the tracers? How long can I keep firing until the barrel begins to melt?"

"You've got to be kidding me," Snakeman said. "Do we look like training manuals?"

"I'm serious as a heart attack." Jones's eyes narrowed.

"Here . . ." Brody closed the Saigon phone book and slid it under Jones's haunches—on top of the pile of ten *other* Saigon phone books *Peg*'s doorgunners used as hatch-stools. "*This* is all you need to know about bein' a door-gunner."

"Protect thy balls at all times." Fletcher was not laughing.

"Ten-plus phone books are usually enough to stop even a zip MG," Brody said. He was talking about unexpected ground fire—random shots at American helicopters as they flew over Void Vicious, en route to distant battlefields, or just on a pizza hop to the rear echelon. "If you get assigned to a ship that doesn't have any phone books lying around, just chuck your flak jacket and sit on *it*."

"But phone books are better," Snakeman maintained. "Not as hard on the hemorrhoids."

"Just don't make it a Vung Tau phonebook"—Brody laughed for the first time—"or a phone book from one of the other villes. It's gotta be a *Saigon* phone book. The others won't stop jackshit."

"The others don't even *have* phones," Jones interrupted, and the cavalry sergeant fell silent again.

"What ya worryin' about, anyway?" Fletcher looked at Jones. "We haven't made any contact in five days. Just sit back an' relax, slick. If and when the time comes, you probably won't even *feel* the bullet with your name on it."

"Oh, bookoo thanks, pal!" Jones replied. "I really needed to hear that, you know?"

As if to accent Fletcher's remark, *Pegasus* suddenly tilted to one side, banking sharply into a starboard descent. Fletcher and Brody were both sure Gabriel had spotted something, but just as they began double checking their weapons—and Jones's face turned a ghostly shade of pale —Gabe The Gunslinger clicked in with, "Headin' south, ladies! Brass Monkey down on Thunder Road, couple dozen kilos north of Saigontown. Fourth Cav catchin' some shit on a counter-ambush. Hold on to your assholes, 'cause there's a hell of a storm struttin' its stuff between us and them."

As they skirted along the ground between two groves of palm trees, Brody remained tense while crouching behind Jones, watching the jungle race past outside. He could not believe that action awaited many miles away—*it was here*, he felt. *Right here—in these trees!* The urge to direct the barrel of his M-16 over Jones's shoulder was almost over-powering. He could feel it—there were Cong waiting in this dark stretch of rain forest.

And then he saw it. Muzzle flashes. Two, maybe three at most.

The rounds—obviously directed at *Pegasus* from some-where below—missed. Brody didn't even see a tracer. "Shots floatin' in on your whiskey," he clicked in at the last moment. Jones didn't see them. Neither did Snake-man, but he was manning the opposite hatch. He whirled around when he heard Treat's transmission.

"Those were sun flashes," the peter pilot acknowledged. "Broken glass . . . a tin can or something."

"I saw 'em," Gabriel clicked in.

"Sun flashes don't leave smoke," Brody insisted.

"I saw 'em, Whoremonger," Gabe repeated. "Don' worry about it—small-time stuff. Probably some farmer pissed off about all the racket—it's approachin' Viet siesta time, you know."

"Besides," the copilot added, "a Brass Monkey slightly outweighs near-misses."

"Don't sweat it, Trick or Treat." Snakeman read the anger in his eyes. "There's always tomorrow."

"Fuck it." Brody flipped his rifle's safety lever back on.

"The little zip probably would've dropped down into an

endless maze o' tunnels anyway by the time Gabe brought us back in for a fly-by. At least now we know we're headed for some truly guaranteed shit."

Brody, his head hanging low now, stared at the floor of the cabin without responding.

"That's just wonderful," Reece Jones joined the conversation with his usual pessimism. "'We're headed for some truly guaranteed shit.' That's just fucking great!"

It was as if they had descended into a raging forest fire.

Forming a gauzelike blanket above the battlefield, huge columns of black smoke rose high among the clouds from several hotspots on the ground, where tanks and APCs burned furiously. Now and then, explosions erupted among the disabled armored tracks, and hundreds of glowing ammo rounds would fly forth like eruptions from a volcano, rivulets of smoke trailing behind them as they arced back to earth.

"Holy shit," Brody muttered from his position behind Reece Jones. The highway—a two-lane, blacktop affair—snaked along the bottom of a deep, zigzagging ravine. A great place for an ambush, and precisely where the American commanders had planned on engaging Charlie. Unfortunately, they had not anticipated that the VC would call on North Vietnamese reserves, which were also in the area. In short, the U.S. troops were nearly outgunned.

Their tanks had taken a heavy toll on the enemy, however, before most of the tracks were knocked out by suicide sapper squads. Had it not been for the arrival of several First Cav helicopters, American casualties would have undoubtedly been much higher.

"Will ya look at that bastard!" Fletcher was pointing down at a scrawny guerrilla clad entirely in black. Fletcher could do no more than point because the Vietnamese was too close to American soldiers for any of *Peg*'s hatch guns to be used, and the ship was swooping in too low and fast on her initial fly-by—the VC was sprinting toward an APC, in fact. He was carrying no firearms, but his body appeared to be wrapped in satchel charges. The two crewmen on the APC were firing a machine gun toward the opposite side of the road and did not see the sapper rushing their position.

"Charlie on your flank!" Gabriel clicked into the outside speaker as *Pegasus* roared a couple of dozen feet above the APC's M-60 turret.

Brody and Fletcher both leaned out their respective hatches and twisted back to watch as the crew members whirled around. But they were too late.

"That bastard was on something!" Snakeman announced after they had witnessed the sapper's daring leap up onto the top of the APC. The VC and both GIs disintegrated before their very eyes in a bright golden flash.

"I'll never understand these people," Jones mumbled as two other gunships raced past on either side of *Pegasus*, heading in the opposite direction. "Sacrificing their lives for a jive-assed tank and two seconds of glory on a no-name stretch of sun-baked highway."

"You don't *have* to understand 'em!" Brody was back beside Jones. He checked the M-60's ammunition belt. "You just have to make sure you're ready to do your job!"

"Get ready to die for Buddha, you little pricks!" Snakeman was leaning into his hatch MG and waving a fist at the guerrillas swarming across the roadway below.

Several other helicopter gunships had already arrived on-station in the nearly two hours it took *Pegasus* to bust blades south out of Binh Dinh Province, and the entire area was becoming a dark pall of smoke. "I hope we don't stack it up in the sky," Brody muttered to himself as they hovered above the lima-lima slicks. He was referring to a midair crash in the dense smoke.

Normally, a ship would not respond to a call for help from so far away—indeed, a ground unit's transmission would never have traveled so far—but as luck would have it, a majority of the area birds were tied up in a bloody skirmish along the coast. The Brass Monkey had been relayed through several commo operators. Gabriel had just happened to monitor the urgent request for assistance. And since Binh Dinh had proved unusually unproductive in recent days, 7th Cav could do without *Pegasus* for an afternoon. Echo Company rarely followed the rulebook, anyway. And Col. Buchanan was lucky just to know the whereabouts of his Chinooks and Skycranes, let alone a Huey or two.

"Is that who I think it is?" Brody pulled a set of folding binoculars from his flak vest as they approached the gully on another fast pass, but Jones confirmed his suspicions long before he had them open.

"Gage Ruckter..."

"*Our* Gage Ruckter?" Fletcher grinned. He had never met the man, but would never forget the look in Treat's eyes when he argued with Reece Jones about the buck sergeant's reputation.

"The one and only!" Brody rammed the case back into its pocket and took the M-60 grips from Jones. As Gabriel brought *Pegasus* down for a low, swerving pass along the western edge of the gulley, Brody fired a long burst down at several Viet Cong as they ran toward a bullet-riddled gunjeep.

Aboard the gunjeep, Ruckter was hopping back and forth from the front to rear seat as he turned the barking M-60 on different groups of the enemy.

"Give 'em hell, Gage!" Brody yelled as *Peg*'s landing skids parted the smoke floating above Ruckter's vehicle. He knew the 4th Cav sergeant could not hear him, but Ruckter looked up when he noticed the friendly fire support.

Ruckter paused ever so briefly to flash a thumbs-up at the low-flying chopper—his right hand was still firing his M-60—then he began jumping from seat to seat again, switching his sights to whichever VC had gotten closest to him. Sparks from ricocheting bullets flew along the jeep's hood and fenders, but Lady Luck must have been sitting on Ruckter's shoulder, for none of the slugs could find him.

Ruckter was not one to give Charlie much credit for marksmanship skills, but he had to remain wary and diligent: a young private lay slumped over the steering wheel beside him. It was Fellows.

Pegasus fell in line behind other gunships already circling the isolated gulley. Well aware of their surroundings, the doorgunners fired only at designated times—almost taking turns, though there were times tracer spray would merge like some giant, glowing letter V.

Finally, the waves of VC were gone. Bodies of a hundred enemy soldiers lay baking beneath the hot Asian sun. Countless blood trails marked the spots where wounded guerrillas had been dragged back behind the tree line.

The enemy had melted back into the thickets, abandoning all hopes of annihilating the Americans—they might have stood a chance against tanks and foot soldiers only, but the ambush team was no match for all the airmobile gunships that had suddenly appeared overhead without warning.

Brody knew it was against S.O.P., but he clicked in

with a personal question. "Can we set 'er down, Mister Gabe?"

They watched the pilots' necks and shoulders seem to tense. Without turning back to look, Gabriel asked, "Everyone okay back there?"

"Zero casualties," Brody responded quickly. "But I got a pal on the ground back there. Ruckter . . ."

"*Our* Ruckter?" A cross between humor and disbelief registered in the warrant officer's tone.

"Same-same." Fletcher entered the exchange.

"Was he W.I.A?"

"Negs, boss. Hero material, though."

"I'm afraid right now we just ain't got the fuel for—"

"He was the supersoldier fighting off Charlie single-handed from that gunjeep, Gabe," Snakeman's voice was cracking with relief now.

"Thought he looked familiar." Gabriel was not bringing *Pegasus* around, though. "But so sorry, Whoremonger. We've gotta beat blades back up into Binh Dinh Promince or my rank's raunchy as a day-old bowl of *nuoc-mam*."

"Just five minutes with the clown?" Brody had to at least try.

"Sorry. I owe you one, Treat." The Gunslinger was insistent.

Pegasus continued to ascend away from the Thunder Road battlefield. Gage Ruckter's "V for Victory" wave would have to do for now.

"I rest my case!" Reece Jones yelled above the increasing drone of rotors as *Peg*'s powerful engine pulled them up through the muggy layers of lowland heat.

"What?" Brody didn't bother to click in, but simply locked eyes with the new doorgunner.

"I said, I rest my case!" He pointed down through the

open hatch. "About that goofy fuck Ruckter: I . . . rest . . . my . . . case!"

Like most army jeeps in The Nam, Ruckter's had a personalized slogan emblazoned across the hood. Brody winced when he saw the crudely painted, upside-down crucifix.

CHAPTER 8

Ten Miles Southwest of Dau Tieng

Capt. Ted Soto's team of nine Nungs was in position, laying dog nearly forty-eight hours before the VC team even showed up.

Soto waited until the guerrillas began setting up the animal before he signaled his men to attack. As soon as the Viet Cong were nearly finished stringing up their tripwires, Soto fired the first M-16 burst, taking out two of the communists himself.

Those who fled in a blind panic set off many of the anti-personnel mines. One Nung was also killed by the claymores, and Soto's ears were still ringing, but, all in all, it had proved a very successful hit. Twelve for the body count in exchange for only one casualty. And, to Capt. Soto, Nung lives were as cheap as Cong.

The problems arose when Soto ordered the enemy weapons, clothing, and equipment to be carted up for shipment to a government laboratory in Tay Ninh City. "For analysis," he always told Sgt. Do Lam Chinh. "Uncle Sammy needs everything analyzed. It gets to be a real pain in the rectal cavity, but it's S.O.P."

"But my men will not bury the enemy," Chinh had argued at first. "It is beneath them. We should just leave them here. Their comrades will return to drag away the bodies after we have gone."

"You don't afford them that opportunity, Chinh," Soto had countered. "You bury the bodies, or—Christ, I don't care—burn the damn things. Just don't leave 'em lyin' around for Charlie to recover. If he can't take home his dead, it's a real morale crusher. Things like that will eventually help us win this joke of a war."

"But you take away their weapons," Chinh's sudden defense of these fallen warriors surprised Soto. "You strip them of their rifles and web belts—even their uniforms. That is no way to dispose of the enemy—men who proved worthy opponents, an enemy who fought courageously in battle."

"Worthy opponents, my ass." Soto had laughed. "The bastards got caught with their pants down—tryin' to ambush you and me, Chinh. Those claymores were bein' set to rip off *my* balls and *yours*, friend. It wasn't as if we fought in hand-to-hand or threw grenades at each other for an hour. It wasn't tit-for-tat out there. I dropped a hammer on two o' the shitheads, and the rest beat feet right into the front sights of you and your men. Real fucking courageous."

Chinh knew Soto was right. But he also knew there was something seriously wrong about the way in which the American captain was handling the affair. "Before, we always leave a couple weapons behind," he maintained.

"Booby traps?" Soto wasn't a butterbar fresh out of O.C.S. himself. He'd been born at night, but not *last* night.

"Yes. Grenades under bodies, or bolo beans inside AK magazine. You know: S.O.P."

"Well, not anymore, Chinh," he had used his best fatherly tone, though it was very possible the Nung was older than Soto by five or ten years. "A booby-trapped weapon might take out one or two VC, but then there's a half-dozen others who can use the damn thing to waste untold numbers of American boys and—"

"Not if you do *good* booby trap," Chinh had maintained. "We show you way to blow the cocksuckers to Bien Hoa and back!"

"We can argue about this 'til it snows in Saigon"— Soto's tone had signaled an end to the discussion—"but I'm a captain and you're the sergeant, and—"

"Okay, *Dai-uy.*" Chinh had waved him silent. "No more argument. But just want you know: Nungs no like how Capt. Soto operate. Maybe you just doing something new . . . something Nungs not used to. Okay. We wait. We wait, we watch, we see."

"I appreciate your vote o' confidence, Chinh." He had slapped the Nung NCO on the back, wondering if Chinh's reply would be as sarcastic as they walked toward the bodies, but the short, stocky, dark-skinned man seemed to give up. He pulled a small mirror and set of tweezers from his thigh pocket, began plucking whiskers on his chin, and said nothing.

"Yep," Soto had continued in a low voice, "I'm just tryin' to follow the latest set o' harebrained orders sent up from MACV, Chinh. That's all."

"Yes, *Dai-uy.*" As he groomed himself, Chinh was carefully watching Soto in the mirror.

That was another thing about these people that irked Soto. Their facial hair wasn't thick enough to grow good beards, in his opinion, so instead of shaving, they'd wait for guard duty and the graveyard shift to pluck each individual whisker. They would usually make every effort to do this in front of one of the American advisers.

"That's why this war is turnin' into such a crock o' shit," Soto said. "The paper shufflers and pencil pushers all want everything analyzed. We oughta just nuke Hanoi and get it over with, you know that? Nuke Hanoi. Then we could round up all the Vietnamese south of the DMZ and put 'em on boats. Put 'em all on boats, take 'em out into the middle of the South China Sea, then sink the fuckin' boats. . . ."

"Sink the boats?" Chinh had asked with a puzzled look creasing his features.

"Right. Sink the fuckin' boats."

"But then nobody would be left, *Dai-uy*."

Capt. Soto nodded with mock gravity. "Yeah, that would be too fucking bad, wouldn't it, Sergeant Do?"

Seventeen-year-old Ninh Kinh Truong stared at the general's photo propped in his lap with his American-made M-16 rifle. Now and then he glanced up at the stars, wondering if the general was staring down, watching over them. Truong was aware of the American Captain and the Nung sergeant talking on the other side of the campfire. The mixture of blue rain-forest mist and smoky curls from the campfire gave them an almost ghostly luminescence.

Truong had been worrying about Chinh lately. "Please guide Sgt. Chinh, General," Truong whispered in hushed Vietnamese to the old, cracked, and faded photograph in its chipped bamboo frame. "Guide him to see the path of least resistance. He is taking all this much too seriously. The Americans . . . the war. I think Sergeant Chinh needs a woman, General. I think he needs some pussy, if you will excuse my frankness. We would all like to be with a girl again, of course, but I think Sergeant Chinh especially needs a woman's hole to rest his head against. . . ."

Truong called his squad leader Sgt. Chinh, after the Vietnamese custom, as opposed to Sgt. Do—the way the Americans preferred to do it.

"The general" was General Phuc Po—a famous Nung

82

warrior who had fought alongside the French against the Viet Minh guerrillas, and was worshiped by the younger men. Many of them, like Truong, carried his picture into battle for good luck. "Please comfort Sergeant Chinh during these troubled times, General," Truong's lips moved almost soundlessly as he watched Chinh and Capt. Soto.

The entire team had become very uneasy since Soto's arrival. There was an immediate friction between the American and their unofficial leader, Sgt. Chinh. The men always followed Chinh's orders to the letter, having implicit faith in his abilities as a jungle warrior, but, as far as Truong knew, none of the other Nungs had ever become really close to him.

The sergeant was almost as legendary as the general himself. Yet he was not one for making friends or for celebrating at the after-action parties that the Nungs often held after completing a hairy mission. Chinh was a quiet man, keeping to himself except for the mandatory briefings, issuing orders, reprimanding someone who made a serious mistake, or patting a hero on the back.

Chinh seemed to be harassed by his own personal demons—some incident from his past, no doubt . . . long before younger mercs like Truong were recruited into the Nungs' ranks. But he was always 100 percent in control during the mission, always accessible to those of his men who had their own problems. Until recently.

The last few weeks Sgt. Chinh had not been himself. The missions did not go down as clean and crisp as usual. Tonight they had managed to zap a ruthless contingent of Cong without the whole affair being executed by the numbers. It was a showpiece counter-ambush, if there ever was one. But they should have been quick in and quick out. As always. True, this was the heart of the rain forest, and they were now king of the jungle, but word traveled fast. Charlie could even now be rushing to the area with reinforcements. It was dark, yet Soto had brazenly started a campfire to announce their presence and their victory over the forces of communism. Now he and Sgt. Chinh were arguing again about S.O.P.

Do Lam Chinh suddenly began barking orders. Something about gathering up all the weapons. Truong couldn't be sure because of the snapping pops and small explosions erupting where moist twigs and rain-soaked branches refused to burn cleanly in the campfire.

With the others, Truong hustled to gather up the AK-47s. Half the men were delegated the task of chopping down bamboo and gnarled saplings that rose to a tangled ceiling overhead, blocking out the stars and forcing a blanket of smoke from the campfire to hover near the ground. Truong knew it would be for the extraction. Instead of humping through the boonies a couple of klicks to one of the nearby open clearings, Soto apparently wanted the chopper to land at this exact location. He was busy with his RTO while the men chopped with machetes and dug with their E-tools.

The task was swiftly becoming as eerie as any jungle mission Truong had ever participated in. Capt. Soto never sent out any LPs—listening posts—to warn the main contingent of VC sneaking up on their position. This served to motivate the Nungs to work even harder and faster, though Truong didn't think it was the American officer's main reason for ignoring perimeter security.

Soto himself seemed to be standing guard. He paced from one edge of the ambush site to the other, M-16 at the ready, eyes scanning the darkness, ears probing the jungle for movement. The true reason quickly became apparent to Truong, and probably the others as well: Less security made for more men to clear the jungle away. Quite a contradiction when one considered how much time Soto and Chinh had wasted arguing.

Truong chopped at the tangled bamboo. He immersed himself in his work, abandoning all hope of trying to get through to Sgt. Chinh. It was a lost cause, he decided. Do Lam Chinh had become the latest casualty of American interference. Besides, Truong was only a Nung, and Nung fighters had always been restricted to the shit details and suicide missions the Arvins refused to undertake. The life expectancy of a Nung private was about as long as that of a pair of rotting jungle boots in the rainy season.

The distant roar of helicopter blades soon reached Truong's ears. They had the lower canopy cleared away moments before the U.S. Army Huey arrived.

The slick hovered directly over their ambush site for a few seconds—its rotor tips barely cleared the tree branches on all sides. Then its belly light flicked on, shining on the ground below. Checking the clearing for stumps and obstructions, no doubt, Truong decided. He stared up at the screaming craft, his gunhand shielding his eyes from the powerful beams of light.

The chopper was slowly descending now, and its rotorblades were snipping off branches as if they were made of cardboard. Before the first sigh of relief was completely out of Truong's lungs, the gunship had set down.

Its rotors continued to flap madly as Capt. Soto waved several of the Nungs toward the pile of rifles. Two privates flew past the AKs, heading directly for the chopper's open hatch. They were getting a spooked feeling about this place, and they were getting the hell out! Truong watched Soto grab both of them and fling them toward the captured weapons. The American officer had his rifle slung now, and his pistol unholstered. He no longer was worried about Charlie. Pistols were drawn only as a last defense, or when administrative actions were bordering on capital punishment. *Combat-zone* capital punishment. Soto's .45 was no match for the Nungs' M-16s and heavy machine guns, of course—it was a purely symbolic gesture. An intimidating one. One that worked. Nungs began carrying rifles, equipment, and uniforms over to the waiting Huey.

When all the matériel was aboard, Capt. Soto began waving the Nungs back, away from the Huey. As their bewildered faces turned toward the icy-eyed American, the Huey's turbines began whining like a wounded leopard and the ship rose up out of Void Vicious, leaving Capt. Soto, Sgt. Do Lam Chinh, and the Nungs behind.

CHAPTER 9

En route to Dau Tieng

"I don't get paid enough to put up with this crap!"

Doc Delgado laughed at Nurse Maddox's complaint. "Honey," he yelled above the helicopter's downblast, "you and I *both* put up with whatever Uncle Sammy *assigns* us to put up with!"

It looked like Lt. Maddox was doing a tap dance—no sooner had she jumped to one side of the cabin than another burst of tracer was crashing up through the helicopter's fiberglass floorboards. "And *you*, Danny-boy, can lick my—" Maddox snapped back when she saw that the medic was still leering at her, even after splinters of lead left small puncture wounds across the swell of her bottom. The nurse's challenge was drowned out by a doorgunner's noisy and relentless attempt to kill the VC riflemen hiding in treetops 50 yards below.

"Honey," Delgado replied, eyeballing Maddox's tight-fitting flightsuit, "as long as I got a tongue . . ."

The doorgunner heard the remark but did not bother to glance black over his shoulder. He was grinning, though, as he poured an impressive stream of twenty- and thirty-round bursts down in the general direction of the unseen snipers.

It was common knowledge among the men of Echo Company that Sgt. Daniel Delgado—the unit's pacifist

Chicano medic and one of the best corpsmen in the First Air Cav Division—and Lt. Lisa Maddox—blond army nurse and rebellious daughter of a big-shot general down at MACV—were a hot item. What made them beloved by the men in Airmobile was their defiance of the old rule that officers should not fraternize with NCOs or enlisted men.

When she and Doc Delgado were caught one night by two horny gunship pilots, word spread to every grunt and NCO in Echo Company. The pilots involved were Cliff Gabriel and Lance Warlokk—two hotdogs both Maddox and Delgado "had the goods on" a dozen times over. So Gabe and Lawless kept the lid on the incident, but harbored secret lust for the sexy angel of mercy. Casualty rates for combat medics were high, they reasoned. It was only a matter of time before Doc Delgado was blown out of the picture. Then they could go back to their old ways and schemes and games, trying to impress Maddox with their airborne abilities and immodest charm.

"Everyone okay back there?" the gunship pilot called over his shoulder without bothering to click in.

"No problem, bud!" Delgado replied. "But you got a couple dozen new windows in the belly of this crate."

"No sweat!" The pilot was satisfied with his instrument board—none of the chip lights was screaming for attention. "We need the ventilation!"

They would count forty-seven bullet holes later. None struck anything vital, apparently. Except for Lisa Maddox's shapely bottom.

"You gonna be okay?" Delgado asked Lisa. He could see by the strained lines creasing her cheeks that she was in some pain.

"Yeah!" she replied, checking over the aid bags. "But it feels like I just took a load o' saltrock *in* the butt! And we're not even halfway to the LZ yet!"

"It's gonna be one of those days!" Delgado was inspect-

88

ing his own equipment. "Them potshot pricks on the ground'll get ya every time!"

"It just means *I* get to be on top tonight." Maddox lowered her voice somewhat. She leaned back and, using the insides of her arms, squeezed the outlines of her breasts together for Danny's benefit.

"*If* we make it *back* tonight!" The doorgunner beside Maddox was no longer firing his hatch-60 and had overheard. He, too, leaned back so that their heads were almost touching. The gunny wore a black patch over one eye and an evil leer. He winked at Lisa with the good eye.

She felt a sudden repulsion—the trooper, in his late thirties, with a bronzed tan that said he'd been in Asia many years, also had a hideous scar across the right side of his face. She had seen his type before. This man would not go back to The World. He couldn't . . . didn't *want* to. He would die here, doing what he enjoyed, doing all that was left to him in this lifetime, here where the women would ignore the scar because their fathers and brothers had them, too—they had grown up seeing such wounds heal.

The gunny's leer was designed to shock Maddox. "Who the hell let *you* work gunships with only one eye?" she shot back, and the doorgunner was the one who was shocked.

"Oh, it's no problem. They don't call me Dead Eye for nothin', ma'am."

The slightest hint of a smile crept onto Lisa's features. "Well, see to it you keep your opinions—and your *winks* —to yourself, soldier!"

"Oh, *yes*, ma'am! No problem—you got it, Lou . . . uh, Lieu*tenant*!" He grabbed the M-60 with both hands and leaned into the weapon's buttplate, lone eye scanning the vast jungle ceiling below for targets of opportunity.

Delgado was staring at Lisa as she in turn watched the doorgunner. The Nam was starting to show on Lt. Maddox's face—in the stress lines at the edges of her eyes, in

89

her fatigued half smiles. The spark had gone out of her eyes lately, too, it seemed. He would have to coax her into a blood test. Maybe it wasn't just the long hours.

Yes, she was growing old in the face. Lisa woke up looking thirty-seven lately instead of her actual twenty-seven, and a sophisticated rage smoldered in her eyes. Her lovemaking abilities had not suffered, although when they found the time to be alone she seemed more violent, always taking control, always trying to hurt him.

"Lima Zulu in dirty sex, ladies and germs," the pilot announced, "and it's gonna be hot." He meant that they would be arriving on-station in thirty seconds or less. "Lima Zulu" was radio phonetic for "landing zone." But the medics and doorgunners knew exactly what he was talking about.

Lima Zulu in dirty sex . . . Did every chopper pilot in the First Division use that LZ prep? Delgado wondered. Cliff Gabriel was not in the pilot's seat, as usual. That is, Delgado was not riding his regular slick, *Pegasus*. In the past, he usually rode into firefights aboard Gabe's ship, but *Peg* was already at the battle scene. Gabriel often used the same announcement. *Lima Zulu in dirty sex* . . .

It was as if they flew into a firestorm. One second, the cool breeze of descent, the next, glowing tracers and whistling ricochets were bouncing about the cabin as their slick flared in for a sideways landing, both doorgunners blasting away wildly.

Grunts on the ground were already rushing up to the ship three at a time. The man in the middle was always wounded—he was being dragged, his arms around the shoulders of wild-eyed friends ducking down so as not to lose their heads to the sharp rotorblades slapping low and fierce.

Delgado recognized Brody and Snakeman. "Where's *Peg*?" he cried as they helped lift a wounded soldier up

90

through the hatch. After Fletcher could do no more, he whipped the slung rifle from its upside-down position across his back and whirled, cutting loose with several three-round bursts, firing back at the hostile tree line.

"Gunslinger already took her back to Tay Ninh," Brody replied, out of breath. A trickle of blood flowed freely from a gash somewhere under his helmet. "She was chock full of wounded, Doc!"

"Holy shit . . ."

They were in the middle of a vast, smoke-choked clearing half a kilometer east of the nowhere ville named Lo Go. Fifty yards away, a sparse tree line extended out from the rain forest along the banks of a dry creekbed. The creekbed snaked its way to the ankle-high elephant grass of the shallow, meadowlike depression they now occupied.

The swirling blanket of smoke was from cooking fires in the village, nearly 2,000 meters distant. The breeze was wafting it directly into the firefight. Life went on as usual in Lo Go. The guerrillas were probably native sons of the medium-sized hamlet.

"I smell Cambodia!" Delgado yelled above the clamor of rotors—five other med-evacs had since pranged into the clearing—as he helped pull the last W.I.A. aboard. Doc was talking about the unmistakable fragrance of Khmer cooking that had traveled on the smoke.

"She's right up the hill there!" Between clips, Fletcher pointed at the ville with his smoking rifle muzzle.

"She?" Lt. Maddox was pulling field bandages from waterproof containers and applying them to wounds in the order of their severity. She had triaged the patients as they were rushed to the ship and went to work on the belly wounds first.

"The Cambodian border, Lieutenant!" Brody turned to assist Fletcher as soon as the last casualty was up and over the landing skids.

"You two coming along or not?" Delgado yelled as Nurse Maddox flipped the pilot a thumbs-up and the craft's tail boom lifted up off the ground.

"There's not enough room!" she argued. The helicopter already was two bodies over the suggested maximum payload.

Grinding his teeth in obvious irritation, the pilot glanced back over his shoulder without saying anything, as several tracers passed in through one hatch and out the other without hitting anybody. He set the ship back down, steam pouring from his eyes and ears.

"There's *always* enough room for a couple doorgunners!" Doc Delgado reached down out of the hatch and latched onto The Whoremonger's wrist. He started to pull him away from Elliott. The gunny on Delgado's side of the ship continued to direct his own shots at sporadic muzzle flashes in the distant tree line.

"We've gotta stay down here and provide cover fire until all the birds get airmobile!" Treat argued.

"That's what the doorgunners are for!" Delgado refused to let go. His eyes scanned the landing zone. Two choppers had already ascended and, in tight turns, were banking back to the southeast, toward Tay Ninh. The remaining craft would be lifting off shortly. He could see no other grunts still on the ground. Even Sgt. Zack and Lt. Vance had climbed aboard the Huey idling farthest from them.

"Get in, now!" Lt. Maddox screamed at them to end the delay, as the hostile fire started increasing dramatically and rounds began punching jagged holes through the Huey's magnesium walls. "Move!" she locked eyes with Snakeman from her unstable crouch beside a soldier whose lower jaw had nearly been torn away. "I'm ordering you two hotdogs into the ship!"

The chopper pilot was beginning to lose his cool. "Either shit or get off the pot!" he advised.

"Flush the fucker!" Fletcher replied as he dove in through the hatch, landing between Lisa's knees. She was knocked back onto her haunches, and Snakeman rose up onto one elbow and smiled back at his buddy. The Whoremonger shrugged and jumped in after him.

The Dustoff's protesting rotors labored hard and faithfully as the craft approached a high wall of trees opposite the VC positions. But a crash could kill the ship's occupants just as easily as enemy bullets. The crew held their breath as the Huey's snout barely rose above several jagged branches.

CHAPTER 10

Northeast of Tay Ninh

Snakeman closed his eyes tightly as the landing skids clipped a limb, but the ship remained airborne and slowly climbed above Void Vicious's outstretched claws. *Pegasus* steadily gained altitude until they were once again above the kill zone.

On the way back to Tay Ninh, they passed two Phantom jets, heading in the opposite direction, faster than the speed of sound.

"And not a minute too soon." Fletcher knew the fighters were en route to the clearing his unit had just been extracted from. They would drop napalm cannisters, 500-pound bombs, and more than a few rockets.

"Shit." Delgado did not bother to glance out either hatch as the dual afterburner roars filled his ears. "They ain't gonna do any good 'cept pulverize some baboons and parrots. Ol' Charlie's already down in his Lo Go tunnel, gettin' a skulljob, gents. He knows the game plan by now."

"You really think so, Doc?" Brody asked. "You really think those Cong were from Lo Go?"

"Whadda *you* think?" The medic was busy trying to close a bleeder.

"Yeah," Treat mulled it over for a second or two. "I think you're right."

"Well, if that's the case, we oughta regroup and return

for the barbecue." Fletcher voiced his opinion with fires raging in his eyes. "It really pisses me off the way things went down back there! Who was that fucking dude, anyway, Treat?"

"The F-4s will finish 'em off," Lt. Maddox said.

"What dude?" Delgado asked.

"A captain climbed into *Peg* with a whole shitload o' Nungs—they were all fucked up pretty bad but still on their feet," Snakeman replied.

"It was truly some weird shit," Brody said, helping with the first aid, as his mind went back to the battle. "I remember seeing a blacked-out Huey speeding away from the LZ as we were coming in—"

"Like a bat outta hell," Fletcher added.

"So we set down with the other ships, and the whole time, in the back o' my mind, I'm thinking, 'Why didn't that slick stay around to help?' but then the shit hit the fan hot and heavy."

"You shoulda seen them Nungs," Fletcher said admiringly. "Now *there's* a class o' ass-kickers who really know how to fight!"

"They were indeed takin' Charlie to town." Brody nodded in agreement.

"Just that there were *too many* Cong in the area." Snakeman caressed his M-16's black fiberglass stock as if it were a woman's thigh. "Too many to handle."

"That captain was definitely in charge. Did you see how the Nungs kept staring at him . . . looking his way . . . ?"

"Yeah. But that one dude . . . I think he was wearin' sergeant's rank," Brody said. "Now *he* was pissed about something. I mean, he was truly steamin'."

"You'd be steamin', too, if Charlie just shot the shit outta *your* unit," Fletcher retorted.

"Yeah." Treat wiped blood-splattered knuckles across his pantsleg. "I guess you're right."

* * *

The wounded outnumbered the angry two to one, Jones reckoned as he looked around *Peg*'s human cargo. Those who weren't bleeding all over his hatch-60 preferred to scamper back into the chopper cabin's farthest recesses, away from the captain squatting in front of him.

Jones stared hard at the officer. His name tag read "Soto." His eyes read rage.

"Looks like your team really walked into a shit storm." Jones harbored no malice against these gung-ho, elite-unit types.

The captain was staring silently at the dark jungle passing by below *Peg*'s sparkling landing skids. He did not respond. He appeared to be in his own little world.

The rotorblades were deafening. Jones decided to raise his voice and try again. "I said it looks like your team really walked into—"

"I heard what you fucking said, asshole." Soto did not bother to glance over at Jones.

"Ahhh"—the apprentice doorgunner's smile brightened, if only artificially—"a good buddy!" He abandoned his M-60 and crouched closer to the officer. "I love to chew the wad with bro's who care," he said sarcastically.

Soto reached over and grabbed the front of Jones's fatigue shirt. "Go fuck yourself, you little shit!" his eyes bulged. He violently pushed Jones away.

"Leave the man alone, Jones," Zack barked, watching the medics work on casualties.

"Aw, I was just tryin' to get to know him, Sarge. The stories this soldier could tell!" The longtime vets were allowed to call Zack Leo, which was short for Leopold. Leo the Lionhearted would do fine, too. Jones was still required to call him by rank, though.

"Just give the cap'n his space." Zack's tone was firm.

"Aw, you hard-core types all stick together, don't you?" Jones glanced back at the sergeant, whose outline was exaggerated by the flickering light from a half dozen aid lamps.

"Eat it like a man, Jones." Zack's reply announced an end to the discussion.

Reece Jones stared long and hard at the captain. Okay, so he would cut the guy some slack—not that anyone had been cutting *him* any slack lately. Life with the glorious First Air Cavalry Division was becoming a real downer, in fact. These gents were seriously into playing soldier.

This damn war is really getting to me. He shook his head from side to side as the lights of Tay Ninh City began to appear in the distance. *I tried for conscientious-objector status, and they laughed in my face simply because of a couple of lousy assault charges on my police record. I was only defending myself back then . . . just like I'm defending myself now,* he reflected.

Jones's college-deferment papers never went through. They never even came back, anyway. There was no foul-up with the draft notice, however. It had arrived at the worst possible time—the same week lucrative job offers were beginning to flow in from the nation's biggest companies.

The only comfort came in knowing there were others in the green machine who had also been screwed by Uncle Sammy's paperwork nightmare. The military bureaucracy managed—quite efficiently, it seemed—to send all the C.O.'s to a combat zone. Saigon was out. We're sorry, they told him, down at the in-processing center on the outskirts of Tan Son Nhut. No slots open right now in Sin City. The Pearl of the Orient was full up. You're headed for the sticks, slick. You get to be a boonie rat.

Those "others" were banding together to plot a way out before they became just another statistic on the nightly

98

news where Walter Cronkite was still mispronouncing Vietnam.

The antidraft GIs were calling themselves Vietnam Vets Against the War, and those who made it back to The World in one piece—and in some cases far from whole—were even starting up a newsletter and support system for those men still in Southeast Asia. Or worse—just arriving.

Jones looked forward to the day when he'd DEROS back to the States. He didn't hope for medals, but surely, by then, he'd have a Purple Heart or two to fling on the White House steps. First, though, he'd stop off in San Francisco. Everyone stopped in Haight-Ashbury for some free love and LSD before joining the hippy caravans to roam the country, free and uncommitted. That's what Reece Jones would do when he got out: let his hair grow down to his ass—he'd promised himself never to cut it again following ETS—buy a Volkswagen van, and journey east to Washington, D.C. Look out, President Johnson!

Capt. Soto glanced over at Jones when the private chuckled in his ear. He had to restrain himself from striking out, from ripping out the kid's Adam's apple. But Jones was just staring out the hatch, out into space, giggling to himself about this or that—nothing directed at Soto, it seemed, so the officer retreated into his own thoughts, trying to figure out what had gone wrong. . . .

Charlie struck less than a minute after the Huey had lifted out all the VC rifles. They had been waiting in the tree line, silent as black cats. For the first time in his career, Soto had missed their arrival.

Soto prided himself on his uncanny ability to sense approaching movement in the jungle, especially in Indochina. There was something weird about these Asian rain forests, but it was an odd sensation his body seemed able to tune into. The hairs along the back of his neck would bristle whenever Charlie was close, trying to sneak up on him in the dark. That nauseated feeling would swirl about in his gut, making him weak-kneed but sending a surge of strength into his gunhand and making his eyesight suddenly eagle-sharp, able to discern even the slightest movement out in the dark unknown. But tonight it had not worked. Tonight his sixth sense had abandoned him.

Tonight the Huey had lifted out of the hastily chopped clearing unmolested—not so much as a single sniper's round chased after her. Then all hell broke loose and the Nungs were scrambling for cover.

For a while they seemed to be holding their own, but no matter how many of the enemy he and his Nungs took out, twice as many seemed to ooze forth from the bamboo to replace them. Finally, it became clear they were being assaulted by a main-force, regimental-size unit, and he directed the RTO to transmit a Brass Monkey.

Luckily, this gaggle of 7th Cav ships had been in the area. Otherwise, his unit of Nungs couldn't possibly have survived the battle much longer.

Things on the team were certainly going to become abrasive after *this* abortion. He would have to talk to the major. He would request another detachment of the brave Chinese mercenaries. There was no way he could go back to commanding American troops. No way in the world. He would end up behind bars in Long Binh Jail, breaking big rocks into little rocks. And he doubted Sgt. Chinh would follow any more of his commands. He would just have to wait and see. A whole new batch of green recruits was the route to go, he was convinced.

Perhaps he could talk to the merc. Explain to him the value of the right people examining the weapons for the military intel they would provide. Chinh would probably spit in his face, of course—and Soto knew he wouldn't be able to blame the man. How could one equate the value of extracting enemy weapons with the loss of life experienced by the Nungs tonight? He would try, though. That was all Capt. Soto could hope to do: try.

Reece Jones stared long and hard at the captain. Something funny struck him—something about the officer's jutting chin and thick brow. "I'll bet you're Gage Ruckter's *papa-san*, ain't ya, sir? Just admit it."

Jones chuckled, but the weak laugh quickly died out, to be replaced by the steady whopping of the rotors overhead. Everyone in the cabin was staring at him. If looks could kill, Reece Jones would already be maggot meat.

CHAPTER 11

South of Dau Tieng SF Camp

The 9th Viet Cong Division, heavily decimated following skirmishes along Minh Thanh Road, fled the battle at Srok Dong and attempted to regroup in well-concealed base areas in the Michelin Rubber Plantation east of Tay Ninh. North Vietnamese replacements arrived to beef up the VC forces for a planned attack on the Special Forces camp at Suoi Da, only to engage unexpectedly with elements of the American 196th Light Infantry Brigade, which was sweeping III Corps' War Zone C for rice and sundry supplies in the U.S. Army's first search-and-destroy missions.

The 2nd Battalion of the 1st Infantry Division air-assaulted into War Zone C on September 14, 1966, officially beginning Operation Attleboro, but there was only light contact with the enemy, and operations shifted to the vicinity around Dau Tieng. After a month of search-and-destroy, the brigade massed for a large tactical sweep. Beginning on October 20, large amounts of rice were uncovered daily, and on Halloween—a date when Trick or Treat Brody especially enjoyed wearing his python-head mask into battle—the 196th discovered documents at Ben Chi Plantation describing possible enemy base camps deeper in the jungle.

Four days later, on November 3, the 1st Battalion of the 27th Infantry, which was now attached to the 196th, landed its Charlie Company without incident, only to later stumble into the 9th VC division's Niner Recon Company.

Aboard gunships, troops were sent north of where Highway 19 runs east-west near the junction of the Saigon River and the Suoi Ba Hao. They landed near a cluster of landing zones known to longtime vets as the Ghost Town Trail, in honor of all the high-casualty firefights that had taken place amongst the area's seemingly endless Buddhist graveyards.

During the assault, Alpha Company of the 27th Infantry's First Battalion was tasked with the duties of physical security at the Dau Tieng airfield, while nine helicopter gunships from the 116th Aviation "Hornets" would scour the area, airlifting two entire companies worth of groundpounders into the rubber plantations in hopes of engaging hostile forces.

At 1000 hours, Bravo Company was airlifted in. They immediately located what was suspected of being a Viet Cong village, hidden behind and nearly surrounded by a wall of 12-foot-high elephant grass.

Charlie had beaten a hasty retreat into the nearby jungle and rubber plantations, however, without firing a single shot, so the American troopers began trashing the huts, outdoor showers, and storage bunkers, and they threw countless items of personal property owned exclusively by VC forces residing in the ville into the Saigon river. Huge caches of rice were also found, but these proved hard to destroy.

An hour later, Charlie Company also landed—but far to the west, below Highway 19—as artillery began softening up the woods in between the two American forces. Alpha Company was still on its way, and the plan—having Alpha and Charlie sweep north, flushing any hiding VC out into Bravo Company's sight picture—required their presence.

As Bravo and Charlie Companies awaited Alpha's arrival, the corps commander, Major General Frederick Weyand, landed in his private helicopter to survey the problems his infantrymen were encountering with the rice destruction. No sooner had the four-star arrived than sporadic shooting could be heard from the direction of Bravo Company. Simultaneously, heavy automatic weapons fire erupted between Charlie Company and a dug-in enemy contingent. The general had arrived just in time to witness a ferocious ground battle: The troopers under his command, expecting to force the VC to flee through the reeds, had walked into an ambush instead.

Gage Ruckter saw the smoke rising along the distant tree line first.

Initially, he thought it was part of the storm front moving in off the northern horizon, but then the dark blue hues of the approaching monsoon became distinguishable from the black-and-gray blanket of drifting gunsmoke.

"Wanna take a look-see?"

He listened to the two pilots of the ash-'n-trash flight discussing the obvious firefight also.

"Probably shouldn't," the peter pilot responded. "Not without gunnies aboard or no Brass Monkey goin' out . . ."

Ruckter breathed a sigh of relief. He craved action, but not *today*, thank you. Today, he'd hitched a hop from Tay Ninh City south to Saigon, where he was scheduled to begin a seven-day, in-country R&R. A full week of "I&I": Intoxication and Intercourse. It just wouldn't do to have his ding-dong shot off by some prick of a Charlie Cong over there in that dark tornado of flying shrapnel and tracer fire. Ruckter wasn't sure if his ears were deceiving him, but he thought he could actually hear explosions now. An animal or two. Yes, several claymores exploding simultaneously —the rolling concussions could mean only one thing.

"Come on, Buddha-buddy." He found himself clutching the good-luck amulet a whore in Pleiku had given him the year before. "Not today. Keep thy chopperjock on a straight-arrow course to our favorite Asian jewel: Saigon."

Garbled chatter was suddenly screaming across several radio bands in the cockpit. Ruckter strained to hear the words, but he needn't have bothered: The cries for help were unmistakable.

A Brass Monkey.

The peter pilot turned back to face Gage. "Are ya game?" he asked, lifting the black visor up to reveal a twinkle in his amused eyes.

"Do I have a fucking choice?" Ruckter responded.

The craft was already diving down toward the treetops.

Gage felt guilty the instant he answered with the sarcastic, whine tone. A Brass Monkey call for help was a priority no one ignored. Similar interagency pleas for assistance had saved his own butt on more than a few occasions.

"Don' worry, soldier," the pilot chuckled. "City o' sorrows'll still be there after this is all over. . . ."

"Should only take a few minutes," the copilot added without looking back. "We're just flyin' relays today, anyway, and don't have much ordnance aboard to drop on Charlie."

"Might have to make a couple extractions, though," the AC reminded him. "Wounded, you know . . . Just depends on how many ships show up."

Ruckter nodded as a flashback consumed him. Fireballs flashed in his mind's eye, and he saw his old unit pinned down at Srok Dong.

Armored personnel carriers blocked the road at every curve—many lay on their sides, burning furiously, their crews either dead or running for cover despite serious burns and gunshot wounds. Charlie was everywhere that day, too. In the treetops, popping up from roadside gulleys —even crawling under their own APCs.

Gage had fired off an entire bandolier of rifle rounds— nearly 300 shells—before he realized how low on ammo he was getting. One bandolier left—and a couple of the twenty-round magazines had fallen out when the ambush first went down and he was blown off the track.

He resolved never to run short on ammo like that again —he promised Buddha and Jesus H. And whoever else might be listening that from that day forth he would carry a rucksack full of 5.56, but right now things were looking grim. Gage Ruckter didn't think he was going to survive this firefight. Even as he switched to semi-automatic to conserve ammunition, he was resigned to the fact his bullets would soon run out.

Then a tank appeared out of nowhere, crashing through several disabled APCs and opening the way for reinforcements. The tank was driven by a sergeant whose crew had been killed. Ruckter and several others jumped aboard and helped push back the Cong until additional help arrived.

The memory left Ruckter breathing hard. He made the sign of the cross, and he wasn't even Catholic. The peter pilot laughed at his antics.

"Looks like we're gonna be the first girl at the party," he joked about their lonely situation.

No sooner had the words left his mouth than a tracer— its flaring glow making it appear the size of a giant green basketball—slammed into the cockpit's main windshield. The Plexiglas spider-webbed. The pilots barely flinched.

Two, three, a half dozen, then countless more rounds crashed through the weakened glass—all ricocheting up through the roof without hitting anything vital. "Gonna be a hot one." The AC gritted his teeth, trying to pull his craft up out of the spray of lead.

It appeared that the Cong on the ground were trying to adjust their aim ahead of each anticipated maneuver. Soon, a dozen riflemen were zeroing in on the Huey.

Several lancelike bolts of tracer arced up hundreds of feet ahead of the craft, converging at a spot it was likely to fly through. Charlie was "leading" on the slick. It was only a matter of time before—

Several rounds punched up through the gunship's snout. The craft began to shake and vibrate. Ruckter feared it would fall apart or explode in midair. Smoke began filling the cockpit and cabin.

"Are we goin' down?" Ruckter pulled the .45 from its holster. He didn't have his M-16, since he was officially on leave. The sidearm was unauthorized, but he refused to part with it.

"Not if I can help it—" the pilot started to say as the craft began skimmering treetops.

The next thing Ruckter knew, he'd been knocked back onto his haunches and the warrant officer's bloody flight helmet was spinning in his lap.

With the pilot dead, the copilot struggled to regain control of the spinning helicopter, but a landing skid clipped several trees, and Ruckter felt his world flip over.

There was a roar of metal against hard-as-concrete water, and the Huey skipped along through blue-green waves on its mangled top. Screams filled Ruckter's ears— the screams of broken rotorblades slamming against one another and tearing loose of their swashplate assembly.

He was suddenly hanging upside down. Somehow he had gotten tangled in a set of monkeystraps hanging from the absent doorgunner's station. The rotorblades had torn free and sliced the cockpit open.

The copilot's body was ripped down the middle. His neck was twisted back grotesquely, his face mangled. He had died with his eyes open. They stared up at Ruckter now.

Water was rushing in through the hatches. Water! They were nowhere near the coast, and the creekbed he'd spotted from the air had appeared to be dry. But the chopper was definitely sinking!

He struggled to free himself from the canvas-and-fiberglass M-60 lifelines, then stumbled up toward the cockpit, his ears ringing from the constant roar of AK and SKS discharges outside. The VC were using the Huey's fuselage for target practice, and he wasn't about to leave the sinking craft with just a lousy .45 automatic.

Chopper pilots were notorious for carrying an arsenal of unauthorized firearms hidden in their cockpits—everything from captured and cut-down AKs to MAC-10s and sawed-off shotguns. Ruckter wasn't disappointed.

He grabbed a German-made MP-40 submachine gun as the ship began to roll over onto its side. The water was already up to his knees.

Several American gunships were crisscrossing the skies overhead now, aware of his predicament, and trying to beat the Cong back with rockets and mini-gun fire until any survivors aboard the shot-down Huey could attempt an escape, assuming there *were* any survivors.

Gage Ruckter wasn't about to let their efforts go to waste.

He kicked out the shattered Plexiglas windshield and discovered the craft had rolled through the treetops at high speed, bounced across a shallow body of water for nearly 50 yards, and come to rest in the middle of a small lake.

The Huey was sinking fast now, as more and more bullet holes turned its fuselage into a sieve. He doubted the lake was very deep, judging by its color and the way in which ripples were moving out from the craft, but he didn't want to take any chances either. "Thanks, buddy!" Knowing he owed his life to the flying abilities of the man who prevented the Huey from crashing on land in a searing fireball, Gage reached down and closed the dead copilot's eyes. "We'll try to get ya outta here after the gunplay's over!"

Ruckter grabbed three ammo magazines from the MP-40, which were tied together with a thick rubber band, then prepared to squirm through the crumpled side hatch, cannonball into the water, and swim for it. He knew there were American troops out there somewhere. But there were also bookoo commies, vying for the chance to hang his severed ears on their web belt.

He hoped he chose the right side of the lake to swim to.

Ruong Nhu Toai's friends were babbling like schoolgirls as they gathered around the boy, playfully fighting over the chance to pat him on the back. The whole affair embarrassed Toai. All he did was what any other dedicated member of the communist youth movement would do: try his darndest to pluck one of the American helicopters from the sky as it passed over.

At fourteen years of age, Toai was not the youngest Viet Cong recruit in the unit, but he was by far the smallest. And the most quiet and modest. That *he* should be the one to bring down a gunship was definitely cause for celebration. The others had fired, too, but Toai—always the clown—had loaded his ammunition clip so that every other round was a bright, glowing tracer. The cell leader himself had watched the burst of bullets crash up through the Huey's belly as it flew over this heavily camouflaged splinter of the Ho Chi Minh Trail. The leader was the first to recognize Toai's accomplishment and the first to congratulate the boy.

110

"You shall receive a medal for felling the American gunship!" the cell leader proclaimed.

Toai was taking all the attention in stride. "All I want to do is race after it," he responded bravely. "To see where it crashed. To finish off the GIs on board!"

The cell leader's eyes narrowed. He had already communicated by radio with other VC units in the area. "I have been informed the Huey has gone down in the middle of a lake beside a battlefield involving the 9th Viet Cong Regiment," the older communist advised.

"Then—" Toai's eyes lit up.

"We are not to get involved in that confrontation." The cell leader's tone grew firm. "Our orders are to continue south toward Saigon. We have a specific mission to undertake once we are within striking distance of the capital."

"But—" Toai was suddenly the hero of the group. He wanted to see the fruits of his labor.

"No argument, Ruong Nhu Toai. You did well. Now do not dishonor your family by arguing with your commander."

"Yes, sir." Toai lowered his eyes to the ground. A leech was nibbling on his big toe, but the boy's tire-tread sandals did not move.

"And as for the rest of you"—the cell leader's eyes scanned the dozen or so cadre members—"there will be no more pot shots taken at aircraft flying over the trail. We must conserve our ammunition. Toai's hit was a lucky one. I doubt any of you could repeat it."

After the adult turned and left to rejoin his radio operator, the other youths swarmed over Toai again, congratulating him on his skillful display of marksmanship.

"You truly have the tiger's eye, Toai." One youth beamed.

"They will soon make you a sniper," another joined in.

"You must show us how you did it!"

"It must have been a very difficult shot, what with all these trees and thick branches. . . ."

". . . The thick canopy obscuring the sky like that . . ."

"You must show us . . . after we persuade the captain to change his mind. . . ."

"It will never happen." Someone behind Toai laughed.

"All I want is to be a good soldier," Toai said, rubbing the powder marks from his rifle's muzzle. "All I want is to make my mother and father . . . my family proud. . . ."

Ruckter thought some monster from the deep must have grabbed his boots, was trying to drag him down to a dark doom beneath the lake's surface. In reality, it was only moss and water reeds clinging to his boots and ankles, but the evil sensation sent a chill through Gage and a scream through his curled-back lips.

He was still too excited to realize what was really going on. Reality was hard to grasp in that lake on the edge of Dau Tieng. Thick smoke floated only a few feet above the lake, making it look as if a menacing black sky were pressing down on Ruckter, trying to smother him. He was beginning to feel like the last living man in the world.

Then suddenly the smoke parted down the middle slightly as a helicopter gunship roared past low overhead. Ruckter watched the smoke rush back in, sucking up the rotorwash, but then the chopper was hovering directly overhead again.

"You're swimming the wrong way!" someone was leaning down out of a hatch and yelling at him, trying to get his attention.

"The pilot!" a doorgunner was yelling, too. "What about the Alpha-Charlie and copilot?" Ruckter obviously didn't look like warrant-officer material to this crew.

"Dead!" he managed to reply, though Gage Ruckter was a man who couldn't swim and chat at the same time, and the effort took him underwater for a moment. He returned to the surface gasping for air and flailing at the ripples until he got his balance back.

"*That* way!" A second man pointed. "Swim that way, bud!"

Ruckter was thinking, *Why don't you guys just pick me up?* but he was too exhausted to open his mouth, much less turn his bewildered thoughts into words; and then a hailstorm of smoking lead from three different banks along the lake's edge was converging on the Huey. He watched it bank away sharply, trying to outrace the bullets as the doorgunner fired back fearlessly.

Already, Ruckter was feeling like he was in a whirling cesspool, trying to remember which way the gunny had pointed. He watched the tracers flying up into the dark sky. Still coming from three different points on shore. He would swim for the fourth point. That was where the Americans had to be holed up. Bullets began dancing across the lake's surface, only a few feet from his head, so Ruckter folded at the belly, lifting his buttocks up into the air, and dove.

A single round hit the heel of his boot—it felt like someone had struck his foot as hard as they could with a baseball bat—but he didn't think the bullet had penetrated his flesh. He wasn't feeling any pain—yet—but that could be because of the adrenaline rush. If he'd been hit, he'd know it soon enough.

Ruckter dove deep—until his hands touched the lake bottom, about 30 feet down—and changed directions underwater. When he broke surface again, he felt he was pointed in the right direction.

CHAPTER 12

Dau Tieng SF Camp

Zack was tearing entire tents from the earth with his bare hands.

"Let's go! Let's go!" his booming voice woke those who were sleeping through the hi-lo scramble siren. "Hands off your cocks and up with your socks, *ladies*!"

"What's the score, Leo?" a groggy-faced Elliott Fletcher emerged with his eyes still tightly closed. He'd just finished a twelve-hour guard-duty shift and only five minutes earlier had drifted off to a much-deserved and needed bout of beauty sleep.

"Brass Monkey just over the hill!" Zack's yelling was giving Treat Brody a headache. "Just across the pond!"

"The swamp?" Fletcher tried to return to his tent. "I ain't goin' back to the swamp!"

"Oh, yes, you are, Snakeoil!" Zack grabbed the top of the Spec-4's tent halves and jerked them free of their stakes.

"Aw, Leo." Fletcher was awake now. He rested his hands on his hips. "Ya didn't have to go and do that. . . ."

"Get the fuck going!" Sgt. Zack was already gone. "Time to polish the Brass Monkey. Some boys from One-Niner-Six call fo' their mama, and tonight youz their motherfuckin' mamas, slickstuff!"

"Come on, Fletch!" Brody grabbed his buddy's wrist.

115

"I'm gettin' good vibes on this one!" In the background, they could hear several gunship turbines winding up. "I feel like we're gonna really kick some ass on this one! You wait and see—you're gonna come back with a hard-on ya can't get rid of, dude. You just wait and see...."

"Wouldn't be the first time." Elliott forced a grin. He glanced over at the predawn glow along the eastern horizon. "But I don't like the goddamned swamp. I haven't liked the swamp since the first day we set up shop here. Dau Tieng can kiss my—"

Brody pointed him toward the helipad. "But it's not Dau Tieng we're beatin' blades to get help—it's some brotha' Americans, dude. Just remember that!" He inspected Fletcher's clothing and equipment at the same time to make sure his buddy had everything he would need. It was not necessary. Fletcher slept with everything on in The Nam.

A dozen heavily armed troopers were trotting, bent over slightly, on either side of Brody and Fletcher as they approached the flightline. Sgt. Zack and Lt. Vance were already aboard the two nearest Hueys.

Brody frowned when he saw Reece Jones secreted in one of the doorgunner positions, waiting with bated breath for his void vet trainer. "Well, fuck me 'til it hurts," Treat grumbled. He had all but forgotten that his current duties included showing in-processing pogues the ins and outs of being a chopper gunny.

"You'll get over it, Whoremonger!" Elliott laughed. He was suddenly shifting into a good mood.

"Ha!" Brody laughed back after they had climbed into *Pegasus* only to find an FNG behind the Snake's Hog-60 as well.

"Aw, shit!" Fletcher hissed.

"Howdy!" the newby waved warmly. "My name's—"

Fletcher cut him off. "Shut the fuck up! I don' wanna know!"

116

"You clowns *up* back there?" It was Gabriel, their pilot. Already, the ship's tail boom was rising off the ground.

"Eat duck!" Fletcher muttered through clenched teeth. To "eat duck" was an insult among doorgunners. It had always been, though no one was ever quite sure why. Brody didn't think the pilots had caught on one way or the other. If they did, they didn't seem to care.

"Right," Gabe the Gunslinger answered back. "Eat duck." As the gunship ascended, he clicked into the intercom with a flat-billed and utterly fowl imitation of a duck.

"What the fuck's *his* point?" Snakeman pointed out the hatch. He was not referring to their AC. "Is the shit-for-brains trying to say farewell with an out-of-tune serenade or something?"

On the ground, Green Beret Sgt. Frisk stood alone atop a double-decker conex bunker beside the helipad, madly playing his fiddle. Eyes locking with the Whoremonger's as *Pegasus* passed low overhead, his teeth flashed ear to ear and his upper torso twisted and turned to some unheard tune the rotorblades were drowning out. "Looks like it's Frisk's way of saying 'Nice to have known ya.'"

"I think that's his way of saying he doesn't feel sorry for us at all," Fletcher countered.

"You're probably right, Snakeman. . . . You're probably right." Brody was grinning back at Sgt. Frisk, but he couldn't understand why. He did not think they were smiling about the same things.

Gage Ruckter's arms felt like they were going to fall off, but he finally reached shore—and without losing the MP-40. Its sling was wrapped around one elbow. His arm was scraped raw and burning, but he had a weapon to defend himself with, and that was all that mattered.

Crawling through shallow water now, he watched an Air Cav gunship swoop past, just overhead. A winged horse was painted across its snout.

Closer by, a human skull was leering down at Ruckter as he clawed his way up onto the lake's muddy bank. Blood-streaked tombstones rose up behind the cranium. After catching his breath, Ruckter realized he was on the edge of a cemetery.

Artillery was still slamming down into the ground just over the hill—one projectile had unearthed a Buddhist graveyard, scattering bones along the side of the lake. The same explosion had ripped a VC soldier to shreds while he sprinted for the cover of several shattered tree trunks. His blood smeared across the grave marker as his remains plopped down into the bomb crater.

"Join the party, Gage-baby!"

Ruckter, who was still staring eyeball to empty socket with the grinning skull, nearly flew out of his skin. And then he recognized the voice and realized the invitation was coming from behind a fallen log a few yards away.

"Brody! Where the hell'd you come from?"

"What is this, Truth or Consequences?" came a second voice. "Get your no-account ass over here, Ruckter!"

Snakeman. Snakeman Fletcher! "What the—"

"Come on!"

"You wanna end up like minced meat in some Charlie Cong's mutt soufflé!" Brody lifted his M-16 an inch or two above the bark and fired off half a magazine with one hand, pistol fashion, laying down some indiscriminate cover fire for his old buddy.

"Fuckin' *A!*" Ruckter gave the mandatory Army approval.

A string of AK rounds danced along the log's top, showering the three Americans with bark. Brody lifted his M-16, fired off the remaining rounds in his banana clip,

118

then pulled a smaller, twenty-round magazine from the bandolier around his neck and slammed it home. The rifle's bolt flew forward with a reassuring *twang!* and the cavalry sergeant turned to face the trio's ranking NCO.

"So whatta we do now?" he asked Ruckter.

"You're askin' *me* for advice?" Gage laughed as a Chi-Com stick grenade exploded nearby. "Ol' Gage-baby was just passin' through, gents! I don't even know where the fuck we are!"

"Dau Tieng, my man!" Fletcher advised him. "Or somewhere in the vicinity of same."

"We were just responding to a Brass Monkey." Ruckter examined his MP-40, opened the breech, and allowed water to drain from the barrel.

"Yeah, we watched your chopper cartwheel into the lake over there. Sorry about the others," Brody said.

"Right . . ." Gage sighed as he readied the submachine gun. "Me, too. But we weren't tight. I didn't even know 'em, really."

"Was it a full crew?" Fletcher asked. "I didn't see no gunnies in the hatch as it flipped through the trees over there."

"Nope. Just me and the chopperjocks." Ruckter's eyes scanned the area from where they seemed to be taking the most fire. "It was an ash-'n-trash."

"An ash-'n-trash?" Brody's eyes lit up. "Were you goin' AWOL, or—"

"R&R." Ruckter was still shaking his head in resignation. "Can you believe it?"

"In-country?"

"Yep. Saigon."

"Ahhh," Fletcher mused appreciatively. "Sin City. Nguyen Hue. The Butterfly Bar. Tu Do Street. Ladies of questionable virtue."

"Boom-boom girls." The Whoremonger sighed as explosions rumbled in the distance. "Short-time girls . . . all-nighters . . ."

Fletcher was peeking out over the log. He slid a fragmentation grenade from his web belt, pulled the pin, and threw it, softball fashion, as hard as he could over the nearest tree line. A chorus of screams and groans followed the muffled blast.

Ruckter sent a burst from his submachine gun at the legs of two guerrillas who suddenly chose that moment to rush the Americans' position. Brody followed up with a grenade of his own, finishing both communists off.

"Man, it sure was a damned good sight to see that fucking gunship swoopin' in to help me *kacka-dau* them Cong bastards on Thunder Road! I never in my life felt so relieved! It's a memory that'll stay with me forever, gents! Such a sight: this great big beautiful olive-drab brute flutterin' overhead like a metallic dragon spoutin' fire out three sides. . . . Thanks, guys," Ruckter said.

"Both hatches and the snout cannon." Snakeman was nodding his head slowly as he pulled frags from his ruck and laid them out in front of him. Brody thought he looked like some mischievous juvenile delinquent on the Fourth of July, getting his cherry bombs and M-80s ready for the annual neighborhood firecracker rumble.

Ruckter stared at the soldier a moment as well, then locked eyes with Treat. "So whatta you two jokers propose we do that'll get us out of *this* clusterfuck?"

"Christ, Gage-baby"—Brody's eyebrows rose innocently—"*you're* the ranking honcho-san. We were just passin' through, too!"

"Respondin' to the Brass Monkey?"

"Roger-that."

"What was the original game plan here?" Ruckter asked.

With bullets ricocheting into their position from three

different tree lines, Brody quickly briefed him on Bravo and Charlie companies' attempt to sweep the area, flushing out what they believed at the time would be a much smaller enemy force. "At least that's as much as the crew chief knew on our way in," he added. "These doggies walked into one helluva ambush!"

"From what we've seen between insertion and sprintin' over to this clump o' trees, they've sustained heavy casualties!" Fletcher said.

"Not a single command officer left standin' on his feet!" Brody sensed nearby movement and glanced above the log in time to spot a sapper with two stick grenades rushing their position.

Treat slammed his rifle across the log sideways and jerked the trigger without aiming, choosing instead to remain undercover while his gunhand guided the M-16 back and forth. The Viet Cong bellied over and crashed face first into a boulder. Neither grenade detonated.

"I think somebody upstairs"—Fletcher referred to the gunships circling the battle scene at a safe distance—"oughta call in reinforcements. Otherwise, Charlie's gonna keep us pinned down here until he outguns us."

"Which is definitely Numba Ten in my book!" Brody flipped clips.

"Roger-*that*!"

The constant, almost rhythmic, rattle of sharp AK cracks was suddenly replaced by a more powerful, ear-splitting roar. The log providing them cover began to shudder and shake.

"Jesus . . ." Fletcher swallowed hard and long.

"Machine-gun nest." Brody's ears perked. "Toward the lake."

"Well, beatin' feet back to the rear is out now." Ruckter's face looked grim.

"Rear?" Fletcher laughed dryly. "There *ain't* no rear here, Rucksack! Charlie's *everywhere*! That's why these guys got chewed up so bad."

Brody glanced back over his shoulder. He could see an awful lot of exposed, motionless bodies out there—bodies that were wearing U.S. jungle fatigues.

"We've gotta take out that damn MG," Ruckter decided.

Brody's eyes lit up. "How?"

Ruckter glanced around. There was no nearby cover once they left the log—only intermittent clumps of elephant grass. "We rush the fucker," he said finally.

"What?" Brody's eyes grew even larger. He was no coward, but he was no idiot either—the VC machine guns sounded a hundred yards away. They'd be cut down for sure.

"All three of us," the 4th Cav sergeant said. "We stagger out charges and veer away from one another."

"No fuckin' way, Rucksack," Fletcher laughed. It was a chuckle laced with mild hysteria. "They'd make *kimchi* out of us!"

"*One* of us has to get through," Gage maintained. "Hey, it's sink or swim," he said. "Sooner or—"

"I'll take *later*!" Snakeman was still shaking his head in disagreement.

"What about you, Treat?"

Before Brody could answer, a madman's war cry reached their ears. All three soldiers tensed—the sound was rushing up from behind them.

His rifle ready to fire, Brody whirled finally.

A fellow American was sprinting up to their position from the cover of several dead bodies 20 yards away. He was carrying an M-60 machine gun in his arms and firing short bursts at the Cong MG nest. "*Sat Cong!*" he began yelling. Kill commuinists. "*Sat Cong! Sat Cong!*"

"Whoaaa, buddy!" Brody tried to wave him back, but he was completely ignored.

Still screaming at the top of his lungs, he didn't even acknowledge the three GIs' presence, but leaped over their log, intent on rushing the enemy position single-handedly.

A burst of glowing green tracers struck the soldier dead center. The glory vanished from his eyes instantly. The infantryman's lifeless body was knocked back down to the ground. His machine gun twirled through the smoky air, striking Gage Ruckter in the face. Its front sight nearly gouged his eyes out.

CHAPTER 13

Dan Tieng SF Camp

Sgt. Chinh and his men could hear the thunderclaps of battle in the distance as they sat along the southern fence-line of the SF camp, oiling down their weapons. Chinh had watched the Airmobile helicopter insertions the morning before. The Americans were obviously mounting a major operation. "Attleboro," he'd heard one of the Green Berets talking about it outside the mess tent. But the Green Berets weren't actively participating in this one. Neither were the Nungs. And Capt. Soto would tell him nothing about the operation.

The gunship troopers were obviously getting themselves into some pretty hairy shit. Chinh had spent the predawn hours squatting outside the commo bunker, rubbing lube oil into his rifle's barrel and stock, listening to the excited radio chatter and finally three Brass Monkeys in a row.

Still, his command of English wasn't all that good, and the Americans were speaking rat-a-tat fast, like machine guns. He couldn't understand exactly where they were or what they were trying to accomplish, but there was no mistaking the urgency in the RTO's voice. This sounded like a battle the Americans were going to lose.

"We should go," he told Soto when the captain passed by in the misty dark, his arms piled high with rolled-up maps and documents.

"MACV needs us somewhere else," the officer responded condescendingly. MACV was always pronounced "Mac-V," but Soto preferred to say each letter individually. Chinh disliked hearing the abbbreviation in any form. References to the U.S. Military Assistance Command Vietnam were usually followed by romeo-foxtrots of one sort or another. "I'm getting the cords plotted right now. You might as well warn your troops to get ready to saddle up. We'll be choppered out before sunrise."

Soto watched Chinh salute, execute a sharp about-face, and vanish in the gloom. As his arms were full, the captain wasn't expected to return the salute. Soto didn't think he would have in any case. The fragile mutual respect that had existed prior to the Cong ambush where Chinh lost so many men was now nonexistent. And the major had declined to give him a new team. "Too many chiefs and not enough Indians as it is now," his C.O. claimed with a dry laugh. "You and your fellow officers oughta get together for a little powwow and discuss the unusally high mortality rate of said Nung-chinks." They both laughed at his little joke, but Soto was fuming as he walked out of the CP. He could feel it in his gut: Sgt. Do was disenchanted with their "working relationship." He had that conspiratorial gleam in his dark, ever-narrowed eyes. Soto had never had any of his officers fragged before, but he was beginning to feel as if such a fate was waiting just around the corner. For *himself*.

Chinh moved from hammock to hammock, silently waking his men. Bright flashes lit up the southern horizon every few seconds—but it wasn't heat lightning. The sounds told him it was close-in combat. Another fleet of gunships roared overhead as he reached the last sleeping figure.

Chinh stared at the phantomlike shapes moving below the stars. The choppers were all blacked out, in anticipa-

126

tion of hot LZs, but there was no hiding the anxious beating of rotors, and the giant, shifting silhouettes against the sky.

Chinh wished he was aboard one of them. At least he'd know where he was headed, what lay waiting for him at trip's end. At least the gunship troopers racing past overhead had a fighting chance.

With Soto, Chinh believed his men didn't even have that.

Gage Ruckter was as mad as a hornet in heat. He wasn't about to just lie there and wait for the Cong to snuff his life out like some cheap candle in the wind.

"I'm gonna turn the tables on Charlie a little bit," he told Brody and Fletcher.

"In other words, you're gonna do somethin' stupid, right?" Treat's expression told Ruckter to forget it.

"Help will be here soon," Fletcher said. "You in a hurry to die?" His outward calm could not mask the fear dancing in his eyes. "Just mellow out. Neil Nazi will figure out something. Sooner or later . . ."

"And you're dreamin'." Ruckter was shaking his head in disbelief. "What's *happened* to you guys?" he asked. "What's happened to the don't-give-a-fuck, nonchalant Whoremonger I used to know? You gettin' chickenshit in your old age, Treat?"

The taunt did not upset Brody. He'd heard it before from better men than Ruckter—soldiers who were eager to mix it up with Charlie but weren't looking at the situation logically. Brody had no shortage of courage—he lived for the taste of licoricelike gunsmoke lining his throat during a firefight, too—but he also wanted to be able to live to fight another day. In Gage's eyes, he saw that temporary insanity again.

"Just shut the fuck up for a minute and catch your breath," he told Ruckter. "Plug your left nostril and get a bead on reality, hero. Think about what you're up against . . ."

Ruckter was apparently in no mood to contemplate the situation further. And he was bored with the conversation. "Here!" He shoved the dead soldier's M-60 into Brody's arms. "Save that for me. I'll be back."

"And where the flyin' fuck do ya think you're goin'?" Fletcher curled up into the fetal position, arms wrapped around his helmeted head, as a barrage of mortars dropped in a crude circle around their position.

"I'm tired o' bein' a sitting duck!" Ruckter screamed back as a long string of bullets tore more bark from their log.

"But—"

"I'm gonna turn the tables a little. . . . I'm gonna take the ambush war to those yellow fucks and see how *they* like it!"

"But—"

Gage Ruckter was already up and running.

Brody chanced a peek. When he peered through the bullet-riddled log's top layer of splinters, his eyes were treated to a jackrabbit's footwork: Ruckter dove an instant after leaving the log's cover.

He rolled, then abruptly flew to his feet, darted in the opposite direction, zigged when you would have thought he would zag, somersaulted through a clump of reeds, low-crawled through some elephant grass, and flew to his feet again, only to jump in the air and bounce off toward the nearest tree line the instant his body struck the ground.

Charlie was apparently startled by Ruckter's hyper antics. He had nearly reached the tree line before a single

128

shot was fired his direction, and by then, it was too late—Gage had made it behind cover.

"Impossible!" Fletcher was laughing. "But *now* what's he gonna do for an encore?"

The rolling blast from additional mortars began walking the field nearby—walking away. They were not trying to zero in on the log any longer. Perhaps they thought Ruckter had been the only one there.

"What the hell's he tryin' to do now?" Snakeman was no longer laughing as he watched Ruckter dive from tree to tree, moving closer to the Cong position.

"Trying to put the fuckers out of their misery," Brody whispered with glazed eyes.

CHAPTER 14

15th Medical Battalion MAST, Outskirts of Tay Ninh....

Lisa Maddox shook with a start when the alert siren began squawking. Some of the coffee in the cup she was holding to her lips splashed onto her chest. a mixture of irritation and hopelessness contracted her features. She threw the foam cup over a shoulder.

"That's us." Delgado sighed. Medic and MAST lieutenant stood and dashed from the mess tent, heading for the Dustoff helipad.

"Doesn't look good." Lisa stared at dark storm clouds massing on the western horizon. The sun was slowly falling behind them, its searing outline a dark, flickering orange. In the east, it was already dark. Stars hung heavy and low in all their tropical splendor at the clouds' edge.

Their med-evac pilot was already cranking up his Huey as they trotted across the tarmac carrying a full load of emergency gear. The metal tarmac's ripples creaked and groaned under the weight of anxious footfalls. Hissing turbines filled the air—several other slicks were preparing to scramble as well. "Must be a bad one," Doc Delgado observed.

Lisa grabbed his arm gently after they jumped up over the landing skids into the cabin and strapped in. "It doesn't feel good."

"It's the storm," Delgado sought to reassure her. "The electricity in their air. I'll bet its even making your pubic hairs stand up, ain't it, honey?"

The peter pilot glanced back over his shoulder as they prepared to lift off. He was smiling slightly, though he hadn't heard their conversation, due to the whirring rotor-blades overhead. Just the sight of Lisa Maddox was enough to excite most chopperjocks. Having her aboard could only be considered a good omen, a lucky charm—*two* lucky charms, actually, and that didn't include Delgado.

There were pilots who refused to have Army flight nurses aboard their ships, of course, considering it bookoo *bad* luck, but not these two. They enjoyed a flash of blond, a hint of shapely curves now and then—though Maddox's Army-issue, mint-green coveralls were anything but flattering. Any "Jody" was a sight for sore eyes to them. And to think that Doc—a mere buck sergeant—was poking this young thing on his time off.

"You're really not worried, are you?" Lisa leaned closer to Delgado as the helicopter rose quickly above the camp's sparkling perimeter of concertina.

He stared at the ship's landing skids as they passed only a foot or two above the razor-sharp barbs. "Of course I'm worried"—he sighed—"but what do you expect me to do about it?"

Lisa followed his gaze. "Well," she began hesitantly, "it's just that . . . well, I was beginning to think . . . the way you've been acting lately. . ."

"Yes?" he locked eyes with her finally.

"I'm beginning to think you're starting to like this job. And don't tell me 'it's what I do.' I don't want to her that, Danny."

"You want to hear something with a bit more . . . substance?"

Maddox paused only a moment. "For a start . . . yes," she said.

132

"What choice do I have? It's not as if I could just split. I want to keep my record clean, so I can . . . make something of myself when I get back to The World, you know?"

"I know, but that doesn't really apply, does it?"

Their words were interrupted by a crescendo of dull explosions in the distance.

"Just thunder," he said.

None of the tension seemed to leave her eyes. "It's not as if this were your first tour in Vietnam," she said. "How many years has it been, Danny—going on three now?"

"*You've* just extended," he pointed out almost accusingly.

"To be with *you*," she reminded him with an elbow jab.

The ship began to shake, and she grasped his wrist. "Sorry 'bout that," the copilot clicked in. "Just turbulence. Looks like a doozy of a storm up ahead. And we're beatin' blades directly into the heart of—"

"What kind of injuries are we looking at?" Lt. Maddox interrupted him as she unlatched, dropped to her knees in the center of the cabin, and set about readying their gear.

"No idea, ma'am. Just got a call for Dustoffs—as many as Tay Ninh could spare. Don' look good, though. . . ."

"It never does," she muttered under her breath.

The ship began to shudder and tremble again—more violently than before. "Lima Zulu comin' up on our starboard," the AC warned. "Looks like a mighty hot one, Lieutenant. . . ."

"Thanks, Mac," Lisa clicked in.

Rain was slashing at the open hatches. The cabin floor was already slick with it. A lightning bolt lanced down close by with an earsplitting thunderclap, leaving a deafening ring to Lt. Maddox's eardrums and her night vision temporarily destroyed. Tracers arced up all around. They had definitely entered two storms. She wondered which one posed the more danger.

They listened to the pilots struggling with the sudden fierceness of the storm—all the while the sounds of the battle below reaching their ears.

"Un-fucking-real." Delgado had to use both hands to hold on to the ship now—it was as if they were in a tornado. The roar of rain coming down on the helicopter's roof and walls was louder than the rotor downblast itself.

"Try it again," they heard the pilot urging as visibility fell to zero. Lightning blinded them. Sheets of rain slapped at their faces.

"Forget it, Joe-Joe." The AC was talking to his peter pilot as if the man outranked him. Delgado wondered who was actually doing the flying. But it didn't matter. "Take 'er outta this soup—ain't worth all our asses, brother!"

"Motion carried," the copilot switched frequencies, advising Tango Charlie they would be unable to land at the battlefield outside Dau Tieng due to zero visibility. They would hover nearby until the storm passed or until they ran critically low on fuel.

The helicopter abruptly ascended, forcing both Doc Delgado and Lt. Maddox against the floorboards.

"Well, scrub *that* med-evac." The corpsman shook his head.

"Those poor boys." Lisa Maddox was holding on to the doorgunner's lifeline support bar now as she stared down out of the hatch, trying to spot the firefight. All she could see, however, was a solid wall of water, swirling down with the rotorwash, a gray funnel in the heart of hell.

At first, Brody thought trees felled by the lightning had come crashing down on either side of him and Fletcher, but the objects diving for cover breathed and cursed.

134

"Welcome to the party!" Snakeman recognized the darkest face of the four: Sgt. Zack's. Beads of perspiration covered the black NCO's shaved crown.

"We were sure you fuckwads were dead!" Lt. Vance was with him.

"You should be so lucky!" Brody replied, as thunder rolled across the heavens above.

"Did you guys hear choppers a minute ago?" Fletcher asked the lieutenant.

"Yeah!" A stocky, bronze-skinned soldier of medium height answered for the officer. "But this storm's too strong." Chance Broken Arrow. American Indian—Comanche, to be precise. A no-nonsense trooper, with several tours of Nam duty under his belt now.

"They're probably hangin' back a coupla klicks out," Leo the Lionhearted finally spoke up. For the first time, Brody noticed rivulets of blood along his thick neck mixing with the raindrops.

"I thought I spotted someone else here with you," Vance said.

"Ruckter, Lou. Gage Ruckter—an E-Five from the Fourth. He was on that ash-'n-trash Charlie dropped into the swamp," answered Brody.

"Ah, yes . . ."

Zack was turning over the facedown corpse lying at one end of the log. He waited for lightning to flash overhead and illuminate the dead soldier's face before gently dropping it back into place. "Sorry, stranger," he muttered to himself. Turning to the lieutenant, he said aloud, "Didn't know him."

"So just exactly where *is* young Ruckter?" Vance withdrew the banana clip from his M-16 and began forcing loose rounds from a thigh pocket into the magazine's open top.

"He took off sprintin' through the open field there"—

135

Fletcher's arm rose only slightly to encompass the oppressive darkness—"carryin' some old World War II submachine gun."

"An MP-40," Brody added.

"Christ." Vance slid the full clip back into his rifle's feeder well and tapped the bottom with the palm of his hand until it snapped securely in place.

"Yeah. That was nearly an hour ago. Charlie was lightin' up the twilight, tryin' to take him down with sheer firepower—I don't know if they got him or not. I never saw any return fire from where we last saw him. . . ."

"But we been keeping our heads down," Fletcher admitted.

"What do you suggest we do?" Brody asked the lieutenant.

"Well, this is the One-ninety-sixth's show, but—"

"But they're kinda hurtin' for decision makers right now," Brody reminded him sarcastically. From what the gunship troopers could see immediately after responding to the Brass Monkey, most of the ground infantry unit's officers had already been killed.

"Right now, I think our best bet is just to ride out this storm," Vance said. "It's keepin' Charlie's movements restricted, too."

"That's exactly why we should attack that MG nest *now*," Zack argued with obvious determination in his eyes.

"How so, Sergeant?"

"Charlie thinks the Americans are soft. He thinks we're dug in for the storm . . . for the night. Ruckter's got the right idea. Take the fight to the VC. Treat 'em to some of their own hit-and-run tactics. The trouble is, I think they canceled Ruckter's ticket." He turned to face Brody. "It's been nearly an hour, you say?"

"Right. He might just be layin' dog, though. Or maybe that German sub-Mag o' his don't even shoot—hell only

136

knows where Gage came up with something like *that* on such short notice!"

"You guys are all fucking nuts!" The fourth soldier who had charged up to their position with Vance, Zack, and Broken Arrow spoke up for the first time.

Reece Jones.

Brody's eyes narrowed. He felt his chin rise challengingly in the darkness. He felt like throwing a punch just for the hell of it. "What?" he asked instead, his tone telling the private he was speaking for the lieutenant as well.

"What the hell are we even doin' out here?" Jones's eyes seemed to glow against the black of night. "We should be back in the rear, searchin' for a shack-up job or short-time girl. *I* should be down in Saigon, damnit! I'm a lover, not a—"

"Don't say it," Zack growled.

"We're *out here*," Vance said, between lightning bolts, "because One-Niner-Six called for help, and we were the nearest GIs around, and I suggest we concentrate on figuring out how to accomplish Sgt. Zack's plan," Lt. Vance said. "I've thought it over, and I agree: We shouldn't wait until dawn. We need to act now—while the storm's got everybody on both sides disoriented."

"Let's not give the downpour so much credit, sir." Zack's voice sounded pained. It frightened Jacob Vance. Zack was the experienced NCO he counted on to keep them alive . . . to pull them through . . . to get this mission accomplished. And now he wasn't sounding so confident anymore. "Charlie's been livin' in these hills all his life," Zack went on. "He's up to the monsoon. He sleeps and screws when it rains. The only thing we got goin' for us tonight is that it's dark, *as well as* raining, and, contrary to popular belief, Charlie does *not* own the night, gentlemen."

"Then it's unanimous." Vance did not ask for other opinions. "We make our move now."

"Hey!" Jones protested as three green tracers floated past overhead and disappeared in the black distance. "It *ain't* fuckin' unanimous, *sir*—with all due respect! I think we oughta wait for Mista Sun to show his face, then we can radio for—"

"Listen up!" Fletcher reached out in the darkness and latched onto the front of Jones's shirt. He pulled the dissenter close so he would be sure to miss none of the harsh words. "Ruckter's one o' my buddies," he said, "and we're going to do everything possible to give him some much-deserved support out there."

"Okay!" Jones pushed Fletcher away, and Vance low-crawled between them. "But I just hope that crazy fuckin' buddy o' yours—if he ain't dead—don't accidentally blow *us* away in the process when we go tiptoein' through the elephant grass to check on 'im!"

"I hope not, too," Lt. Vance snapped loudly, "'cause *you're* gonna be walkin' point, slick."

CHAPTER 15

Jungles outside Dau Tieng

Gage Ruckter had been sucking rainwater for going on two hours now. It was raining so hard, in fact, he'd almost lost his bearings. In the jungle, monsoon downpours were no big problem—there was usually enough of a canopy overhead to filter out the storm, leaving only a fine mist and preserving visibility, for the most part. Here, though, he was crouching behind tombstones and charred treetrunks, trying to keep the enemy machine-gun nest in sight—but there was little cover this far from the main tree line to shelter him from the rain. The VC, on the other hand, *did* have a thatched splinter of the rain-forest ceiling above to protect them. Ruckter was relying on the incessant lightning to keep Charlie guessing—the Asians' night vision hampered, their eyes following the shifting collage of shadows and wondering which might be the American.

Surely they knew Ruckter was coming to get them.

The storm was hampering his own progress, of course. Now and then, when he cowered against the fierce, stinging sheets of rain, he became disoriented and would have to wait for the VC to fire off a wild round or two before he could get his bearings again.

Now was just such a time.

He was standing against a lone tree—the highest one

away from the main tree line. The MP-40 had no stock extension, for it was a rather compact submachine gun, though it was heavy. Waiting for an outgoing tracer to mark the exact location of the MG nest again, Ruckter felt awkward bracing for a carefully aimed shot, with nothing to rest against his shoulder, but he didn't have long to hold his breath.

As lightning flashed directly overhead, he spotted three Viet Cong between several stacked and heavily camouflaged logs. One had both hands on an old, French-made Hotchkiss. Another was keeping the long belts of machine-gun ammo untangled. The third held binoculars to his eyes. He was scanning the hedgerows Ruckter had first sprinted into after leaving Brody and Fletcher.

Trying to keep his bursts down to two or three rounds each, Ruckter fired at the trigger man, then shifted an inch to the left, attempting to take out the spotter.

All three Vietnamese were catapulted backwards as the rounds crashed into their chests.

Ruckter ran as hard as he could toward the three, but they lay motionless in the muck when he slid up to their trench.

He'd been keeping careful track of how many rounds he fired with the MP-40, and he was sure he had five left. Somewhere, he'd lost all the extra magazines except one. He switched ammo clips so that a full complement of rounds was ready to go. By light from the silver bolts spider-webbing across the heavens, he saw that there were three AK-47s to choose from, if he desired added firepower.

Slinging the MP-40, he dropped to one knee amongst the dead communists, drew the commando knife from a sheath taped to his calf, and began slitting throats.

* * *

Young VC apprentice sharpshooter Ruong Nhu Toai would never be able to recite the communist chain of command to you. He was not even sure if communism was what he wanted to dedicate his life to, though he was well aware that he had *risked* his life for Ho Chi Minh and the honcho-san's hammer-and-sickle ideals. But Toai was not sure his heart was truly with the North·Vietnamese cause.

Toai, though he didn't stay awake nights worrying about it, considered himself more a nationalist than anything else. If only his brother Vietnamese in the north could come to an understanding with the strongmen in Saigon, perhaps peace would return to his homeland. Reunification was the answer, Toai was convinced—not communism. The people would not stand for communism. Too many restrictions. Saigon, the southern capital, would *certainly* never cooperate. But such were problems for old-timers with more wisdom than himself to ponder.

Toai did not talk about his feelings. They did not really matter, in the long run—in the big scheme of things to come in Indochina. All the young rifleman wanted was to please his parents in Hue, the Imperial City, where he'd been "drafted" by the Viet Cong and sent south on the Ho Chi Minh Trail to fight the Arvin.

He wondered if his parents would hear that he'd downed the American helicopter. It would make them proud, he was sure. Though they considered themselves apolitical, his parents seemed to side more with the guerrillas, if only because they wanted the Americans out of their country. His parents worshiped the emperor's memory above all else, and didn't feel there was anything outside Hue left to fight for; but, as insurance against the chance the South

Vietnamese army might try to force Toai into uniform as he approached draft age, his father began saving to send the youth out of the country to Taiwan or Hong Kong to attend school. Not an easy feat for a chopsticks manufacturer.

Then the VC breezed through town one midnight and snatched Toai away first.

"You did not shoot down any gunships today," a taunting voice filtered through the thick bamboo.

Toai was busy cutting a shelter from the rain with his machete. He glanced up to see his friend Thieu. The VC had kidnapped Thieu the same night they got Toai. Thieu was having a hard time of it. The cadre members picked on him a lot, which was not unusual—considering his first name was the same as the South Vietnamese president's. But he was determined to become a good VC soldier. Just like Toai. When Thieu emerged from behind the bamboo, he was wearing a combination poncho lining and oversized mosquito net. The net had obviously been originally made to be draped over a bed or sleeping cot. It gave Thieu a somewhat comical appearance, which was enhanced when one took in the ancient Viet Minh carbine he was carrying.

Toai smiled at Thieu. "It has been less than twenty-four hours." He laughed as the rain beat down on them. "And all the action is miles away at Dau Tieng. I can still hear it."

"Yes," Thieu said, though all *he* could hear was thunder booming overhead.

"Teacher gives me no chance to shoot down another. You heard him warn against 'wasting ammo trying to match Toai's lucky shot.'"

"But you are a good shot." Thieu squatted beside his childhood friend. "An *excellent* shot."

"Yes," Toai admitted without arrogance. He was well aware of his skill with a rifle—he worked hard at this "craft" every day, and preferred shooting to following in

142

his father's footsteps in the chopsticks business. "Even the helicopter pilots defy me by avoiding the area," he said matter-of-factly, "but it is only a matter of time before Teacher realizes we are needed more at Dau Tieng than down in Saigon."

They had called their commander "Teacher" ever since being assigned to this, their first field unit. At least it was classified as a field unit by the VC, but their commander seemed to spend more time teaching them communist ideology and the evil ways of Western influence and imperialism than actually engaging any of the hairy-armed long-noses in combat.

"Do you miss Hue?" Thieu asked unexpectedly as Toai finished fashioning his natural umbrella in the high wall of bamboo.

"Hue?" he stood there unmoving, the raindrops sliding down his pith helmet and falling from his nose.

"Yes, Hue." Thieu's expression became one of agitation. "Surely you have not forgotten your home . . . your family. And what of—"

"I think of them every day . . . every night," Toai admitted, "but—"

"But?" the storm was making Thieu impatient.

"Being here . . . being a part of the war is more important."

"You told me you do not care one way or the other for communism. You told me—"

Toai gently placed a hand over Thieu's mouth. He glanced around, but Teacher was nowhere near—only the men sleeping in hammocks suspended from rubber-tree branches. "Communism, no. But we must rid Vietnam of the foreigners. After that, we can return to our families. After that, everything can return to . . . the way it once was."

"There has always been war," Thieu reminded him.

Toai frowned. "Perhaps you are right. That makes what I am saying all the more important."

"I don't understand, Toai."

Such a child. Toai smiled, shaking his head slowly. "*We* will be the first to make Vietnam totally free," he said. "Don't you see that? *We* shall be the true heroes. Peace will finally come to this land, Thieu, and *we* will be the ones who have brought it. It will be . . . glorious."

"Do you miss Linh?"

Toai's smile faded, and his eyes dropped from the dark sky above, where he had been seeking stars but was rewarded only with the ceaseless rainfall. "Of course I miss her." Carefully, he pulled his diary from its plastic wrapper and showed Thieu what he was using as the bookmark: a laminated photo of a young Vietnamese woman.

Thieu stared at the long black hair and dark eyes, the nervous smile. "Linh . . ." he whispered.

"Yes," Toai said proudly. "It took me weeks to find a shopkeeper who would develop the film without telling father." That was because the photo showed Linh naked to her slender waist. She was holding her bare breasts, lifting the taut nipples for the photographer, Toai.

"Your mother would kill you if she ever saw this." Thieu giggled.

"The Americans might kill me, too," Toai replied, lifting the picture to his lips. "So what? We all must die. Another life awaits us, Thieu."

Thieu stared at the photo. Linh's breasts were modest, but he had never seen such huge nipples before! He thought back to all the days they had spent following her around Hue, flirting. He never imagined such wonderful breasts lurked beneath Linh's tightly wrapped *ao dai*. "She is two years older than you," Thieu reminded him.

144

"Yes, but I shall marry Linh when I return victorious to the Imperial City."

"I believe you shall," Thieu said encouragingly. "May I look at the photo again?"

Laughing softly, Toai handed it over.

CHAPTER 16

Jungles outside Dau Tieng

"Hell, if I'd o' known we had party crashers, I'd o' brought a couple more souvenirs back with me!"

Gage Ruckter flew through the night, landing boots-first in the muck between Brody and Fletcher. He slammed down the three captured AKs with fierce momentum. Zack winced as one of the stocks cracked loudly.

"Was that *you* knocked out that MG nest?" Lt. Vance appeared startled by the buck sergeant's sudden appearance. The group huddled around the new arrival.

"You know any other heroes trompin' about out there right now?" Ruckter lifted one of the Soviet-built rifles and tossed it to the officer. "There's a Hotchkiss back there, too—that's what the zip mothers were usin', but I accidentally smashed the action with one o' my shots. Didn't figure it was worth humpin' all the way back over here with."

"Definitely Silver Star material." Zack glanced back at the lieutenant, as if the officer should make a written note of it. Vance simply stared back, dumbfounded.

Before he could respond, Ruckter said, "I don't want no damn medals, Lou. Just a decent M-16! Then point me in the right direction—"

"And let go of his leash!" Jones muttered.

Ruckter's expression softened. His eyes scanned the rest of the soldiers, seeking out the source of the familiar voice.

They came to rest on Jones, and he squinted. "Reece-baby?" he asked. "Is that really fucking you?"

"Yep," came the single-word reply.

The others were probably expecting to see a sudden bearhug. Instead, Ruckter unloaded with a roundhouse punch.

His fist connected solidly. Jones went down, out cold.

"Hey!" Vance rushed forward on his knees as red, white, and green tracers crisscrossed the night sky only a few feet overhead.

"The dumb fuck owes me a hundred bucks, sir." Ruckter assumed the expression of a crime victim. He began rubbing his knuckles as Zack checked on Jones.

"You didn't have to hit him," the lieutenant argued. "Especially in front of me! What if he wants to press charges?"

"Sure I did, sir. And don't worry—he won't. Reece Jones is nothin' but a back-stabbin' little worthless piece o' shit."

"I think we get the jist of your feelings toward Pvt. Jones," Vance said. "Now why don't you start acting like a sergeant, and—"

"No sweat, sir," Ruckter moved over to the dead soldier's body—the one who had tried to assault the enemy machine-gun nest earlier, only to get blown off his feet. "I think I've gotten Reece the Grease out of my system. For now."

"Good," Vance replied.

Brody turned to Snakeman. *Reece the Grease?* his eyes seemed to say. *Well, that explains everything. . . .*

Gage turned to Brody. "Hey," he said, "where's this guy's M-60? Didn't I leave it with you and the Snakeman for safekeeping?"

"We put it under the guy's body," Fletcher said. "To get it out of the rain."

                                    *   *   *

"We're going to give it another shot."

"Okay." Lisa Maddox nodded. But she thought the chopper pilots were crazy. The storm seemed worse now than when they had had to abort the first time.

Her free hand grasped Danny Delgado's wrist as the Huey tilted to the left, swinging around back toward Dau Tieng and the storm.

Doc glanced at a string of bright stars hanging out one hatch, but the night quickly became a black blanket of clouds again, and rain was soon lashing at the doorgun, as before.

The lieutenant's free hand was checking syrettes in her aid bag. Painkiller. She felt like jabbing herself with a handful of them. This was not working out. This was definitely not working out at all.

But wasn't that how it *always* happened with two lovers? Especially in a war zone. Two years of sneaking around and goofing off, hopping in and out of each other's rack, trying to set records with each other while the war went on, almost unnoticed. Then, the instant you got serious, talking commitments and mortgages and some kind of future, reality and the true impact of your surroundings set in, and the days suddenly became weeks, the weeks months. Everything was dangerous now—no longer a lark . . . the mission's hours a millenium of stress and uncertainty.

"This sucks, Danny-boy."

"We'll get through it." Delgado squeezed her hand.

"Lima Zulu in dirty sex, ladies and germs!" The peter pilot's voice came back to them over the intercom, lifeless and plastic.

Delgado drew the .45 automatic from his holster and

dropped to one knee beside the port hatch. He could sense it immediately—again, they were not landing.

The AC had pulled the chopper's snout up. The craft was ascending . . . circling back around. "Don't look right, Mac . . ." They heard the peter pilot complaining. "Everything's different down there. . . ."

"Yep . . . they've changed positions on us. I'm not even sure what happened to the old LZ. Looks like it fucking washed away, Jed."

"What a royal clusterfuck."

"Yep. I knew I shoulda joined the Navy."

"At least they're smart enough to bring out the boats when the shit starts to flow this deep."

"Yep."

Below, only 50 or 60 yards down, Delgado could clearly see the American and Viet Cong positions in the flashes of lightning, despite the heavy rainfall. It appeared there were several separate skirmishes going on, actually —all along one side of the swamp. Out of restless desperation, he fired an entire clip—seven bullets—down at a cluster of pith helmets, well aware he was beyond the pistol's maximum effective range. But he was angry—angry at Charlie, angry at his present predicament in life—and he had to take it out on somebody or something. Perhaps the fact that they were flying over the target and he was shooting almost straight down would help. Before he could tell if any of the rounds had struck home, though, the AC was banking sharply to the right and Delgado's face was pelted with sheets of rainwater.

A burst of green tracer was chasing up after the Huey, and the AC struggled with the controls, trying to outmaneuver the subsequent bursts of glowing white rounds that followed.

Potshots were floating up from different spots, trying to hit the craft, but one particular rifleman on the ground, far away from the main cluster of VC positions, seemed especially persistent.

"Are we gonna land or what?" Delgado yelled up at the two warrant officers in the cockpit.

"Good question!" the copilot shot back as they swung out far from the original landing zone.

Lisa was following Doc's example. She took the M-16 from its makeshift emergency-armament compartment against one wall and dropped to both knees beside the opposite hatch. "Well, if we're not going to land," she cried, "take us over the spot where that goofy little bastard with the green tracers is at!"

"Your wish is my command, Lieutenant. . . ." the pilot pulled up so abruptly that Maddox was thrown back onto her bottom again. Under his breath to the warrant officer beside him, he added, "Fucking cunt."

Ramming a thirty-round banana clip into the rifle, Maddox heard every word, but she ignored them. It didn't matter anymore. The void was calling to her. Tonight's the night. Fuck 'em all!

She yanked back the M-16's charging handle, chambering a live round. Then, on semi-automatic, she began firing down at the patch of black where the VC sharpshooter's tracers were originating.

Toai dove from the huge boulder, but not quickly enough.

Splinters of lead dug into his buttocks, and he was unable to suppress a loud, startled cry. He rolled toward the trees as the American Army gunship made a low pass directly overhead.

Before scampering from sight beneath the thick foliage, he caught a glimpse of the woman hanging out the side hatch—a round-eyed woman with white hair . . .

"Choi-oi!" he yelled, rubbing the superficial wounds on his bottom.

"We should get back to the unit!" Thieu was frightened. He never imagined that, in this pitch-black darkness, they would ever be able to attract the attention of an enemy helicopter. He had forgotten what a good shot Toai was.

"I think I've hit it!" Toai was not listening to what his friend said. "I wish it would make another pass. If it does, I will get it this time for sure!"

"But your weapon! You lost your rifle!" Thieu observed. "And you are bleeding!"

"It is not bad—it doesn't even hurt!" Toai was riding high on the adrenaline rush. And the woman—he had never seen such a thing before in his life!

"She looked like the messenger of death!" Thieu's thoughts mirrored his own. "Did you see her hair—all white!" In Vietnam, white is the color of mourning—the prominent color at funerals.

Lt. Vance slammed the receiver of the PR-25 radio.

"They say they can't get Dustoffs in here because of the storm!" he snapped. "'Zero visibility,' or some such shit!"

Raindrops pelting his grimace, Leo Zack glanced up at the dark skies. "Makes sense to me," he said.

Another young lieutenant had made his way to their position from the ranks of wounded infantrymen 50 yards away. Except for a seriously wounded captain, he was the only officer left from the two companies originally inserted into the area. "We've gotta get a med-evac for the captain!" he insisted. "There's no way he'll last until dawn!"

"I don't know what to tell you," Vance said. "'God,'" he motioned toward the field radio, "says 'No Can Do.' We're on our own."

"And I suggest we make our first priority trying to secure this side of the cemetery," Zack said. "That swamp forms a natural boundary we can guide on. If I take some men over to where the rubber plantation ends and the jungle begins, then work our way back over the next couple hours . . ."

"Icing every guerrilla you come across . . ." Vance nodded.

"Right. Then we'll have that high ground there secured . . . maybe even before the sun comes up, if we're lucky, and we work fast."

"Then we'll have an LZ for the slicks to land in!" the infantry lieutenant's disposition improved as the possibilities began to register.

"Right," said Vance.

"Okay, let's quit pullin' on our puds." Zack started to climb over the log. "The main thing is to get a move on before Charlie starts beefin' up—"

A cacophony of high-powered discharges lit up the night. A string of muzzle flashes set the trees and hillsides glowing directly behind the trench where Ruckter took out the first machine-gun nest.

Zack fell back into their arms.

"Jesus, Leo!" Snakeman yelled.

"Machine guns!" Brody was already firing back with his M-16. "They came back with more machine guns—at least three of 'em. I'm countin' at least *three* of 'em, Lieutenant!"

"You all right, Leo?" Vance had one eye on Brody's actions, and the other on Zack.

"You are one *lucky* motherfucker, sarge!" Snakeman said.

"If it was me, I probably woulda got my face punched out and my balls liberated!" Gage was sliding his MP-40 up over the tree's bullet-riddled bark.

"Could I maybe have some motherfucking assistance over here?" Brody had fired off an entire magazine and was now lying on his back behind the log as he ejected the empty clip and rammed home a fresh one. Tracers flew back over his face in reply. "You clowns sound like a bunch o' old ladies tonight!"

"Eat it like a man, Whorehouse," Leo the Lionhearted responded.

"Five, four, three, two . . ." After each trigger squeeze, Gage Ruckter was still counting down the number of bullets remaining in the submachine gun he had taken from the pilot in the downed helicopter. After "two," the weapon jammed. "Damn!" he hissed, throwing it down. "Where's that M-60? Gimme that M-60 over there!" He noticed that the dead soldier had brought along only a single hundred-round belt of cartridges. It was draped, Pancho Villa-style, across his chest.

"Here!" He slid the belt free himself and handed the loose end to the Air Cav lieutenant. "Make sure this shit don't get tangled up on nothin', sir!"

"Uh, right!" the officer complied without hesitation. Ruckter began firing ten- and fifteen-round bursts at the muzzle flashes 50 yards away.

"There's movement out there, Gage!" Brody warned. "Bookoo movement—can you see it? To your right . . . fire to your right, brother . . ."

"I can't see it, but I can *feel* it!" Ruckter yelled above the barking hog.

"Somethin' bad-ass terrible is goin' on out there!" Snakeman Fletcher tensed.

Suddenly, it seemed as if every enemy muzzle in the area was directed at them. Ruckter, Brody, and the others hugged the earth as the already chewed-up log began disintegrating further. Soon, there wouldn't be much of it left to afford any cover.

154

"Try callin' in some arty, Lieutenant!" Ruckter told Vance. "Call the damn rounds right in on top of us if you have to!"

Vance and the infantry officer glanced back at the RTO. The specialist was lying on his back, next to the dead machine-gunner. His face was a mushy pulp where one of the first MG bursts had struck it dead center.

"We're truly fucked, sir," Snakeman Fletcher said as he reached out, grabbed the PR-25, and dragged it back against the smoking log.

The field radio was riddled with at least a dozen bullet holes.

CHAPTER 17

Perimeter, Dau Tieng Cemetary

"Do you think they will come back looking for us?"

"Be quiet," Toai told Thieu, as they lay on the rocks overlooking the cemetery. "There is someone . . . something out there. Can you see it move?"

"No," Thieu replied in a terrified whisper. "I see only blackness."

"Watch the tracers in the distance . . . at the firefight," Toai told him. "Watch the tracers, but watch them only out of the corner of your eyes, and you will see it . . . in the foreground: movement. Someone . . . or something moving through the cemetery. *There!*"

Thieu started. "You are trying to frighten me!" he whispered harshly.

"They might be only ghosts," Toai admitted. "We need not worry about *them*. You do not fear dead soldiers, do you, Thieu? Spirits with their heads cut off and doomed to run around in circles for eternity, and have little time to bother with mere mortals such as you and I."

Thieu avoided the question. "Do you think the helicopter will come back?" The helicopter was what really worried Thieu. A minute splinter of lead, ricocheting among the rocks during its last pass twenty minutes ago, had struck Thieu in the cheek. He had never felt such pain before in his life; he had had a rather pampered childhood.

"If it does, I will shoot it down."

"I believe you, but I am afraid the ghost woman will shoot *me* again, first!"

"There it is once more!" Toai lowered his rifle and pointed straight ahead, into the solid pitch-black darkness.

"I see *nothing*!" Thieu made no effort to hide his irritation.

Toai pulled a small aluminum cylinder from a cluster in his pack. "Do you feel brave?" he asked Thieu.

"What are you planning to do?" The other youth stared at the odd-looking container. In the dim glow of crackling lightning, it seemed to be 3 or 4 inches long, and less than an inch in diameter. One end was stuffed with a wad of cardboard. The other had some sort of black, abrasive sandpaper across it.

"This is a flare. I found them on one of the dead Americans last week. Teacher told me it is not regular Army issue, but something from the civilians."

"Civilians?"

"The dead soldier wore fatigues, but maybe he had civilian friends in the United States who sent them to him. It doesn't matter. Something is out there. You think I am just playing games. I do not play games with a battle going on only half a mile away, Thieu."

Holding its top out away from his face and pointed toward the field of elephant grass separating them from the distant firefight, Toai scraped the flare's sandpaper bottom against a rock.

With a loud *woooooosh!* they watched a small, glowing projectile burst forth and shoot up into the heavens. It arced out over the closest edge of the clearing and exploded into a sizzling ball of silver that floated on the breeze for a few seconds, illuminating everything beneath it for nearly a hundred yards before flickering out.

"Oh-oh," Toai clutched at his rifle.

"Buddha be with us," Thieu whispered as they found themselves face to face with a tiger. The boy's stared at it, and the beast stared back.

"We've lost radio contact with the grunts on the ground, Lieutenant!"

Lisa Maddox stood frozen in the port hatch, M-16 rifle in one hand, the other clenched in a fist. She heard nothing the pilot was saying. "I want that bastard!" she muttered under her breath. "You hear me? Can you take us around for another pass?"

Delgado and the peter pilot exchanged pained glances. "We've already been over that stretch of rubber trees a dozen times, Lieutenant," the warrant officer said.

"Then make it *two* dozen!" Maddox screamed, firing the rifle down into the dark indiscriminately now.

Delgado's sad smile was one of resignation. Lisa had the big gun. Twirling his index finger in a circular motion near his temple to describe what he felt her current mental condition was, he then lifted his hand over his head and imitated a cowboy lassoing a cow—the signal to take the ship back over the cemetery's south edge one more time.

Delgado approached Lisa cautiously from behind. "I think you already got him, honey," he whispered into her ear.

"Bullshit, lover!"

He could see that her eyes were bulging as she peered out the hatch, down into the dark. Doc backed away slowly. She would be all right. He'd seen this before in grunts on the ground—after a vicious firefight, after Charlie had eluded them again She would snap out of it . . . with time.

Though it would be nice if they *could* spot that Cong

159

rifleman who was using the red cross emblazoned across the Huey's belly for target practice. Just one more time. He'd take up one of the hatch hogs himself, and rip the sucker to shreds. Yes, it would be nice. . . .

Delgado moved back to the cockpit. "Maybe you should just set us down outside the kill zone," he told the pilot. "Me and the lieutenant. We'll walk in."

"That's not how we usually do things around here." The copilot was shaking his head from side to side.

"Damnit, man!" Spittle flew from the corpsman's lips. "There's men down there who need a medic's help. We're not doin' anybody a shit's worth of good chasin' our tail around up here in the night."

"I think we could arrange it," the AC decided. Delgado got the immediate impression he just wanted to counteract his copilot. "Which side would you want to set down on?"

"How 'bout—"

The helicopter bolted like a bucking bronco. The snout and tail boom dropped, while the cabin's midsection buckled, rising. Both Delgado and Maddox were thrown off their feet.

The cockpit became filled with trouble sirens and bells as chip alarms began activating all across the ship. From the corner of his eye, Delgado spotted a burst of green tracer floating alongside the hatch, trying to keep up with the slick.

"There's your boyfriend!" he told Lisa.

Maddox rushed to the opposite hatch, but by the time she looked down, the last of the tracers were riding the storm currents with them—the bullets' source no longer visible. "Damn!" she protested.

Delgado suddenly had no more time for her self-pity. He returned to the cockpit. "We goin' down an' dirty?" he asked the aircraft commander.

"She's smokin' awfully bad," came the terse reply, "and we've lost the pumps to half our fuel cells. . . ."

"The hydraulics are *alllll* screwed up," the peter pilot chimed in.

". . . But I think we can get 'er back to Tay Ninh in one piece, Doc."

Delgado sighed loudly. "I pity those poor bastards down there." He closed his eyes tightly.

"There's other slicks were headed in," the AC reminded him. "Maybe one of them made it down in one piece."

"Anything over the net?"

"Nah, they're playin' the secret-shit, silence-counts game."

"The only way to go."

"I guess."

Lt. Maddox's countenance softened as they flew farther and farther away from the firefight. Slowly, she lowered the M-16 and began to tremble. She was suddenly feeling foolish and helpless, and needed somebody to hold her—to tell her it was okay . . . that it was all over.

When she turned to Delgado, Lisa screamed instead. The medic's entire back was soaked with blood.

CHAPTER 18

Jungles outside Dau Tieng

Working as a team, it took Brody, Snakeman, and Gage Ruckter just under an hour to low-crawl among the wounded and locate a working field radio.

"How close do you want to bring it in?" Fletcher asked Brody, who in turn looked to Ruckter.

"Right in on the perimeter," Ruckter responded.

"There's critically wounded men out there," Brody reminded him. "If you really wanna call that a perimeter."

It was hardly a perimeter. Their defenses were a staggered network of fallen logs and hastily dug trenchlines—the former all but totally bullet-riddled, the latter shallow and rarely interconnecting.

"No choice." Ruckter deliberated for only a few seconds. "If we don't get some arty in here and get it in here *now*, there isn't going to be *any* of us left breathin' in the morning, let alone the wounded. Can you figure out the cords of our location?" He handed Fletcher the map.

"I was top dog in my A.I.T. field-nav class!" Snakeman said grimly.

Watching him plot with the help of the steady lightning, Brody began switching frequencies on the Prick-25. Fletcher was a good doorgunner, but doorgunners in Echo Company didn't have much opportunity during their tour to

163

play boonies grunt and try their hand at calling in an artillery strike.

"Ready?" He glanced up at Treat.

"Send it."

Fletcher called in three sets of numbers. They would bombard the southern, northern, and eastern reaches of the cemetery, trying to keep the shells out of the tombstones lest the Saigon government raise hell over desecrating the resting place of the area residents' ancestors. Never mind that the area residents were more than likely hard-core Cong. Family was family.

Five tense minutes passed, then it was as if hell *had* risen. First they heard the cannon shells whistling down over their positions, then great geysers of sand and dirt exploded only a few dozen yards away. Shrapnel screamed past over their heads. Powerful concussions rolled across the land. Charlie was pulverized for nearly an hour.

Some 250 artillery shells later, Treat Brody slowly came out from beneath his helmet. Blood was trickling down along his earlobes and dripping into his mustache from his nostrils.

He waved the cloud of mosquitoes away from his face. "Jesus." Fletcher noticed the bugs, too. "They're still around, even after a barrage like *that*."

"And so, apparently, is Charlie!" Ruckter pointed to several black pajama-clad sappers running along the edge of the swamp. He drew the pistol from his hip holster and fired off all eight rounds.

One Viet Cong was knocked off his feet. Another stumbled into the swamp and sank out of sight. The other five or six began sprinting.

"Assholes!" Brody brought up his rifle and sent a ten- to fifteen-round burst after the Viet Cong. An instant later, there was a bright explosion when one of them triggered the satchel charge he was carrying.

164

"All that for nothing." Fletcher referred to the artillery.

"We probably didn't do a whole lot o' damage to those bastards," Ruckter said, "'cause they're dug in so well."

"Just blew a bunch of tree gibbons outta their monkey suits!" Brody pointed at small piles of fur scattered along the tree line. "That's all."

Slowly, one, then two, then a third enemy machine gun began strafing the American positions again. Between the long MG bursts, the three cavalrymen did their best to move among the injured, performing first aid and assessing the damage.

One thing became obvious early in the game: Whether by skill or pure accident, Charlie had succeeded in killing or critically injuring nearly all of Bravo and Charlie companies' senior noncommissioned officers. Ruckter appeared to be the most experienced sergeant left—that they were aware of, anyway. Vance, who was back with Zack and Jones, trying to hold down the southernmost perimeter, was probably the most combat-experienced officer—Charlie Company's captain was nearly dead, and the only other officer on his feet, a lieutenant fresh out of OCS, was showing courage and dedication, but little in the way of combat know-how. The infantrymen who had been airlifted into battle less than forty-eight hours earlier were fighting without leaders. They were simply trying to survive now.

"Oh, man!" Brody felt his gut belly-flop as they dropped down into a new defensive position. Five soldiers lay dead in the bottom of the dead trench.

A sixth was propped up against the earthen wall at the trench's edge. His left forearm was missing. With his right hand, he was clutching at a jagged belly wound—trying to keep his intestines from slithering out. A helpless, disgusted look molded the man's features—as if he were trying to keep his insides from getting dirty, but failing miserably.

165

"It's okay, buddy. It's okay!" Brody and Snakeman rushed to his side.

Ruckter sniffed at the air. The injuries had obviously just been inflicted in the last minute or so. He could still smell the sulfur in the air. One of the sappers had rushed through the perimeter and thrown a satchel into the trench.

On a hunch, Ruckter checked the dead more closely. He pulled the smallest body away and threw it out, facedown, into the mud. An M-16 bayonet was still implanted in his chest. "VC!" Gage responded to Brody's questioning look.

"Looks like your buddies got the bastard before they died, pal!" Fletcher helped Treat lay the man on his back. Then they went to work. Elliott tied the tourniquet across the soldier's biceps; Brody pulled the twigs and shrapnel out of his exposed intestines, then placed a bandage over the wound without trying to force the organs back inside the man's stomach cavity.

When the wounded soldier realized he was among living, breathing Americans again, he finally passed out. "You're gonna make it, buddy," Fletcher whispered into his ear. "You're gonna make it. . . ."

"Any of you carryin' morphine syrettes?" Brody asked.

"I *wish*," Ruckter answered.

"It's times like these we could sure use a fucking corpsman," Fletcher was fuming as he stared down at their handiwork. He didn't think it would be able to save the soldier in the long run—not if he had to spend much more time in this hell hole.

"I've been hearin' those med-evacs circling around up there, Snakeman!" Brody said. "They're *tryin'* to get in, but this fuckin' storm, man . . ."

"Yeah, you can't fault the slicks." Ruckter wiped dead mosquitoes from his sweaty forehead. "Have you *seen* all those tracers flyin' upstairs? I'm surprised we haven't had

166

more med-evacs droppin' in an everlovin' ball o' flames, you know?"

"Well, I could sure go for a certain sight for sore eyes." Fletcher described his battlefield fantasy: "Doc Delgado trotting up through the mist and gunsmoke with aid bags draggin' in both hands!"

"Full o' morphine!" added Brody, who was aching himself now from numerous minor shrapnel and ricochet wounds.

"Yeah!" Ruckter threw a fist in the air, carrying the motion. "So are we gonna stay with this guy, or what?"

Brody was still holding the soldier in his arms. He glanced down and went white. The man was no longer breathing. He was dead.

Bullets danced along the trench's rim, sending Ruckter and Fletcher both down on their knees and elbows. "Jesus H!" Snakeman cried as bullets crisscrossed their position, sending mud and clods of dirt flying into his face.

He lifted his M-16 above his head, pistol-fashion, but at the last moment decided not to pull the trigger—there were too many friendlies around, and he couldn't even see where the enemy rounds had originated.

"Holy shit!" Fletcher grabbed Ruckter's arm and pointed.

Sprinting toward their position in a wild charge, several dozen Viet Cong were overrunning the perimeter defenses, bayoneting the wounded men they passed and encountering little resistance. A few soldiers rose up and engaged the VC in hand-to-hand combat. Here and there, wrestling duos quickly disappeared off to the side.

There was no shortage of communists. They would soon reach the trench, and the three Americans probably didn't have enough bullets left between them to make a difference.

"It's been nice knowin' ya, Treat!" Snakeman Fletcher

patted his best friend on the back, then began wrapping an empty ammo bandolier around his knuckles, preparing for their last stint of hand-to-hand.

Strangely enough, Brody the Whoremonger wasn't very worried, though. Above the din of explosions and constant automatic weapons fire, he heard an odd noise approaching. It sounded like a fiddle.

CHAPTER 19

Perimeter of Dau Tieng Cemetery

Sgt. Do Lam Chinh thought he heard music, but he could not be sure. Still, he motioned for his men to exercise extreme caution and remain as silent as panthers on the prowl. Sgt. Chinh was able to say all this with mere hand signals because his men—what was left of them—had been together for a long time. They worked like a finely tuned, precision-crafted machine. They knew the motions as well as they knew the phases of the moon, and they knew which phases it was safe to fight under and which were best to avoid, as well. Tonight was not a good phase at all: The moon was a mere crescent, hanging low along the horizon, and orange as a cat's eyes. It was a grave robber's moon . . . a moon beneath which ghouls and panthers prowled. It was not a moon honest men could fight under with any hope of winning.

But the Nungs trusted Chinh. And Chinh was loyal to the finest warrior he had ever known in The Nam: Green Beret Sgt. Frisk.

Capt. Soto would have his head over all this, of course, but Soto was of no consequence right now. Despite all the fighting only a klick or two away, the captain was hard at work in one of the underground bunkers in the heart of Dau Tieng's Special Forces outpost, plotting some rat-fuck F.O.B. for tomorrow. Tonight was what really mattered.

Frisk had taken a squad of Green Berets out to the grave-yard to try to help out the infantrymen. And he had asked Chinh to bring his Nungs along, too.

"Take them the long way around the swamp," Frisk had told him. "Through the northern edge of the cemeteries in sector seven."

The cemeteries in sector 7. Plural. Bookoo. More than just one graveyard to prance through.

That was what Chinh's men really hated about Dau Tieng. It was sacred ground to the thousands of Buddhists in Tay Ninh Province who needed a place to bury their dead and worship their ancestors. There was not one but many interlocking cemeteries in the region. Vast fingers of the Michelin Rubber Plantation pressed against the jungle's edge, and in between the fingers lay graveyards that varied in age and size depending on which field of elephant grass you were walking through. Some were well taken care of; others were overgrown with weeds and creeping probes from the jungle itself. Chinh's men were often tripped up by wait-a-minute vines clinging to the low tombstones.

"We are going to insert along the southeast sector," Frisk had told him, "and work our way north by northwest. The largest group of GIs still hangin' in there are clustered around Big Boy. That's where we'll be."

"Right, Sergeant."

"Big Boy" was a huge, 12-foot-tall blue-gray statue of Buddha that stood in the middle of one of the most ancient cemeteries—some of the graves were 800 or 900 years old, the province chief had told Chinh.

"You work your men down to our position, taking out as many of the Cong bastards as you can."

"Of course, Sergeant."

"By the time we rendezvous at Big Boy, we oughta have a better idea of how things stand, okay?"

"Yes, Sergeant."

"And quit calling me 'Sergeant,' okay Chinh?" The Nung nodded in noble reply. "Just call me 'Sarge.'"

It had been a joke. Chinh, nodding with his most gracious smile and troubled eyes, did not get it. "Okay, Sarge."

Now they lay behind scrub brush on a low hill overlooking Big Boy, and there was obviously a large body of enemy soldiers dug in between them. Chinh alone could make out fifty or sixty AK bayonets being swung into place.

The VC were preparing to rush the Americans before the storm got any worse.

The rain had stopped momentarily. The wind still screamed at the earth, though, tearing at the uniforms of both sides, and now and then a mortar would enlarge a mud puddle. High walls of black cloud rose up in the night like a castle's walls erected around the maze of clearings and rubber trees near Dau Tieng. The clouds seemed to be waiting for something. Chinh wished he could view the storm from on high, in a helicopter or jet fighter.

From his vantage point, he could not see any of the American troops, including Frisk's element. Below the Nungs' hilltop, a deep gulley dipped, then rose to another, lower hill. The VC were massing just below its summit. Beyond, a patch of rubber trees, then the fields of elephant grass and tombstones extending several miles to a winding ribbon of trees, and, finally, thick, nearly impenetrable jungle.

Chinh signaled for one of his corporals lying a dozen feet away to fire a flare. It would tell Frisk that the Nungs were attacking, and would also pinpoint the enemy's exact position.

The corporal hesitated. Chinh's eyes burned into the man, but another soldier at his side nudged the sergeant.

"This is wrong," he whispered. "We are only inviting our own annihilation. They outnumber us fifty to one."

Chinh did not speak immediately. His eyes showed surprise that the man dared challenge him—and on the verge of battle, at the edge of their sworn enemy's position! "Are you taking over this squad?" His lips barely moved. Chinh sensed the indecision . . . the shifting of loyalties among his other men. He could see it in their faces.

"We have agreed amongst ourselves." The soldier was a sergeant, like himself. "No man here wants to die for the Americans."

"We are not dying 'for the Americans'" Chinh hissed. "If we die, we die for Vietnam—not for any of the long-noses!" Chinh did not fully believe his own words. He loved Frisk as a brother, but some of the other Americans —like Soto—he could easily do without. He tried to remind himself they were in his country as guests, that they were making sacrifices of their own to keep Vietnam free of communist tyranny. But he could not thoroughly convince himself of this.

"Don't die for the foreigners, Sergeant. . . ."

"Shut up!" Chinh snapped back, gunhand resting on the holstered .45 hanging from his web belt.

Episodes like the one in which Soto gave extraction priority to a slickful of captured assault rifles instead of wounded Nungs were bound to stay fresh in the minds of his men. That they were ambushed shortly after the helicopter rose away into the night did not help matters any. Soto could not be behind the ambush, of course, but his poor judgment had cost Chinh's people dearly. The memory made it easy for Chinh to understand his men's motives, but not to approve of them. He was a sergeant. There was a mission waiting for them to accomplish. And he'd be damned if he would fail in front of Frisk.

"Many of the men do not even care to die for 'Vietnam,'" the younger sergeant said. "We feel our needs would better be served by a separate state. A separate home for the Nungs."

"Your home may very well be hell"—Chinh's eyes narrowed until they appeared almost closed—"if we do not proceed soon. You and 'your people' are picking a stupid time to rebel and declare your independence from Annam. Even if we turned back now . . . even if we *tried* to return to Dau Tieng, I doubt our movements would go undetected. It is a miracle we got this far. Either way, we will get into a fight. We might as well be fighting for something." Chinh motioned for the corporal to fire the flare again. "Only schoolgirls retreat from something they have started," he muttered.

Once more, the soldier hesitated.

Chinh's hand slid off the holster's rainflap. He laid his rifle down gently. With his left hand, he pulled a flare from his own ruck. Then, with his gunhand, he suddenly drew his pistol and shot first the sergeant beside him, then the corporal who had refused to launch the flare.

A bright light burst over the Viet Cong positions suddenly. One of the other Nungs had fired a flare for Chinh. The sergeant shot his own skyward as well. Other dull pops sounded. Soon, four silver balls of light were floating over the raging firefight, and half of Chinh's men began their charge down toward the communists.

They were not doing as instructed! Brave acts, indeed, but foolish—oh, so foolish. Chinh fired off an entire magazine at the startled guerrillas lying below, killing five before they could seek alternate cover. *Then* he began his charge down the hillside, bayonet fixed. Chinh was yelling, but no one was listening to him.

The monstrous blast catapulted him backwards, over the hilltop and on top of the Nung sergeant he had executed. A dozen of his other men lay in various stages of disabling

173

pain along the summit. The first wave of Nungs who had charged down the hillside were all dead, victims of a trip-wire.

"Oh, no . . . no!" Chinh exclaimed in horror. It was all going down wrong.

The VC were no fools. They had strung several clay-mores along their rear approaches. Just in case Green Berets or Nungs or some other fanatics were creeping through the wait-a-minute vines, bent on throwing a sur-prise party.

Chinh jumped to his feet and struggled back up to the summit, over bodies and debris. His squad of ten men had been decimated. Half appeared dead—few could have sur-vived such traumatic wounds: severed arms and legs, a missing head here, an entire lower torso gone there . . .

He fired his rifle on full-auto until the bolt locked back on an empty chamber, then he ejected the banana clip and struggled to slide a fresh magazine into the weapon. His fingers would not work. He was shaking.

Finally, the clip slid home, and he was firing again—picking off Cong quite easily, left and right, from this high vantage point overlooking their position. But then the flares began going out one by one, and the cloak of dark-ness fell over the graveyards and elephant grass again.

Tracers crisscrossed the tombstones, and another volley of flares floated out over the scene. Larger flares, this time suspended beneath silk parachutes, dropped by the gun-ships circling overhead. In their flickering shards of gold and silver he could see a squad of Americans zigzagging through the tombstones, rushing toward a pinned-down in-fantry position farther away. The runners were wearing green berets, but he did not recognize Frisk.

A soldier was groaning at Chinh's feet, and he dropped to one knee to check the man's injuries. Bullet wounds to the stomach—painful, but he would live, if Chinh could get him back to the SF camp. Quickly, he pulled a half-empty ammunition bandolier from around the soldier's neck and began wrapping the wound, trying to stem the flow of blood. The soldier was regaining consciousness now. "Direct pressure!" Chinh told the man, grabbing his hand and placing it where the makeshift bandage covered the worst part of the injury. It was the only first aid Chinh could remember right now.

Still carrying his rifle in one hand, he threw his back against the man, and slowly lifted him up over a shoulder. "Direct pressure!" he said again. "Do not let go. I will get you back to the compound. Just do not let go, do you understand me?"

"I will not . . . let go, Sergeant Chinh. . . ."

"That is an order!"

"Yes, Sergeant. . . ." Then the Nung threw up on Chinh. The Sergeant felt blood, mixed with rice and beansprouts and *dau xanh banh lot*, dripping down the small of his back beneath the edge of his flak vest. "I am sorry, Sgt. Chinh," the soldier gagged, and coughed and vomited again.

"It is all right," Chinh replied, "just do not swallow! Do you understand?"

He could feel the Nung nodding as he climbed the hillside, but there was no verbal reply, and Chinh suddenly halted in his tracks.

"Check those two over there!" The words left his lips automatically as he spotted a Nung stumbling through the drifting smoke 20 yards away and became aware of movement beside a pile of decapitated bodies.

"They are all dead!" came the strained reply. The man was disoriented, shellshocked. At this moment, he cared nothing about anybody but himself.

"Now!" Chinh fired a three-round burst across the ground in front of the man's stumbling boots.

"*Yes*, Sgt. Chinh!" That seemed to wake him up. His eyes darted about, seeking the bodies Chinh referred to. Then he began running up to them and tripped and fell onto his hands and knees. But he continued, crablike, toward the wounded.

Chinh's attention returned to the VC at the hill's crest below. He was surprised they hadn't already raced up the hillside, competing for his men's heads. The squad of Green Berets was keeping them busy, it seemed. And perhaps Charlie thought they had enough additional claymores spread out to protect their flank in the event of a secondary assault by the Dau Tieng mercenaries.

Most of the Cong were gone from the gulley, anyway. They were streaming over the low rolling hills into the nearest cemetery itself, attacking the Americans with bayonets and engaging the survivors in hand-to-hand combat. For the most part, the only things left in the deep, dry gulley were the VC bodies Chinh and his people had killed before the corporal, eager to show his courage, had tripped the claymores.

An image formed in Chinh's mind, only to vanish on the fetid breeze swirling up from the gulley. He saw a U.S. Army bulldozer moving across the silent battlefield. The sun was riding the western horizon, crimson and bloated. It was setting. A whole day of peace had already passed, the body count had been taken, the American and Nung corpses had been removed. Blood trails were being followed through the tombstones and bamboo—usually to a spot where they mysteriously ended with no Cong body to account for. All that was left in the bottom of the gulley were the communist corpses that had *not* been dragged away in the night. Dozens of them.

In his vision, Chinh watched the tractor bulldoze Charlie down into the bloody mass grave, then proceed to cover up all evidence that there had ever been a fierce firefight outside Dau Tieng. Dust rose from the gulley as the tractor driver toiled endlessly through the day and into the evening. The dust was thick and at times hid the sun. The dust appeared red to Chinh.

There was blood on the sun.

Chinh's eyes searched for tripwires. Several strands of fishing line reflected the elusive shards of flarelight. He would stand no chance trying to make his way down through the booby traps. His only regret was that he'd been unable to warn his men in time.

The Nung he had yelled at was carrying another wounded comrade away from the ridge's kill zone. His energy and coordination back, he trotted toward Chinh despite the heavy load.

That was it. Four of them. Four left out of ten. If only they had waited until the corporal fired his flare. Chinh would surely have spotted the tripwires, and they could switch to one of the alternate tactics. But regrets were for fools and Americans—the Nungs couldn't afford them. And Buddha didn't seem to care.

As much as it hurt his pride, Chinh was now forced to abandon his Green Beret blood brother. Frisk was on his own. Chinh's first priority now was to get these two wounded soldiers back to Dau Tieng and proper medical attention.

Then he would whittle the post's perimeter guard force down to the bare essentials, and return with more Nungs. The next time he would approach from the east. And Chinh would commandeer a goddamned chopper if he had to! He refused to have Frisk's blood on his hands as well as that of his men.

"What do we do now, Sgt. Chinh?" The private stood in front of him now, gasping for breath, another enlisted man over his back. "Where do we go?"

Chinh stared long and hard at the soldier. The Nung was

obviously placing his last trust in Chinh. Chinh hesitated. He was torn between two courses of action—fighting or fleeing—as the adrenaline surge peaked.

"Sergeant?"

Eyes blinking back tears, Chinh turned quickly so that the private would not be witness to his loss of face. "We return to the camp!" he said. "We get some help! Then we come back!"

It was painful for the Nung sergeant to turn his back on the battle—very painful, indeed. But he had no choice. His loyalty to Frisk almost outweighed his dedication to his own squad . . . almost stopped Chinh in his tracks, lured him back to fight to victory or the death. . . . But it was something else that froze the Nung NCO in his tracks.

Movement down among the dead Viet Cong. Someone was rushing from corpse to corpse, gathering up weapons.

An American.

Chinh squinted hard—the soldier was a big man. He looked like Capt. Soto, but his back was to the Nung. So Chinh couldn't tell for sure.

Before his face appeared again, a flare drifting overhead broke free of its 'chute and plummeted to earth. Darkness enveloped the cemetery again, and the only thing Chinh could see was the flare's wispy gray trail in the sky, merging with gunsmoke rising from the scarred earth.

CHAPTER 20

Jungles outside Dau Tieng

Air! He needed air!

The Viet Cong soldier's hands were locked on Treat Brody's throat tighter than vise grips. He'd never imagined that an Asian hardly half his weight could be so strong.

Air! If only he could get in one more gulp of air. Brody felt himself blacking out. His knees were buckling.

They had swarmed down through the clearing, firing from the hip, and overrun the American positions swiftly. Brody was the first to be targeted at his pit. Two VC body-tackled him, while a third attempted to thrust a bayonet through his heart. The blade struck one of the clips in the bandoliers crisscrossing his chest. That had saved him, bought him enough time to pivot, bend, and kick out.

The guerrilla with bayonet mania dropped into the mud with a broken jaw, unconscious.

Brody had whirled then, flinging one of the other sappers off—directly into Gage Ruckter's arms. The 4th Cav sergeant slit his throat. Treat watched blood spurt from the Viet Cong's neck. The communist's eyes burned into Brody—defiant even in death.

Two more VC came flying through the air, feet first—both aiming their boots at Brody's face. One missed entirely and sailed out over the ridge of muddy anthills. The other crumpled against Brody's chest. The sheer momentum forced Whoremonger backwards over the ridge.

His helmet went flying, the back of his head struck what had to be the only dry strip of earth in Dau Tieng. Flares —not stars—spiraled in front of his eyes, and the one bastard was trying to choke him out.

Air! He needed air!

He stopped trying to break the Cong's grip on his throat and began slapping the palms of his hands against the VC's ears.

Nothing. No effect whatsoever.

Brody was fast losing his strength. He punched at the flaring Vietnamese nose in front of him . . . watched it flatten . . . break . . . squirt blood laced with mucus. . . . But the man's grip on his throat did not ease up.

Brody reached down and grabbed the soldier's crotch. He twisted as hard as he could, then, summoning what little strength he had left, brought up his knee hard. Brody knew it was the last move he would be able to make.

Almond eyes crossing, the Vietnamese groaned and dropped to his knees, releasing Brody's throat.

Scampering back on his hands and boots, crablike, the cavalry sergeant sucked in the hot, bug-infested air. His chest heaved, and the feeling in his arms began to return, but his joints still gave out.

Brody crashed onto his back. A childlike cry escaped him.

He drew the rain-soaked pistol on his hip and tried to aim it at the guerrilla's face, but he couldn't keep his hand and arm from shaking. The .45's front sight jumped about, falling on Americans behind the Cong, men wrestling in the mud, corpses with sparkling bayonets implanted in their rib cages and rifle butts swinging back and forth in the muggy air over them.

He pulled the trigger anyway, but nothing happened.

180

The safety! Little voices in his head were screaming. *Flip off the safety, you stupid shit!*

Brody's thumb came down on the safety lever, then he jerked in the trigger—well aware there was no way he'd hit the motionless VC: You never jerked a weapon's trigger. *Gentle*, he said to himself.

The Whoremonger knew he always carried a live round in the pistol's chamber. No soldier worth his salt wore a .45 in any other manner. But the hammer had slammed down without a discharge. *Misfire!*

Had the rain fouled his weapon? Treat tried pulling the slide back to chamber the clip's top round, but his arms were still too weak, and then a giant was zigzagging amongst the VC, knocking them silly with vicious elbow punches from their blind sides.

Frisk!

"Where's your fucking fiddle, Sergeant?" Brody heard himself asking in a businesslike tone, and then he dropped back, blacking out before he hit the mud.

"Hold still, damnit!"

Lisa Maddox's hand began trembling again, and the tweezers pushed the sliver of lead in deeper before she could securely grasp hold of it.

"Jesus, woman!" Doc Delgado flinched. "You tryin' to treat me or put me in traction?"

Two emotions swirled through the Army nurse. She wanted both to slap the side of his head and to hug him. "I'm sorry." She heard the words leave her lips but couldn't remember forming them in her head. "It's just that . . ."

"Don't say you're nervous in the service. I'll get some

181

fuckin' housegirl to pull the rest of 'em out." He was only half joking.

". . . I'm just not used to . . . to treating someone I actually know. Someone I *care* for. . ."

"Well . . ."

"There. That's the last one, anyway." Maddox set down the blood-streaked surgical tweezers in a bedpan littered with bits and pieces of former bullets. Delgado was sitting on a gurney. He wore his trousers and jungle boots, but no shirt. Lt. Maddox stood behind him. Beside her was a bright lamp positioned to shed light on the dozen or so minute puncture wounds across the medic's back—puncture wounds inflicted when a lone bullet from the ground had struck a bulkhead in the med-evac and shattered into fragments, many of which found their way into Delgado.

"You sure bleed a lot, Doc"—another corpsman handed Delgado a new fatigue shirt—"for just a few 'ricochets.' Like a stuck pig, in fact."

"And you can take your opinion and *stuff* it, Mercer. *Hey!*" Delgado noticed that he hadn't been given the correct shirt. Painful as lower torso movement was for him, he turned just in time to see his good-luck jungle jersey being trashed. "You do that and I'll slice your nuts off, then slamdunk what's left into a vat o' rubbing alcohol!"

"Ooooooo!" Mercer winced at visions his mind began conjuring up. "Perish the thought!" Holding the shirt out at arm's length and pinching his nose shut with his free hand, the corpsman returned the torn and bloodstained rag.

Delado took a moment to survey the shirt—it really *was* a mess. He shook his head in resignation, dropped the clean shirt on the gurney, and slid the old one on. "Ahhh . . ." He seemed rather pleased with the fit.

Maddox and Mercer exchanged looks of mild revulsion.

"Okay, let's get the lead out," Delgado said.

"Huh?" Mercer asked.

"I just *got* the goddamned lead out!" Lisa was still holding the last sliver in the palm of her hand. She dropped it into the bedpan, and it rolled around with a threatening sound for a few tense seconds.

"I mean, back to battle!"

"How 'bout a cup o' coffee first?" Maddox appeared drained, both emotionally and physically.

"No time for shit like that, honey." He cast her a look designed to elicit as much guilt as possible. "There's men *dyin'* out there . . . *friends* of ours!"

"We don't have transportation, hero!" she reminded him. "Let's get a mug o' brew, and by the time it all fizzles out maybe we can grab an ash-'n-trash down to Saigon . . . anywhere! I'm righteously in the goddamned mood to go AWOL! Do you hear me, lover?"

"*You*, Lieutenant?" Mercer asked with wide eyes and lower jaw dragging.

"Don't talk that way in front of the kids." Delgado cast Mercer a just-kidding grin. "You'll give 'em ideas. And the wrong impression, Mom."

Lisa Maddox frowned.

"You hear them rotors idling out there?" Delgado cupped an ear with his hand, seemingly ignoring her. "Those are Gabe the Gunslinger's blades, baby! I saw him prangin' in for fuel a few minutes ago." He pointed through the Quonset hut's two miniature windows. "When you were operatin'."

"*Pegasus?*"

"Double-yeps."

Maddox bent over to peer out the windows. Mercer stared at her shapely bottom, then quickly glanced away when he noticed Delgado was watching him. Amused, Doc kept his eyes on Mercer, and when the corpsman stole a look over at Delgado a second time, the buck sergeant raised and lowered his eyebrows several times in a Groucho Marx imitation. Mercer's hand flew over his mouth so that he wouldn't laugh out loud.

"I don't think Gabriel wants any dead weight," Lisa said. "I don't think he wants to attempt any more hot LZs tonight either."

The sound of men arguing reached their ears as the lieutenant was speaking. Several men. Many Vietnamese, and what sounded like only one American. Maddox thought she recognized Cliff Gabriel's voice among the bilingual din of threats and counter-threats.

Delgado started toward Lisa's side, buttoning his shirt up and fastening his web-belt holster on the way over.

The Quonset hut's swinging double doors flew open suddenly. Gabe the Gunslinger—minus his gun—burst in, hands raised in surrender.

Lisa's hand came to her lips but she did not scream, as Mercer was sure she would. He cringed more in anticipation of the dramatic and mandatory shriek than because of any perceived threat from the intruders.

Doc Delgado thought they were North Vietnamese at first. Instinctively, his hand dropped to the holstered pistol at his side, but he removed it and relaxed a bit when one of the Asians waved a rifle at him.

An M-16!

The NVA didn't carry M-16s. Delgado squinted. The eyes of the five Vietnamese behind Gabriel narrowed suspiciously in reply.

"Don't I know you?" Delgado pointed at the gunman wearing sergeant's stripes. "You're one of the Nungs."

"He's Sgt. Chinh!" Maddox recognized him, too.

"What the hell's goin' on here, Chinh?" Boots placed apart, Delgado's stance became a defensive one, but he rested both hands on his hips, bewildered.

"They wanna go back to the fighting!" Gabriel told him. "They want me to take 'em back in *Peg*!"

"And what's wrong with that?" Delgado listened to himself with a puzzled expression, but the words continued to flow anyway—after all, he was one of the walking wounded now, and was allowed to make no sense whatsoever if he wanted to. "That's only being a good soldier, mister . . . isn't it?"

"*Pegasus* is deadlined until further notice!" Gabriel barked back. "We took all kinds of flak on that last pass. I swear, Uncle Sammy better get his shit together out there, or the crapola's really gonna hit the fan, Doc!"

"That's the impression *I* got too, Mr. Gabe." Delgado turned around and lifted his fatigue shirt so that Gabriel could see the colorful flock of butterfly bandages Lisa had applied.

"Fuckin-A!" added Mercer in the background.

"We have to go back!" Sgt Chinh spoke for the first time.

"And why is that?" Gabriel's eyes swelled in mock suspense as he stared down at the angry Nung.

"We have obligation," Chinh said, undeterred. "Sgt. Frisk out there. Your people, too—Lt. Vance, Sgt. Leo, and the others: Whorekiller and Snakegod! Bookoo VC back there, Doctor Delgado! *Bookoo!* You *bic*? In cemetery!"

"But my ship's temporarily outta service, Luke," Gabriel said, brushing the M-16 barrel out of his face, "so kindly get that fucking thing outta my—"

Chinh jabbed the muzzle into Gabe's left nostril again. "I lose almost all my men!" the Nung told Delgado. "Only four live. Only two still standing—I find these men on guard duty. I relieved them so we can go back. This man, Mister Gabriel—he chickenshit. He no want to fight Viet Cong. He a . . . a flyboy fairy!"

"A *what*?" Mercer bellowed.

"I can assure you, Sgt. Chinh"—Delgado was shaking

185

his head again—"that if Gabriel says *Pegasus* is down for repairs, then she's fucking down for repairs. You'll just have to wait and—"

"Then we walk!" Chinh yelled. "No time for bullshit jackaround. Men dying! My friends . . . yours too! How can you stay here, chatting with . . . with *womens*?"

Doc glanced back at Lisa. She was frowning and tilting her head to one side in anticipation of his response. "Come on!" he told Chinh, knocking the barrel down out of Gabriel's nose as he headed through the door. "I'll get us some fucking transportation if it kills us! Mac oughta have his bird flightworthy by now—he's as certifiably *dinky-dau* as they come!"

"Wait for me!" Lisa Maddox rushed past Gabriel, an anxious expression on her face. She threw him a dirty wink on the way out.

CHAPTER 21

Jungles outside Dau Tieng

Toai had been squatting with his rifle propped between his legs, muzzle pointed up at the night sky, when the tiger growled from its perch on the ledge above theirs. Toai immediately forced the trigger down with his thumb.

A short burst flew skyward, the rifle's butt began bouncing against the rock outcropping beneath their haunches with each discharge, and Thieu yelled as the barrel tipped out of control, sending a tracer or two close enough to have shaved off his mustache, were he old enough to grow one.

"Shoot him, Toai! Shoot the goddamned thing!" Thieu yelled, never thinking to raise his own rifle.

"I've dropped it!" Toai shouted back. "I dropped my AK and can't find it!"

It was darker now. The crescent moon had set, and now clouds were obliterating even the dim starlight.

But Toai had no problem making out the glowing green eyes leaning out over the ledge 5 or 6 feet above his head.

Toai stared up at the tiger. The tiger stared back down at Toai. Then it let out the longest, most bloodcurdling roar either Toai or Thieu had ever heard.

"Oh, Buddha!" Thieu started trying to climb down from their ledge, which was very dangerous, of course, since to reach this point they had had to traverse the hilltop leading to the cliff from the opposite side, then drop down from the ledge on which the tiger now stood.

Thieu fell.

"Are you okay?" Toai called down to him. There was no answer except a low, nearly inaudible groan.

Toai looked up at the ledge again. The eyes still glowed. His foot nudged something and, where he'd least expected to find it: the rifle.

Toai fought the urge to throw his arms up and scream at the big cat in an attempt to startle the damn thing—frighten it off with the unexpected noise. He'd probably have Bengal stripes all over him like white on rice.

Slowly, he dropped into a half squat so that his fingers could reach for the AK, but before he could grab the weapon, a gunship roared past a mere 10 or 12 feet overhead.

Toai had never even heard the rotors; it was flying so close to the contours of the earth. The tiger ducked and sprang to a higher outcropping of shale, dodged the shadowy threat, and disappeared as mysteriously as it had arrived.

"Thieu!" Toai yelled down to his friend. "I'm coming down to get you! Are you all right?"

Another series of low groans greeted the query.

Toai slung the AK-47 over his shoulder and began climbing down the side of the hill. The cliff was not sheer —there were many large boulders and protruding scrubbrush to hold on to—but it took Toai all of half an hour to descend the modest 25 feet.

Thieu would live. In fact, Toai could find no visible fractures or serious injuries. Thieu was just shaken up.

"Come on, I'm not about to carry you, that's for sure!" Toai helped Thieu onto his feet and commenced brushing off his friend's clothes.

188

"That was sure a close one," Thieu finally said. He began spitting dust out of his mouth.

It was beginning to rain again. Toai wondered where he could find enough dust to eat amidst all this mud. "Let's go!" he urged Thieu to hurry. "I have a bad feeling that that creature is still lurking nearby."

"My ankle hurts," Thieu complained. "I think I twisted it."

"You'll make it back. You don't even have any real injuries—except to your pride, perhaps." Nevertheless, Toai took his best friend's arm and hoisted it over his own shoulder for support.

This is how Uncle Sammy's green machine tries to work: An Army division usually consists of 5,000 to 20,000 soldiers. Three to five brigades or regiments make up a single division. There are three to five battalions in each brigade, with one battalion consisting of 400 to 800 men, grouped into four to six companies. Ideally, there are 80 to 150 men in each company, divided into three to five platoons, with twenty to forty men in each platoon. Two to four squads make up your average RVN platoon. If you have nine troopers per squad, you're flying high; if you have three, times are tight and you're as undermanned as it gets. Five to seven was the average.

At Dau Tieng, none of this meant water-buffalo dung. The 196th Light Infantry Brigade had been whittled down to that last notch above zero—men who were just hanging on, trying to survive. Nearly all of their commanders had been killed by the Viet Cong during a vicious series of hastily planned but highly successful ambushes. That members of 7th Cav's Echo Company happened to answer the Brass Monkey call for help would only further confuse and bewilder military archivists, for the troopers of Echo Company itself rarely knew how many GIs were in town for the duration and how many were just passing through.

Charlie Company of One-Niner-Six happened to have 131 men in it before the firefights at Dau Tieng. Each rifleman carried only 240 rounds—about twelve clips—along with two smoke grenades and four frags. The machine-gunners were allowed a thousand rounds, and each squad carried three claymores and tripflares divided among the men. None of this ammunition lasted very long during the opening rounds of battle that first week of November, 1966.

Most of the Americans were just happy to make it through the night—and find themselves alive to fight another day.

Frisk opened the tiny vial and waved it under Brody's nose until the Whoremonger came to.

"Damn!" Treat began coughing.

"Works every fuckin' time." The big Green Beret smiled broadly.

"Where the hell *am* I?" Brody's eyes focused on Frisk first, then on his gunsmoke-laced surroundings. He stared at the vial again. "What *is* that shit?"

"Good idea!" Sgt. Frisk kept Brody flat on his back when the Cavalry NCO attempted to sit up. "But actually, it's just fermented fish sauce."

"Nouc-mam?" Brody's nostrils wrinkled in disgust.

"Better than that!" Frisk glanced around, but the situation still appeared under control, so he returned his full attention to the shaken doorgunner. "A special concoction of the indigenous persuasion," he whispered with a sly grin. "Someday this war's gonna be over, and I'm gonna be a millionaire . . . gonna be rich, Trick or Treat. Gonna market this crap . . . sell it to the CIA."

190

"As what?" Brody glanced around, recognizing some faces, blanking on others.

"Secret shit."

"Oh. . . ."

Fletcher was beside him now. "You okay, Whoremonger?" he asked, but there was no real look of concern in his eyes.

"I . . . I think so." Brody checked his arms and legs. Everything seemed to be intact. "What's happening? What's the . . . ?"

It all began coming back to him then: the VC surge, the bayonets, the hand-to-hand combat, and one particular little scrawny gook with vise grips for hands, trying to choke him into never-never land. The doped-up guerrillas, and someone serenading the troops.

Frisk's fiddle.

"It took some doing," Snakeman briefed him, "but we beat Charlie back. We ain't got no commo; we ain't got no extra ammo, either. We ain't got diddly-squat—but we're hangin' in there, bud."

Brody looked up at Frisk. The Green Beret was holding a submachine gun in both hands. Brody's eyes scanned the man's web belt. Nothing was hanging from his pack, either. "I heard . . . violin music," he said uncertainly, then his eyes darted to the other men's faces, waiting for them to react with laughter.

Frisk was the only one to laugh. His right hand moved back to pat the bottom of his rucksack. "In the pack, Oh-Honorable Whore-san."

"I *knew* I heard one. . . ."

"Frisk gets frisky unless he's got his fiddle." Another Special Forces NCO appeared at the edge of Brody's field of vision. "Superstitious slut."

Brody watched the two Green Berets exchange knowing grins.

Lt. Vance and Leo Zack joined them. "So what's the game plan?" a voice behind them asked. Brody recognized Reece Jones's voice instantly.

Vance looked to Zack. Zack glanced over at Frisk. "You've got the most ammo," Leo told the SF commando, nodding at the numerous ammo bandoliers crisscrossing his chest. Five other Green Berets were with Frisk. Each man was heavily armed with bandoliers—and with a half dozen magazine pouches on his web belt.

"But nothing interchangeable with your sixteens." Frisk cast Zack an apologetic look.

"No sweat," Lt. Vance said. "When the VC come down on us again, we'll resist 'til we run out of bullets. . . ."

"Which won't be long," Jones observed sarcastically.

". . . Then we'll play it by ear," Vance continued without affording Jones so much as a glance.

"Well, first thing we can do is start policing up all the firepower donated to 'the cause' by Ho Chi Minh's nephews there." Frisk motioned toward the dead VC. "I see plenty o' AKs. They'll do for a start."

"What do you think Charlie's gonna do for an encore?" Vance's question was an open one.

The men with Frisk all began to respond at the same time—each had a theory. The trooper nearest Vance pointed to a tracer-laced skirmish taking place only a hundred yards away. "The VC aren't much more organized on this thing than the one-ninety-sixth was when they stepped boots-first into the shit, Lou," he said. "Eventually, they're gonna regroup and start sweepin' the area over here."

"Then they're going to figure out there's a whole *shit-load* o' survivors over here they've got to contend with, and—"

"So I suggest we start building up some kind of make-shift defenses"—Frisk glanced over at the ominous black

192

shadows moving across the skies—storm fronts merging again, coming together over the northwestern edge of the battlefield, over the swamp—"before Charlie gets his act together and—"

A lone white tracer floated up to Frisk, missed his head by inches, and ricocheted off Reece Jones's helmet. Brody and Vance watched the tracer bounce up into the night, arcing away. "God*damn!*" Snakeman Fletcher laughed. Reece was hugging the ground—a good move, since several dozen additional tracers followed the first after a mere heartbeat's delay.

Everyone except Frisk and the Green Berets joined Jones on the ground. "You okay, Reece-baby?" Gage Ruckter asked with a grin.

"Screw you, Rucksack!" Jones directed an obscene gesture at the cavalry sergeant.

"I wish people would quit calling me that." Ruckter shook his head in resignation.

Frisk's arms were waving wildly. He was directing his men this way and that. With the occasional lightning flash to show the way, they were hunting the VC in the dark. Treat Brody marveled at the array of exotic weapons the Green Berets were using—he couldn't identify a single one, although he could tell that most were submachine guns of European manufacture. One might have been East German, but that was only a guess.

A force of forty to fifty Viet Cong was slowly moving toward them now. Walking upright, the black-clad Asians reminded Brody of paintings he'd seen of the American Civil War, where it sometimes appeared routine for combatants to walk into battle, firing directly at one another without taking cover. They gotta be on dope, he decided, rising up on one knee to let fly a ten-round burst from one of the AKs lying in the mud.

The air became a sudden flurry of beating rotors as two

helicopter gunships swooped down low over the escalating confrontation. They were heading directly for the VC, and several flares burst in midair behind their tail booms.

Four red-hot lances—tracers from the Huey doorgunners—dropped through the night and began scattering the communists. Gage Ruckter stood upright and cheered. With one hand he waved a fist. With the other, he fired an M-16 he'd come up with somewhere, pistol-fashion.

"Was that *Pegasus?*" Snakeman asked Brody.

"I don't think so!" Treat yelled back between three-round bursts of his own. A satisfied look crept across his features as several Cong in the front ranks went down in the mud.

"I thought I saw some white pussy up there!"

"Maddox?"

"Yeah!"

"Could be." Brody was laughing now as he switched magazines. "Was she firin' one of the doorguns?"

"I don't think so! I just saw some blond hair through the hatch. Maybe it was some clown from Delta—but it looked pretty long to be just some swingin' dick's."

"Lisa keeps hers up on top of her head in a bun," Brody said knowledgeably.

"How the fuck would *you* know?" Ruckter scampered over to Brody's side, and they both sent a long burst of lead at the enemy before resuming their chat. "And who the hell is *Lisa?*"

"*Lieutenant* Lisa Maddox." Vance dove into the mud on the other side of Brody. "One of the flight nurses."

"Oh . . ." Ruckter seemed intrigued but, at the moment, he was more preoccupied with a jammed round. He slammed the ejector lever several times with his palm, without success. "Fuckin' toy!" He abandoned the rifle and took an AK from the stack beside Jones.

One of the gunships was making a swing around, and

Brody noticed that there was full cargo aboard—grunts in the cabin. But these were Asians!

"Nungs!" Fletcher spotted the no-nonsense faces as well. "Those gotta be Nungs from Dau Tieng!"

"Sgt. Chinh!" Frisk yelled. He seemed surprised.

"Maybe we can finally get a medic in here!" Jones said.

Several of the men stared at him without saying anything. There were only two categories of Americans in their little cluster—the dead and the living.

As if on cue, every soldier with a firearm opened up on the VC's last known position as the slick ferrying Maddox, Doc Delgado, and the Nungs flared in for a blacked-out, no-lights landing.

The first trooper to un-ass was Sgt. Chinh. From the air, he had spotted the Viet Cong as well, and he immediately directed long bursts from his M-16 at the guerrillas lying behind an old, dried-out rice paddy berm. The next Nung down out of the chopper hatch was a corporal. He carried the Nungs' battle flag: a skull and crossbones floating on a black field.

Brody could see smoke drifting up from the corporal's rifle even before the Asian was in a position to fire, and he felt he knew what the explanation was: the Nungs of Dau Tieng were a superstitious lot. In preparation for battle, they would carry *joss* sticks taped to the barrels of their rifles—three sticks each if they suspected the American advisers were sending them out on a romeo-foxtrot. If the *joss* stick was blown out before it could burn down on its own, a bad omen of gargantuan proportions was in the offing. Even carrying General Phuc Po's photo into battle might not be able to offset the bad *joss*.

Brody felt good about this Nung and his trio of *joss* sticks. They had not gone out until the corporal jumped down into the gunship's powerful rotorwash. To be extinguished in that manner *had* to be okay in Brody's book.

After all, what could harbor more magic and bewitch more grunts than beauties like *Pegasus* and the other fleet slicks, whose job it was to save Brody and better men than he from the likes of Void Vicious?

Brody felt the gunship calling to him. The last Nung had jumped out, and now Lisa Maddox was climbing down over the landing skids. Doc Delgado was already on the ground and running toward the wounded with his aid bag.

Brody watched the doorgunner pour an incessant stream of lead and tracers into the VC positions. Some Cong jumped up and charged—a few of their rounds managed to strike the helicopter, but there was no loss of power, no smoke, no explosion. The gunny effectively muted most of their futile attempts to destroy the ship. A scream reached the men clustered in the clearing, though.

The doorgunner was finally hit.

Brody watched him tumble back, into the middle of the cabin.

The machine-gunner manning the opposite hatch-60 rushed to his aid, only to be hit as well.

Brody was quickly on his feet. Frozen in place, he glanced back over a shoulder for some reason. Lt. Vance and Sgt. Zack were directly in back of him. They both waved him toward the craft. "Get aboard and see if you can help!" Leo yelled.

Brody responded with a what-about-you? expression, and Vance's wave became more violent. "Move it!" he told Treat. "We're needed down here."

"Get your ass on that slick!" Leo the Lionhearted boomed. Then the night air went white with a thirty-round full-auto burst from his M-16.

Running as hard as he could, Brody watched Zack's bullets fly past, knocking several VC, who were also running for the chopper, off their feet. One was a sapper. His

196

satchel charge slid past the ground at Brody's feet but failed to explode.

"Welcome aboard!" the copilot motioned Brody in through the hatch as he scrambled up over the landing skids. Already, the tail boom was lifting off the ground and dull thumps signaled that the Huey's nose cannon was sending M-79 rounds into the Cong ranks. A grinding roar filled his ears and Brody felt good inside. He recognized the sound: Two XM-21 mini-guns were mounted in the helicopter's snout as well. The weapons were capable of firing 6,000 rounds of seven-point-six-two per minute, and had a ten-degree pivot enabling them to automatically track 5 degrees off center, side to side.

Brody's eyes scanned the cabin as he scampered for the nearest hatch hog. He could see the ship was a UH-1C— probably the most maneuverable of the Huey models, able to fly 100 knots when the weather wasn't a factor. This girl was definitely faster and more powerful than the earlier models put out by Bell. She had two rocketpods on each side, with seven 2.5-inchers in each pod, aimed and launched electrically by the skyjockeys in the cockpit.

Brody noticed that the copilot's neck and back were drenched in blood, but he appeared to be functioning okay.

"You all right, mister?" Brody yelled up to him as he gave the M-60 a once-over, then slammed a fresh belt of ammo into it. Warrant officers were referred to not as "sir" but as "mister"—a military quirk that amused everyone involved except the lieutenants and captains, who couldn't figure out what all the enlisted men constantly seemed to be smiling about.

"It's not mine," the peter pilot pulled the blood-soaked fabric away from the flesh along his shoulder, then released it. "It's Gunny Pace's!" the pilot explained. "Charlie really splashed him all over the place. Make sure he's history, or we'll head back to Tay Ninh City *rikky-tik*."

"He's history," Brody muttered softly, refusing to look twice at the mutilated corpse. It no longer had a head.

Brody concentrated on killing as many Cong as was humanly possible, as the chopper rose up above the tree-tops and circled around the kill zone.

"For Gunny Pace," he growled against the clamor of empty brass rising up around his jungle boots. "I ain't got no *joss* smoke to make no goofy offering to Buddha and the Void, brother," he stared at the silver puffs hanging in front of the M-60's muzzle. "*These*'ll have to get you over the rainbow and into second heaven!"

On the ground, the soldiers lying behind logs and the debris of war listened to Vance issuing perimeter directives as they dug foxholes in the mud. The Viet Cong had, at least temporarily, pulled back. Frisk and his Green Berets were checking the nearby tombstones within a hundred-yard radius and dragging wounded Americans back to the main clearing beneath Big Boy.

Snakeman Fletcher stared up at the huge, 12-foot-high statue. Things were not looking good, and Elliott didn't like his fate resting in the hands of a chipped and smiling Buddha—he didn't care how old it was. "I should have tagged along with Treat," he muttered.

"Huh?" The soldier slamming his E-tool into the mud inches from Fletcher's was Reece Jones.

"I said *fuck* this shit!"

"Yeah, I hear ya, pal. We shoulda both beat feet over to that gunship. I'd rather go out in a ball o' flames any day than die in the muck of some Buddha-forsaken place called . . . What the hell's this place called?" He turned to the soldier digging behind him.

"Dau Tieng." Gage Ruckter produced an ear-to-ear smile without slowing his pace.

"Aw, fuck . . ." Jones sighed, startled the NCO was so

198

near. "You gonna pound me again, Sgt. Ruckter?" he asked.

"Not if you behave, ya no-account shit," came the reply.

"See what I mean?" Jones spoke to Fletcher. "How are we supposed to win a ground war in Southeast Asia with these gung-ho hard-core types leadin' us into battle?"

"You're cruisin' for a bruisin', Reece-baby." Ruckter began assaulting the earth with renewed viciousness.

"Well, I just shoulda beat feet over to that Huey," Fletcher repeated. "That's all I can say!"

"You need something to cheer you up, troop!" Jones dropped his folding shovel in the muck and sat on the fox-hole's crumbling edge. From a thigh pocket, he pulled several waterlogged brochures. "You need some readin' material."

"When you gonna see the light, Reece-baby?" Ruckter asked. "That 'vets against the war' bullshit ain't never gonna get you nothin' 'cept ten to twenty at hard labor in LBJ. Did you know that, smartass?"

"It's my future, Sergeant-sir, ain't it?" The soggy flyers came apart in Jones's hands, and he went back to digging.

Ruckter was still shaking his head. "And you used to be such a good Joe," he said. "Regular hero material. What the fuck happened to you, Reece-baby?"

"If you don't quit callin' me 'Reece-baby,' I'm gonna—"

"You're gonna what?" Ruckter challenged, leaning his shovel back over a shoulder.

Jones said nothing, but dug harder and quickened his pace, throwing his anger and frustration into his work.

Ruckter set his shovel down and brought out a pack of cigarettes. Because they were in the middle of the kill zone, he didn't dare light it, but he wanted some tobacco to chew on. He handed one to the Green Beret, Frisk.

199

"Jonesey used to be such a good Joe," he told Fletcher. "Did I ever tell you we were together back in Srok Dong?"

Elliott wasn't really interested but, still digging, he said, "Nope, Gage-baby . . . I don't think you did."

A stray round ricocheted into their position, skimming across the mud puddles with a nauseating echo. The group squatted down in the growing foxhole and peered out from under their helmets, trying to spot the source of the shot.

"So anyways"—Ruckter turned back from the search until he was facing Jones—"what the flyin' fudge was we talkin' 'bout, partner?"

"Srok Dong." Jones sighed.

"Ah, yes . . . the battle for Srok Dong," Ruckter recalled. He glanced back over his shoulder at Snakeman. "You shoulda been there, *amigo*," he said. "We really kicked Charlie's butt."

"Bravo Troop got their asses ambushed by the Two-seventy-first VC Regiment while returning down Route 13 to Loc Ninh," Jones suddenly felt compelled to tell the story. "After bridge-repair duties."

"Four of our own tanks were destroyed," Ruckter added. "Many of the track commanders were decapitated on the spot. . . ."

"We called in gunships to reinforce, of course." Ruckter's shoulders were tensing with each new battlefield description. "Even some Chinooks . . ."

"But it took 'em awhile to get there," Jones added.

"Charlie Troop sent in their tanks and APCs, piled high with grunts eager for a fight. By the time they arrived, the roadway was blocked with our own disabled tanks."

"We were pinned down at the far end of the convoy," Ruckter continued, "away from the help. Charlie started showering our position with mortars. . . ."

"By the time Charlie Troop arrived, the entire road was clogged with mangled metal."

"And the lead tank from C Troop was a death wagon," Jones continued. "The entire crew topside, as well the gunners inside, were killed by the exploding mortars. The turret had been disabled. The only man still alive was the driver, and he was badly wounded."

"He rammed the tanks blocking the roadway. . . ."

"And got through," Jones said. "Opening the way for the rest of Charlie Troop."

"When that first tank pulled up, we dragged the dead out, and five of us joined the driver," Ruckter went on.

"He was a sergeant," Jones added with emphasis.

"We operated the turret manually, and sent over sixty rounds into Charlie's positions while crashing through all the disabled tanks in an attempt to reopen more of the roadway."

"You talk just like a goddamned traffic cop, Gage, you know that?" Jones asked him, and Ruckter paused as if he'd just heard or seen a ghost. He cast Jones a peculiar look, then said, "Ram it in and break it off, shit-for-brains."

"Sounds painful, dickbreath."

Ruckter just sighed and resumed digging. Bullets were bouncing into their position again from all over, but he was ignoring them now—just standing there. Digging. Yes, it was sounding painful, indeed.

CHAPTER 22

LZ, Dau Tieng

"What's the situation?" Nurse Maddox asked fellow lieutenant Jake Vance after the gunship ascended and its downblast died away.

"It's bad," Vance replied. "More for me than you, though," he added. "I've got more dead in this clearing than living or wounded—and they're not even my men!"

"One-ninety-sixth?"

"Right! You probably better check on those two guys over there first. They're pretty bad—stomach wounds, and I think the white guy's going to lose that hand. . . ."

"Okay." Lisa was already starting over toward them.

". . . We've got a captain out there somewhere," Vance continued. "One of the wounded who stumbled in here just before you landed told us about him. I guess he's hit pretty bad. We just can't find him."

"You can't find him?" She was down on one knee between the two grunts.

"This is one of the most screwed-up situations I've ever been in," Vance admitted, as the helicopter with Brody aboard began flying tight circles over their clearing, dropping bursts of tracer down into the jungle and rubber-tree ceiling. Maddox was already pulling a poncho liner up over the face of the soldier whose wrist was nothing but shreds of cartilage and whose intestines glistened in the flarelight. He was gone. "There's a hundred . . . maybe two hundred troops scattered throughout this cemetery for all I know, and—"

"*These* cemeteries," Lisa corrected him. "Doc told me there's six different Viet graveyards sprinkled throughout the Michelin Plantation."

"At least," Delgado said. He was helping her stabilize the black soldier now.

"Well, anyway." Vance ducked as the gunship swooped lower than before, dropping smoke bombs and CS cannisters directly on top of the Viet Cong.

"Fuck," Delgado muttered as his ears picked up the distinctive pop of CS cannisters. "That goddamned Brody!" But the wind was blowing away from them, and the silver clouds of tear gas swirled about the VC positions only. Soon, they could hear many of the communists coughing and gagging. Several defiant rifle bursts flew up toward the gunship, though. It appeared the CS was having the desired affect: bringing tears to the guerrillas' eyes, for they couldn't seem to shoot very straight now.

"Frisk is over there," Vance continued, "the Green Beret sergeant . . . he's going to take some of the Nungs and go looking for the captain. . . ."

"We've gotta get this guy out of here," Doc Delgado was working frantically to save the black infantryman. Vance watched the grunt's eyeballs flutter and roll into the top of his head several times as he clung to life. He'd seen the look before—and always just before the wounded warrior stepped into his next life.

One of the Nung soldiers remained as close to Delgado as a shadow. He carried a PR-25 radio on his back. "You want me call Mac now, ma'am?" he asked Lt. Maddox.

Lisa glanced up at the threatening skies. She could smell the rain moving back in, taste it on the air. "Yeah," she said, "get 'em back down here." They had to get a move on before the weather turned nasty again, grounding the helicopters and sentencing the W.I.A.s still on the ground to certain death.

The initial plan differed from the usual med-evac operation in that Delgado and Maddox were unsure what they'd find on the ground when they got there. Vance, Zack, and Brody's people had no communications, so they were unaware a Dustoff was coming in. It was doubtful the grunts on the ground would rush up to the slick with their wounded in tow, as was the usual procedure. It'd surely be a hot LZ, with every swingin' dick under fire. Maddox could not even be sure there were any Americans left alive down there. The Nungs weren't too confident about Frisk's chances. That they'd found the men of Echo Company struggling to survive the Americal ambush as well was icing on the ricecake.

The current plan was to have Maddox and Delgado assess the exact situation and stabilize as many patients as possible while Brody flew gunny slot aboard the gunship, laying down as much cover fire from above as he could. Having the slick airmobile, its hatch guns blasting away and doing them all some good, was a better prospect than allowing the ship to sit idle while the men on the ground readied their wounded for transport. The chopper crew would be sitting ducks. They were safer in the air.

When ready, Maddox would call for Mac and Gabriel to come back in. They'd on-load the casualties, transport them back to Tay Ninh, and return for more. With any luck, Frisk and his team would have located the captain by then.

Once he was confident they'd done all they could for the black soldier on the ground, Delgado checked on the other, less seriously wounded men. He counted a dozen gunshot victims. Before the slick was even flaring in for its second landing, he determined that nine of them could remain on the ground for the time being—and help Vance and the others to defend the cemetery hilltops until reinforcements could arrive in the morning.

"I just hope The Brass have got reinforcements coming," Delgado muttered to the lieutenant as the gunship pranged across several low grave markers on its sideways slide through the overgrown elephant grass.

He could see Brody firing the hatch-60 nonstop into the suspected VC positions, but the slick was receiving little return fire. Most of the guerrillas still seemed to be suffering the ill effects of the tear gas. Delgado was thankful the Cong did not have masks.

Neither did most of the American troops.

"Let's go!" Maddox urged Jones and Fletcher to hustle the wounded toward the helicopter. It stood in the middle of the clearing now, its rotors still flapping at near full power, its turbine screaming like a banshee.

"Tell Whoremonger to get his ass back here!" Delgado ordered Fletcher.

Maddox, who was helping one of the wounded men limp toward the Huey, halted in her tracks and turned to look back at Doc. He was not moving. "You're not coming?" her eyes burned into him.

"I'm needed more on the ground right now," he said, bringing an immediate smile to the faces of Vance and Zack. "That guy with the leg wound there"—Delgado pointed to one of the W.I.A.s limping over to the chopper —"he's not that bad off. I told him to take over the Hog-60. I want Brody down here on the ground with us!"

An odd look twisting her expression, Lisa nodded and climbed mechanically, speechlessly, up into the helicopter, never taking her eyes off Delgado.

After she was aboard, Doc turned toward one of the wounded GIs. Delgado blocked everything else out when there were bullets to be plucked and blood to be stopped. He buried himself in his work.

Brody sprinted back across the clearing and rejoined what was left of Echo Company. "I love that guy like a brother." He stared at Delgado. "I knew he'd find some way to get out here to help us!"

"Yep!" Fletcher was lying prone on one side of Brody. Ruckter and Jones were on the other. Bullets were beginning to kick up mud and dirt near their heads again. "It's amazing how pussy can motivate a man to do heroic crap when you least expect it!"

"That's what war's always been about, Snakeman!" Ruckter rose to one knee and fired off several rounds from the AK on semi-automatic. The assault rifle finally ran empty. Ruckter checked the mud at his knees, but there were no extra ammo magazines anywhere nearby.

"Then why haven't I had a decent shot o' leg in the last six months?" Snakeman complained. "I'd at least like to sample some of the *spoils* of war if I'm gonna risk my balls over 'em!"

Ruckter didn't seem to be listening, however. He gently laid the AK-47 down in the mud and slid the MP-40 submachine gun from its slung position over his back, flipped the safety off, and resumed killing commies for Christ.

CHAPTER 23

Perimeter, Cemetery, Dau Tieng

Ruong Nhu Toai had been laying dog for several hours now and he was ecstatic.

Teacher had had a change of heart. Or at least he had received new orders—a change of plans. The unit Toai and Thieu were assigned to would not be proceeding south to Saigon after all. The capital would have to wait. Common sense had finally caught up with the local Viet Cong hierarchy: Their 9th VC Recon Company had nearly been annihilated after prolonged pitched battles with the Americans near the Dau Tieng Special Forces camp. Toai's unit would be needed to help turn the tables on the U.S. infantry, now that cavalry Airmobile forces were being introduced into the fray.

The unit's more experienced jungle fighters were at that very moment probing the Americans' staggered defensive perimeters in preparation for a surprise secondary assault at pre-dawn. Toai, Thieu, and many of the younger recruits were positioned along the trails between graveyards—a last line of security in the unlikely event the besieged Americans were sending out probes of their own.

Toai was not really sure what he should do if he spotted an American, though. They had no radios or fieldphones with which to communicate with their superiors. And the helicopters! There were gunships cruising low overhead everywhere.

"What are you doing?" Toai whispered harshly through the bushes to Thieu, who was positioned a few meters away. They had been guarding the same spot without incident now for nearly six hours, and, for the last few minutes, Thieu had failed to observe the VC's strict code of silence while in the bush.

"Nothing!" Thieu whispered back. Toai smiled to himself. His best friend sounded irritated.

"Then quit make so much noise!"

"*You* are the one doing all the talking!" Thieu shot back. Strangely, the bushes clustered around him had fallen mysteriously silent again. "It is *you* who will attract the enemy's attention, not I!"

"Ha!" Toai replied skeptically, but he said nothing else. His ears perked and his eyes narrowed—he detected movement several dozen meters beyond Thieu's place of concealment.

Toai rubbed at his eyes. He was beginning to see things in the dark, obviously. It had happened to him many times in the past during training—especially after several hours in the bush with no moon above to aid in distinguishing which shadows were actually moving and which just appeared to be moving.

As he squatted in the bushes now, listening to the sounds of combat nearby and the constant flapping of gunship rotor-blades on the night air and the returning rumble of menacing thunder approaching from several different directions, Toai waited for his chance.

Sgt. Do Lam Chinh motioned his men forward.

Chinh knew there were VC nearby. The hairs standing

up on the back of his neck told him so. Charlie was here! Somewhere within the sphere of his highly trained, finely tuned vision.

But Charlie was simply not moving. These were well-disciplined troops. Or else they were sleeping. Chinh smiled to himself: If that was the case, it was snooze-and-lose time.

And then he spotted it. That wisp of almost ghostly luminescence floating above a cluster of bushes, then flittering from view the instant he tried concentrating on it—that thinly veiled puff of blurred color swirling about against the pitch-black.

Chinh flipped the M-16's safety off and raised his rifle to his shoulder as the cluster of bushes grew nearer. The bush was moving now. Moving ever so slightly. His trigger finger tightened.

Toai's palms were sweating fiercely.

He set down the American-made clacker, wiped his hands on his trousers, and picked up the firing device again. He could see shapes moving in the distance now. He could make out the distinct outline of three heads bobbing slightly up and down in the dark as they approached.

Something moved overhead, too. Swollen storm clouds, blotting out most of the stars.

Toai could tell by the shapes he saw that the soldiers wore boonie rats. He could tell by their height that they were Asian—Arvins or, more probably, Nungs from the Dau Tieng outpost. As the outlines drew closer, enlarging, becoming more stocky than normal South Vietnamese troopers, he decided they were Nungs.

They were walking directly into the kill zone he and

211

Thieu had set up before concealing themselves in the brush. Toai's lips moved silently as he counted to himself: three, two, one. . . .

Toai slammed his hands shut over and over. His ears filled with the businesslike click and buzz of the clackers as they detonated dual claymores.

A deafening explosion lit up the night. The bright flash illuminated the outlines of half a dozen Nungs!

Toai heard a startled Thieu scream out as the thunderous blast was immediately followed by a sudden cloudburst overhead.

Damn! Toai picked up the other clacker and attempted to set off the last two claymores as the downpour nearly blinded him—he'd misjudged the Nungs' position in relation to where Thieu had planted the anti-personnel mines: All the Nungs had been blown off their feet, but Toai could not be sure they were directly in the deadly path of the screaming ball bearings.

When he set off the second set of claymores, the flash revealed that one of the Nungs had managed to struggle back on his feet. He was wearing the chevrons of a sergeant and seemed only stunned at worst. Others were stumbling around behind him, trying to get up also. Toai's suspicions were confirmed: The Nungs had evaded the main brunt of his lethal traps. But it wouldn't happen a second time. Now they were directly in the kill-zone.

Toai watched the Nung sergeant disappear beyond a wall of thick smoke and swirling shrapnel.

The two VC recruits, Toai and Thieu, were frightened. They were more terrified than they had ever been before in their lives.

Teacher had not allowed the successful detonation of four claymore anti-personnel mines to go unrewarded. He was convinced beyond a doubt now that, in Toai, he had a warrior of unusual talent and courage. Toai had insisted that his good friend Thieu was invaluable in pulling the ambush off and, though Teacher appeared skeptical about this, he allowed the duo to remain together.

Teacher's idea of a promotion was an assignment to the teams of machine-gunners. Both of them. Toai was ecstatic at first. Thieu wanted to lop off his best friend's head. Duty with the machine-gun squads involved just about as much danger as could be found in a war zone. The survival rate beyond three or four months was not very high: A machine gun was a highly prized, very valuable weapon to the Viet Cong and NVA hierarchy—worth much more than a mere foot soldier or two, by all means! Machine-gunners and their ammo men were required to stay with their machine guns at all costs. Machine guns were heavy weapons, and lugging them around all day and night could be exhausting. Running with them over your shoulder or across your back when the American jets swooped in to decimate the MG nests was truly the pits. Thus, the reason for the high mortality rate among machine-gunners.

It was sort of like being the captain of a warship in time of conflict: You might as well go down with your ship, because you'll probably be executed afterward anyway if any harm comes to your charge.

It was a no-win situation. Therefore, machine-gunners were encouraged to survive every encounter with the enemy at all costs.

If Toai had found adventure and excitement while soldiering with the Viet Cong along the Ho Chi Minh Trail, he now found dread and terror at Dau Tieng. Duty as a machine-gunner would surely be the death of him—he had never been so close to the fighting, the actual exchange of hot lead, before. Taking potshots at unsuspecting gunships and detonating claymores from a hiding place were crazy enough. But to have someone so angry at you on a personal and perpetual basis . . . someone who was actually trying to put a bullet between your eyes or in your heart or through your belly quickly broadened Toai's perspective regarding combat and belied the romance of the battlefield ballads his cell of recruits had often sung during their motivated marches down the Ho Chi Minh Trail.

This was totally different! His chances at earning a body bag back to Hue had obviously increased tenfold. And, knowing the communist forces' supply system as he did, Toai did not doubt his corpse would end up in some martyrs' mass grave in Hanoi or Haiphong—if they didn't just dump his napalm-charred bones in some roadside gully here outside Dau Tieng.

"Thanks so much, Toai!" Thieu elbowed him sarcastically as a fifty-year-old guerrilla showed them how to load, care for, and fire a Soviet-built machine gun. "If it was not for your talent for taking pot shots at American helicopters and killing Chinese mercenaries with claymores, we would not be in this fix now!"

Thieu had never been a dedicated fighter. His favorite pastime was complaining about something or other. Tonight was no exception.

"I was under the impression we had been put in a machine-gun squad on the front lines solely because your mother had the 'wisdom' to name you after the president of South Vietnam!" Toai tried to camouflage his unrest and fear with feeble attempts at humor.

"Nguyen Van Thieu was not even in the Presidential Palace when I was born—and you know it!" Thieu retorted icily.

214

"Perhaps I could use my influence as hot-dog, stand-out recruit to get you a transfer back to the rear echelon. Where the girls and old *mama-sans* piss on punji stakes and pack black-powder stick grenades for the true jungle guerrillas."

Thieu hesitated for only a moment, then a grin finally creased his ashen features. "No, thanks."

The old man who was showing them how to operate the even more ancient Degtyarev locked eyes with Toai. He could tell that both teenage recruits were more than nervous. They were terrified.

"You fear the Americans?" he asked.

Toai did not answer immediately. Was this man one of Teacher's plants? A spy? Someone sent to test him . . . to see if he could take the stress? Possibly.

Another tracer whizzed past Toai's ear, exploded in the bark of a nearby tree, and showered them with red splinters of glowing lead. Toai no longer cared what anyone thought. He wasn't old enugh to be a bona fide hero yet. He was still a kid, and no one knew it more than Toai himself. "I fear the bullets," he said. "I don't care *who* is firing them: the Americans, the puppets of the Saigon regime, or even our own people. Bullets are bullets. I want to die an old man."

"Like me!" The aging insurgent laughed. His smile revealed only a single tooth hanging from his upper gums.

Toai and Thieu both found themselves laughing back, but it was the old soldier's comical appearance more than anything they found humorous. His toothless grin was what set them off. "Yes!" Thieu agreed. "Like you!"

The old soldier nodded proudly. He could not hear what Thieu had said because of all the noisy discharges on the hillside below them now, but he could read the youth's lips. He knew they found his smile amusing.

215

Toai nudged Thieu with an elbow to silence him. This old man had been fighting the French long before the Americans ever arrived—and the Japanese before that! He might be a goofy-looking oddball, but he'd killed more foreigners than they'd had pimples.

He was laughing along with them now—laughing at himself—but no one would care if he lopped off their heads. Old *papa-san* was a revered jungle fighter with a mean rep from way back. A legend in these hills. Scourge of Dau Tieng. Terror of the graveyards, keeper of the cemetery. No one would miss two bamboo-green recruits.

This man was a legend among the 9th Viet Cong Regiment. They should be honored he was taking the time to teach them how to survive in Dong Minh Chau.

The hill behind them was not steep, but it was covered with dense tangles of mahogany and thick scrub brush. There were thorns everywhere. The foreigners would catch hell trying to rush the machine-gun nests. The gunships were making life on the plantation miserable, of course, but the insurgents were heavily entrenched. And napalm posed the only real threat. It was raining again. The storm would keep the jets grounded. Soon the Hueys would return to the barn as well.

Dark as it was, the VC positions on this edge of the swamp were such that they had an unobstructed view of the Americans' movements. Other small hills rose up along the western confines of the cemeteries, and guerrillas moving forward along those hills kept the scattered groups of Americans pinned down, too.

A reinforced battalion of North Vietnamese shock troops was rumored to be en route across the Cambodian border to lend assistance to the local insurgents, but none of the older VC put much stock in that story—similar ploys by 'The Brass' to keep their men motivated and fighting had been used countless times in the past. And the NVA never showed.

The Viet Cong fought until they were tired or out of ammo or dead, and, in the morning, their commanders gave them a cock-and-bull spiel about how the NVA troopers had encountered a contingent of U.S. Army troops on the way over, or had been driven back by a monsoon typhoon, or had some bridge blown out from under them by the Green Berets, or had gotten lost in the dark or devoured by fire-breathing dragons. And everyone dismissed it as just another cruel joke of being born Vietnamese and went on with the mission.

CHAPTER 24

Perimeter, Cemetery, Dau Tieng

"This bites the big one, Gage!"

"Yeah." Ruckter ate mud in his attempt to flatten farther against the earth. Brody had their current dilemma nailed to a tee. "This truly bites the big one, Treat, ol' boy!"

Machine-gun bullets were slamming into the ground on all sides. Viet Cong were opening up on them from positions the Americans didn't even know were under VC control a minute ago. A splinter of lead jabbed Brody's thigh—it felt like some punk back on his old block had poked him with a straight razor, then fled into the crowd.

"The little bastards are comin' out of the woodwork, Gage-baby." Jones's voice.

"Yep, Reece, my man—the scrawny yellow fucks are definitely comin' out o' the woodwork!"

It had started out as a simple hit team. Frisk had taken his Nungs and some Green Berets out on a broad sweep through the adjoining graveyards in search of the wounded captain, and Brody's people were tired of being targets for the three VC machine-gun nests. For the last hour they'd been nothing more than sitting ducks in a shooting gallery, and the cavalrymen were getting fed up.

Vance had agreed that they should send out two squads to try to take out the nearest MG pit first. Then they could work on the other two. It would sure help chopperjocks

Mac and Gabe when they returned to pick up the captain —whom Brody and the others were beginning to believe was more phantom than fact, for the wounded soldiers all asked about him, but nobody seemed able to locate the man.

Going after the machine-gunners without air support had turned out to be a mistake, however, for now there were suddenly *five* MG nests to contend with.

"Where'd they all come from?" Jones asked.

"That's the million-dollar question," Ruckter muttered.

"I'd settle on a million-dollar wound!" Jones countered, referring to the gunshot or shrapnel injuries that were serious enough to earn one a med-evac slick out of combat and a freedom flight back to The World but, one hoped, no permanent disabilities.

"I'll give you a million-dollar wound *in the mouth* if you don't can it!" Fletcher threatened.

"Mellow out, Snakeman," Brody urged. "Remember who the real enemy is around here!"

"Well, I just don't like fightin' in the battle with a commsymp college radical from Berkeley-U ridin' my ass!"

"God*damnit*!" Ruckter had been trying to fire his MP-40, but managed to get only two rounds off before a cartridge jammed in the ejection port. "Fuckin' piece o' German shit!"

He dropped the submachine gun and glanced back over his shoulder as the leg lieutenant entered his peripheral vision. Not Vance, but the butterbar with no time in grade. He was low-crawling up to them from the bomb crater's other side.

"Where the hell did *he* come from?" Ruckter asked Brody.

"He's been with us all along, Gage! Get yo' head outta yo' ass, boy!"

"Shit . . ." Ruckter muttered. He was mad. He felt like making a crude remark about the worth and value—or lack thereof—of new lieutenants, but thought better of it. He eyeballed the officer's shiny new M-16.

"Anything I can do to help?" The lieutenant's eyes were naturally drawn to Ruckter—the biggest man there. He ducked just as several tracers flew past, narrowly missing him.

"Yeah!" Ruckter's hand shot out. "Gimme your fuckin' weapon, Lou!"

The officer hesitated, then, nodding as if he considered the request reasonable, surrendered the rifle without protest. Feeling suddenly inadequate, though, he drew his sidearm and held it poised by his head, barrel pointed straight up. Safety first!

Every enlisted man there observed the exchange. No one laughed. No one said a word. They just stared at the lieutenant for a moment, then they returned to the matter at hand.

The lieutenant maintained a low profile for the next few minutes, then quietly disappeared alone into the vast, shimmering sea of elephant grass. He was out of place here—a trained but inexperienced leader amongst combat-hardened vets. If he opened his mouth once or attempted to give a single order, they'd eat him alive.

Probably headed back to the main LZ, Brody decided. Where it's a bit safer, though not by much. Brody hoped he'd make it back alive.

Lisa Maddox was anxious to get back to the graveyards.

They'd off-loaded all the casualties, only to discover that several VC bullets in the helicopter's tail boom necessitated immediate repairs and deadline time at Dau Tieng.

"A half hour, Lieutenant!" Gabriel was not optimistic even about that. "Just gimme a half-hour."

"I'm not sure they've *got* a half hour out there, Gabe! What about *Pegasus*? Can we take *Pegasus* instead?"

"*Peg*'s out of the question," he replied quickly. "She'll be down until at least tomorrow. I have to order a part from An Khe, and the next scheduled ash-'n-trash isn't until 0400 hours."

"Fine!" Maddox snapped, pivoting on her heels. "That's all I wanted to know." She started toward the mess tent. "Just give me zero-five to grab some brew and I'll be right back."

"Like I said, ma'am"—Gabriel slowly wiped his oily hands with an o.d. green handkerchief—"take up to thirty if you want. Ain't no way we're gonna get this crate off the ground sooner than—"

"*Fine!*" she threw a hand in the air without looking back.

"What's her problem?" The crew chief joined Gabriel. "That time of the month or something?"

"Fucking cunt." Gunslinger tossed the handkerchief in a tub of gun-cleaning solvent and resumed patching bullet holes.

Lisa stared down into her Styrofoam cup.

She searched for Danny Delgado's face in the jet-black coffee, but no mystical sign came to her. This was her fourth cup in ten minutes. What was she trying to do? Overdose on caffeine?

The mess sergeant was staring at her strangely. It couldn't be that he wanted to shut down the mess tent— she knew for a fact he kept it open twenty-four hours a day. Perhaps he hadn't seen a white woman in six months.

He was walking over toward a huge tank of coffee. "Get you another cup, Lieutenant?" he asked in a warm, friendly voice that just *couldn't* have come from such a bear-chested, mean-looking man. Could she just be imagining all this? Was she becoming paranoid?

"No, thank you, Sergeant," She forced the words out. "This one makes my quota."

"Fresh tank just completed a brew cycle." He tapped the army-issue blender.

"No, thanks."

Lisa stared down into the coffee at the bottom of her cup long and hard. She swirled it around and saw the ceiling fan twirling slowly for an instant. Then she saw her own reflection. Tears were running down her cheeks.

"Everything okay, ma'am?"

Damnit! she thought to herself. *The old coot's still staring at me.* But she couldn't raise her head to face him. Lips trembling as she fought to keep the sobs in, she waved him out of her world, nodding that she was okay.

Lt. Maddox couldn't help thinking about Delgado, out in that rat-fuck of a battle. He needed her, and so did the rest of the men lying wounded.

Gulping down the last of her coffee, she wiped her cheeks, rose, and headed for the choppers, determined to make Gabe move his ass.

CHAPTER 25

LZ, Dau Tieng

Frisk found the wounded captain under a pile of bodies.

Many of the officer's men had perished in hand-to-hand combat trying to save his life. Now he'd be going back to Echo Company's LZ for extraction and a slick ride back to Tay Ninh City.

It wasn't easy getting him back there. Luckily, Brody and Ruckter were successful in assembling most of the Americans at an old B-52 bomb crater midway between the swamp and Big Boy. They would wait it out there until the Dustoff slicks returned.

It was raining again, but the brunt of the storm seemed to be holding back for now. And the Cong were quiet—a few potshots now and then, only one mortar probe. That was all, Jody baby. Probably massing for one final all-out assault, Jones grumbled. But he was probably right.

"What the hell?"

Brody glanced up. Something small and black and metallic was spiraling down directly on top of them with a smothered flutter.

A Loach!

The small observation chopper landed with a hushed whisper. There was no dust kicked up because everything was mud, water, or blood.

"What the hell?" Zack and Ruckter rushed up to the

helicopter. Lt. Vance, spotting the colonel's eagle before the others, rushed between the two cavalrymen.

He didn't salute, but also asked, "What the hell?"

"Don't you men have any commo?" the colonel asked. "We've been trying to reach you for over twenty-four hours!"

"We're with Echo Company, sir!" Vance was not eager to admit too much, but his lips kept moving. "Seventh Cav of the First Division. . . ."

"Airmobile?"

"Yes, sir!"

"Well, what's the poop, soldier?"

"We responded to a Brass Monkey, sir," Vance began.

"I know that!" the colonel snapped impatiently. "And we appreciate it! Just get to the meat of this buttfuck, will ya?"

Snakeman smiled, and Brody elbowed him hard as their lieutenant began the battlefield briefing.

"We've got Victor Charlie on that ridge and that ridge and that one, and probably all across those hills up on the other side of the swamp as well as—"

"Where's my Charlie Company captain?" he interrupted Vance and faced Ruckter and Frisk, the two biggest men in the bomb crater. "Have any of you men seen my captain?"

"He's right here, Colonel," Jones motioned the tall, gray-haired officer over to a body sheltered from the wind and rain by two tent halves lain together without the stakes.

"Is he alive?"

"Barely." Vance remained by the colonel's side. "We've got a med-evac returnin' *rikky-tik*!"

"Returnin' *rikky-tik*?"

"Yes, sir!"

"Well, what's the fucking delay, Lieutenant? We spotted some slicks on the way over here—they were beatin' blades in the other direction! Can you explain that to me?"

226

"We just found the captain here a few minutes ago, Colonel," Frisk puffed his chest out, trying to intimidate the officer. "*After* the last Dustoff left." When that didn't work, he made a show of tilting his beret a cocky degree or two—throughout the recent hostilities, he'd been able to hold on to it. But that, too, failed to impress the officer. The old petrified fart's been in This Man's Army awhile, Frisk decided.

"The other birds have been havin' trouble gettin' in here, sir!" Zack said. "Charlie's been takin' a lot of potshots at them and—"

One of those potshots suddenly struck the colonel's helmet, knocking him off his feet.

Frisk watched the glowing rifle round bounce up into the night sky like a sputtering flare. The sight made him think of sparks thrown from railroad tracks at night as a train passes over them.

"Sir!" Vance screamed. "Are you all right?"

The colonel was still wearing his helmet. Frisk dropped to one knee beside the officer and ran his thumb against the deep groove the bullet had left. "Lucky for you"—Frisk was not laughing, but his eyes seemed to gleam—"that round was fired from quite a ways off. These steel pots aren't worth shit when it comes to stoppin' a rifle slug o' that caliber!"

"How do you know *where* it was fired from!" yelled Vance as he helped the colonel to his feet. "I didn't even hear it coming!"

"Neither did I, Lou, but the distance obviously took some of the punch out of it, or I guarantee you it would o' left a squeaky-clean hole the size of a nickel right about *here*!" He tapped the groove left in the colonel's helmet.

They didn't have much more time to discuss the potshot. Dull thumps in the distance cut the conversation short.

The first mortar struck the colonel's Loach dead center. It exploded like a small volcano, sending hundreds of rounds of tracers arcing out into the night. Fireballs also rose up toward the dark heavens.

"Aw, shit!" Brody heard the colonel pounding his fist in the mud. "Took me six friggin' weeks to get that Loach!" Within minutes, it had melted into the muck.

Buddha must have been laughing down at them from the castle-like storm clouds drifting overhead, for the rains did not resume falling until the Loach had burned itself out and was little more than a flattened heap of misshapen magnesium and fiberglass in the middle of the clearing.

The colonel stared at the small wisps of smoke rising from the wreckage. All he could do was shake his head in silence.

The mortar attack lasted until the Loach no longer looked like a Loach. Vance theorized that Charlie sent in his mortars in hopes of preventing the Americans from using the light observation helicopter against them in the near future.

In that, the VC were successful.

Several snipers kept the men pinned down the rest of the night. By midnight, the lightning storm returned in all its intensity, and again, the medical-evacuation slicks were grounded.

With an amber, pre-dawn glow along the eastern horizon seven hours later, the roar of approaching rotors alerted the Americans to a welcome change in the stalemate. No one had slept throughout the night—mainly because of the miserable weather, but also because of the harassment fire from VC snipers and the constant threat that Charlie would mount a surprise attack on their position.

The assault never came, but even with a taunting hint of sunrise in the east, thick black clouds directly overhead kept the battlefield dark and wet.

"Dustoffs!" Brody announced unnecessarily as the first slick came into view a half-mile beyond the low tree line. Already, they could see bursts of green VC tracer floating up toward the Hueys from a tree line 200 yards away.

Brody's people responded with a deafening din of automatic rifle fire directed at the Viet Cong positions, and the med-evacs continued to come in, despite heavy hostile flak.

Treat hoped to see *Pegasus* in the lead, but she was not present in the first fly-over, and there were no other ships on the horizon.

It didn't really matter, though. A chopper was a chopper, wasn't it? He ejected a half-spent banana clip, inserted a fresh magazine, then began reloading the B.C. until it was back to max with thirty rounds.

The first Huey to flare in was hit by ground fire almost immediately. Tracers from five different directions stitched across her belly, even with the Americans unloading everything they had into the trees. Brody did not know the ship, but he thought he recognized the pilot's unique method of trying to dodge ground flak. Gabe The Gunslinger. It just had to be.

"Welcome to Moonbase One!"

Brody could hear one of the grunts talking with the pilot on the radio. Moonbase must have been his cynical reference to all the B-52 craters dotting the barren landscape. Barren except for bones from a few graves the VC mortar barrage had ripped open. He could not hear the pilot's reply, if there was one.

The enemy rifle fire abated suddenly, but, just as the chopper was about to touch down, another burst struck its cockpit dead-center.

The gunship's snout dipped, striking the ground, its rotor tips gouged into the earth, and the huge machine seemed to bounce 50 feet up in the air before crashing onto its side.

Dense smoke rolled out to engulf the bomb crater where the Americans had taken cover. They could no longer see the Dustoff. But they could hear the sounds of metal crumpling, fiberglass snapping, the rotorblades ripping down into the collapsing cabin. And screams. Screams from someone trapped inside.

CHAPTER 26

LZ, Dau Tieng

The peter pilot managed to squirm out through the crumpled wreckage and run for cover. Bullets flew toward him from a dozen different directions, but he sprinted across angel's wings this morning, for only a tiny ricochet's sliver struck his back, and he would not even notice it until a day or two afterward.

He would later tell commanding officers that, in his haste to escape the smoldering wreckage, he had not noticed what happened to the rest of his crew. Except for the pilot, Mac, of course. Mac was a goner. Mac was just so much *joss* smoke on the evening breeze.

The med-evac slick lay on its side, smoking heavily, but it failed to burst into flames—as every Huey that Brody had ever seen go "down-n-dirty" in the past had done. One of the doorgunners remained standing in the open, exposed hatch, his M-60 disconnected from its fiberglass lifeline and in his arms now. He was sending long, steady bursts back at the Viet Cong in the trees. He almost felt like aiming a tracer or two at the retreating peter pilot, but Charlie was the target of his rage now.

Vance couldn't understand why he was remaining with the helicopter like that.

Snakeman and Ruckter were already running out from cover to help the copilot, who had tripped and crashed flat

231

on his face into some thornbushes. Brody, Zack, and Jones defied Lt. Vance's orders and sprinted out, under intense enemy fire, toward the crippled gunship itself. She was not *Pegasus*, but they knew for a fact that Cliff Gabriel was aboard, and it was against the Gunslinger's Law to let him burn to death just because his ankle was caught between the collective pitch-control lever and the cyclic friction adjuster. No, that just would not do.

Doc Delgado wasn't sure whether Lisa was aboard this Dustoff or not, but he wasn't about to wait to find out. He watched Gabriel finally roll out through the cockpit's shattered front windshield, his flightsuit charred and smoking on the right side.

"Doc! *No!*" Vance was still screaming at everyone to stay behind cover, but the medic zigzagged around the cluster of soldiers dragging Gabe through the mud, away from the craft. Behind Vance, down in the belly of the bomb crater, the American colonel was crouched over one of the radios.

". . . At X-Ray Tango Foe-wer eight six six eight niner, how copy?" he was yelling into the PRC-25's mike. "I say again: Dump everything you got, into the whiskey . . . X-Ray Tango Foe-wer eight six six eight niner, over. . . ."

Doc Delgado arrived at the ship's mangled fuselage just as mortars began raining down all around the crash site.

Merging concussions knocked the corpsman off his feet before he could get to the chopper's hatch. Smoke was pouring out of the Huey now, but he heard no flames crackling and saw no fire. Deafening blasts from the exploding mortars rolled over him, ripping his clothes to shreds. He was dazed and shaken, and Frisk and some other Green Berets began dragging him away from the ship.

The doorgunner remained in the hatch, firing away like

232

there would be no tomorrow. His courage both awed and angered Lt. Jake Vance.

"No fuckin' chopper's worth your ass!" the cavalry officer yelled above the din of walking mortars. "Get out o' there, soldier!"

The gunny screamed something in reply, but his words were drowned out by the succession of explosions.

A mortar slammed into the earth directly behind the helicopter, and the gunny slowly disappeared from view as a wall of smoke settled over the wreckage.

Seconds later, he was back on his feet, however—face and chest bloody, but flak vest still intact, knuckles still bone-white as his hands whirled the smoking M-60 left to right, right to left, firing until the barrel began to melt.

Vance stared speechlessly at the machine gun's glowing muzzle.

"Charlie!" someone behind the lieutenant was yelling. "We got Victor Charlie on the whiskey!"

"Oh, my God!" Vance murmured as he turned to face the hundred or more black-pajama-clad guerrillas running toward their position from the hills beyond the swamp.

"Pull back!" he issued the order. "Everyone pull back!"

"We've gotta get this man aboard the Dustoff, Lieutenant!"

Vance turned to find the colonel helping carry a stretcher out through a wall of bamboo. The bamboo separated the makeshift LZ and crash site from the bomb crater where they had weathered the storm. The wounded Charlie Company captain was on the stretcher. Face white as chalk, he was trying to sit up, but his elbows would not support him, and he fell back again.

"We've gotta get this man on board that slick!" the colonel yelled again. He was only now seeing the mangled Huey for the first time—only now realizing there was no possibility the craft would be able to lift off again under its own power. "We've . . . gotta. . . . Aw, fuck!"

A half-dozen grunts were down on one knee on either side of the two arguing officers now, firing their rifles at the attacking Viet Cong.

"There's no way!" Gabriel wrestled himself free of the men trying to drag him back behind cover. "I'm okay! *I'm okay!*" he yelled. Then, to the colonel: "There's no way! Forget it!" He motioned toward the critically injured captain. "Take him back!"

"But we've gotta—"

"No way!" Gabriel was wondering when the wreckage smoking in front of their very eyes was going to register with the colonel. "We're down-'n-dirty! Kiss it goodbye. . . ."

"Get out of our way!" the colonel insisted. And then it hit him. The shock. The reality of it. The chopper lying on its side.

He glanced down at the captain.

"It's dead, Captain!" Gabriel sighed. "I'm sorry—the bird's dead."

"But just hang in there!" the colonel dropped to one knee as a storm of rounds began kicking dirt into the wounded officer's face. "Just hang in there and—"

But the captain's eyes closed upon realizing the hopelessness of the situation. His eyes closed, and he dropped back into the poncho-liner stretcher. The bird was down-'n-dirty, and the captain had dropped dead as well.

"Come on! Let's go!" Lt. Vance was shouting. "Let's get out of here!"

Gabriel turned to face the smoking chopper and nearly passed out. His arms began waving wildly above his head as he spotted Delgado being dragged, semi-conscious, away from the Huey. Doc Delgado, but nobody else.

"Let's *MOVE IT*!" Vance began pushing Gabriel and the colonel.

"We can't!" Gabe screamed back. It was obvious from the look in his eyes that he had expected to see more than just Delgado scrambling from the helicopter.

The Viet Cong were only a hundred yards away now, and they outnumbered the Americans a hundred to one! They were approaching fast in a wild, disorganized swarm.

"Whadda ya mean, we can't?!" Vance looked like he could strangle the warrant officer.

"Lisa!" Gabriel was being held back by two Green Berets now. "Lt. Maddox is still in that chopper, Jake!"

"We've got reinforcements coming in from Charlie-Three of the 21st!" the colonel slammed down the radio receiver.

"Good," Vance nodded. He placed a hand on Doc Delgado's shoulder. "Anything?" he asked the medic.

The doorgunner's still blastin' away at 'em. Man, I don't know who that gutsy bastard is, but he sure deserves a Medal of Honor if we ever get his ass out of this mess!"

"His ammo's bound to run out soon," Vance muttered. "How much fucking ammo can a med-evac slick carry, anyway?"

They all lay clustered around the bomb crater's rim, rifles trained out 360 degrees. The bomb crater was a good 40 or 50 feet in diameter, and 10 feet deep. Fifty dazed and battered Americans lay prone along the rim, shoulder to shoulder, holding off what seemed like thousands of the enemy.

After the Americans were forced to retreat from the crash site back to the bomb crater, which offered the most cover, the VC succeeded in cutting them completely off from the clearing where the crippled helicopter lay.

Sgt. Delgado was on a side of the crater's ridge facing the crash site. He held powerful binoculars to his eyes.

"Any sign whatsoever of Lisa?" Vance asked.

"None." Delgado replied without visible emotion. "She must be dead, Jake. I haven't seen any movement at all, except from the gunny. . . ."

"Let's keep our fingers crossed," Brody said supportively. "That gunny wouldn't have stayed with the ship through all this unless he thought Lisa had a chance."

"She must be trapped inside the cabin," Snakeman suggested.

"It's the only possible explanation," Vance agreed. "Or else she would have hopped out with Gabe. I've seen Lt. Maddox in some pretty tight situations—she's not your typical damsel-in-distress type."

"She can handle her ass." Delgado nodded somberly.

"I never even heard her scream," Brody sighed. "Not a single scream. . . ." They were both thinking about the other hideous cries for help that had come from inside the helicopter immediately following the crash. A man's cries. Someone who was in extreme pain.

The screams lasted a good five minutes, then stopped. The doorgunner never left his post—never even looked down at the victim, whoever he was. It was as if the gunny knew the injured man had no chance.

But five minutes of agonizing misery. Five minutes . . .

"Alpha Company has just landed," the colonel informed them. He was still on the radio.

"Where?" Fletcher raised his head and glanced about sarcastically. "I don't see no fucking Alpha Company, *sir*!"

A lone bullet struck Snakeman's helmet. It sent the steel pot twirling through the air, and Elliott flying backwards into a mud puddle at the bottom of the bomb crater.

"Fuck!" he shook his head after sitting up. Blood was streaming down from a minor but messy scalp wound.

No one ran immediately to his aid. "For your informa-

236

tion, *Specialist*," the colonel said dryly, "Alpha's been inserted over an hour's march away!"

"An hour!" Vance glanced at his watch: 1300 hours. Sixty minutes after high noon already. The Indians had missed their Hollywood cue.

"An hour!" Fletcher imitated his platoon leader.

"Quicktime," the colonel added. "And Charlie-Three of the 21st is comin' in from Tay Ninh on nine gunships!"

"It's about fucking time!" Brody slammed a fresh magazine into his M-16.

With this pronouncement, it began raining again. "Oh, great!" Fletcher stood up in the middle of the mud puddle. He sounded suddenly happy despite all the hostilities. "Buddha grants the Snakeman a shower. First one since this fucking operation started!"

"You take the cake, Snakeman!" Reece Jones shook his head. Inside, he was laughing, but outside, he was too tired to cough up the chuckle. "You definitely take the cake."

"And I eat it, too!"

"Here come the wingnuts!" Delgado's binoculars spotted several dark shapes moving in fast from the southeastern horizon.

"Yo!" Snakeman waved a fist in the air as two F-4 Phantoms swooped low over the bomb crater. "Flyboys, finally!" The jet fighters' wings waved up and down, back and forth, as they roared past, leaving sonic booms to roll across the land in their wake.

"I eat this shit up!" Snakeman yelled as he rushed to police up his steel pot and rifle. The rifle was at the bottom of the mud puddle. He snatched it up and scurried back to his position on the crater's rim.

On their second pass, the planes dropped napalm and several 500-pound bombs on the Viet Cong positions. Four more Phantoms swooped in, assessed the deteriorating situation, and unleashed more devastating 500-pounders on the enemy positions.

"The crash site!" Delgado yelled at the colonel. "Tell 'em to pepper that tree line near the crash site—drive Charlie back, so we can get down to Lisa—to Lt. Maddox!"

"I'm tryin'!" the colonel shouted back above the roar of six jets' afterburners kicking in as the Phantoms dealt Victor Charlie all the wrong cards in Nam's ultimate game of mindfuck.

"This is mindfuck to the max!" Fletcher cheered the Phantoms on. "I'm really eatin' this shit up!"

"We know!" Reece Jones did not sound as enthusiastic, but he was aiming at silhouettes in the trees, and actually trying to take out snipers who, in turn, were attempting to shoot down the Phantoms.

"Eat it like a man, Snakeoil!" Zack called out.

"Well, hell's bells," Ruckter stared long and hard at Reece Jones as he shot sniper after sniper out of their treetop perch. "Looks like just maybe we're gonna be able to make a soldier outta you yet!"

Alpha Company finally arrived at approximately 1700 hours, an hour before the sun began flattening orange and majestic along the western horizon.

Most of Brody's people were sorely hurting for ammo, but the infantrymen of Alpha had no intentions of replenishing the Air Cav's supply, or that of One-Niner-Six's Bravo and Charlie Companies either—what remained of them. Not immediately, anyway. Instead, Alpha began setting up defensive positions farther out from the initial battlefield. They wanted to get up out of the graveyards—and with good reason. Nearly all the scattered cemeteries were in the low ground. Charlie held the overlooking hills rising up on three sides. Only the rubber plantation on the east was no man's land: a free fire zone.

Vance had already suggested that Frisk take some of his men down through the orderly rows of rubber trees in search of an escape route—just in case they were unable to get gunships in and the VC mounted another attack.

Frisk complied, but it now seemed unnecessary. The Phantom jets had decimated almost all of the enemy machine-gun nests. The Viet Cong ground troops that had surged forward following the med-evac crash were now pulling back to the shimmering fields of deep elephant grass.

"Whatta ya think, Lou?" Brody and Delgado confronted Lt. Vance after the Phantoms had been pounding the hillsides for nearly an hour. Doc swung his binoculars toward the crippled medical-evacuation helicopter.

"Any sign of that doorgunner?" Vance asked.

"None," Delgado responded dejectedly.

"He's been watching like an eagle since sunup," Brody said.

"I know. . . ."

". . . And no movement whatsoever."

"They musta got the gunny, too," Delgado muttered.

"But you still wanna beat feet out there to check on Lt. Maddox."

Delgado was scanning the hillsides now. Sporadic shots were still being fired down on the Americans from on high, but they had endured that harassment since their arrival at the Brass Monkey and were almost getting used to it—if that was possible.

"You got it, Lou."

"Okay," Vance finally agreed. The threat of being overrun by a thousand VC guerrillas did not seem so ominous anymore. And now they had air support. Phantoms. That changed everything! "Just watch your asses."

"How many troops you planning to take along?" The colonel had joined them now.

"Just us two," Brody said.

"The dynamic duo." Vance's smile was a grim one.

The colonel's nod was a newcomer's surrender. "Okay," he said. "Lieutenant, have your men lay down lanes of fire along those—" he started pointing toward the hills from which they'd been receiving the most harassment.

"Consider it done." Vance brought his attention to three cavalrymen who were setting up an M-60 along the bomb crater's northern ridge.

"Fine, just so long as we—"

"Ah!" Brody was the first to hear rotors flapping in the distance. "A perfect diversion!"

They ran out to the crippled chopper as soon as the first slicks began flaring in to Moonbase One's red-hot LZ.

Toai's vision was slightly blurred. Now there were two gunships, not one, lying on their side down in the middle of the clearing between the cemeteries. He lowered his AK-47, rubbed at his eyes, then placed the stock against his shoulder again.

Toai shook his head, but was unable to clear the fog. It was still raining, but only lightly now, and there should not be any fog swirling down through the hills and tombstones —the rising sun had already burned it away. That much he had seen with his own eyes! He found himself wishing Comrade Thieu was by his side, so he could ask his friend whether he was having the same problems with his vision.

Toai brought his sights down on the two Americans running out to the crippled med-evac. He hesitated, lowered

240

the rifle, rubbed his eyes again—and yelled down at the Americans, 75 yards away.

"You die, *du ma!*" he screamed at the top of his lungs.

Then Ruong Nhu Toai fired off the entire magazine, delighting in the brilliant shades of green dazzling as the tracers soared down toward their target.

Toai did not watch to see whether either American fell in his tracks. He was trying to eject the ammo clip instead, but it was jammed. And he had no backup.

CHAPTER 27

Cemetery, Dau Tieng

Bullets bouncing between their jungle boots, Doc Delgado and Brody slammed into each other as they dove beside the helicopter's warped fuselage for cover.

"You okay?" Delgado grabbed one of Treat's shoulders.

"Yeah . . . yeah, I think so, Doc!" Brody moved his chin from side to side, then shook his head. "'Least I don't *think* anything's broken."

Quickly, they rose into cautious crouches and moved up to the cabin's hatch as another burst of rounds kicked up dirt 30 feet away.

"One thing's for sure," Delgado said. "That rifleman up there can't shoot worth a shit!"

Brody glanced down at a gash in the heel of his boot. "Well, he sure tried anyway. . . ."

Delgado was about to ask him to elaborate when two gigantic shadows passed overhead. The air above became a sudden fury of chopping vibrations. "Puff . . ." Doc whispered. "Puff the Magic Dragon . . ."

"Jolly Greens!" Brody was sure glad to see the twin-rotored CH-47 Chinooks. They drifted past, 40 or 50 feet above the downed med-evac, and slowed to a hover directly above the hillside from which the muzzle flashes and puffs of smoke had originated.

Huge Gatling guns mounted in the hatches of each Jolly

243

Green Giant, as grateful grunts usually called the choppers, went to work, chewing up the dense foliage from hillcrest to summit.

The AK-47 went silent.

Brody watched in awe as the helicopters remained over the area for several minutes, dumping tens of thousands of rounds into the treetops until several tracers touched off fires.

"Ain't that beautiful!" He stared up at the giant smoke rings left by the Chinooks as they widened their circles and began flying over some of the other nearby battlefields. At night, the thousands of rounds fired by similarly equipped aerial workhorses during their "Viet Cong hunting parties" often appeared as glowing red lances sweeping the jungles below. From afar, miles away from the carnage and devastation, the sight was spectacular and often haunting. Some soldiers began calling the ships Puff the Magic Dragon, for surely one of the mythical fire-breathing beasts could not have wrought more death and destruction.

"Bad news!" Delgado was standing over the hatch now.

For a second, Brody had forgotten why they were originally there. He whirled to face Doc. "Don't tell me—" But the dread was not there—it was not in his eyes.

"Empty," the medic's features became deep, worried creases. "The ship's empty. No Lisa. No doorgunner. Just one K.I.A. up front. In the cockpit."

"Mac?"

"Yep."

"Aw, fuck. . . ."

"Let's check that gulley down there," Doc pointed toward a ravine opposite the sloping graveyards, which had not been visible to the soldiers in the bomb crater.

"I think we should report back to Vance first, Doc," Brody grabbed his arm, sensing that universal urge to go

244

AWOL when matters of the heart interfered with the priorities of combat.

"Suit yourself," Delgado jerked his elbow away, and started walking back toward the bomb crater. "I was hoping you'd say that. I didn't want to have to prove nothing on my own. I'm a lover, not a fighter. . . ."

Brody's head tilted to one side. He didn't understand. He'd thought Doc and the lieutenant were tight. Maybe Maddox was old business.

"Vance can organize a search party!" he called after Delgado. "Bookoo guys with a radio and heavy weapons'll accomplish a whole lot more than just the two of us ever could!"

"Right. . . ." Some stray sniper rounds kicked up dirt at the medic's feet, but Doc kept walking as if he was in another world. Whoremonger could not see the tears streaming down through the ash and dust on his face.

Shortly before dusk, one of the Chinooks—its ton or two of ammunition disgorged now—returned to the crash site and dropped into a hover several dozen feet above the crippled Huey med-evac.

Crews specially trained to retrieve downed helicopters and other aircraft dropped from the Jolly Green on ropes, guiding giant cables and chains into place. Swiftly—for the occasional potshot sniper was still busting caps in their direction—the men worked at spinning a metallic web around the twisted helicopter.

Within a few hectic minutes, their task was complete, and the Chinook ascended, pulling the Huey up with it. Brody's people watched the impressive operation from start to finish as they attempted to provide cover fire against the VC riflemen still darting through the nearby woods. The

245

second Chinook circled around as well, but it could be only one place at a time—and radio communications between the two craft and the cavalrymen on the ground was almost nonexistent.

With the destroyed Huey being carried off into the sunset, Vance and his troopers set about trying to locate Lt. Maddox and the missing doorgunner.

"Anybody have any idea what the gunny's name was?" Ruckter asked.

"Nope," Delgado responded. "And I hate to say this, but I think there's a distinct possibility Charlie took more than two prisoners last night."

"What?" Brody asked.

"There was physical evidence in the cabin that three, possibly four, individuals were wounded during the VC assault."

"'Physical evidence?'" Frisk sounded skeptical. "What are you, Doc—fuckin' Sherlock Holmes or something?"

"Bet you wanted to be a detective when you were a kid, right, Doc?" Brody stepped between the two men. "Then you got drafted and Uncle Sammy made you a medic and wham-bam-thank-you-ma'am, you're here in The Nam with the rest of us. Now admit it: how close am I, huh?"

"There were three splash marks," Delgado tried to explain as Vance and the colonel went over their tattered and waterlogged maps of the area, seemingly uninterested.

"Splash marks?" Frisk folded massive arms across his chest in a show-me stance.

"Where the bullets exited their bodies," Delgado said grimly, "and the blood following the lead out splattered against the wall behind them. . . ."

Both Brody's and Frisk's smiles faded. "Then we're probably wastin' our time searchin' for these people, anyway, right?"

Fletcher and Jones watched the last of the Dustoff slicks

246

lift off into the sizzling dusk. On board, they carried the wounded from Operation Attleboro—so many wounded, in fact, that there was no room left on board for Echo Company or about fifty of the American troopers.

The cluster of clearings and interconnecting graveyards where Operation Attleboro had taken place was now a smoking landscape of charred tombstones and jagged tree-trunks. The Phantoms with their napalm and 500-pounders had seen to that. Charlie took a beating at this free-fire zone outside Dau Tieng. The U.S. Army managed to hold its ground despite a series of devastating ambushes initially. Jones wondered how long it would be before Uncle Sammy ordered American someplace else, abandoning the real estate to Ho Chi Minh again. Would all those men have died in vain? Or would the loss of a company commander wake up The Brass—from Disneyland East and Puzzle Palace to Washington and the Pentagon—to the unending quagmire developing in South Vietnam.

"My people will remain here at the bomb crater," the colonel told everyone. "Until we can get some fresh grunts in here to sweep the area and clean out the hard-core VC holdouts. My people will hold this cemetery and the grids between those two hilltops." He pointed into the setting sun, then toward the eastern horizon. "I'll stay with them. I figure on two, maybe three, more days here to take an accurate body count and ensure that the Cong aren't just lying in wait beyond the bamboo there. You know how overconfident they can get with those goddamned tunnels of theirs. . . ."

"*Real* overconfident, colonel," someone in the back of the group called out.

Nobody laughed.

"Okay, let's saddle up!" Vance announced, slapping his map briskly into a thigh pocket.

The men all glanced around. There were no gunships, tanks, or jeeps anywhere in sight.

"Poor choice of words," the lieutenant frowned at his own words, as the others had done. "Let's move it," he amended the command. "Back toward Dau Tieng!"

The blood trails at the med-evac crash site had led back in the direction of Dau Tieng. Vance and his men were able to follow these down for nearly a mile through the straight rows of trees on a vast rubber plantation, then the clues suddenly stopped in the middle of a small clearing. The rubber trees here had been cut down long ago—definitely before Operation Attleboro. Probably a year or two earlier, in fact. The clearing was about 25 yards in diameter.

"Do you think they extracted 'em?" Jones asked.

"The Cong don't have choppers, stupid!" Fletcher retorted.

"They probably just now—right here, I mean—realized one or more of their P.O.W.s was leaving behind a blood trail," Frisk said. "They either treated all or one of them there where the blood stops, I'd say, or . . ."

After a short pause, Vance said, "Or what?"

Frisk frowned. He wasn't sure, but there was certainly something odd about this whole affair. "Your guess is as good as mine," he finally said.

There were twenty-one men with Vance's party. The lieutenant was down on one knee, checking the clearing carefully. He had feared this might happen. But in anticipation of just such an obstacle, he had had the re-supply slicks bring in several PRC-25 radios. His group now carried four of them. "Absolutely no sign which way they went," he concluded.

"Oh, the little buggers were thorough," Frisk admitted. "But I'd say they headed due west, away from Dau Tieng —as far away from any large concentration of American and Arvin troops as they could get."

"Toward the Cambodian border and sanctuary," Snakeman concurred in a bitter and unforgiving tone.

"That's exactly why I think they went the opposite way," Vance told Frisk, ignoring Fletcher, "because they know I've got Green Berets like you augmenting my forces. But I'm taking no chances."

"Don't tell me." Jones's face became a pained expression of extreme grief.

"Yep," Vance nodded. "We split up. Five troops per squad. I want at least one Green Beret in each squad. . . ."

"Me and Treat don't need no green weenies on our team," Fletcher protested. "We're mean, lean fightin' machines, and—"

"Shut up, Snakeman," Brody muttered.

"Okay." Fletcher feigned a sudden, uncharacteristic meekness.

"I don't doubt your abilities to survive out there"— Vance specifically addressed Fletcher, then let his eyes roam around the group—"but these men from Special Forces all possess skills and training you don't get in your everyday infantry A.I.T., okay? It would be a poor command decision on my part to keep them all grouped together. Unless, of course"—the lieutenant glanced over at Frisk—"*you* have a problem with your A-Team being broken up, Sergeant."

"No problem whatsoever, sir," Frisk said. "They ain't *my* A-Team—they're all a bunch o' outcasts. I was gettin' kinda tired o' hangin' out with the perverts, anyway." He blew a kiss at the nearest Green Beret, and the commando passed gas in reply.

"Well, Charlie's gonna know we're nearby now for sure," Frisk added, shaking his head in mock resignation.

"All right, then," Vance said. He grouped four men with Zack and four with himself. An E-7 Green Beret was given four others. "Sgt. Brody, you and Ruckter and Frisk can keep Snakeman and Jones in line."

Delgado appeared to be odd man out. "We'll take Doc," Brody said.

"You got any problem with that, Sergeant Delgado?"

Delgado stared at Reece Jones for a moment, then allowed his eyes to fall to the ground. "No problem." He looked emotionally exhausted to Treat Brody.

"Okay, then," Vance gave each group a direction to take. "Let's move out. We search until you can't see in the twilight anymore—that oughta give us about forty, forty-five minutes. If you find something, fire a flare—the rest of us'll come trottin'. If not, we all meet back here at no later than 1900 hours."

"If we're gonna meet back here," Frisk said, "we better leave one man behind to make sure we don't return to a spider web o' tripwires and booby traps. I guarantee you Charlie is watching us right now."

Vance whirled around. His eyes scanned the endless rows of identical rubber trees. He wanted to ask "where?" but then he understood.

"This is Charlie's domain," Frisk answered for anyone who didn't. "Don't think that just because he's on the run, he won't take a break, lay back, and see if he can't throw a punji stick or two into your day."

"Good advice." The lieutenant scratched at the stubble on his chin. "Now let's move out."

Snakeman Fletcher cast Vance a bewildered look. "Don't we get to synchronize watches?" He reminded the

250

officer of a kid in a candy store, waiting anxiously for the latest batch of baseball cards to come in.

"You're not wearing one." Brody's reminder was accented by a solid punch to the biceps.

At the edge of the rubber plantation, the land dipped, and Brody's squad found themselves staring at another Buddhist cemetery. This was the largest they had seen thus far. Ancient tombstones extended up and over several hillsides in the distance as the valley rose and widened. Tall trees atop the ridgelines to their left and right gave the valley a closed-in, eerie feeling. The waist-high elephant grass rising among the tombstones made it appear as if no humans had set foot in the cemetery for a hundred years. Low storm clouds, black and ominous-looking, rolled overhead.

"No birds," Snakeman whispered. "I don't hear no birds, Treat. . . ."

"Bingo!" Sgt. Brody dropped to one knee and aimed at a Vietnamese male running through the tombstones directly ahead of them, about 50 yards out. "*Dung-the-fuckin'-lai*, you sonofabitch!" The command to halt left Brody more as a whisper.

The subject was obviously VC: His AK-47 silhouette was proof-positive. Brody fired a single shot, and a puff of dust rose from between the man's shoulder blades. He dropped out of sight.

"Lucky shot," Snakeman muttered, unimpressed, though his eyes seemed to dance a bit with excitement.

"Let's go check him," Brody started up into the graveyard.

Delgado and Frisk were both examining a smooth stretch of earth beside the last row of rubber trees. "We've

251

got another blood trail over here, Treat!" the Green Beret said.

"And chatter on the squawkbox," Jones, who had been given the Prick-25, complained. He lifted the receiver and placed it against his ear, hoping no one was calling their squad.

Gage Ruckter was whirling as well. Another suspected guerrilla was zigzagging up through the grave markers 20 yards uphill from the first. He was carrying a heavy backpack, but the 4th Cav sergeant could see no weapon.

Ruckter's MP-40 submachine gun came down off its shoulder sling and he took aim at the Viet Cong's back, but before he could fire, the man dropped out of sight. "Damn . . ."

He slid the weapon over his shoulder again, deciding that the pistol in his web belt holster would be more fun at what appeared to be developing into a close-in combat range, complete with all *kinds* of affordable cover— namely, the wide diversity of concrete and metal tombstones.

"Brody!" Jones called out before Treat could get very far.

"Yeah?"

"I've got Vance on the horn! He wants us back at the main clearing, ASAP!"

"What?"

"He wants us back at the main clearing, ASAP!" Jones repeated.

"I heard you the first time! Did you tell him we've made contact?"

"Yeah! He said he didn't care—it was from higher authority: Get our asses back to the main clearing, or face immediate court-martial!"

"Jesus . . ." Treat slid to a stop. What the fuck could go wrong next?

"You die, *du ma*!" a scrawny Vietnamese youth wearing black calico trousers and a tiger-stripe shirt popped up from a tunnel's spider-hole entrance 30 yards away. He began firing at the Americans with three- and four-round bursts from an AK-47. "Welcome to graveyard *you*!" he screamed between discharges.

Brody recognized the voice—it was the same one he had heard yelling "You die, *du ma*!" earlier.

"'Welcome to graveyard you?'" Fletcher repeated derisively as he automatically returned the rifle fire. "What kinda fuckin' shit is *that*? Let's get the bastard, Treat!" But the sniper had disappeared behind some tombstones.

Brody was torn between two courses of action: pursuing the gunman and following orders. "Radio to Vance that we're pinned down by a sniper and unable to pull out!" he yelled to Jones.

"I already told him that!" Jones was curled up in the fetal position behind a large grave marker, using the radio as cover. "He says to do our best!"

"Let's go!" Brody yelled to Fletcher, but Snakeman was already halfway to the area where the sniper was last seen.

"What took you guys so long?"

Lt. Vance was steaming, but Brody and Snakeman both had good excuses: They raised their hands, and the army officer's jaw dropped when he saw the deep gashes. "What the—?"

"Booby trap," Snakeman muttered.

"We were pinned down by sniper fire, too," Brody reminded the lieutenant of Jones's earlier radio transmission.

Rifles poised for the unexpected, they had raced toward the tombstone where the VC guerrilla dropped out of sight, Fletcher explained. At first, all they found was a freshly dug grave. But then they noticed what appeared to be a low crevice along one side of the narrow pit's floor . . . a crevice barely big enough for a scrawny Viet Cong to slip through.

Both cavalrymen jumped down into the grave simultaneously. That was when the spring-activated traps, hidden behind a false wall camouflaged with brown rice paper, swung out at them. The traps consisted of nails hammered through wooden planks so that they protruded several inches. The planks were pressed back against old mattress springs, which were double-twisted to pack more punch.

Not very sophisticated, the devices allowed Brody and Fletcher that extra moment to bring their hands up to protect their faces, but the nails had still managed to rip into their palms.

"We never did find the little Cong bastard," Fletcher told Vance. "Just a couple drops o' blood."

A U.S. Army officer suddenly appeared from behind some rubber trees. He had obviously been listening carefully to everything the two soldiers said. He did not seem very impressed by or interested in their story, however. Brody instantly got a bad feeling about the man. Fletcher whipped a half salute on the old boy.

"This is Captain Soto," Lt. Vance said.

"You the reason we got called off that search back there?" Brody sounded like he was speaking man to man.

Vance stepped between Brody and the officer. "Captain Soto is adviser to the Nungs over at Dau Tieng Special Forces camp."

The huge Green Beret standing behind Jones stepped forward as well. "Top claims he's a real ass-kicker."

"Evenin', Frisk," Soto accepted the compliment with a slight tip of his boonie hat.

"What's the meanin' o' this, Cap'n?" Frisk asked. "Why you callin' off *our* fun?"

254

"Some of my Nungs are gettin' the shit stomped out of 'em just a couple klicks on the other side of those hills there. I'm on my own. There's only a quarter-strength strike force at Dau Tieng as it is. I need some men. Lieutenant Vance has just supplied them."

"Us." Frisk frowned.

"You," Soto confirmed.

"We were searching for someone important down there," Brody cut in.

"Sgt. Brody. . ." Vance muttered in a cautious tone.

"Lieutenant Maddox and a missing doorgunner. Lieutenant *Lisa* Maddox. Possibly some other crew members, as well—we're not sure yet."

Soto glanced over at Vance. "That blond broad?" he asked. "The Army nurse?"

"Same-same."

"Christ. Well, if I know the Cong, she's tits to the wind by now. You might as well give her up as M.I.A. but Presumed Dead."

Brody glanced back over a shoulder, expecting Doc to lunge at the officer.

"Where's Sgt. Delgado?" Vance must have anticipated the same move, and Treat nearly tore a neck muscle checking over both shoulders.

Frisk and the others whirled as well. "He was right behind me!" Reece Jones exclaimed. "I swear!"

"Reece!" Brody's eyes bulged. "If you let some fucking VC sapper team snatch our best corpsman, I'm gonna—"

"I *swear*, Sarge! He was right behind me. I mean, shee-it! He was a goddamned sergeant! Am I supposed to baby-sit *every*body around here?"

"*Is* a goddamned sergeant!" Snakeman quickly corrected him.

"Doc Delgado the medic?" Captain Soto asked.

"Yeah." Brody turned to look down the trail they'd just

255

come up, hoping against all odds he'd see Delgado lingering in the shadows: A depressed Delgado was better than a dead Delgado.

"Hell." Soto's laugh was one of mild disgust. "Everyone knows Doc Delgado's been pokin' that Maddox broad. The Cong didn't kidnap your medic, sergeant—he's a hostage to love!"

"And what the flyin' *yin-yang* does that mean, *sir*? You tryin' to say Doc walked into one o' Charlie's traps and got taken—"

"I'm not tryin' to say that at all. We called you off that search just when, apparently, you got hot on the trail of some clues, right? Delgado wasn't about to give it up without a fight. . . ."

"You mean you think—"

"Doc Delgado's gone over the hill, slick. He's gone AWOL over a piece o' ass!"

CHAPTER 28

Cemetery, Dau Tieng

Delgado crouched behind a cluster of leaning tombstones. This was not going to be easy at all. Not at all.

He was on his own now, and Charlie was still up there somewhere, prancing around on the high ground, just waiting. He knew the VC were nearby—he could smell them, just as he'd been able to smell them on every battlefield he'd ever fought on in Vietnam. The VC were taunting and toying with him. Any moment now, they would put a rifle slug through the middle of his forehead. But maybe —just maybe, they'd make Lisa let out a scream first, or push her into the open for a second to flash some thigh before attempting to cancel his ticket. That would be all the time he needed.

Delgado harbored no plans to die for Lisa Maddox. This was not a suicide mission. But he owed the woman.

Delgado's eyes scanned the tombstones rising up into the green hills. There must be a million of them! he thought. Where to begin?

He had bugged out from Brody's squad an hour ago. Already he'd been crouching behind these tombstones, waiting for something to happen, going on fifteen minutes now. Vance and the others would probably come looking for him soon—depending on how serious the other mission happened to be. There was only one thing left to do.

Delgado stood up and began walking nonchalantly through the graveyard, inviting Charlie to draw a bead on him.

"We've gotta go back and search for Doc." Brody stood his ground.

"Oh, you don't have to worry about that," Capt. Soto said. "When I get back from this rat-fuck, I'll make sure Delgado's name is on every AWOL roster from Saigon to Cincinnati! Did you know they've got MPs who do nothing but beat the bush looking for deserters, Sergeant? And I'm talking here in The Nam! Not some cushy, white-hat job back in D.C."

Brody didn't seem interested, but Soto kept talking—in part, perhaps, because he sensed the cavalry NCO was not going to comply with his orders to abandon the corpsman. "They've actually got this detachment assigned to MACV's War Room—about thirty guys—and all they do is follow up leads about deserters from all the armed services. Did you know that? Oh, they'll just love this one . . . they truly will: Danny Delgado, notorious lady's man . . . seducer of members of the Army's Nursing Corps . . . bender of U-Sarvee rules . . . legend in his own mind. Yep, they've got this detachment of badass MPs down in Sin City. . . . All they *do* is track down goofy grunts like Delgado who think they're one up on Uncle Sammy, who think they can beat the system. They call these MPs the Dirty Thirty. And I assure you: They don't call 'em that for nothing. They're U-Sarvee's Finest." USARV—The United States Army Vietnam.

Brody laughed at the "Dirty Thirty" label, and Soto grinned back, but Lt. Vance got the distinct impression that the two soldiers were not smiling about the same thing.

258

"We'll help your Nungs, Captain," Brody said finally, "but first, there's a graveyard, a real big motherfucker, a coupla klicks or so down through that grove o' rubber trees, and we're gonna take every swingin' dick in this clearing and make one last sweep of the trail between here and there. I'm gonna find Doc before Charlie *or* the MPs do. . . ."

"We're going to find Lisa, too," added Snakeman Fletcher, "and the doorgunner."

". . . And then we'll help your Nungs, sir," Brody completed the terms of the deal.

Capt. Soto stared at Vance: The lieutenant obviously hadn't made a decision about what was going down. Soto didn't like the weird look in his eyes.

He scanned the odd collection of warriors and jungle fighters standing in overconfident, semi-defiant poses behind Brody. Every last one of the inglorious bastards had his gunhand resting on the triggerguard of his weapon. Would they actually blast him out of his boots over some two-bit, taco-bending medic? He decided calling their bluff wasn't worth it.

Soto didn't bother challenging Sgt. Brody about the way things were being decided here today, in this little rubber plantation clearing deep in the heart of never-never land. It really didn't matter. Not even to Soto, who would be listed as the victim if any UCMJ proceedings were ever to come out of it. This was The Nam, damnit. Nowhere country. It wasn't even a war. The rules didn't apply—and if they did, men made them up as they went along. Soto had to give Brody credit for the show of force, the display of bravado. He wasn't sure if, twenty years earlier, he'd have been able to do the same thing himself—stick up for a buddy, a blood brother.

"Fuck it," Soto muttered.

"My sentiments exactly," Vance said without any visible

259

trace of emotion. Turning his back on the captain, he started down the trail.

Reece Jones lost his ear the moment they reached the cemetery. A bullet ricocheted off the tombstone in front of him, threw concrete chips into his face, and ripped his right ear away in a spray of crimson before Brody or the others even knew what happened. Jones dropped to the ground, cupping the side of his face with his hands and rolling back and forth on top of a grave mound, but he did not cry out. The echoing discharge reached them an instant later. Then the scream.

It was not Reece Jones's scream, but the VC sniper's. "You die, *du ma!*" the taunt filtered down through the grave markers. It was followed by several more shots, which kept the Americans pinned down behind the Buddhist burial markers for a minute or so.

"What the hell does *du ma* mean?" Jones spat out the words. Sitting up against one of the tombstones, blood rolled down along his chin and neck. For the first time since Ruckter had known him, he seemed genuinely fighting mad.

"Motherfucker!" Snakeman translated.

"It means motherfucker?" Jones shot back.

"Yeah!" said Gage. This would have normally been his cue to rag Reece Jones about whatever they were discussing, but the 4th Cav sergeant actually felt compassion for the soldier now.

Must be all the blood, he decided. *Jones didn't look like such a die-hard antiwar radical now, with blood caked in his hair.*

Frisk was already beside him, bandaging the shredded hole in his head. "Anybody see where the ear went to?" the

260

Green Beret asked seriously. "Maybe I can sew the fucker back on."

"The *mother*fucker!" Jones sought to correct. "The *du ma*! You hear me, Charlie?" he rose up into a low crouch and screamed over the tombstone. "The *du ma*, you scrawny little shit! You shot off my ear and I'm gonna waste your ass now! Payback's a real bitch, Charlie-san, you hear me?!"

"Don't give the zip the satisfaction o' hearin' how pissed you are, Reece," Brody told him.

"Anybody see the ear?" Frisk was checking the ground now, but the ear appeared to be history.

"You die, *du ma* GI Joe!" the sniper cried again. As if to punctuate the warning, another magazine of AK rounds peppered the burial plots all around the Americans. Sparks showered them. Slivers of lead sliced into more than a few low-crawling men.

"Anybody get a bead on the asshole?" Ruckter asked. "Anybody actually see where he was shooting from?"

"*I'm* ready to go hunting Cong." Soto had joined the club. He patted Jones on the shoulder.

"Anybody see the friggin' ear?" Frisk was getting desperate. "Watch where you're walkin', men! Don' nobody step on this soldier's ear!"

"There it is!" Snakeman called out. "There's Reece's ear!"

Fletcher and the Green Beret nearly collided trying to get to the object Elliott was pointing at.

"*That's* not no ear, you shithead!" Frisk threw a smashed mushroom back over his shoulder as a tracer struck the marker beside his face. "God *damnit*!" Fragments of lead ricocheted amongst the men, and his hand slammed against a superficial cheek wound.

"Sorry, Reece," Fletcher tilted his head and shrugged

261

his shoulders as Jones's obvious anticipation turned to disappointment.

"Just think, Reece-baby," Ruckter felt the devil in him coming out in the trickle of blood reaching his chin. "At least you'll get a Purple Heart outta this fiasco."

"Just what I always wanted." Jones's reply was a sarcastic one.

"It's what I'd call a million-dollar wound, my man!"

Jones's eyes lit up. His head flew in Ruckter's direction. "Million-dollar wound?" he cupped his ear, winced but held on despite the bolts of pain—the thought had never occurred to him.

"Yep. . . ."

"You mean I'm goin' home?"

"You ever seen any one-eared grunts humpin' the boonies, slick? Huh? Now have ya?"

"I'm goin' home?!"

"Looks that way. . . ." Gage turned, his eyes searching out Vance. "Wouldn't you say so, Lieutenant? Wouldn't you say Goofy here got himself a million-dollar wound . . . a slot on the freedom-bird manifest . . . a ticket back to The World?"

Vance hesitated. He didn't seem quite as enthusiastic as Ruckter. After all, he was responsible for the men. His eyes scanned the ridgeline above them, but there were no muzzle flashes . . . no puffs of smoke. "Yeah," he said finally, "I guess you got yourself a meal ticket home, Private Jones."

"I'm goin' home!" Jones waved his fist in the air defiantly. Several shots rang out, but none of them came close.

"You die, *du ma!*" the Viet Cong sniper yelled down from on high.

"Screw you, ya zip sonofabitch!" Jones stood up in full view of the rifleman and directed obscene gestures at him

262

with both hands. "I'm going *HOME*! And you're stuck in this cesspool, ya cheapshot *lifer*! You're *stuck* here in the asshole of the earth!"

Frisk and Ruckter rushed to pull him down.

"But first you gotta make it outta this hell hole!" the Green Beret reminded him. "And this *is* a cemetery, honeychile!"

Jones sank down onto his haunches and dropped his head between his knees. He wanted to throw up. He wanted out.

Permanently.

Brody's people remained pinned down as night fell over the cemetery.

The VC played on the Americans' traditional fear of graveyards. Every few minutes, they would emit terrifying screams without warning, or throw rocks at the cavalrymen and Green Berets. Brody was convinced that more than one guerrilla was harassing them—the distances between spots, where sappers dressed in white appeared for brief periods of time, was just too great. Charlie was not treating them to your garden variety of haunted-house special effects. He was so good at playing the ghost that Brody wondered if perhaps just one or two of the apparitions floating through the trees might not have been genuine spirits darting from shadow to shadow. After all, this was a burial ground in a country at war—a very ancient burial ground, at that, and a land where large numbers of people had been dying violently for a thousand years.

"What's our strategy, Trick or Treat?" Fletcher asked.

"I can't figure out what Charlie's game plan is," Brody whispered. "If he's tryin' to scare us outta here, then why is he doin' his damndest to keep us pinned down?"

"Good question." Capt. Soto was between them now. "I say we start acting like soldiers and send some Lurps out there to get our bayonet points across. This 'Charlie owns the night' crap is shit!"

"I say we stay planted until sunrise." Vance rolled from behind his tombstone to where Soto sat against a wooden marker. "They know this place. We don't."

"If we stay where we're at, they're gonna *plant* us six feet under, *Lieu*tenant," Soto was fast losing his patience. "If you aren't in the mood to mix it up a little with Charlie, at least we can try and see where that blood trail goes. I'm assuming there *is* a blood trail, right? Didn't someone mention a motherfucking blood trail?"

"Over there, sir." Fletcher pointed toward some rubber trees.

"Besides," Soto continued, "my Nungs are waitin' for me to return with the cavalry, remember?"

"I remember," Vance's teeth flashed in the dark.

"I thought cemeteries were always supposed to have full moons," said Snakeman. "Isn't that a rule of nature or something?"

"It *would* be nice to get a little light," Brody muttered.

"Anyone got any flares?" Soto asked.

"Nope," Frisk replied. Everyone else remained silent.

"I say we stay put at least until pre-dawn." Brody held out his bandaged hands.

"Yeah." Fletcher did likewise. "Where there's one booby trap, there's bound to be more."

"We'll never catch any of these little monsters in the dark, anyway," Ruckter said. "I vote we wait."

"I second it," Reece Jones said.

"I'm afraid I have to side with the captain," Frisk told them.

"Traitor," Jones muttered under his breath, but everyone ignored him.

"Look, Captain Soto has been real *understanding* here tonight," Vance said. "He could be *telling* us what we're gonna do, instead o' listening to our opinions," his voice sounded as if it were aimed at Jones. "So let's show some respect around here, okay?"

Soto didn't give the men a chance to answer. "Let's go, Sgt. Frisk. The rest of you hold down the fort. We're going to scout around a little."

"Rodg," Vance responded. "How long do you think you'll be out?"

"What are you?" Frisk asked with a wink. "My *mama-san*?"

Delgado low-crawled between grave markers until his elbows were raw and bleeding, but the extra caution was paying off: He was halfway through the cemetery, and Charlie hadn't spotted him yet—or hadn't let on that he had. The Viet Cong seemed preoccupied with the squad back at the plantation's edge. Good ole Brody—he'd returned.

A blood-curdling scream only a few yards behind Delgado sent the hairs rising along the back of his neck. He froze, but then some sporadic rifle shots rang out, and he heard the rounds impact against grave markers in the distance. *Those crazy Cong.* He slowly shook his head. *If only I had a minute to spare . . . where Buddha and Jesus Christ would both turn their backs while I smoked one Victor Charlie off the face of the earth. Surely the world would be a better place without—*

His fingers snagged something, and Delgado's heart seemed to freeze: tripwire!

Now his heartbeat was racing. How much tension had

he put on the wire before realizing it was there? Would the damn thing detonate if he backed off?

He held his breath, trying to think. Three or four of the VC were firing down the hill now. Laughing and screaming and waving small white sheets in the trees . . . shooting off entire magazines.

A tracer bounced along on the ground near Doc's face —a *red* tracer. The Americans used red!

He turned slightly, realizing two things instantly: The VC sappers were running toward him in the dark, and, far off down the hill, one or two of Brody's people appeared to be mounting a surprise attack on the guerrilla ghouls.

Without moving his hands, Delgado rolled onto his side, against the nearest tombstone—trying to make himself as small and invisible as was humanly possible.

He almost cried out when the four Viet Cong charged past, right through the tripwire!

Doc felt the wire snap and spring back against his wrist. Another guerrilla trotted past, and Doc curled up into the fetal position, expecting the worst, but this one did not see him either, and no explosion tore him in half.

He would probably never know why the wire was put there in the first place. Perhaps the explosives—if there were any—had deteriorated due to wind and rain. Perhaps they had been disconnected accidentally. Perhaps the VC only connected them when they were expecting U.S. patrols through the cemetery. He didn't have time for maybes. Two silhouettes were moving cautiously up through the dark, following the maze of trails between tombstones. Delgado could tell by their size that these two were Americans.

He rolled back farther into the shadows, out of sight behind the nearest grave marker.

Delgado wasn't ready to be rescued yet.

266

* * *

Brody nodded off and Snakeman gently elbowed him awake again.

"Thanks, Fletch," he whispered.

"No thanks necessary," came the soft reply. "Purely selfish reasons: If you fall asleep, I'll surely be right behind you in the quest for deep Zs. No doubt about it. Then we'd really be up shit creek."

"We have to keep each other awake." Brody nodded in full agreement. He glanced toward the east. Already, the slightest hint of a false dawn was emerging beyond the heavy fog and swirling mists. "It'll only be an hour now, at most. . . ."

Snakeman and The Whoremonger were on the pre-dawn 3 A.M. to 6 A.M. watch—probably the worst in any grunt's opinion. The potential for nodding off was certainly there. In The Nam, that could turn terminal—it could mean the deep sleep.

Frisk and Soto had yet to return. Charlie stopped sniping down at them around the time Brody and Fletcher relieved Ruckter and Jones.

"Aw, man," Elliott shook Brody awake again, "we got trouble. . . ."

"What . . . what is it?!" Treat's head flew up. "I'm awake—*what is it?*"

"Something . . . something's wrong!" Fletcher realized they'd both dozed off after all.

Brody sat up straight. "Yeah," he began trembling and readied his M-16, "I can feel it too."

"Wake up the others."

"Right."

There was an unnatural stillness at one end of the clearing—where Frisk's Green Beret friends were clustered near a cement crypt. The men were not moving. They were not moving at all! In the field, few enlisted men find comfort sleeping on the cold ground. They toss and turn. There's always someone tossing or turning.

Vance felt it, too.

He was up in a crouch even before Fletcher reached him.

Pistol out, he cautiously approached the men clustered at the far end of the clearing. As he stepped over his own men, Vance observed that they automatically stirred, moving out of his way. Many sat up, grumbling softly. Others sat up stone cold silent. The Green Berets were still not moving at all.

Vance almost slipped in the sticky pool of blood. He threw up his hands, trying to keep his balance, and a face popped out from behind a tombstone 10 feet away. It was one of the Viet Cong, and he was pointing a rifle directly at the lieutenant's chest.

Try as he would, Vance could not keep his balance on the slight incline. His boots slipped out from under him, and he dropped onto his haunches as the VC bullet tore through the space where his chest had been only the blink of an eye earlier.

"You die, too, *du ma!*" the sniper screamed. His threat drained away into a hideous, little laugh, and he vanished as suddenly as he'd appeared.

A strange desperation seizing him, Vance reached out, grabbed the nearest Green Beret, and pulled his body over. "Damnit, man!" the lieutenant screamed. "Wake up!"

Blood gushed from the severed neck onto Jacob Vance and, with the bottoms of his jungle boots, he pushed the decapitated corpse away, back into the mud.

None of the other Green Berets had heads left, either.

CHAPTER 29

Deep Jungle, Dau Tieng

Lisa Maddox lay bound and gagged at the bottom of the snake pit.

There were thirty or forty of the reptiles slithering over her arms and legs, beneath her body, across her face, but it seemed like there were hundreds. They were obviously not poisonous, for she had been in the pit several hours now without being bitten.

The first twenty or thirty minutes had been the worst, of course. Her screams muffled by the empty ammo bandolier wrapped tightly across her mouth, she lay there helpless, hands bound behind her back, ankles tied together with a broken bicycle chain, as the curious serpents probed her body. But without striking.

She had even, while trying to sit up, fallen back on her elbows, squishing one—and she was still not bitten. That was when it hit her: None of the reptiles was venomous. This was just one of the Viet Cong's more entertaining ways of having fun . . . of trying to soften her up. But for what? Surely they knew they had no big intelligence catch here—she could reveal no great military secrets, even under torture.

She was, she thought, just an Army nurse. What good could she possibly be to them, except, perhaps, as a propaganda tool? She imagined the headlines: "American female in North Vietnamese custody"; "American female combatant released by Hanoi as goodwill gesture." But, if she died of cardiac arrest, she'd be useless to the goons.

She stared at the serpents. Falling back on the phase of her nursing training that involved snakebite treatment, she realized that none of the snouts bouncing against her face resembled that of a two-step krait viper, an Asian cobra, or any of a hundred other well-known Indochinese species that could easily kill a husky foot soldier, let alone a petite nurse weighing in at only 120 pounds or thereabouts. These snakes were obviously of the harmless garden variety.

She was amazed at how dry their scales felt. Lisa had always envisioned snakes as being slimy, filth-covered, and disease-ridden creatures. These, actually, felt quite clean, almost pleasant—so long as she kept her eyes closed.

With her eyes closed, a few dozen snakes rolling over her felt like some new massage technique. If she ever got out of this mess, perhaps she could open a "snake parlor" in Saigon, or perhaps on safer turf; like Bangkok or Singapore. She'd make a killing. Japanese tourists go for all the new fads; just think of all the great pictures they'd get, she decided.

Maddox couldn't believe she was actually entertaining such thoughts. *If she ever got out of this mess?* That was certainly wishful and foolishly naive thinking. She was a prisoner of the enemy. *Be realistic, girl, she decided:* You're dead meat.

The blindfold had fallen away a couple hours earlier, and her captors had made no attempt to replace it. There would have been no great effort involved, but she was happy to be able to see again. She could see that she was in an underground chamber of sorts, and that the snake pit was only a 3- or 4-foot-deep, bathtub-sized cavity in the tunnel's earthen floor.

Her captors—a squad of what appeared to be seven low-ranking VC sappers—had treated her harshly at first, with kicks, shoves, and long torrents of abusive language, little of which she understood, although it was certainly of a threatening nature. But they had paid her little attention since throwing her into the pit. There appeared to be an ongoing flurry of activity in other areas of the tunnel complex, and she was, at least temporarily, placed on the back burner.

She was not sure where the tunnel was located. There was a constant, muffled shaking of the reinforced dirt walls, which sounded like surface bombings, but she couldn't be sure.

The Viet Cong had blindfolded her immediately after pulling her from the downed helicopter—where her arm had been caught in the wreckage but not seriously injured. She was not sure what had happened to the craft's door-gunner, who did a heroic job of trying to keep the communists at bay, or the RTO who had come along in an attempt to deliver two PRC-25s, but she somehow felt they both were wounded during the capture. A final eruption of close-in discharges, sudden shouts, and screams, and the fact her uniform was covered in blood seemed to confirm her assumption.

She had witnessed the blades slam down through the cockpit, too, chopping off both of Mac's arms. Watching him lie there, trying not to cry out as blood spurted from his severed limbs, had been hideous. That Lisa was pinned in the wreckage and unable to help had been equally disturbing. It was a memory she would carry with her until her own death. Which, she was well aware, might not be that far down the road.

She didn't know where the two men—the radio operator and the doorgunner—were now. She'd been separated from them immediately after their escort from the crash site. Maddox had heard no English since being brought into the tunnel.

The Cong had force-marched her and the other P.O.W.s for about an hour to get to the underground complex. The blindfold had been in place nearly the whole time. There was something about the area they were walking through. She could smell the rubber trees. And she could *feel* the graves. Charlie had not taken her far from Dau Tieng— Maddox was sure of that. They were still in or near the vast maze of cemeteries dotting the rolling hills of War Zone C. To think she was lying on the same level as thousands of skeletons had an unnerving effect on the lieutenant. She wondered which came first: the VC tunnels or the VC cemeteries. If it was the cemeteries—if the tunnels were constructed afterwards, that alone told her more than she wanted to know about the attitude and motivation of her Asian enemy.

They had not raped her yet. She had heard them discussing it enough during the last hour: when they would finally do it to her, who would be first, how many different ways they would do it to her, and how many different ways she would do it back. She didn't speak fluent Vietnamese, but there was no mistaking some of the choice words. And the tone in which they were spoken was universal—it was the same degrading mixture of grunts and facial expressions men used worldwide. The VC did not consider her a great prize or even a possible negotiating piece at all. An unusual catch, perhaps, but they would have their fun with her, and then she would be discarded. These soldiers had probably never heard of the Geneva convention. Here, she had no rights. This tunnel snake pit—after they had their way with her—would most likely become her grave as well.

She stared at the earthen walls, wondering if arm and leg bones had protruded when the tunnel was first constructed, and if they had to be plucked out before final inspection.

Rainfall. Lost in her thoughts and muted fears, she suddenly imagined a thunderstorm, a monsoon downburst. Then Maddox shook her head, startled out of her daydream. She tossed her wet hair back, out of her face—the odor making her nauseous as she realized one of the guards was urinating on her.

Trying to wiggle out of her bonds, the gag broke lose. "You bastard!" she yelled. "You filthy, fucking bastard!"

But the guerrilla merely spat on her, shook his penis a couple of insulting times, turned away, and disappeared amid a chorus of background laughter.

"Damnit!" Strands of hair fell back over her eyes, and she tried to force them back again. The blond locks refused to cooperate. *Damnit!* She thought of Hanoi and Laos, and of all the American P.O.W.s who must be undergoing the same, if not even more humiliating, treatment.

"You call one of my men 'filthy fucking *what*?'"

A jagged shadow fell across her urine-streaked face, and the lieutenant looked up to see a black-pajama-clad Vietnamese in his late sixties or early seventies staring back down at her with an amused grin. "A bastard!" she cried. "He is a bastard! And so are *you*!"

"And 'ba-stard' means what, please?" He dropped into a squat along the edge of the pit.

"Whore's child!" Maddox suspected a trick question, but she didn't care. She could not remember ever having been so angry before.

"Ahhh...." the aging cadre leader bowed ever so slightly and nodded. "Yes...ba-stard," he broke the word into two clear syllables, and added, "We shall see how many little 'ba-stards' *you* produce for *us*." Then he turned

273

and walked out of sight, muttering "ba-stard" over and over.

Gangbang. That was the word that came to Maddox's mind first, following this short but rather explicit conversation. She would not be saved by someone of years. His old, dried-out eyes held more of a sadistic twinkle than those of even any of the younger men.

These goddamned Asian heathens, she thought. But then she found herself wondering if her treatment would be any different were she held in Europe or Africa. Probably not.

"We should kill you." The aging VC guerrilla had walked back and was standing at the edge of the snake pit. "But my commander... he says if you are nurse, you don' die today."

"I'm a nurse," she nodded.

"Maybe tomorrow... next week fo' sure, but not today."

"Are you taking me to Hanoi?" Maddox hoped she did not sound too hopeful. If they took her into North Vietnam, she might get some media coverage, which would ensure her long-term survival. Until the war ended. If it ever did. She'd make the official P.O.W. lists, which the War Room kept an eye on—as opposed to the M.I.A.s, whom most of Washington presumed were dead.

If they kept her here in the south—or worse, in Laos— she'd end up rotting away in some godforsaken jungle camp.

"Hanoi?" the old man laughed. "We wait for fighting to stop," his thumb flew up to indicate the battles still raging above ground a mile or so away. "Then we take you to PRG hospital."

"Hospital?"

"We have many wounded... many dying. Your planes

274

kill many PRG soldiers last two, three days. Many survive, but they have bad injury—from napalm fire, you know?"

Maddox nodded. She knew. Napalm. She would be treating napalm victims. And Lisa Maddox hated burn cases. They were the worst.

CHAPTER 30

Cemetery, Dau Tieng

Vance stared at the decapitated corpses beginning to bloat beneath the steaming, tropical sun. He could not have moved them into the shade even if there *was* shade—the VC snipers still had the Americans pinned down.

"Don't worry about it, Lieutenant," Zack seemed to read Vance's mind. "'Cause they sure as hell don' mind the heat."

Vance did not answer, but simply glanced down at the ground and nodded.

Jones stared past several grave markers at Ruckter. Gage happened to look up at the same time, and the two soldiers locked eyes. A burst of rounds danced across the cemetery's edge, and everyone proned out except them. "Did ya get your quota last night, Sarge?"

"What the fuck you talkin' about, Reece?" But Ruckter followed Jones's gaze back to the headless bodies, and knew. "You've gotta have a screw loose somewhere to say somethin' like *that*, ya little sorry-assed *shit*!"

Not only had the corpses been decapitated, but crucifixes were carved into their chests. Upside-down crosses. Or so they appeared. The wounds were very jagged, though none of the Green Berets had resisted—they all died in their sleep, it appeared. Perhaps the crosses were not crosses at all.

277

"I think you know exactly what I'm talkin' about."

Ruckter's expression became that of a man whose questionable past was suddenly catching up with him.

"Knock it off, you two!" Vance yelled as another dozen or so bullets chipped at nearby tombstones. Ruckter seemed somewhat relieved by the interruption, but his eyes still burned into Reece Jones.

"Come on, Sarge!" Jones kept it up. "Tell the lieutenant about your old Satan-lovin' days! 'Bout due for a sacrifice, weren't ya?"

"You're so full of shit, Jones. I don't know how all those goofy stories got started—probably some disgruntled antiwar *draftee* who got told by some sergeant to burn shit or something—but if I ever find out—"

Soto and Frisk interrupted him this time. They came zigzagging down through the gravestones, bullets kicking up dirt at their heels. "Let's move it!" Capt. Soto was pointing away from the cemetery they had just searched, and up through the rubber plantation—toward the bomb-crater encampment and helicopter crash site.

"Move it where?" Vance rose to one knee, and Zack urged caution: Charlie was really pouring on the sniper fire now. Ricochets tap-danced through the dirt where they lay.

"Back to the colonel's CP. This here's nothin' but a crock o' shit!"

"Any sign of Delgado or Maddox?" Leo asked.

"None!" Frisk said. "I think those blood trails just belonged to Charlie, 'cause this is a Cong graveyard, and them trails just stop dead up there. There's nothing else to go on: nobodies, no tunnel, no nothing."

"So fuck it," Soto said. "Let's get out of here while we can."

"There's more Cong over that hill there." Frisk pointed back into the heart of the ancient cemetery, "than you can shake chopsticks at!"

278

"What about these guys?" Zack motioned toward the headless corpses. Frisk's mouth fell open.

"I'm sorry, Sgt. Frisk," Vance started to explain. "It happened during the night. We didn't even—"

"Leave 'em!" Soto yelled. "Now let's go! We can have a team return to secure the bodies as soon as reinforcements arrive for the post-op sweep. Now come on!"

"But—" Frisk started to protest. Then he saw the company-sized force of VC swarming down through the upper rows of grave markers a hundred yards away.

"Aw, man . . . we truly got some hardship troubles here!"

Ruckter was pointing the other way—down the trail of rubber trees that led back to their bomb-crater command post. A large contingent of Viet Cong was also running toward them from the plantation grounds.

"This way!" Capt. Soto pointed at the tree line jutting out from the jungle's edge.

The Americans left the small clearing separating the cemetery and rubber plantation, and ran into the rain forest, Charlie's bullets following them all the way. But Brody's people made it behind cover without a single injury.

Almost immediately, as the trees became more dense, they came across a winding trail. "No trails!" Soto insisted. "They're all booby-trapped—no doubt about it!"

"Probably!" Vance yelled back, "but what other choice have we got?"

"If we waste time cuttin' through the vines and crap with machetes," Sgt. Frisk agreed, "we'll be cold meat within the hour. *They* know this stretch o' the jungle, cap'n—don't forget that. *They* know it better than we ever could!"

"Volunteers?" Soto's eyes scanned hesitant faces as the men stared down the narrow, hostile-looking trail. Slight wisps of mist clung to the earth for as far as the eye could see. They would never be able to spot any tripwires in time. Especially on the run.

Snakeman Fletcher answered the captain by sprinting past. He fast disappeared out of sight down the trail. Brody rushed to follow, but Soto held out a hand.

"Not so fast," he said. "Give him a couple seconds."

"In case he trips a claymore?" Frisk pushed past the officer. "So the rest of us won't catch the flak as well?" The Green Beret gave Soto a disgusted look, then was gone.

Brody nodded to the captain—he knew the officer was right, but military strategy didn't mean shit today. Brody's buddy was involved. Snakeman meant more to him than proper procedure. "We'll be okay, sir!"

The others quickly followed.

Soto urged Vance, who was down on one knee directing semi-automatic shots at the approaching VC, to fall in line. The lieutenant didn't need much encouragement—he was just waiting for the disputes to stop and the crowd to clear out.

In a flash, he was gone.

Dropping out of sight, into a squat, Soto quickly brought out two fragmentation grenades, pulled their pins, and propped them under small pie-sized rocks in the middle of the trail so that their handles wouldn't pop out until disturbed. Some in the fast-approaching herd of guerrillas would surely disturb the rocks, engaging the frags' firing mechanisms. A good, spur-of-the-moment booby trap, Soto nodded, pleased with himself.

He took three more grenades out of his ruck, waited until the first wave of Viet Cong was within throwing distance, then pulled out the pins and heaved the frags as hard as he could.

Before they even exploded, Soto had already vanished

down the murky jungle trail, trying to catch up with the others.

His pistol extended at arm's length, Doc Delgado slowly eased himself down into the tunnel's spiderhole entrance.

They were called spiderholes for two reasons. First, most had camouflage coverings, which, if one really used his imagination, resembled those of the trapdoor spider's. Second, nearly all of the tunnel entrances were filled with spider webs.

Delgado quickly learned that the second explanation was more applicable to the chamber he was descending into now. He tried to avoid the webs, but as soon as his boots reached the first level, his elbows snagged a thick, gauzelike section of webbing, and a squadron of 4-inch bamboo spiders swiftly dropped onto him.

Most found their way into his collar and began scurrying across his neck.

Most men would have commenced somersaulting back up to the surface while slapping their shirt as hard as possible and screaming like a wildman. Not Doc Delgado. He froze.

His sudden inactivity did not have the desired effect. Excited by his intrusion into their dark domain, the hairy green spiders rushed about him in a frenzy, exploring and inspecting every wrinkle in his uniform, every unbuttoned pocket, every shiny object. Two began climbing up into his hair. A third was trying to cram itself into his ear—

Sweat began rolling down Delgado's body—it was almost too much to take. But it was also too late to change his tactics. They were all over his upper torso now, and the medic was well aware that the bite of a bamboo spider, though rarely fatal, would surely disable him. If he bolted

281

and they *all* bit him, the multiple stings just *might* prove deadly.

So Delgado continued to freeze. He held his breath as one spider clung to his lips, its two hairy forelegs slowly probing his nostrils. Delgado willed his heart to stop beating so furiously—surely that was what was exciting them. He could hear his own heartbeat in this dark, confined shaft. Or so it seemed. Perhaps that was why the spider clinging to his earlobe was trying so desperately to make Delgado's inner ear his new home.

Then he felt it. On his inner thigh. The first bite.

Unable to control his muscles, he felt his mouth tensing, his head falling back with the pain—and that was when the two spiders clinging to his hair encountered each other, embraced in combat, and fell away.

He began trembling violently—not because of the bite, but because the sensation of a dozen spiders crawling all over his body was too much for Delgado to stand. The creature on his ear was gnawing at his lobe—but it was surely a prerequisite to a full-blown bite, and Doc's hands shot up, trying to pull himself out of the hole.

One immediately latched onto the fingers of his right hand, biting them several times, and he was forced to change strategy. He dropped.

Delgado dropped the 5 or 6 more feet down to the second level of what was now obviously just an old, unused tunnel, and he rolled. He rolled hard, trying to crush the horrible creatures, trying to slap them flat, until he was rolling through space.

Delgado dropped into an underground pool, and felt himself sinking into inky blackness—slapping away, air bubbles bursting forth from his lips, and sinking.

It was obviously an underground storage cache that the VC had abandoned because moisture had seeped in from the water table or from a nearby natural chamber. Over the years, a pool had formed.

Delgado's boots touched bottom. Rotting crates collapsed beneath his feet, and he pushed away, struggling back up to the surface.

Nobody will believe this, he was thinking as water surged into his lungs, and he tried to hold on . . . just another couple of feet. . . .

He broke surface with a wild splash, his body rising up out of the water nearly to his waist, and he was still thinking about his buddies back in Echo Company, and how he wanted to survive this so he could tell them about the spiders, and how he couldn't believe he was going through this hell for a woman. Survival became of the utmost importance to Delgado now. People had to learn about this . . . to know how powerful love really was. How insanely it could spur otherwise rational men to do some of the most stupid things imaginable.

The spiders were gone now, but he was already feeling weak. His stomach was cramping up from their needle-like injections of venom. His calves were cramping up, too. He wouldn't be able to stay afloat much longer.

It was pitch black in the underground chamber—no glow from the entrance several dozen yards around a distant bend in the tunnel—but he knew he was not alone.

Rats.

Dozens, if not hundreds of them. He could hear their gentle squeals increasing to an excited frenzy. On all sides. Waiting. Waiting on the limestone ledges surrounding the pool. They were hungry. And they were waiting for him.

But Doc's legs were really beginning to cramp up now. Soon, he would sink. If he kept exerting himself like this, the venom from a half-dozen spider bites might be pumped directly into his heart, and he didn't want to envision the consequences.

He vomited onto the black water in front of his face and felt better, but then the exertion took its toll, and he began feeling dizzy.

That was it. He wouldn't be able to dog-paddle around in circles much longer.

The rats' anxious cries rising in intensity all around him now, Delgado began swimming for the closest source of the revolting squeals.

Snakeman had been running only five minutes, but it had been a full-wind sprint and it seemed to have taken five hours. The trail wound around huge rain-forest trees that rose up out of sight into the green gloom of tangled canopies overhead, and it wound through an interlocking maze of vines and otherwise impenetrable bamboo as well.

Elliott slid to a halt as soon as he entered the small clearing. There seemed to be no other trails leading in or out of the place.

Brody and the others soon caught up with him, nearly knocking Fletch closer toward the hideous display set up in the middle of the mist-enshrouded clearing.

"My God. . . ." Vance whispered as he, too, nearly ran into the men sliding to a stop behind Snakeman.

Shafts of weak sunlight filtered down through a break in the jungle ceiling. The mist made each shaft appear a sleepy bluish-green. The shafts all fell across a soldier. A soldier whose nude and desecrated body had been nailed to a teakwood cross.

The American's head was missing—lopped off with a machete, it appeared. The makeshift crucifix was suspended upside down from vines and hung over a smoldering campfire. The flames had burned the dead man's shoulders and neck a charcoaled black.

Slowly, Capt. Soto walked up to the body and lifted a shiny object attached to the dead man's boot. It was a dogtag. Most GIs in The Nam carried their dogtags tied to their boots instead of around their neck.

"Quintana," the Nung adviser read the name. "Anybody know him?"

Lt. Vance stepped forward. "Quintana was the missing doorgunner."

CHAPTER 31

Jungle, Dau Tieng

Impenetrable stocks of thick bamboo surrounded the clearing. They could not get out, but the Viet Cong could not get in either, unless they came down the trail. Vance had Jones and Ruckter positioned where the trail opened out into the clearing. They were equipped with the group's only M-60 and two rucks full of ammo. So far, they had expended only a half-dozen bursts—to advise Charlie that the clearing was off limits and the trail was closed to local traffic.

It quickly became a stalemate. The Viet Cong were not about to lose any more men by sending them to certain death down the trail. And Charlie couldn't lob mortars into the clearing—the thick, triple-canopied ceiling overhead prevented that.

So they would wait.

Even if the Americans from the 196th Americal arrived with reinforcements, they would never find this trail. Unless the soldiers holed up in the clearing had a radio. That would be bad for business. The communists would just wait and see.

For now, it would become a game of wits.

"This *proves* I wasn't behind any of that devil-worshiping crap." Ruckter made Jones look him in the eye after they'd sent another long burst down the trail—just to advise Charlie they were not low on ammo and more than willing to rock and roll if Victor Charlie was in the mood to dance.

"Coulda happened while you were out with those Green Berets," Jones countered. "That poor dude might've been waitin' for us out here for *days*! Coulda been you did it when—"

"Jesus, Jones!" Ruckter shook his head in resignation. "Don't you ever give up? That body's still fresh—it's still got blood drippin', for Christ's sake!"

"For *Christ's* sake?" Jones glared with disbelief at the 4th Cav sergeant.

"If you wanna place blame on the basis of zilch, why don't you consider Soto? Or even Frisk—that goofy fiddle-playin' Green Beret?"

"Capt. Soto?" Jones narrowed his eyes at Gage suspiciously.

"Sure," Ruckter whispered as the men 20 feet behind them began digging defensive positions along the clearing's perimeter. "Wasn't it Soto who was gone for eight or nine fuckin' hours last night, when those Special Forces guys were beheaded? Shit, it coulda even been Brody and Snakeman—*they're* the two who supposedly fell asleep on duty! They've been hangin' on in this country for how many years now? That *alone* would drive better men than them *dinky-dau*. Jus' admit it."

"But they claim they didn't fall asleep!" Jones countered.

"Bullshit. You and I know they did. The entire company's exhausted. No one could stay awake last night—especially since the Cong didn't throw anything at us after the moon went down. Even Charlie went to sleep! I'm tellin' you—no one could stay awake . . . not even Whoremonger and his sidekick. No one expected them to. It was just a formality. They fell asleep on duty, and you and I

288

know it, and if they didn't, then *they* should be your prime suspects—not me."

"But—"

"And what about Doc?"

"Delgado?"

"Yeah. He's still out there roamin' around in the night, searchin' for his true-blonde cunt, ain't he? He's a god-damned trained and certified combat medic, ain't he? Hell, man . . . he coulda snuck into camp and sliced them boys up without Brody and the Snake noticin' even if they *were* awake! Doc would be an expert at that kinda crap. He could slice your head off without *any* noise, chump. He knows how to do it—I've seen them corpsmen go to town on corpses sometimes. They really know their business, brother. . . ."

"Fuck. . . ." Jones turned inward, seeking an explanation, but there were none.

After a heated argument between Soto and Jones—Jones no longer would work the MG with Ruckter, refusing to be paired with someone he considered to be a madman—the captain assigned him to bury the decapitated door-gunner by himself. The men slept sitting up that night, with their backs to the thick treetrunks, their faces poised to catch any sudden movements from the others.

Gunners at the MG nest were changed every hour. Three other men remained awake to watch the perimeter. Soto and Vance exchanged turns staying up with their enlisted men—they agreed one or the other officer would always remain on his feet. Frisk had been busy for the last six hours, trying to make contact with the Americal colonel back at the main CP.

Three of the radios had stopped bullets on the hectic race down through the trail and were no longer working. A fourth had also been struck by lead, but a bad battery was its downfall. Frisk was repeatedly using the fifth to make contact with any American forces, but no one was answering.

Could the 196th and its support units have pulled out without mounting a search to locate Vance's people and Capt. Soto?

Frisk didn't think so, but anything was possible. Perhaps the colonel *had* tried to reach them by radio. Maybe he had given them up for dead.

If that was the case, the remnants of Echo Company wouldn't last for long. They were outnumbered by probably hundreds to one, which was usually the case anyway —but this time they had no air support, no artillery, no reinforcements coming. This time they were on their own. Abandoned by the mighty Green Machine of the U.S. Army.

Charlie would wait until the 196th had pulled out completely. Then the VC would bring in their young suicide sappers and spare no expense wiping out the small pocket of resistance.

At 0400 hours, Vance swallowed his last handful of caffeine pills and advised Soto he could try and sleep for the next few hours—until the sun rose, or Charlie mounted an attack. Whichever came first.

An hour later, the American-made grenade rolled through camp, bounced off the dozing Capt. Soto's elbow, and detonated 5 feet away from the officer.

CHAPTER 32

Deep Jungle, Dau Tieng

Delgado was suffering with both a fever and the chills—or so it seemed. As he made his way down the jungle trail, he was perspiring heavily, yet seized with sudden tremors that made his knees buckle. He would drop to the rain-forest floor, shaking so hard he couldn't breathe, then finally recover and move on after a few minutes.

Several of the rats had bitten him before he could outrace them back to the spiderhole and climb out of the tunnel. Delgado didn't know whether the rats were rabid, but he was aware their bites had transmitted *some* sort of infection. The fever was testimony to that.

He made his way back to his medical pack and began injecting himself with an assortment of syrettes and larger needles.

Five minutes later, convinced he had done all a lowly corpsman could possibly do, Delgado lifted his helmet from beneath one of the palm fronds and turned it over. From within the steel pot's plastic liner and cloth straps, he removed an item. Mint green and radiant against the setting sun's crimson rays, Lisa's panties, his good-luck charm, flapped gently in the breeze. And he hadn't even worn the helmet down into the rat- and spider-infested tunnel!

Somehow finding the energy to smile at the memory of their last lovemaking session, he draped Lisa's panties across his face, dropped back into a pile of dead palm fronds and passed out.

He awoke in the dark.

A small bird lay nestled against him. One of its wings was badly broken. Its good wing flapped wildly as Delgado began to move. He reached down and gently grabbed the black and white magpie, smoothing its feathers down and running his lips against the back of its head, whispering soothing words until the bird calmed down a bit.

While Doc was sleeping, it must have dropped down into the palm fronds beside him and taken comfort in the medic's body heat.

He contemplated setting the little creature's wing, but then he remembered where he was . . . what his circumstances were. Delgado set the bird down and shooed it away down the trail. "Fly home, little one. . . ." he whispered.

The bird glanced back at him tentatively, then it limped off, finally disappearing round a bend in the trail.

Doc stared after it for a long time, too tired to move, regretting he hadn't put forth more effort to treat the poor thing. After all, he was a healer, wasn't he?

He stared down at his palms. They were puffy and swollen where the rats and spiders had bitten him, but at the least the chills had subsided. He was nursing a hell of a headache, but the fever broke sometime during his slumber on the palm fronds.

There was a sudden squeal down the trail—a bird's terrified chirp. It was a death whistle, Doc know.

Someone had killed the defenseless little creature. Delgado heard muffled laughter. It had been a pleasure kill.

Doc slid noiselessly back into the fronds and waited.

Clutching his pistol in both hands, the slide's top against his lips, he sat there frozen while the two Viet Cong soldiers walked by.

After they had passed, he aimed at the closest one's back, but hesitated. It would be too easy—another pleasure kill—and they could serve a better purpose than just contributing to the jungle floor's carpet of rotting plant and animal matter.

He would follow them. They wore no heavy rucksacks, which indicated that their camp or base of operations was nearby.

Perhaps the two VC would lead Doc Delgado to Lisa.

A sniper was plaguing the men now.

Not a minute had passed since the grenade blast threw a shower of rocks and dirtclods on the slumbering Capt. Soto, and already VC-green tracers were zipping into the clearing. It was the rifleman who was fond of shouting "You die, *du ma!*"

"I'm gonna get that sonofabitch," Jones growled, his gunhand massaging the olive-drab bandage where his ear used to be.

"I've got a plan." Ruckter slid up on his elbows beside Reece.

"Get away from me, you crazy bastard!" Jones yelled, trying to seek cover elsewhere, but suddenly Capt. Soto was between them.

"Either one of you see where that grenade came from?" he asked, the obvious rage forcing his bullet-grey eyes to bulge slightly.

"I'm assuming it's the same little shit who's shooting at us right now, Cap'n!" Ruckter said almost sarcastically.

"It was an American-made frag!" Soto countered. "An

M-26. I heard the damn thing go off with my own ears. . . ."

"Must be nice." Jones was still massaging the bandage.

". . . And one of ours!" Soto continued. "My eyes were closed, but I wasn't asleep, goddamnit!"

"What exactly are you tryin' to say, Cap'n?" Ruckter locked eyes with the officer.

Soto broke the trance and stared at Jones. "I'm sayin' I think someone right here in present company maybe went and—"

Frisk slid up to the men. "Where'd that fuckin' frag come from?" he asked.

A flurry of bullets from the Viet Cong sniper sent them all scurrying for better cover. The rifleman had somehow moved rapidly through the dense trees and was now firing down on them from the other side of the clearing. They knew it was the same man because he was still yelling the threats in pidgin English and Vietnamese slang. It was the same voice.

Suddenly, Frisk popped up and fired off an entire magazine from his own captured AD-47, sweeping the maze of bamboo walls. He swept in the right direction—the last four slugs slammed into the sniper.

Into his rifle, rather.

Sparks flew off the rifle's barrel, and the stock exploded as it took the brunt of a three-round burst.

Brody caught the whole thing through his folding binoculars. "Fantastic shooting, Frisk!" He had watched the sniper's weapon disintegrate. But before Treat could bring up his own rifle, the Vietnamese dropped back out of sight, stunned.

"Did you see the look of disbelief on that dink's face?" Frisk turned toward Brody, who nodded.

The two soldiers low-crawled over to Soto and Vance.

Fletcher, Ruckter and Jones were nearby. "I've got an idea." Frisk stared at Jones's M-16.

"I don't like the way you're lookin' at me!" Reece snapped back.

"How new is that '16 you got there, troop?"

Jones cradled the rifle closer, holding it to his chest so no one could jerk it away. "It's *brand* new. Why?"

"Hand it over," Frisk demanded.

"No way!"

Glancing over at Brody, Frisk said, "Put me together five or six bolo beans, Whoremonger." Then he lunged forward and easily relieved Jones of his M-16.

"You prick!" Jones's lips curled back from his teeth. He was again fighting mad for a change. "What the hell am I supposed to defend my fuckin' self with if Charlie comes and—?"

Frisk nodded over at the M-60 lying beside the trail where Ruckter had been sleeping: "You've got a machine gun there, haven't ya?"

Frowning, Jones turned his back on the Green Beret and hurried over to the heavy weapon—anything to get away from those crazies.

"Will C-4 do okay?" Brody had his ruck open and a small cube of the plastic explosive exposed. He was already pulling bullets from their cartridges and dumping 70 to 80 percent of the powder out.

"C-4's fine." Frisk nodded. "Now hustle. I want those bullets back together and in the top of a twenty-round clip *rikky-tick*, slick! And just eighteen rounds total. Leave me two spaces on top. Our friend *Du Ma* just lost his AK, and I wanna place an irresistible little gift at his doorstep."

Vance stared at the shells Brody was reassembling. Bolo beans, some called them. After filling the brass cartridges with C-4 and crimping the necks so tight the lead would be unable to leave the shell on discharge, the explosion would most likely kill whomever fired the rifle. At the very least, it would erase his face and leave him something to think about all the rest of his days.

"How are you gonna convince him it's a legitimate loss on our part?" Vance was skeptical. They couldn't just throw it out at Charlie and say, "Here! Here's a freebie on Uncle Sammy!"

"Simple." Frisk was on his feet. "Brody," he said, "as soon as I make my way out there to where we last saw the little prick, I'm gonna pop up, and you're gonna accidentally mistake me for a Victor Charlie, and you're gonna unload a full clip into the trees all around me. Think you can do that without punchin' my ticket, sweet-thing?"

"No sweat!" Brody nodded confidently, slipping the last bolo bean into its magazine.

"Then I'm outta here!" Frisk grabbed the magazine, forced two white-tipped tracers into its throat, then slammed it into the M-16, and disappeared through the trees.

Within two minutes, he was in the general vicinity where they had last spotted the Viet Cong sniper. As planned, Frisk popped up, firing off two quick rounds toward the VC positions. Simultaneously, Brody began peppering the trees close to Frisk.

The men watched two white tracers leave Frisk's rifle convincingly enough, then the Green Beret walked into the path of Brody's bullets!

Like a baton, he flipped the M-16 into the air, end over end. All eyes seemed to be on the rifle as it rose then fell among the branches.

By the time it dropped into some bushes, Frisk was gone.

Lisa Maddox watched the two Viet Cong guerrillas drop down through the tunnel entrance. They didn't even need to use the bamboo ladder that led to the surface.

She turned to avoid their eyes, for they were the same two who always directed vulgar looks at her whenever they returned from jungle patrols or details of one sort or another. The same two who always made a point of walking close to the corner where she was tied up, playing with their crotches when they passed.

The lieutenant was no longer in the snake pit, but bound to an ammo crate in an out-of-the-way corner of the tunnel. And she had been working on the strips of twine that kept her wrists together, constantly twisting them back and forth. She thought she just might have them loosened enough now to slip free of. But then where would she go? Several of the sappers were always present.

Then Lisa Maddox's world exploded. There was a loud *pop*! and out of the corner of one eye she spotted a cannister rolling across the floor spewing silver smoke: tear gas.

A third person was dropping down into the tunnel entrance—she could not make out his face because of all the smoke; she couldn't even tell whether he was American or Vietnamese. And then she rolled onto the earthen floor as yellow flames began lighting up the tunnel: A pistol was discharging.

One of the VC began firing his AK in response, but all the rounds were stitching the ceiling, and dust began raining down to mix with the billowing clouds of blue smoke.

Maddox rolled toward the tunnel entrance as a gang of Viet Cong stormed the gunman, knocking him off his feet back into the ammo-supply cache. She froze as several more sets of tire-tread sandals flew by. And then Lisa looked up.

There was no one nearby. She had no idea how she would ever be able to make it up the ladder with her hands tied behind her back, but nothing was impossible. She had to try! Blinding shafts of sunlight shone down through the gunsmoke like a sign from God.

"You're a goddamned Army lieutenant, girl," she muttered under her breath, unable to hear her own words as more discharges exploded nearby. "You can do it!"

Her ears ringing from the many gunshots, her mind recalling all those bedroom conversations she and Delgado had shared, Lisa rose unsteadily. Her arms were still tied behind her back and, starting toward the bamboo ladder leading up through the spiderhole trapdoor, she lost her balance and stumbled.

"Damn. . . ." she muttered, feeling blood drip from a scraped elbow. The small of her back ached, too, as if it had been pricked with a needle. Voices were screaming in the distance, but she could not make them out because her ears still rang like church bells.

She twisted and turned, trying to get back to her feet again, and the twine holding her wrists together snapped. Her hands came free, and that was all the extra incentive Lisa Maddox needed.

She grabbed the bamboo ladder and flew up into the sunlight, three and four rungs at a time.

Delgado did not feel like he was in his environment. This was not his cup of tea.

He twisted and turned, kicking out, slamming away with the pistol barrel, but the skinny old man riding his

298

back like a cowboy on a bucking bronco wouldn't let go on the thick St. Christopher's medal chain around his neck.

The medic's .45 was empty, but he refused to release it. As he staggered from one side of the underground tunnel to the other, crashing into the reinforcing supports and ammo crates, he kept pistol-whipping the old man on his back. The old man choked back, trying to strangle the American intruder.

Immediately after dropping into the tunnel and firing off his eight rounds, Delgado had disarmed the youth with the rifle. Smashing his skull in with the butt of his own weapon, Delgado then sprayed a dozen AK rounds out in a wide arc, killing every Viet Cong in the chamber except for the old man. The old man was obviously a cell leader of some sort, and he had experience under his khaki belt, for Doc never saw him coming. Now the senior sapper was trying to kill him with an old choke-hold maneuver—either that or he was attempting to snap the American's neck.

Bending over as far as he could while still maintaining his balance, Delgado charged a wooden buttress near the tunnel's entrance ladder. He ducked, and, channeling all his power into forward momentum, forced the old man's face against the thick teakwood support beam.

Groaning loudly, the VC released his hold on Delgado and slid down off the corpsman's back. He crumpled onto the earthen floor.

Delgado pivoted, intending to bring the rifle down hard —to buttstroke the Cong elder to death—but he hesitated. The old man's right eyeball had been smashed flat by the teakwood beam. His skull was fractured as well. Blood trickled from his nose, ears and lips.

Delgado dropped to one knee and, glancing around to make sure no one was sneaking up on him from behind, quickly examined the old guerrilla's face. "You'll live, *Papa-san*," he muttered, dropping the man's head back into the dust. "You've only got one eye left now, and that skull fracture just might do you in in the long run, but for the next month or so you're going to be more trouble to your men than you're worth. You're gonna wish you *had* died."

Then he turned and checked behind some of the huge ammunition crates in the underground cache. He could find no sign the VC had been holding prisoners here. There was no evidence at all that Lisa was ever down in this tunnel.

"Lisa!" he called her name anyway. Along the wall opposite the chamber's spiderhole entrance, a series of smaller tunnels burrowed down into the earth's dark bowels. "*Lisa!* Can you hear me?"

He listened hard for muffled screams . . . kicking sounds . . . metal against wood . . . flesh against earth . . . *anything*! But it was useless. Doc Delgado's ears were still ringing. He wouldn't have been able to hear Lisa if she was groaning off on a pelvic ride of multiple orgasms directly on top of him.

The medic climbed up the bamboo ladder and paused at the tunnel's entrance. The shoot-out had attracted no other guerrillas yet. He glanced around. No movement in the trees. Nothing to indicate Lisa had even been within 10 miles of this spiderhole. . . .

Then, climbing out of the tunnel entrance now, he saw it clearly in the thick layer of dust beside the trapdoor's coffee-can hinge: a bare footprint, small enough to be a woman's.

Toai watched the big American running off through the trees. Toai was terrified. They had shot his AK-47 right out of his hands! Teacher was going to kill him. And here this lumbering Green Beret had nearly caught him . . . had

300

nearly finished him off. Thank Buddha his men mistook him for guerrillas in the trees, and fired on the counter-insurgent, or Toai would be only so much hogfeed right now.

Toai stared at the shiny, new M-16 lying on top of a bush only 15 feet away. The big Green Beret had dropped it when his own men began shooting at him. The Green Beret had dropped, too—like a sack of rice. They had hit one of their own men!

Perhaps if he could sneak out there and retrieve not only the M-16, but the green beret and two ears off the giant commando, Teacher would not be so harsh on him. Toai wavered on his feet, trying to make a decision.

Suddenly, Toai found himself darting out into the open, toward the fancy American-made automatic rifle. Keeping bent down low, he snatched the sling and paused a moment to scan the ground for the Green Beret's body—but there was no sign of it. Somehow the big GI had survived, or was crawling off along the jungle floor, wounded. Toai didn't have time to linger and investigate.

Bullets were zinging in all around now—the Americans had spotted him!

Toai ran deeper into the woods, carrying his new war trophy. He began laughing uncontrollably at the ease with which he'd grabbed the weapon, but it would have been so much better to bring Teacher a green beret and two ears as well.

With his binoculars, Treat Brody caught a glimpse of the Vietnamese sniper darting off through the trees like an antelope. Then the youth was gone—another hostile shadow in Void Vicious to contend with.

Sgt. Frisk slid up beside Brody on his knees. He was breathing hard. "Did the little shit take the bait?" he asked.

"Worked like a charm," Brody grinned.

"Fuckin-A." Frisk slapped a meaty fist against his palm. Now it would only be a matter of time before they heard a facelifting blast follow the metallic twang of an M-16 charging handle at work.

Lisa Maddox stumbled through the brush, trying to get as far away from the underground tunnel as she possibly could. Already, she had nearly been re-captured by a patrol of Viet Cong moving through the woods. But the VC had been trotting at a brisk pace—and she was able to hear them coming in time to duck down near some palm fronds.

Her chest heaving, Maddox lay back against a tree trunk, trying to catch her breath. Staring up at the rain forest's multilayered ceiling, she could see parrots flying about. Huge parrots, painted every color of the rainbow. It seemed so calm up there, high in the jungle's canopy. . . . Perhaps she could just build a treehouse, like Tarzan and Jane, make friends with a pet gibbon, and refuse to come down until the war was over.

When her strength began returning, she rose up onto her elbows and noticed the dead bird for the first time. A black and white magpie, its head had been twisted off. She stared at the tiny, frail bones protruding from the broken wing. Law of the jungle, she thought. Only the strong survive here. . . . Maybe it wouldn't be such fun living in a tree-house after all.

She rose to her feet and glanced around. Only the one trail. Lisa had almost forgotten which way she came from —which way the tunnel was. She couldn't be that careless again!

But then she started feeling faint. Dizzy and faint . . . weak. The small of her back was damp. The adrenaline was beginning to ebb, the pain starting to lance up from her hips, out through her breasts. Her nipples felt erect suddenly, taut with pain.

302

Dau, she heard a Vietnamese woman's voice back in the hospital in Qui Nhon. *Dau* means pain.

Lisa felt she knew *dau* now.

She ran her knuckles back along the small of her back and came away with blood all over her hand.

She had been hit down in the tunnel. One of the lucky bastards had got her. "Damn!" she muttered, thinking this was not how it should end at all . . . this was not how a bullet wound should feel. She could not feel the hole, just a dull, throbbing pain, slowly increasing in intensity.

The lieutenant forced herself back onto her feet. She started down the trail, unable to remember now which way the VC tunnel was.

Suddenly the trail opened up into a dark clearing, deep in the heart of the rain forest. Instead of mushrooms, tombstones rose up here. Another cemetery.

"No!" she screamed at the confusing dead end. "I will not die here! Not in this . . . in this. . . ."

She whirled around, and found she was facing still another mist-enshrouded clearing, also crowded with grave markers. "*No!*" she screamed again, dropping to her knees, eyes tightly closed, fists clenched in anger. She dropped onto her side and began sobbing.

CHAPTER 33

Jungle, Dau Tieng

Toai ran his fingers along the M-16's smooth black hand-guards and felt a tingle swirl through his system. He'd lost his AK-47, but now he had a more prestigious weapon. No Viet Cong was allowed to carry an M-16 unless he had taken it off a GI he had killed personally. And that was exactly what he would tell Thieu and the others.

In the safety of his treetop perch, he pushed the magazine ejector button, and slid the ammo clip out. The rounds looked shiny and new.

Toai carefully took them out of the magazine, piling them in his lap, then withdrew a box of old, greening, and moldy cartridges he had been carrying in the bottom of his ruck since beginning the long trek down the Ho Chi Minh Trail. He had found the box of shells up near Hue, at an American air force crash site, and had no idea how old they were, or whether they would even fire, but he was sure they would. Everything made in America was built to last.

The teenage VC took all the old shells from the torn and crumbling box and forced them down into the well-oiled unscratched M-16 magazine. Then he carefully placed the new bullets into the box, closed its lid tightly, and replaced it in his pack.

He would save the shiny new bullets for a special occasion.

Toai wanted to see how well the fancy M-16 worked. He also wanted to learn if the old bullets were still any good, so he jerked back the rifle's charging handle, listened to a live round slide into the chamber, observed that the fire selector was already on SEMI, and aimed down at the clearing at cemetery's edge, 75 yards away.

He fired one shot, and watched a puff of dirt rise in the middle of the clearing. Not bad! he thought, watching the GIs along the clearing's perimeter scramble for cover and peer forth over their fallen logs and piles of dirt, seeking him out.

The old shells had apparently retained their spunk.

It was clear that most of the Americans below thought he was in the opposite tree line. Why they thought so was unclear to Toai. Perhaps his bullet had not hit the center of the clearing at all, but struck a tree above and beyond it, only to ricochet back down amongst the cavalrymen before sending up its telltale puff of dust.

There was only one way to find out for sure, he smiled. Toai could see one soldier in particular. The smallest in the group, he was lying prone beside an M-60, staring out in the wrong direction like all the rest.

Toai flipped the rear sight into its long-range mode and aimed at the GI's head. He took in a deep breath, slowly exhaled, then gently squeezed the trigger.

The American soldier seemed to rise up off the ground several inches. He began screaming, and rolled away from the spot where the trail met the clearing. Blood spurted from the soldier's hand up into the air in a fine spray.

Toai grinned with satisfaction. Not a head hit, but not bad at all from that distance. And everyone knew the wounded could be more trouble for an infantry commander than the dead.

306

Toai slid down his tree and began hiking back to the tunnel complex. His stomach was beginning to growl, and one couldn't have that while on the prowl.

He might even show Thieu the photo of Linh today— that's how good a mood Toai was in.

Reece Jones rolled all the way to the middle of the clearing before realizing how vulnerable to more bullets he now was. Sgt. Frisk flew from cover, grabbed an arm and a leg, lifted the wounded cavalryman's right side completely up off the ground, and drag-carried him back to one of the trenches.

"My finger!" Jones was yelling defensively, as if to excuse his actions. "That *du ma* sonofabitch shot off my goddamned finger, Sarge! *Look at it!*"

"I know! I know!" Frisk tried to calm him down. "Let me see it! Settle down."

Vance braved the possibility of additional rounds and dove beside them. "How bad is it?"

Jones held up his left hand. Blood was still squirting from where the ring finger had been severed. "Good. Keep it right there!" Frisk said. "Keep it elevated, you hear me?"

"My God," Vance had seen a thousand dead bodies since arriving in Vietnam, but it was these smaller wounds that always made him feel like throwing up.

Frisk was working frantically to wrap a bandage around the small stump. An ivory-white splinter of bone protruded where the finger had been smashed off by an unseen slug of lead.

"Damn," Vance bit into his lower lip. "I sure wish Doc was here! Can't we get him anything for the pain?"

"I can bop him over the head a couple times, sir," Frisk said with a straight face, "but that's about it. . . ."

"I'll be all right, Lieutenant," Jones was keeping his own face pressed against the earth in an attempt to fight the throbbing bolts lancing up and down his forearm.

Brody was beside them now, too. "We'll get that son of a bitch, Reece!" he said. "I *promise* you we will—if it's the last thing I do!"

"I thought you clowns planted bolo beans in that fucking '16!" Tears welled up in Jones's eyes as he fought the intense pain.

"I thought so, too," Frisk eyeballed Brody. "What the hell happened, Whoremonger?"

"I packed enough C-4 in those shells to blow that fucker beyond Bien Hoa!" Treat retorted with concerned eyes. "I *swear*, guys! I know what I'm doin' when it comes to bolo beans. That little scrawny fuckwad out there must be carryin' his own bandolier!"

"Just the thought I got dinged by one of our own rifles hurts almost as much as the missing finger!" Jones told them.

"Unfortunately," Frisk muttered.

"Yep," nodded Snakeman, who was among them now, too. "That weren't no AK crack. It was definitely one of ours."

"Shit." Jones was shaking his head violently now. "Any other day and I'd a been med-evac'ed the hell out of here long ago, you know that?"

"I'm sorry, Reece." Vance was shaking his head too. "I feel personally responsible for—"

But Jones cut him off. "I'm not asking for your sympathy, sir. It's not your fault. . . . It's just that . . . well, this certainly sucks the big one. . . ."

"You can say that again," Frisk nodded.

Jones's lips started to part with the mandatory and expected comedic reply, but he fell silent instead.

"Sgt. Brody," Vance said, "I want you and Fletcher to man that '60 over there. I'm startin' to get a feeling. . . ."

Brody and Fletcher both nodded. "I hear ya, Lou," said Snakeman.

"I'm gettin' the same feeling," Brody was already on his feet and racing across the clearing, bent over.

"You going to stay with him?" Vance asked Frisk.

"Yeah, no sweat, Lou—we'll be okay."

"Okay. I'm going back to the other side of the clearing. My asshole hairs are beginnin' to perk, and that always means the pucker factor is about to increase dramatically."

"Right. . . ."

Frisk watched Vance low-crawl swiftly across the clearing. He felt the lieutenant was just overreacting to Jones's ugly-looking wound. Personally, Frisk did not feel any change coming on, but you couldn't be too careful.

"How you feeling?" he asked Jones.

"Like an idiot who just got his finger blown off."

"Yeah. . . ." Frisk was almost done wrapping the wound. "Sorry I don't have any painkiller. You're just going to have to rough it until we get out of this mess."

"I'll make it all right."

"If the pain gets really bad, think about being drowned in cunt juice. . . ."

"Cunt juice?" Jones cast him an incredulous look.

"Yeah . . . cunt juice. It has a soothing, numbing effect, and has always worked for me."

"That's all I need is for Charlie to put a bullet through my hard-on next, Sarge. . . ."

"'Twas just a suggestion, bud. . . ." Frisk's eyes scanned the tree line in all directions. Zero movement. And he was in a talkative mood. Blood always brought words to his mouth. "So tell me what brings you to The Nam, soldier?"

Reece Jones slowly looked up with lines of utter disbe-

309

lief creasing his features. "Are you serious?" he asked slowly.

"Sure. Serious. What's the poop?"

"I was drafted," Jones said simply.

"Oh," Frisk sounded disappointed. "I didn't know they let your type in the air cavalry."

Jones's head tilted the other way. "Are you for real?" he asked.

Frisk's smile faded. "Look," he said, "to tell you the truth, I'm just trying to make conversation. Forget it. Just lie there in pain, suffering like an idiot. Don't talk. Don't try and take your mind off the pain. Just lay there basking in your misery. Just—"

"Okay, *okay*!" Jones rolled onto his side and faced the Green Beret. "As a matter of fact—and I know you'll just eat this up—I'm from a family with a long and respected military background," he began.

"You?" Frisk asked with disbelief. "Nah. . . ."

"Right. Believe it or not. My father killed Chinese in Korea; my grandfather killed Japanese in Saipan. *They're* still alive. My oldest brother died in Mytho in '64. Riverine duty, before it was official."

"I'm sorry," Frisk glanced away.

"My Numba Two brother died in Pleiku, Tet '65. Long-range Lurps got caught in an over-the-border counter-ambush."

"What?" Frisk locked eyes with him again.

"My Numba Three brother died in Saigon six months ago. VC terrorist bombing. Open-air cafe, down on Tu Do Street of all places."

"Jesus, Reece. . . ." Frisk was almost at a loss for words, but not quite. "I really *am* sorry. But how could Uncle Sammy go and draft your ass over here, too?"

"Yeah, I was in-country when the last one went down. Missed the funeral. Me and Ruckter were kickin' ass and

310

takin' names down in the Mekong Delta. My brothers all volunteered."

"Oh, man . . . what a blow." The Green Beret took a few seconds to think it over. "Yeah, that would really be a low blow for me . . . for *anyone* to take. I'm really sorry, man . . . but aren't you a sole surviving son, or something like that by now? Aren't you protected by—?"

"I'm from a big family," Jones was nodding in the negative. "Three more brothers after me . . . younger brothers. Three more after yours truly."

"I guess now I can understand why you're all tangled up in this VVAW bullshit."

"Yeah. . . ."

"You should tell Ruckter what you just told me. Maybe then he wouldn't be on your case all the time."

"Screw Gage Ruckter. I don't have to explain *anything* to *anybody*."

"Yeah . . . I suppose you're right, pal. All I can say is . . . well, hang in there." Frisk looked like he was getting ready to leave. "You have to stick up for your rights. . . . You have to fight for what you believe in."

Jones held up his bandaged hand. "I'm really tired of fighting, Sarge. I really am. . . ."

Broken radio transmissions on the main net urged Ruckter to notify Vance and Soto that something was up. The two officers were beside the PRC-25 radio almost instantly.

"What is it?" Vance asked.

"Listen. . . ."

"I need . . . I need. . . ." But the transmissions faded abruptly.

"Could you hear anything else?" Capt. Soto asked Ruckter as he stared up at the stars overhead. They'd been trying to raise the CP now for several hours, still without success. There had been no movement from the VC, except to resume blasting away at the Americans whenever movement was spotted within the clearing. The stalemate continued. Vance and Soto were praying that the Americal's 196th would get the lead out, sweep the area and locate them. Charlie's command people were obviously also taking their time deciding what to do about current developments on the rubber plantation. "Was anything else said?"

"Just—"

"Listen!" Vance cut in, turning the volume up ever so slightly.

"I need . . . I need . . . help. Please. . . ."

"Is it a woman's voice?" Soto asked.

"I can't tell," Ruckter said. "It's pretty deep . . . throaty and low . . . rasping almost."

Again, the transmission ceased. "Mark down what frequency you picked that up on," Vance said.

"Right. Do you think it might be VC, sir?" Ruckter asked. "Trying to bait us or something?"

"I don't know, Gage." Vance appeared even more exhausted than the rest of them.

"I didn't detect any accent," Soto told him.

Vance turned and started back toward the machine-gun nest. "Just keep me posted," he said.

Behind the officer, Sgt. Frisk was playing his fiddle. Vance gave him an irritated look, but the Green Beret sergeant merely responded with a smile, a nod, and a semi-casual tip of the beret.

"You tryin' to bust my chops, or just drive Charlie *dinky-dau*, Frisk?" Vance asked.

"Really, sir, this will help Jones over there. He knows fine classical music when he hears it."

"He's the only one who does," Vance low-crawled out

312

of sight, still shaking his head. No other commander would put up with this crap. Any other commander would have confiscated that damn fiddle by now and busted it in two.

Vance hated himself at times like this. Why couldn't he be a hardass, like all the other officers?

Five minutes later, the first mortar fell onto the clearing. The muffled explosion sent a shower of smoking hot shrapnel over the Americans' helmets, but Vance's head count showed no injuries.

"Get ready to tuck your head between your legs and kiss your ass good bye!" Frisk called out. A captured AK-47 propped ready and waiting across his thighs, he had begun playing a more frantic, desperate tune on his fiddle.

"You should know!" Jones responded, but in his gut, he knew the Green Beret sergeant was right. The mortar had obviously been a signal for the VC to move.

A few seconds later, they began swarming down through the trees.

Brody was the first to spot them, and he quickly began knocking down targets of opportunity with his M-60. Frisk threw several grenades at shadows darting through the tombstones, and Ruckter rose to one knee and began firing an AK-47 on semi-automatic.

"Cheap piece o' shit!" He quickly dropped prone after only two or three shots. The rifle had jammed.

"Here!" Frisk surrendered his own AK as Ruckter was about to bring the MP-40 submachine gun down from its slung position across his back. Frisk drew his pistol. "I get the feeling we're gonna be doin' an awful lotta close-in fightin' just 'bout *rikky-tik*, anyway!"

Only one Viet Cong managed to break through the wall of solid lead being laid out by the dozen or so roaring

M-16s and other assorted automatic rifles. Soto himself tackled the communist as he rushed toward Brody's M-60 with a stick grenade in each hand.

As if angry with a dance-floor partner, Soto grabbed one of the guerrilla's wrists and, helped by the momentum of his own sudden speed across the open space, flung the Cong off his feet and completely out of the clearing. The guerrilla crashed into a wall of bamboo, fell back out of sight, and almost got off a scream before both Chi-Coms exploded, sending bits of bone, flesh, and gristle back into the clearing.

The thick foliage and dense network of trees worked to the advantage of the Americans—it was very difficult for the VC to work their way toward the clearing without using the narrow trail, and Brody had *that* covered well with the barking M-60.

Ten minutes later, bullets were still flying, though.

Whirling, Vance spotted movement along the northern perimeter and nearly shot Ruckter in the back of the head when the 4th Cav sergeant also rose to one knee. But Ruckter hesitated, too, as the figure zigzagged through the tombstones and bamboo stalks, getting closer and closer without stopping an M-16 bullet.

"Doc!" Brody was the first to recognize him.

Like a ghost floating in through the graveyard mists, Delgado emerged from the swirling blanket of gunsmoke drifting in the trees.

"*Doc!*" Snakeman Fletcher flew through the air, grabbed the medic's arm, and dragged him down behind cover.

"Where the hell have you been, boy?!" Brody could barely believe his eyes. Delgado looked dazed and shaken.

"I . . . I got. . . ." He wasn't sure how much trouble he was in, but, even in his present mental and physical state,

314

he was coherent enough to know he'd better play it safe. "I . . . got . . . separated from . . . you guys. . . ."

"Separated?" Brody laughed.

"That's sure a fuckin' understatement!" Fletcher slapped the corpsman on the back.

Brody hadn't been this happy in weeks, but his smile quickly faded. Soto and Vance were making their way over to Delgado through the incoming bullets and whistling ricochets.

"Is *this* the NCO behind this whole goddamned mess?" Capt. Soto was asking while propped on his elbows beneath the crisscrossing lead. The question was unnecessary. Soto knew the medic on sight.

"Guilty," Doc stared into the officer's eyes for a moment, then glanced away. He was obviously of the opinion he had nothing to prove to anybody.

"Any luck finding Lisa, Doc?" Brody asked. "I mean . . . any luck finding the lieutenant . . . Lt. Maddox?"

Delgado slowly shook his head from side to side.

"Damn. . . ." Fletcher muttered.

"As soon as we're outta this clusterfuck," Soto began, "I'm bringin' you up on charges, mister!" His bullet-grey eyes bored into Delgado.

"What?" Brody and Fletcher both gauged the captain's expression. Vance remained neutrally silent, well aware that Doc was in deep trouble for bugging out under fire.

"What charges?" Ruckter asked.

"AWOL," Soto sounded adamant. "You didn't get fuckin' 'separated' from *anybody.* You went AWOL for a piece o' ass, sergeant, and my men suffered for it. A lousy piece o' dead cunt. And as soon as we get extracted outta this abortion, I'm gonna see to it you spend the next twenty years breakin' big rocks at LBJ!"

"That's fine, captain," Delgado said without emotion. "Just don't have a coronary over it, okay sir?"

Soto seemed disturbed by the medic's reaction—or lack of it—to his threats of disciplinary action. "Did you hear what I *said*, soldier?"

Delgado reached out and grabbed the front of Soto's shirt and pulled the officer closer, until their noses were rubbing in a threatening manner. "You used to be an ace kinda guy," he said slowly, eyes still glazed over, but fist iron tight. "You used to be a real ass-kicker, Soto. You never struck me as a company man. What the fuck happened to you?" He pushed the captain away roughly.

Vance winced. Soto ground his teeth. "This isn't the last of it, Doc," he said, as the fighting suddenly died to a trickle.

"Fine. Make an appointment with my secretary."

Fuming, Soto moved toward the other side of the clearing.

CHAPTER 34

Jungle, Dau Tieng

That night was filled with screams.

The Viet Cong guerrillas were trying to mindfuck the unyielding cavalrymen with taunting, frightening yells. The sniper was still out there, too, despite the bolo beans, yelling "You die, *du ma*!" and dropping three- and four-round M-16 bursts down into the clearing from the safety of a treetop 50 to 75 yards away.

When the sun rose, two of the men were missing.

"Vanders and Minolti," Brody informed Vance. Two of the Echo Company newbies. None of the old-timers knew them very well.

"Think they bugged out?" Vance asked Fletcher and Ruckter, who'd had last watch before dawn.

"Not on our shift," Snakeman nodded grimly. "We would have noticed, Lou. I guarantee it."

Vance stared out at the fog moving through the tombstones. "Volunteers," he said softly. "I need volunteers for a search outside the perimeter. . . ."

"*Outside* the perimeter?" Jones asked. Everyone heard his swallow despite the occasional rifle discharge echoing through the woods.

"I'll go," Frisk volunteered.

"Me, too," Brody rose his rifle.

"I'll go alone," Frisk said. "It'll be faster. I can cover more ground."

Brody looked to the lieutenant.

"Take Sgt. Brody with you. There's no hurry."

"Okay, sir. . . ."

"Just beat the bushes a couple dozen yards out or so, just in case they snuck out to shit in private and sat on a punji stick or something." Vance was not trying to sound funny.

"Right. . . ."

They found the two newbies only 20 feet away, propped up against two grave markers, as if meeting for a friendly round of cards. Both held the infamous Ace of Spades First Cav death cards in their hands. The cards read: "Compliments of the First Team: Our business is killing, and killing is good."

Their uniforms had been removed, and blood dripped down from deep gashes where their throats had been slit. Their weapons were missing, as were their genitals. A crucifix, fashioned from two long pieces of bamboo, hung upside down between them.

Whoever killed them had switched their heads and cut out their tongues.

Reece Jones hit Ruckter in the face as hard as he could. Reece Jones was left-handed, but, since he'd just lost the ring finger of that hand, he threw the punch with his right. It wasn't nearly the best roundhouse the world had ever seen.

Ruckter sidestepped the brunt of the somewhat expected

assault, grabbed Jones's injured hand, and twisted it hard until the man went down on both knees, grimacing in pain. "What's your fucking *problem*, Jones?!" Gage yelled.

"I know you did it!" Jones swung with his right hand again, aiming for Ruckter's groin. Gage simply stepped back, out of the way, and twisted harder. Jones fell face first on the ground, screaming in agony.

"Back off, Ruckter!"

Gage glanced up to find Lt. Vance holding a rifle on him. "My papa told me never to point a weapon at anybody unless I was planning to use it, sir," Ruckter's remark was a blatant challenge. but Vance wasn't into mind games.

"Drop Jones's hand . . . slowly . . . then drop your holster." His rifle was already on the ground. Ruckter slowly, cautiously complied on both counts. "Now the MP-40," Vance added. "Take it down off your back . . . slowly, Gage."

"I didn't kill those men, Lieutenant," Ruckter locked eyes with the officer.

"I don't think you did either, Sarge," Vance admitted, "but this is turnin' into a real bona fide drive-in horror flick, and I can't take the chance." He stared down at Reece Jones. "I want your weapons, too, Reece," he said.

"What?" Jones cast him a questioning look.

"I just keep gettin' this bad, nagging gut feeling about you, friend . . . and like I said: no chances."

Frowning, Jones threw his rifle down. "I'm small-time," he said. "I don't rate a motherfucking pistol."

"Brody."

"Yes, sir?" Treat was trying not to get involved, but it looked as if his number had just been called.

"You get to watch 'em tonight."

"I'd really rather not, sir. . . . I mean, I'd really rather—"

"And I'd rather be gettin' a skulljob down in Saigon, but we can't always have what we want, now, can we, Whoremonger?"

"No sir, I guess we can't."

"Fine. The rest of you men dig in and crash. Somethin' tells me it's going to be a long night."

Vance and Sgt. Frisk spent the next day trying to raise the 196th CP on the radio again, but all they got was static.

"The battery's runnin' low, too, Lou," Frisk shook his head.

"Yeah. . . ."

During the twelve hours until dusk, only twenty or thirty rounds dropped into the clearing. None of the men was wounded. Everybody was learning the routine.

"Charlie must really be planning something big for us," Brody worried.

"You know what?" Vance said. "I think that last big F-4 raid on those hills took out most of the local VC infrastructure. It's only a guess, but I think there's no one out there but a bunch o' punk kids takin' potshots at us 'cause they've got nothin' better to do . . . no one to tell 'em what *else* to do."

"But there was sure a lot o' the bastards swarmin' down on us at first, sir," Brody reminded Vance. "Remember?"

"Yeah," the lieutenant admitted. "But bookoo Indians and no chiefs, that's all."

Frisk then volunteered to attempt a one-man mission right through the enemy's lines. "I could make it back to the colonel and brief him on our situation here," the LRRP specialist maintained. "Then I could lead him and the cavalry right back here. . . ."

320

"Could you bring us a couple radios that work while you're at it?" Fletcher grinned dryly.

"We wouldn't need new radios if I could make it through and get some help. Let me try, Lou. It's what I'm trained for."

"Forget it." Vance nixed Frisk's idea. "You'd never make it. We're completely surrounded—it's shoulder-to-shoulder zips out there, even if they are just a shitload o' doper buck privates with no time in grade. What we need is—"

"Lieutenant! There it is again!" The newby who was monitoring the radio turned the volume up and the squelch off. Intermittent transmissions silenced the static long enough for the men to hear the soft, throaty voice gain.

"It's her!" Brody said. "It's her again."

"What makes you think it's a woman?" Vance asked.

"It's a woman's voice, all right. . . ." Upon hearing the confident words, they all looked up to see Doc Delgado standing there. "It's Lisa."

"I'm sorry, Gage."

"It's okay, Reece-baby. I'd have probably suspected me too, under similar circumstances.

Ruckter and Jones were shaking hands and reslinging their weapons because, overnight, another newby was snatched out of the corral. Brody and Fletcher verified they had kept one eye on the two suspects and on each other the entire night. And no, they had not seen what happened to the newby who'd spent all day monitoring the radio, only to get stabbed in his sleep and dragged off to an appointment with Machete Man after dark. "It's a big clearing, lieutenant—and we've only got two eyes each."

The newby's head had been lopped off 30 or 40 yards

outside the clearing, but whoever killed the young soldier then dragged him back to some nearby grave markers, propped him upside down against the tombstone, and rammed another bamboo crucifix into his rectum.

The turn of events—though not all that unexpected—was leaving Brody's people somewhat tense. An it-can't-happen-to-us-old-timers mindset took over, and the vets blocked out what had been happening to the newbies. Frisk was a constant reminder of what had happened to five Green Berets, but the men refused to think about *that*.

"Oh-oh, Lieutenant. . . ."

"What?!" Vance whirled around to confront Brody's voice. He was getting tired of surprises.

"We got trouble. . . ."

Fletcher broke the news. "Soto and Frisk are missing."

Frisk staggered back into camp at dusk that evening. He was carrying Capt. Soto over his shoulder.

Fletcher checked the officer's pulse before Frisk dropped him like a sack of potatoes. "He's dead," Snakeman said.

Sgt. Frisk nodded. "Stone cold."

"What the fuck happened?" Vance asked.

Frisk stared at the lieutenant, then bent down over Soto's body and ripped open the dead man's bloody shirt. Around his neck was a black rawhide strip attached to a small ebony upside-down cross.

"Frisk, you fucking deaf, or what?" Vance yelled.

A string of bullets danced across the clearing, and they all dropped out of sight, behind cover.

"That motherfucker was behind all the weird mutilations," Frisk began, pointing at Soto's body. And then he explained the story from the start. . . .

322

In the middle of the night, Frisk had spotted Soto moving up through the mists, toward the perimeter. Oddly enough, he had never felt threatened, and he watched more with curiosity and fascination as the man he recognized to be Soto entered the clearing's edge, paused over one of the new men, then, with silent precision, delivered a karate chop to the temple and dragged the unresisting newby back into the bamboo.

Intrigued, Frisk failed to sound any alarm, but followed Soto back out through the dark. When he saw Soto slam a survival knife down into the American's heart, Frisk charged.

Soto put up quite a fight, and a somewhat startled Frisk ended up on the bottom—unconscious from some very fast karate moves.

When Frisk came to, Soto had already hacked the other soldier's head off and desecrated his body. Frisk jumped up again, and this time Soto fled.

Both men ran deeper into the jungle, somehow managing to avoid the nearby Viet Cong, and Frisk finally caught up with Soto about 200 yards away from the body.

They fought, but Frisk played dirty, and this time Soto ended up on the bottom. Frisk twisted his arm and got the story out of him. Cursing, then laughing and crying in turns, Soto babbled incoherently about powers of darkness helping him fight only if he offered the blood of his own kind. He was proud of the heads he'd collected.

"He just flipped out, I guess," Frisk said. "The pressure of working in deep jungle with men who hated him finally pushed him past the breaking point."

"The Nungs hated him? Vance asked.

"Right. Chinh told me Soto gave his men all kinds of shit—downright sacrificing many of them, in fact—so he could cover his bad command decisions. Fucker lost his guts months ago."

"*Our* Captain Soto?" Doc asked sarcastically. "Mister Clean?"

"Yep," Frisk glanced at the officer's body lying near the middle of the clearing.

"Sonofabitch," Reece said.

Frisk was carrying an AK-47 rifle over his other shoulder. He slipped the sling off, and let the weapon drop onto the ground.

"So far you haven't told us how Soto got his ticket punched," Snakeman said.

Frisk's brows came together as he stared directly at the doorgunner. "There I was sittin' on the crazy fuck, keeping his arms pinned down, and I looked him in the eye and told him we were going to get up and walk back to the clearing, nice and cooperative-like. Next thing I know, the goofy shit grabs at my AK-47, we fight over it for a few seconds, and he turns the barrel against his chest and jerks on the weapon. Well, naturally, the damn thing discharged."

"Hhmph," Vance was examining Soto's chest. "Five times?" he asked.

"The selector was on full-auto."

"Hhmph. . . ."

The sound of rotors fast approaching in the distance cut the recap short. Fletcher and Brody exchanged tense glances: Dare they hope for a miracle?

"Oh yeah," Frisk added belatedly. "While I was out, I phoned in a Brass Monkey. That's why I've been gone all day, Lieutenant." He turned to face Vance. "The cavalry should be on their way."

"You did what?" Vance sounded cheated out of glory. "You *phoned* it in?"

"Once I found myself outside of Charlie's cordon," Frisk explained, "I quick-timed it back to the old CP."

"You made contact with the colonel?" Vance asked in disbelief.

324

"Yeah," the Green Beret did not seem very elated himself. "Help is on the way, ladies. . . ."

As if to dispute his claim, muzzle flashes began erupting in a treetop 50 yards away. M-16 rounds began whistling into the clearing. Every man gathered around Doc spotted the puffs of smoke this time. A dozen rifles came up, and the boys from Echo Company nearly chopped the palm tree down with hot lead.

The sniper was catapulted out of the palm fronds.

The Americans watched him falling to the ground—arms and legs flailing, M-16 twirling end over end just out of the guerrilla's reach.

"You think that was the same bastard who snatched up the M-16?" Ruckter asked Frisk.

"I don't know, brother," came the dull reply. "And right about now, I really don't give a flying—"

"Brody," Ruckter cut in again, "somebody's gotta reteach you how to make bolo beans, dude."

Treat Brody gnawed on his lower lip without responding. He wondered what could possibly have gone wrong. "Does C-4 have an expiration date?" he asked Frisk, only half seriously.

"You die, *du ma*!" Reece Jones called out, and the others laughed as the airborne sniper's body lifted a huge puff of mushroom dust in the distance. The VC rifleman was finally down for the count, five bullets in his belly.

Aboard the gunships came reinforcements, and among the reinforcements were specialists trained in the art of isolating and tracking down radio transmissions.

Lt. Lisa Maddox had obviously stumbled across either the RTO from her original med-evac flight, his radio, or both. Intermittent transmissions from the army nurse had been received over the last forty-eight hours, but she sounded incoherent and dazed—a woman lapsing into shock.

"Help. . . ." the pleas were mere whispers now. "Please . . . help . . . me. . . ."

"She's obviously wounded," Vance told Doc Delgado as they watched the communications technicians working. "Probably suffering from shock and extreme loss of blood."

"We almost get a fix on her," one of the technicians told Vance, "and then she stops transmitting."

"If only she'd just keep keying the mike," the other specialist said. "Just for ten . . . even five minutes. We'd have her grid identified, then you could begin a ground search."

"We got trouble!" Frisk went tense, and most of the men nearby dropped into a crouch. The VC had pulled back, melting phantom-like into the bamboo as helicopter reinforcements arrived, but the Green Beret had spotted a flash of metal in the distant tree line. "Everyone down," he motioned toward the radio technicians, "and that means you guys, too."

But all Frisk had now was his pistol—useless at this distance. "Gage, gimme that goofy German piece o' shit you're always carrying!" he told Ruckter.

The 4th Cav sergeant complied, sliding the MP-40 submachine gun down from across his back.

Frisk flipped the safety off, aimed at the treetop, and pulled the trigger.

The submachine gun exploded, smoke enveloped the Green Beret, and he and Ruckter were both knocked to the ground by the terrific concussion.

At the same time, a muffled explosion came from the treetop Frisk had been aiming at, and Thieu the VC

326

recruit dropped to the ground—his shiny M-16 shattered by the bolo bean, his face erased by the searing blast.

"Oh, man, he's fucked up bad!" Ruckter rolled over to find Frisk gasping for air. The Green Beret's face was terribly burned, and a hole the size of Brody's fist sent blood spurting from his left breast.

Ruckter stared at the ghastly wound. He stared down at the mangled MP-40, then back at the jagged shards of metal protruding from the wound again. "My God! Frisk, I didn't know! My God!"

Delgado was working frantically to stem the flow of blood, but with little luck.

Blinded by the explosion, Frisk reached out and grabbed the nearest body. Treat Brody. "Yeah, Sgt. Frisk!" Brody said, "it's me, Brody! I'm right here!"

"Get . . . me . . . Jones," blood bubbled from Frisk's lips. "Get . . . me . . . Jones!"

"Jones!" Brody yelled.

"I'm right here!" Jones was already by Frisk's side. "I'm right here, Sarge!"

Frisk's powerful hand grabbed the front of Jones's shirt, pulling him closer. "I trust you, Reece. . . ."

"I trust you, too, Sarge. Hang on."

"After you . . . about your brothers . . . I got to . . . trust you. . . ."

"Right, Sarge! I trust you, too!" he repeated.

Frisk pulled Reece Jones down ever closer, until his ear was against the dying Green Beret's lips. "The vio— . . . the vio—" Blood filled Frisk's throat, and he began to choke and gag.

"What, Sarge? What was that? Something about . . . the fiddle! What about the fiddle, Sarge?"

Frisk still had a good grip on him.

"Violin . . . yours. I . . . want you to . . . have it. Take care . . . of it . . . for me."

327

"Right, Sarge. Sure . . . sure! I'll protect it with my life, man . . . I really will."

And then Sgt. Frisk's heart gave out. His hand released Jones's shirt and fell against the earth with a dull thud.

Reece Jones could not keep the tears from filling his eyes. He turned to the other men for support, but most of them had already left, turning away from the pain of loss. Only Treat Brody remained by his side.

"Fucking all that for . . ."

"Yeah. At least he left part of him behind."

They watched Delgado drape a poncho liner over Sgt. Frisk's face, and Jones's eyes drifted over to the radio technicians, where Vance, Ruckter, and the others had gathered.

"We're packin' it in," he could hear one of the specialists saying. "I'm sorry, but she just didn't key the mike long enough. We couldn't get a fix on the transmission, and she let her battery run down. The radio finally went dead, guys. There's nothing more we can do."

CHAPTER 35

Special Forces Camp, Dau Tieng

"I can't believe this, Treat," Reece Jones stared at the papers he'd found hidden inside the small violin case stuffed at the bottom of Frisk's rucksack.

"Well, now you've got something to leave your grandchildren, my friend."

Reece drew his face back to gauge Brody's expression.

"Just kidding," Whoremonger took Sgt. Frisk's fiddle and strummed it a couple times. "Just don't feel like it's an heirloom from old George Washington's time."

"Handed down generations from his grandfather to his father to him. . . ."

"Hhmph. That's funny. Frisk always treated it like a toy . . . just like a goddamned toy, you know?"

"Oh, no," Reece Jones disagreed. "Sgt. Frisk loved this violin. He loved it with all his heart, my friend. I could tell. I could see it in his eyes . . . in his smile whenever he played. . . ."

Jones knew he would just keep the violin and learn to play when he returned to The World. Maybe he could hook a cord up to the thing, give it an electric twist, and join a rock-'n-roll band. Rock-'n-roll bands were using electric strings more and more these days.

If not, he'd hang out at the VFW in Thornton, Colorado, and strum rock tunes in honor of the greatest Green Beret he had ever known.

Doc Delgado stared at Choi-oi but didn't seem to actually see what the dog was doing. He heard men laughing as they waited to board the choppers for the ride out, and realized they were laughing at Choi-oi. And then he realized what the crazy mutt was doing: humping his helmet.

Delgado's helmet was in the middle of the clearing, propped up against his rucksack and some other equipment, and the dog was humping the steel pot like crazy.

"Choi-oi! Delgado yelled. "Knock it off, you little pervert!" Any other time, the sight might actually have been funny to Doc as well, but today he was too depressed. They were leaving Dau Tieng soon. He was leaving Lisa. Abandoning her. Wherever she was. The thought of leaving her body to Void Vicious made Danny sick deep inside.

He had watched the radio technicians load up all their gear only an hour ago. They, too, had given up.

The U.S. Army had given up on the army nurse as well. Lt. Lisa Maddox was now officially on the roster of Missing In Action in Southeast Asia. M.I.A.—Presumed Dead.

The thought of her body lying out there in the jungle somewhere, alone and unguarded . . . rotting . . . just lying beneath the merciless tropical sun, was nearly enough to make him vomit.

Danny Delgado would never be the same again.

"Hey, Brody! When you gonna teach that bastard mutt o' yours some manners?" someone called from behind an M-60 in one of the rising gunships. "Don't know why the fuck we ever brought him along!"

Delgado glanced back at Choi-oi. The dog was still humping his helmet.

Doc watched Treat Brody walk up and try and snatch the steel pot away, but Choi-oi appeared to be in the mood to play. The mutt tipped the helmet over, poked his snout inside, and came out with Lisa's mint-green panties.

Delgado had forgotten about them.

"Hey!" Doc yelled and began chasing after Choi-oi alongside Brody as the dog jumped around in circles, just barely managing to stay out of the medic's reach.

"Sorry, Doc!" Brody dove toward the mongrel several times, but without success, as the men boarding gunships in the background cheered on Choi-oi and booed the two cavalrymen.

"Come here, Choi-oi! Come here, boy!" Delgado coaxed.

Choi-oi lingered just out of reach, throwing the panties up in the air once, and poking his snout through one of the leg bands as it came down. The dog actually seemed to be grinning.

He pranced around the two cavalrymen in circles, always managing to stay just out of reach.

Suddenly, Snakeman Fletcher came flying through the air. He tackled Choi-oi with ease, and the dog and cavalryman tumbled through the dust. Choi-oi yelped in uncertainty and fright. Fletcher laughed his head off.

Delgado and Brody quickly piled onto the two, and Doc grabbed the panties.

The idea struck all three men at once.

"Choi-oi!" Delgado yelled.

Choi-oi jumped to his feet and backed away cautiously, wanting nothing to do with the three suddenly serious-looking men.

"Come 'ere, Choi-oi. Come 'ere, boy!" Brody pulled a smashed cigarette butt from a pocket, held it out and slapped his thighs, and the dog finally responded.

Snatching up the panties, Delgado hugged the dog as

well, then held Lisa's panties against Choi-oi's snout and chops. "Lisa, Choi-oi! Lisa!"

Choi-oi barked, and Doc rubbed the panties in the dog's face for a few more seconds. "Lisa, Choi-oi! Do you remember Lisa?"

"Sure you do!" Brody and Fletcher both responded, nodding their heads eagerly. Choi-oi barked what appeared to be an acknowledgment.

"Go find Lisa!" Delgado made as if to throw the panties out of the clearing, into the trees, and Choi-oi lunged in anticipation. The dog slid to a halt when the undergarments failed to leave Doc's hand.

"Go find Lisa, Choi-oi!" Doc made as if to throw the panties again, and this time, sniffing the air in a businesslike manner, Choi-oi let out a long howl, and raced off down one of several nearby jungle trails.

"Let's go!" all three cavalrymen sprinted out of the clearing.

When they finally caught up to Choi-oi, his face was buried in a pile of palm fronds on the edge of another graveyard. His rump was up in the air, his stub of a tail wagging furiously.

Delgado spotted the severed head first.

"My God. . . ." Brody and Snakeman stared at the dead radio operator's open eyes. Ants were crawling all over what little flesh remained on his face.

But Lisa was still alive.

She lay propped between the decapitated body and the dead PRC-25. "Please . . . help . . . me," she was still whispering into the radio microphone. Both of her hands were shaking violently.

"It's okay, honey," Delgado lifted her up into his arms.

"It's okay, baby—you're safe now. You're with Danny-boy. . . ."

Lisa refused to let go of the microphone. "Please . . . help . . . me. . . ."

"You're going to be okay, Lisa!" Delgado gently laid her back down and began checking her for injuries.

"Is she okay, Doc?" Brody asked.

"It looks like she's lost a lot of blood. . . ."

"Bullet in the back," Snakeman watched Doc run his finger through the tear in her shirt.

"Yeah. . . ." Delgado sighed, "but she's going to be okay. We've found her now. She's going to be okay. . . ."

"Danny-boy?"

Lisa was looking up into his eyes now. She seemed to recognize him finally. "Is that you, Danny-boy?"

"Yeah, Lisa . . . it's me, honey. . . . We're gonna be takin' you to the field hospital soon. Just hang in there, okay? Hang in there!"

Choi-oi rushed up and nearly knocked them all over in his zeal to resume licking Lisa's face.

"Choi-oi?" she asked softly. "Is that you, Choi-oi?"

Choi-oi barked in response. "The one and only," Brody answered further for the mutt.

Lisa's eyes were beginning to focus on them all. "He . . . found . . . me? *Choi-oi* found me?"

"Yep," Doc Delgado nodded down at the grinning mongrel. "Choi-oi found you when all the resources of the U.S. Army couldn't. Can you believe it?"

Choi-oi, sensing his cue, moved in to lick Lisa again, but she pushed him away playfully and hugged Doc as hard as she could.

Snakeman and The Whoremonger backed away a few feet.

"I can't believe it." Fletcher nudged Choi-oi out of the way.

"What?"

"A goddamned happy ending, man. A happy ending in The Nam for a change."

"Yeah. Truly mind-boggling, ain't it?"

Choi-oi let out a yelp and ran circles around them. He didn't seem to be taking it personally that the obvious hero here was suddenly being ignored.

Jumping up against Delgado's back with his front paws as a diversionary tactic, Choi-oi snatched the mint-green panties hanging from the medic's back pocket, and ran off into the rain forest, barking with glee, the waistband caught around his bullet-scarred ears.

EPILOGUE

At midnight on November 4, the Suoi Cau Regional Force camp was attacked by elements of the 272nd Viet Cong Regiment. Mortar barrages walked through the 196th Infantry CP, and, though the initial assault was repulsed, six more enemy attacks would follow during the next twenty-four hours. The U.S. 27th and 31st infantries would join the fighting, as would the 101st North Vietnamese Regiment, which was augmenting the three VC regiments, including the 70th and 271st. The American First Infantry Division contributed an entire brigade to the battle, and soon the 173rd Airborne Brigade and 4th Infantry Division joined the fray alongside 25th Infantry Division units. Several air cavalry units answered countless calls for help, and the skies over Dau Tieng were olive drab with rotor-to-rotor gunships. The final stages of Operation Attleboro were in full swing. And the 9th VC Division couldn't take it anymore.

A week later, the insurgents had retreated west, across the border into Cambodia, seeking sanctuary in the dense, dark rain forests of Svay Rieng Province. By November 15, Operation Attleboro would be officially over.

GLOSSARY

AA   Antiaircraft weapon

AC   Aircraft Commander

Acting Jack   Acting NCO

AIT   Advanced Individual Training

AJ   Acting Jack

AK-47   Automatic rifle used by VC/NVA

Animal   See Monster

AO   Area of Operations

Ao Dai   Traditional Vietnamese gown

APH-5   Helmet worn by gunship pilots

APO   Army Post Office

Arc-Light   B-52 bombing mission

ArCOM   Army Commendation Medal

Article-15   Disciplinary action

Ash-'n'-Trash   Relay flight

Bad Paper   Dishonorable discharge

Ba Muoi Ba   Vietnamese beer

Banana Clip   Ammo magazine holding 30 bullets

Bao Chi   Press or news media

Basic   Boot camp

BCT   Basic Combat Training (Boot)

Bic   Vietnamese for "Understand?"

Big-20   Army career of 20 years

Bird   Helicopter

BLA   Black Liberation Army

Bloods   Black soldiers

Blues   An airmobile company

Body Count   Number of enemy KIA

Bookoo   Vietnamese for "many" (actually bastardization of French *beaucoup*)

Bought the Farm   Died and life insurance policy paid for mortgage

Brass Monkey   Interagency radio call for help

Brew   Usually coffee, but sometimes beer

Bring Smoke   To shoot someone

Broken-Down   Disassembled

Buddha Zone   Death

Bush ('Bush)   Ambush

Butter Bar   2nd Lieutenant

CA   Combat Assault

Cam Ong   Viet for "Thank you"

Cartridge   Shell casing for bullet

C&C   Command & Control chopper

Chao   Vietnamese greeting

Charlie   Viet Cong (from military phonetic: Victor Charlie)

Charlie Tango   Control Tower

Cherry   New man in unit

Cherry Boy   Virgin

Chicken Plate   Pilot's chest/groin armor

Chi-Com   Chinese Communist

Chieu Hoi   Program where communists can surrender and become scouts

Choi-oi   Viet exclamation

CIB   Combat Infantry Badge

CID   Criminal Investigation Division

Clip   Ammo magazine

CMOH   Congressional Medal of Honor

CO   Commanding Officer

Cobra   Helicopter gunship used for combat assaults/ escorts only

Cockbang   Bangkok, Thailand

Conex   Shipping container (metal)

Coz   Short for Cozmoline

CP   Command Post

338

CSM   Command Sergeant Major
Cunt Cap   Green narrow cap worn with khakis

Dash-13   Helicopter maintenance report
Dau   Viet for pain
Deadlined   Down for repairs
Dep   Viet for beautiful
DEROS   Date of Estimated Return from Overseas
Deuce-and-a-Half   2½-ton truck
DFC   Distinguished Flying Cross
DI   Drill Instructor (Sgt.)
Di Di   Viet for "Leave or go!"
Dink   Derogatory term for Vietnam national
Dinky Dau   Viet for "crazy"
Disneyland East   MACV complex including annex
DMZ   Demilitarized Zone
Dogtags   Small aluminum tag worn by soldiers with
   name, serial number, religion, and blood type imprinted
   on it
DOOM Pussy   Danang Officers Open Mess
Door gunner   Soldier who mans M-60 machine gun
   mounted in side hatch of Huey gunship
Dung Lai   Viet for "Halt!"
Dustoff   Medevac chopper

Early Out   Unscheduled ETS
EM   Enlisted Man
ER   Emergency Room (hospital)
ETS   End Tour of (military) Service

Field Phone   Hand-generated portable phones used in
   bunkers
Fini   Viet for "Stop" or "the End"
First Louie   1st Lieutenant
First Team   Motto of 1st Air Cav
Flak Jacket   Body armor
FNG   Fucking new guy
FOB   Fly over border mission
Foxtrot   Vietnamese female

Foxtrot Tosser   Flame thrower
Frag   Fragmentation grenade
FTA   Fuck the Army

Gaggle   Loose flight of slicks
Get Some   Kill someone
GI   Government Issue, or, a soldier
Greenbacks   U.S. currency
Green Machine   U.S. Army
Gunship   Attack helicopter armed with machine guns and rockets
Gurney   Stretcher with wheels

Ham & Motherfuckers   C-rations serving of ham and lima beans
Herpetologist   One who studies reptiles and amphibians
HOG-60   M-60 machine gun
Hot LZ   Landing zone under hostile fire
Housegirl   Indigenous personnel hired to clean buildings, wash laundry, etc.
Huey   Primary troop-carrying helicopter

IC   Installation Commander
IG   Inspector General
In-Country   Within Vietnam
Intel   Intelligence (military)
IP   That point in a mission where descent toward target begins

JAG   Judge Advocate General
Jane   Jane's Military Reference books
Jesus Nut   The bolt that holds rotor blade to helicopter
Jody   Any American girlfriends
Jolly Green   Chinook helicopter

KIA   Killed in Action
Kimchi   Korean fish sauce salad
Klick   Kilometer
KP   Mess hall duty

Lai Day   Viet for "come here"

LAW   Light Anti-Tank Weapon

Lay Dog   Lie low in jungle during recon patrol

LBFM   Little Brown Fucking Machine

LBJ   Long Binh Jail (main stockade)

Leg   Infantryman not airborne qualified

Lifeline   Straps holding gunny aboard chopper while he fires M-60 out the hatch

Lifer   Career soldier

Links   Metal strip holding ammo belt together

Loach   Small spotter/scout chopper

LP   Listening Post

LRRP   Long-Range Recon Patrol

LSA   Gun oil

Lurp   One who participates in LRRPs

LZ   Landing Zone

M-14   American carbine

M-16   Primary U.S. Automatic Rifle

M-26   Fragmentation grenade

M-60   Primary U.S. Machine gun

M-79   Grenade launcher (rifle)

MACV   Military Assistance Command, Vietnam

Magazine   Metal container that feeds bullets into weapon. Holds 20 or 30 rounds per unit

Mag Pouch   Magazine holder worn on web belt

MAST   Mobile Army Surgical Team

Med-Evac   Medical Evacuation Chopper

Mess Hall   GI cafeteria

MG   Machine gun

MI   Military Intelligence

MIA   Missing in Action

Mike-Mike   Millimeters

Mike Papas   Military Policemen

Mister Zippo   Flame-thrower operator

Mjao   Central Highlands witch doctor

Monkeyhouse   Stockade or jail

Monkeystrap   See **Lifeline**

Monster   12-21 claymore antipersonnel mines jury-rigged
   to detonate simultaneously
Montagnarde   Hill tribe people of Central Highlands,
   RVN
MPC   Money Payment Certificates (scrip) issued to GIs
   in RVN in lieu of greenbacks
Muster   A quick assemblage of soldiers with little or no
   warning
My   Viet for "American"

Net   Radio net
NETT   New Equipment Training Team
Newby   New GI in-country
Numba One   Something very good
Numba Ten   Something very bad
Nuoc Nam   Viet fish sauce
NVA   North Vietnamese Army

OD   Olive Drab
OR   Operating Room (Hospital)
P   Piasters
PA   Public Address system
PCS   Permanent Change of (Duty) Station (transfer out of
   RVN)
Peter Pilot   Copilot in training
PF   Popular Forces (Vietnamese)
PFC   Private First Class
Phantom   Jet fighter plane
Phu   Vietnamese noodle soup
Piaster   Vietnamese Currency
PJ   Photojournalist
Point   The most dangerous position on patrol. The point
   man walks ahead and to the side of the others, acting as
   a lookout
PRG   Provisional Revolutionary Govt. (the Communists)
Prang   Land a helicopter roughly
Prick-25   Pr-25 field radio
Profile   Medical exemption
Psy-Ops   Psychological operation

PT Physical Training
Puff Heavily armed aircraft
Purple Heart Medal given for wounds received in combat
Purple Vision Night vision
Puzzle Palace The MACV HQ building

Quad-50 Truck equipped with four 50-caliber MGs
QC Vietnamese MP

Rat Fuck Mission doomed from the start
Regular An enlistee or full-time soldier as opposed to PFs and Reserves, NG, etc.
REMF Rear Echelon Motherfucker
R&R Rest and Relaxation
Re-Up Re-enlist
Rikky-Tik Quickly or fast
Rock 'n' Roll Automatic fire
Roger Affirmative
ROK Republic of Korea
Rotor Overhead helicopter blade
Round Bullet
RPG Rocket-propelled grenade
Ruck(Sack) GI's backpack
RVN Republic of (South) Vietnam

Saigon Capital of RVN

SAM Surface-to-Air Missile
Sapper Guerrilla terrorist equipped with satchel charge (explosives)
SAR Downed-chopper rescue mission
Scramble Alert reaction to call for help, CA or rescue operation.
Scrip See MPC
7.62 M-60 ammunition
Sierra Echo Southeast (Northwest is November Whiskey, etc.)
Single-Digit Fidget A nervous single-digit midget

343

Single-Digit Midget One with fewer than ten days remaining in Vietnam

SKS Russian-made carbine

Slick Helicopter

Slicksleeve Private E-1

Slug Bullet

SNAFU Situation normal: all fucked up

Soggy Frog Green Beret laying dog

SOP Standard Operating Procedure (also known as Shit Output)

Spiderhole Tunnel entrance

Strac Sharp appearance

Steel Pot Helmet

Striker Montagnarde hamlet defender

Sub-Gunny Substitute door gunner

TDY Temporary Duty Assignment

Terr Terrorist

"33" Local Vietnamese beer

Thumper see **M-79**

Ti Ti Viet for little

Tour 365 The year-long tour of duty a GI spends in RVN

Tower Rat Tower guard

Tracer Chemically treated bullet that gives off a glow enroute to its target

Triage That method in which medics determine which victims are most seriously hurt and therefore treated first

Trooper Soldier

201 File Personnel file

Two-Point-Five Gunship rockets

UCMJ Uniformed Code of Military Justice

Unass Leave seat quickly

VC Viet Cong

Victor Charlie VC

Viet Cong South Vietnamese Communists

VNP Vietnamese National Police

344

Void Vicious   Final approach to a Hot LZ; or the jungle when hostile

Warrant Officer   Pilots
Wasted   Killed
Web Belt   Utility belt GIs use to carry equipment, sidearms, etc.
Whiskey   Military phonetic for "West"
WIA   Wounded In Action
Wilco   Will comply
Willie Peter   White phosphorus
Wire   Perimeter (trip wire sets off booby trap)
The World   Any place outside Vietnam

Xin Loi   Viet for "sorry about that" or "good-bye"
XM-21   Gunship mini-gun
XO   Executive officer

'Yarde   Montagnarde
ZIP   Derogatory term for Vietnamese National
Zulu   Military Phonetic for the letter Z (LZ or Landing Zone might be referred to as a Lima Zulu)

All Sphere Books are available at your bookshop or newsagent, or can be ordered from the following address: Sphere Books, Cash Sales Department, P.O. Box 11, Falmouth, Cornwall TR10 9EN.

Please send cheque or postal order (no currency), and allow 60p for postage and packing for the first book plus 25p for the second book and 15p for each additional book ordered up to a maximum charge of £1.90 in U.K.

B.F.P.O. customers please allow 60p for the first book, 25p for the second book plus 15p per copy for the next 7 books, thereafter 9p per book.

Overseas customers, including Eire, please allow £1.25 for postage and packing for the first book, 75p for the second book and 28p for each subsequent title ordered.